W9-CQW-147

PU SONGLING

STRANGE TALES FROM MAKE-DO STUDIO

Translated by Denis C. & Victor H. Mair

FOREIGN LANGUAGES PRESS BEIJING

First Edition 1989
Second Printing 1996

ISBN 7-119-00977-X

Published by Foreign Languages Press
24 Baiwanzhuang Road, Beijing 100037, China

Distributed by China International Book Trading Corporation
35 Chegongzhuang Xilu, Beijing 100044, China
P.O. Box 399, Beijing, China

Printed in the People's Republic of China

CONTENTS

Preface

Strange Tales from Make-Do Studio is an outstanding collection of classical Chinese short stories, but its author Pu Songling was a little-known figure during his lifetime.

Pu Songling (1640-1715), styled Liuxian (Earthbound Spirit) and sometimes called the Recluse of Willow Spring, was born in what is now Zibo City, Shandong, to a declining landlord-merchant family. His father Pu Pan was a man of broad learning who had a disappointing official career. Pu Songling was a bright, studious child, and his father took pains to foster his talents. At nineteen he placed first in three consecutive regional examinations. No one could have expected that he would repeatedly be rejected in subsequent provincial examinations. At the age of seventy he still wore the dark gown of a poor bachelor of letters. Except for a few months clerking for a magistrate south of the Yangtze when he was thirty-one, Pu Songling lived his whole life out of favor, teaching in a country school-room.

Out of the poverty and austerity of his unfulfilled life, Pu Songling learned to identify with the common people in their sufferings. Unlike most feudalistic literati, who looked down sympathetically on the people from positions of privilege, he stood among the people and pondered their fate. For the ill-treated he argued cases in court, and for the indignant he raised his voice. Seeing peasants lie ill for want of medical care, he compiled a book of prescriptions to help them help themselves. Seeing them ignorant and without access to schools, he compiled *Common Characters for Everyday Use* to help them study on their own. To enhance the practice of agriculture, he gathered the fruits of past farming experience to write the *Book of Husbandry and Sericulture.* Among the literati of China's feudal past, men as concerned for the lot of poor peasants as Pu Songling were few and far between. Of course his thinking could not help but reflect the feudalistic education he received from an early age. But this was secondary to the progressive, democratic nature of his thinking.

From his approach to the writing of *Strange Tales from Make-Do Studio* we can see how close were Pu Songling's ties to the people. Diarists of the time tell how Pu Songling collected folk tales by setting out tea for passers-by in a pavilion next to Willow Spring in Pu Village, imploring them to tell their new and strange stories. The country people called him a "story maniac." His fondness for stories about werefoxes, immortals, ghosts, and goblins prompted the country people to warn him playfully: "Be careful the werefoxes don't get you with their spells." Obviously many stories in his book were collected from popular sources. Friends and relatives who knew of his hobby were glad to send unusual folk tales to him. Eventually he amassed nearly five hundred of them. From Pu Songling's manners of collecting some stories and writing others himself, we can say that *Strange Tales from Make-Do Studio* is a crystallization of shared wisdom.[1]

Strange Tales from Make-Do Studio is closely tied to folk

[1] See the materials collected in *Pu Songling yu Minjian Wenxue* (*Pu Songling and Folk Literature*) pp. 24-32, Shanghai Wenxue Chubanshe, Shanghai. 1985.

literature, but ultimately it is not a book of folk tales, because it is imbued with Pu Songling's particular passions and ideals. This is why Pu Songling called it his "book of isolated indignation."

In reading *Strange Tales from Make-Do Studio* the first question that strikes us is: "Why did Pu Songling make up all those ghost stories? Some people say his enthusiasm for ghost stories stemmed from belief in outdated superstitions. This view is untenable. True, certain elements of fatalism and feudal superstition are treated with approval in the stories, but Pu Songling had more socially compelling reasons to write about ghosts. The late Ming and early Qing was a time of great upheaval for China's feudal society. In 1644 the corrupt Ming court was overthrown by Li Zicheng's army of peasant rebels.[1] Aristocratic leaders of the Manchu nationality, in collusion with Wu Sangui, the Ming general garrisoning Shanhai Pass, robbed the peasant army of its victory and established China's last feudal dynasty—the Qing. The Qing rulers overcame the various nationalities of China with the help of widespread slaughter and pillage, thus stirring up fierce flames of resistance. In order that the ruling elite of a small minority people could rule a huge nation, suppression and obliteration of resistance became a key means of protecting its government rule. This was the background for an unprecedentedly ruthless system of suppression—the "literary inquisition." In the circumstances Pu Songling faced, he and his whole family might well have been executed if he had spoken out, but the outrage that swelled within him could not be pent up forever. Thus his thoughts could not help but turn to

[1]Li Zicheng (1606-1645), leader of a late-Ming peasant rebellion. In 1644 his army of peasant rebels took Beijing and toppled the Ming dynasty.

toward the realm of the mysterious and fantastic, to kindred spirits that waited in shaded groves and dark valleys, to stories of werefoxes and ghosts that could vent his secret indignation. Nothing could have followed more naturally. What was more, numerous stories of werefoxes and ghosts had been handed down since ancient times in China. Song dynasty scholars had put together the 500-fascicle collection *Far-Ranging Records of the Taiping Reign*, which contained many stories of werefoxes, ghosts and spirits. This collection laid the groundwork for the writing of *Strange Tales from Make-Do Studio*.

But whether Pu Songling wrote of werefoxes, ghosts, spirits or demons, the true subject of his writing was people. The stories of *Make-Do Studio* appear in the guise of the supernatural, colored with an uncanny strangeness. But this strangeness is not the freakishness of the old marvel fiction. These stories are strange without being freakish, marvelous yet in tune with human feelings. Their unpredictable events are tied to the personalities of ordinary people. The marvelous depictions of young women, in particular, have a lively brilliance, with characters that stand out in clear relief and bold coloring. The genuineness of their feelings wins our esteem and touches on our true concerns.

Of course many of these young women are figures with a positive place in the feudal order, such as Feng-xian and Hu Fourth-maiden, who encourage their husbands to seek fame and riches. But the ones that especially draw our attention are the rebellious women who dare to transgress the code of feudal propriety and fight to throw off their feudal chains. The writer did not create these unusual female figures just for novelty's sake. Through them he could express his outrage at the ways of the world, and his unique perspective on society's problems; he could explore paths that might lead to a better society. Thus most of Pu Songling's female figures tend to pose challenges to accepted practices of feudal society.

Women were the most deeply oppressed segment of feudal society. The fourfold authority of government, clan, religion, and husband pressed down on them like a great mountain, keeping them submissive and hardly able to draw a breath. Even the freedom of women to talk and laugh was constrained by the rule: "Women are not to speak in raised tones, or to expose their teeth in laughter." In direct opposition to this, Pu Songling created the character Yingning, a vivacious girl who is not afraid to speak out and laugh. Wherever Yingning goes, one hears the sound of laughter. The author captures images of her look and mood as she reacts with laughter to differing circumstances. The unfading mountain flower in the story is an unmistakable emblem of her beauty of character. In an authoritarian setting that suppresses laughter, Yingning throws back her head and laughs with an unabashed frivolity that plainly clashes head-no with feudal propriety. Later, Yingning leaves her remote, flower-bedecked valley and comes to the unclean realm of ordinary mortals, where such laughter becomes impossible. "She would not laugh, even when teased." This contrast makes the challenge posed by Yingning's laugh even more obvious.

The feudal landholding classes put a high value on dominant men and submissive women. "In women lack of talent is a virtue." Pu Songling reversed this by writing of many young women whose intelligence and judgement far surpass their men. The incompetence of the girl-scholar's husband in "Miss Yan" prompts her to dress in male clothing, win top honors in an examination, and become an outstanding official, outdoing her husband in everything she sets her hand to. The author plainly created this story to criticize the mistaken notions of male superiority prevalent at the time and demonstrate that female intelligence was capable of great things, if only given the right opportunity, in spite of the long-standing effects of a repressive system. What was more, the talents of many women would put scholarly males to shame.

Feudal propriety ruled that "men and women are forbidden to pass objects from hand to hand." But Pu Songling went against the current to write of close friendships between men and women. In "Ghost Girl Xiaoxie" the girls Qiurong and Xiaoxie show up in young Scholar Tao's study and play whimsical pranks on him: they tug his whiskers, pat his cheeks, or tickle his nose with a feather to make him sneeze. Sometimes they sneak up behind him and cover his eyes with their hands, then hide in a corner trying to stifle their laughter. The reader chuckling over their antics is liable to forget that they are ghosts. The theme of "Fox-Fairy Jiaonuo" is also an affirmation of undying friendship between a man and a woman. Such sincere, pure relationships between the sexes were impossible given the unclean realities of the time, yet people longed for them. Besides relationships of husband and wife, or between lovers, this story demonstrates a wish for simple, open-hearted friendship between the sexes, which can sometimes be more precious than an ordinary love affair.

The feudal classes vociferously proclaimed marriage to be a weighty event that required obedience to "the bidding of one's parents and the words of a go-between." Pu Songling followed the opposite course and wrote many stories of free love between young men and women, surpassing earlier romantic fiction in the boldness and strength of desire they express. For the sake of love Sun Zichu ignores the ridicule and abuse of others ("Precious"); Nie Xiaoqian is unable to find love while alive, but she continues her indomitable search for happiness in ghostly form ("Nie Xiaoqian"); Liancheng gives her life to gain the love of one who understands her, and through the strength of love comes back to life again ("Liancheng"). What eventually brings these young people together is as much an ideal arrangement of the author as it is their own victory through struggle.

Strange Tales from Make-Do Studio brings to life a large number of remarkable female characters, brilliantly prefiguring the gallery of young women who frequent Grandview Garden in *A Dream of Red Mansions.*[1] The emergence of these independent-minded young women in fiction indicates that China's feudal society was in its decline. the moribund condition of the feudal system was exposed for what it was: life was becoming impossible, not just for the oppressed classes, but also for the young men and women of the ruling classes. Thus each of the characters in the stories breaks away from feudal restrictions in their own way, foretelling the breakdown of the feudal structure. This is our understanding of the book's significance in social terms.

Pu Songling was not only an incisive critic of society as it actually was: he wrote of his highest ideals as well. What others dared not conceive of, he conceived of. The wings of his imagination took him to places no one else could go.

His imaginary flights differ from the absurd concoctions

[1] *A Dream of Red Mansions* is a classical novel by Cao Xueqin. "Grandview Garden" is the large pleasure garden in the novel, where the young members of the aristocratic Jia family live.

of the old marvel fiction in the following ways:

1) His imaginary flights have a sharp critical edge:

The forward-thinking fiction of the past includes many pieces which expose the workings of feudal officialdom. But the stories in *Make-Do Studio* have an approach all their own. They do not simply give a straightforward account of crimes committed by feudal officials. Instead, they create illusory settings in which the nature of feudal officialdom is more profoundly exposed. "The Cricket" exposes the endless hardship which the tribute system brought upon the people. But Pu Songling does not waste many words describing the desperation of people who could not hand over the required tribute. He describes a child who is in such desperation that his spirit leaves his body and transforms itself into an item of tribute—a fighting cricket. This cricket is finally presented to the imperial palace, where it overcomes the "famous generals" presented from all the other parts of the empire. It even overcomes an intimidatingly large rooster, much to the glee of the nabobs at court. But underneath this glee are the blood and sweat and resentment of the people. Such an exposé is more touching than a straightforward treatment of a family destroyed for failure to pay tribute. "Dream of Wolves" uses imaginary means to show the cannabalistic nature of feudal officialdom, in all its bloody savagery, and concludes: "I am forced to admit that beasts in official robes are everywhere in the empire." Few works of fiction in past times spoke out so forcefully against feudal officials.

2) His imaginary flights convey heartfelt praise:

Strange Tales from Make-Do Studio uses the techniques of fantasy to portray idealized characters. Pu Songling's were-foxes, immortals and flower spirits are approachable and warmly human, yet noble and high-minded. In "Huanniang" for instance, the girl Huanniang was devoted to the lute from an early age. One hundred years after her death, she still regrets not having learned lute-playing in direct succession from a famous teacher. On hearing Wen Ruchun's beautiful playing, she imitates it in secret until she completely masters his skills. In the course of learning the lute, both she and Lianggong fall in love with Wen. This could naturally have fostered the mutual jealousy of a love triangle, but Huanniang does not know what jealousy is. Instead, she exerts her wit and talents to win happiness for the man she loves, bringing Scholar Wen and Lianggong together in a blissful marriage. This done, she smiles and steals away. This contrasts markedly with the war of wits and trickery that really went on among people then, and the suspicion, jealousy, hypocrisy, and indifference among families. The moving thing about these love stories is how the author's imagination opens a window to the inner beauty of his characters.

3) The author's imagination evinces a powerful quest:

The real and the ideal are a unity of opposites. Pu Songling hated the dark reality of his times and harbored ideals of a better life. But he did not rely on utopian visions to embody his ideals: instead, he attacked the benightedness of the monarchy, and at the same time made his stories an outlet for his hopes of easing society's ills. The book's imaginary flights are a guest for understanding. Consider the questions some of the stories in the book raise:

Why is it the rule in society to invert beauty and ugliness? Might there perhaps be a "city in the sea" where men of talent win an honored place, and each can make use of his ability? ("City of the Rākṣasas")

Why, in so many seats of government, do beasts in robes

and scholars' caps hold sway? Can there ever be a magically powerful ruler who cares enough to free his people from harm? ("The Ruler")

Why is the world of men, as well as the palace of dragons, under dominion of evil demons? Is it possible that somewhere between heaven and earth a paradise might exist? ("Wanxia")

Why do civil examinations hold back brilliant scholars and favor mediocrities? When will the results be audited by Zhang Yuanhou, who would make sure that men of genius assume their rightful place? ("Yu Que")

In other stories we find one woman made anew by the exchanges of her heart for another's ("Judge Lu"), and another disfigured so her innocence may be protected ("Courtesan Ruiyun"). Many of the stories tell of young men and women who break the stifling bonds of feudal propriety. All demonstrate that Pu Songling, though he lived under a corrupt monarchy, never gave up his bold quest for another world. Although the goal of his quest was somewhat obscure, it was admirable in spirit.

4) The author's imagination gives form to thought-provoking messages:

Pu Songling's stories use language sparingly, but yield a great deal of meaning on careful reading. Though other writers wrote of ghosts just as he did, he manages to convey more of a message. His stories are efforts to encapsulate certain lessons of experience or reflections on life. "Painted Skin" is one of the most famous of his stories, and the words "painted skin" have become a synonym for duplicity that wears an outwardly human face but is inwardly demonic. "Witchcraft" and "Nie Xiaoqian" are a thought-provoking study on how fixity of human purpose can overcome demons. "The Taoist of Lao Mountain" is rich with messages that cannot be summarized by the simple moral—"easy paths lead straight into brick walls."

Pu Songling's flights of imagination give his stories a fascination all their own, and they produce artistic effects that other works do not have. To accommodate their unusual characters and ideas, the stories have to be built along unique creative lines. They carry on the technique and form of ancient marvel fiction and wonder tales, but they are developed much beyond this. Their fantasies do not depart from truthfulness, and their marvels are woven cleverly together with normality. Lu Xun, in his *History of Chinese Fiction*, writes:

> Though the *Strange Tales from Make-Do Studio*, like other collections of the period, are merely stories of the supernatural—of fairies, foxes, ghosts and goblins—the narratives are concise and meticulous in the tradition of Tang Dynasty stories, so that all these strange events appear very vivid. Sometimes the author describes oddities belonging not to the world of fantasy but to the world of men, and minor incidents are so well-recorded that readers find them fresh and interesting.

This is an overall view of the stories, but each of them has its own particular coloring. Some of them construct fantastic realms, and some strike out into the unknown. Some use tiny incidents as windows on larger things, and some seek reality in figments of imagination. There are uncanny coincidences, interplays of forces and transcendence of time and space. A nimble play of fancy and an unbounded field of imagination combine to build the scintillating world of these stories.

Pu Songling's treatment of the age-old subject of love,

for instance, sparkles with originality. Writing four or five different love stories might not cost an author much effort, but to write over a hundred love stories, as Pu Songling did without covering the same ground, is certainly no easy matter. Though we must admit that "Liancheng" bears some similarity in plot to the play *Peony Pavilion,*[1] such stories as "Yingning," "Precious," "Ghost-Girl Xiaoxie," "Ghost-Maiden Huanniang," "Ghost-Girl Wanxia," "Bird Nymph Zhuqing," "Linen Scarf" and "Fish Demon Bai Qiulian" are radical departures from previous models of romantic fiction. "Fairy Qing-E" in particular seems to have grown magically from a plot of ground that only the author could tend. The feudal code of propriety deprived young men and women of any chance to meet with each other. If they "tunneled through walls" to be with one another, they were "despised by parents and townsmen." In a setting like this, Huo Yuan feels regard for Qing-e but has no way to see her. Then Pu Songling lets him meet a priest of great magical powers who gives him a little spade. With this spade he digs straight through one wall after another, straight to Qing-e's secluded room, where he spends the night beside her. With the same spade Huo Yuan also drills into the rock face where Qing-e is kept captive, rescuing her from the tyranny of her father. The magic spade is the key element in the story. As a symbol of power it expresses the ardent wish of young men and women to penetrate the walls erected against their love. It expresses their long-felt demand to break through the barriers of rigid decorum. Pu Songling's remarkable plots evince his individual creativity and his progressively dem-

[1] *Peony Pavilion* is a romantic play written by the noted Ming playwright Tang Xianzu.

ocratic thinking. This is what gives his stories enduring life.

Chinese and Western scholars through the years have found much to praise in the streamlined, evocative style of *Strange Tales from Make-Do Studio.* This is one of the remarkable things about the book. The stories are short —in general little over a thousand characters and at most a few thousand. Yet they are surprising for their abundant content, their intricate reversals of plot, and their depth of thought. These stories are reminiscent of Chinese miniature landscapes, in which fist-sized mountains and ponds the size of a cupped hand impress as with scenic grandeur. What is more, each story has its own realm of thought, unlike all the rest. These stories stand rightly at the peak of China's classical short fiction.

In short, *Strange Tales from Make-Do Studio* is a book remarkable in many respects—for its characters, its ideas, its artistic conceptions, and its power to fascinate. Since its appearance, it has been a popular favorite, and its success as a work of the imagination has attracted the notice of scholars overseas. Over the years its stories have been translated and retranslated into many foreign languages. From this we can see that *Strange Tales from Make-Do Studio* has become a shared treasure, not just of the Chinese people, but of all the world's people.

Wang Jisi and *Liu Liemao*

[illegible]

[illegible] Wan, Quan [illegible]. Two [illegible] desks with [illegible] cushions had been set up in front of the hall. [illegible] was already seated at the [illegible] from the head of the room. Master Song sat down shoulder to shoulder with him. On each desk were a pen and a [illegible]. Suddenly a slip of paper bearing the composition topic [illegible] before his eyes. The eight words [illegible] were "One man, two men: with intent, [illegible] not [illegible]

1. CANDIDATE FOR THE POST OF CITY GOD

MY brother-in-law's grandfather Master Song Tao, a local recipient of a government stipend for bachelors of letters, was lying sick in bed one day when an officer bearing a summons and leading a white-blazed horse came to him and said, "You are requested to be present at an examination."

"The civil examiner has not yet arrived; how can an examination be held out of the blue?" asked Master Song.

The officer fended the question off by insistently urging him to go. Master Song climbed weakly onto the horse and followed him along an unfamiliar road till they came to a walled city that looked like the seat of a king's authority. Before long they entered a magnificently built official residence. A group of ten or so officials sat at the head of a hall, none of whom he recognized except the God of War, Guan Yu. Two low desks with floor cushions had been set up in front of the hall. A bachelor of letters was already seated at the place farther from the head of the room. Master Song sat down shoulder-to-shoulder with him. On each desk were a pen and a writing pad. Suddenly a slip of paper bearing the composition topic glided down before his eyes. The eight words on it were "One man, two men: with intent, without intent." The two scholars completed their essays and presented them to the group at the head of the hall. One part of Master Song's essay read: "When a good deed is done with the intent of getting a reward, goodness is not to be rewarded: when an evil deed is done without intent, then evil is not to be punished."

The deities passed the essay around, and there was no end to their praise of it. They called Master Song forward and announced their decision: "There is an opening for a city god in Henan province that you are qualified to fill." Only then did Master Song realize what was happening. He bumped his head pleadingly on the floor and sobbed: "Since you deign to grant me your most partial appointment, how dare I stubbornly decline? But my old mother is in her seventies and has no one to look after her. Please let me be with her until she lives out her appointed span of years: then I will be at your service."

An emperor-like deity commanded that his mother's longevity entry be checked. A clerk with a long beard brought out a record book and, after leafing quickly through it, reported, "She has nine years left on earth."

Guan Yu resolved the general indecision by saying: "No trouble. Have Scholar Zhang hold the seal of appointment in his stead until the nine years are up. That will be fine." Then he turned to Master Song and said, "Even though you should assume your duties right away, in order to promote benevolence and filial obedience, we will grant you a nine-year extension this time. When that period is over we will summon you again." He then spoke a few words of consolation and encouragement to the unsuccessful candidate. The two scholars kowtowed and left the hall together. The unsuccessful candidate shook Master Song's hand and accompanied him to the environs of the city. He volunteered the information that his name was Zhang,

人生
百行孝為
先明義開
宗第一篇
注涕陳情子
假日歡承萱
草喜延年

coming from Changshan. His parting gift was a poem which escaped Song's memory except two of the lines: "With flowers and wine, spring is always here; without candle or lamp the night itself is bright." Master Song mounted his horse, said goodbye and left. As he entered his own neighborhood he felt himself waking up as if from a dream.

At that time he had been dead for three days. His mother heard moaning in the coffin and helped him out. Half a day passed before he could speak. Song asked about Changshan and learned that, sure enough, a scholar named Zhang had died there on the same day that he had.

Nine years later his mother died as expected. As soon as Song had finished making her funeral arrangements, he bathed and then entered his bedroom and died. That day his in-laws, who lived just inside the west gate of the city, saw him riding a horse with engraved harness and crimson trappings, followed by a large number of coaches and horses. Song walked into their hall, bowed once and left. In their astonishment they failed to realize that he was a ghost. They ran to his neighborhood to ask about him, only to find that he was already dead. Master Song left a short autobiography but, unfortunately, nothing remained of it after the disorder that swept our land.[1] Here I give only a bare outline.

1. At the end of the Ming dynasty (1368-1644) and the beginning of the Qing (1644-1911).

2. THE MURAL

WHILE staying in the capital, Meng Longtan of Jiangxi and Master of Letters Zhu once happened upon a monastery. Neither the shrine-hall nor the meditation room was very spacious, and only one old monk was found putting up within. Seeing the guests enter, the monk straightened up his clothes, went to greet them and showed them around the place. An image of Zen Master Baozhi[1] stood in the shrine-hall. On either side wall were painted fine murals with lifelike human figures. The east wall depicted the Buddhist legend of "Heavenly Maidens Scattering Flowers." Among the figures was a young girl with flowing hair[2] with a flower in her hand and a faint smile on her face. Her cherry-red lips were on the verge of moving, and the liquid pools of her eyes seemed to stir with wave-like glances. After gazing intently for some time, Zhu's self-possession began to waver and his thoughts grew so abstracted that he fell into a trance. His body went adrift as if floating on mist; suddenly he was inside the mural. Peak upon peak of palaces and pavilions made him feel as if he was beyond this earth. An old monk was preaching the *Dharma* on a dais, around which stood a large crowd of viewers in robes with their right shoulders bared out of

1. A monk who lived during the Northern and Southern dynasties (420-589).

2. Her hair was not bound up, signifying that she was unmarried.

respect. Zhu mingled in among them.

Before long, he felt someone tugging furtively at his sleeve. He turned to look, and there was the girl with flowing hair giving him a dazzling smile. She tripped abruptly away, and he lost no time following her along a winding walkway into a small chamber. Once there, he hesitated to approach any farther. When she turned her head and raised the flower with a beckoning motion, he went across to her in the quiet, deserted chamber. Swiftly he embraced her and, as she did not put up much resistance, they grew intimate. When it was over she told him not to make a sound and left, closing the door behind her. That night she came again. After two days of this, the girl's companions realized what was happening and searched together until they found the scholar.

"A little gentleman is already growing in your belly, but still you wear those flowing tresses, pretending to be a maiden," they said teasingly. Holding out hairpins and earrings, they pressured her to put her hair up in the coiled knot of a married woman, which she did in silent embarrassment. One of the girls said, "Sisters, let's not out-stay our welcome." At this the group left all in a titter.

Looking at the soft, cloudlike chignon piled atop her head and her phoenix ringlets curved low before her ears, the scholar was more struck by her charms than when she had worn her hair long. Seeing that no one was around, he began to make free with her. His heart throbbed at her musky fragrance but, before they had quite finished their pleasure, the heavy tread of leather boots was heard. A clanking of chains and manacles was followed by clamorous, arguing voices. The girl got up in alarm. Peering out, they saw an officer dressed in armor, his face black as lacquer, with chains in one hand and a mace in the other.

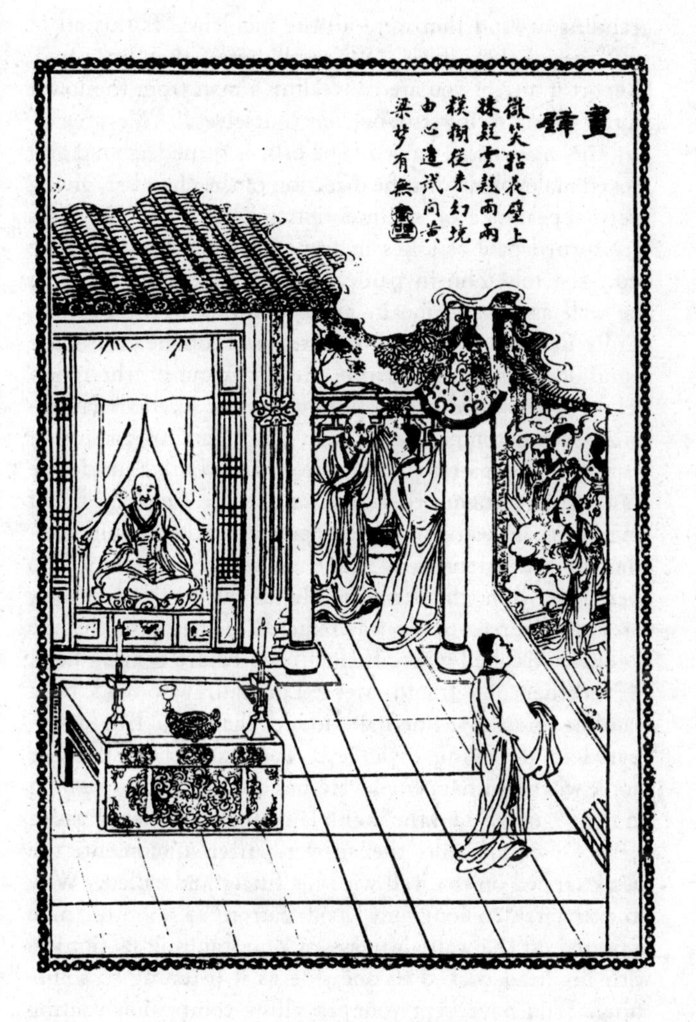
畫壁
微笑拈花壁上
姝鬟雲鬟兩兩
模糊從來幻境
由心造試向黃
粱梦有無

Standing around him were all the maidens. "Is this all of you?" asked the officer. "We're all here," they answered. "Report if any of you are concealing a man from the lower world. Don't bring trouble on yourselves." "We aren't," said the maidens in unison. The officer turned around and looked malevolently in the direction of the chamber, giving every appearance of an intention to search it. The girl's face turned pale as ashes in fear. "Quick, hide under the bed," she told Zhu in panic. She opened a little door in the wall and was gone in an instant. Zhu lay prostrate, hardly daring to take a little breath. Soon he heard the sound of boots stumping into, then back out of the room. Before long, the din of voices gradually receded. He regained some composure, though the sound of passers-by discussing the matter could be heard frequently outside the door. After cringing there for quite some time, he heard ringing in his ears and felt a burning ache in his eyes. Though the intensity of these sensations threatened to overwhelm him, there was no choice but to listen quietly for the girl's return. He was reduced to the point that he no longer recalled where he had been before coming here.

Just then his friend Meng Longtan, who had been standing in the shrine-hall, found that Zhu had disappeared in the blink of an eye. Perplexed, he asked the monk what had happened. "He has gone to hear a sermon on the *Dharma*," said the monk laughingly. "Where?" asked Meng. "Not far" was the answer. After a moment, the monk tapped on the wall with his finger and called, "Why do you tarry so long, my good patron?" Presently there appeared on the wall an image of Zhu standing motionless with his head cocked to one side as if listening to something. "You have kept your travelling companion waiting a long time," called the monk again. Thereupon he drifted out of the mural and down to the floor. He stood woodenly, his mind like burned-out ashes, with eyes staring straight ahead and legs wobbling. Meng was terribly frightened, but in time calmed down enough to ask what had happened. It turned out that Zhu had been hiding under the bed when he heard a thunderous knocking, so he came out of the room to listen for the source of the sound.

They looked at the girl holding the flower and saw, instead of flowing hair, a high coiled chignon on her head. Zhu bowed down to the old monk in amazement and asked the reason for this. "Illusion is born in the mind. How can a poor mendicant like myself explain it?" laughed the monk. Zhu was dispirited and cast down; Meng was shaken and confused. Together they walked down the shrine-hall steps and left.

The Chronicler of the Tales comments: " 'Illusion is born in the mind.' These sound like the words of one who has found the truth. A wanton mind gives rise to visions of lustfulness. The mind dominated by lust gives rise to a state of fear. The Bodhisattva made it possible for the ignorant persons to attain realization for themselves. All the myriad transformations of illusion are nothing but the movements of the human mind itself. The old monk spoke in earnest solicitude, but regrettably there is no sign that the youth found enlightenment in his words and entered the mountains with hair unbound to seek the truth."

3. THE THEFT OF A PEACH

WHEN young I went to the prefectural seat to take an examination and happened to be there on Spring Festival (Spring Begins). According to custom, on the eve of this day all the shopkeepers decorated their storefronts and organized a musical procession that went through town to the *yamen* of the provincial treasury. This was called the "Spring Performance." Some friends and I went to take it in. The streets were lined with walls of spectators. At the head of the provincial treasury hall sat four officials in red silk robes facing each other, two each on the east and west. I was too young then to know their names and titles. All I could hear was the clamor of voices mingled with the din of the procession outside. In the middle of all this a man with loads on a carrying pole led a long-haired boy to the front of the hall. He seemed to be announcing something, but I could not make out the words in the waves of intermingled sounds. I could see, however, that the people at the head of the hall were laughing. Then a black-robed servant ordered them in a loud voice to perform an act. As the man got ready to play, he asked, "What act shall I perform?" The officials spoke a few sentences among themselves. A clerk came down and proclaimed their wish to know his best trick.

"I can transform living creatures," he answered. The clerk relayed this to the officials. After a moment he came

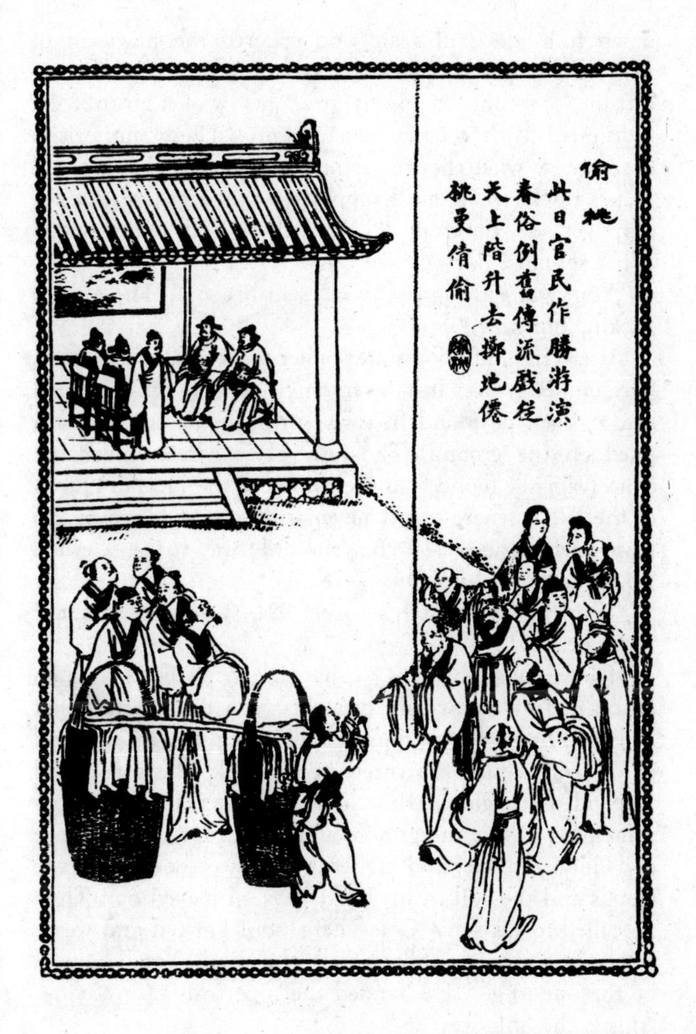

偷桃
此日官民作勝游演
春俗例舊傳流戲徃
天上階升去擲地僊
桃更倩偷

down from the hall again and ordered the magician to materialize a peach. The latter agreed to do so, but taking off his coat and laying it over his wicker trunk, he murmured with feigned resentment, "These authorities don't know what they're saying! The ice out there is still inches thick: where am I supposed to get a peach? But if I don't get one, Im afraid I'll make these lords angry at me. What should I do?"

"You've already agreed to it," said his son. "There is no backing out now."

After grumbling for quite some time, the magician said, "I've mulled it over from every angle. Where on this earth can a peach be found in early spring when snow is still piled on the ground? The only place where one could conceivably be found is in the garden of the Mother Queen of the West, where plants never wither or shed leaves, no matter what the season. But the only way to get a peach would be to steal it from heaven."

"Humph!" exclaimed his son. "Can you scale a ladder up to heaven?"

"I have magic for this," came the answer. Whereupon he opened his trunk and brought out a coil of rope that appeared to be several hundred feet long. He got one end of the rope ready and threw it upwards. The rope stood suspended straight in the air as if it were hanging from something. As he flung more and more rope upwards, the end climbed higher and higher until it was soon lost in the clouds and the coil in his hands was all played out. Then he called to his son: "Come here, son! I'm old and weak. My body is too unwieldy to make the climb. You'll have to be the one to go." He handed the rope to his son saying: "this is the only way up."

His son took the rope reluctantly. "You must be out of

your mind, old man!" he said in exasperation. "You want me to grab onto a flimsily rope like this and climb into the blue yonder. If it breaks when I'm halfway, there won't even be any bones left of me."

Patting the boy's back, the father urged him to act, "My claim has already been made. I can't take it back now. Would you please go? And don't take it so hard. If you steal one and bring it back, they'll be sure to give us a handsome reward, which I'll use to get you a beautiful wife." The son took hold of the rope and ascended swayingly hand over foot, like a spider on its filament, until he entered the cloud layer and was lost to sight. After some time a bowl-sized peach fell out of the sky. Overjoyed, the magician presented it to those in the hall. The officials took turns examining it for quite some time without being able to tell whether it was real or fake.

Suddenly the rope fell to the earth. "This is awful!" exclaimed the magician. "Someone up above cut my rope. How will my son hold on there?" In a moment an object hurtled to the ground. It turned out to be the boy's head. He held it up and sobbed: "He must have been caught stealing the peach by a guard. It is all over for my boy." Before long a leg fell earthwards, followed by the remaining pieces of a dismembered corpse. The grief-stricken magician gathered up the pieces, placed them in his trunk and snapped it shut, saying "I had only this one son. He was with me in all my wanderings. Now, compelled by his father's command, he has met an unexpected and horrible end. I have no choice but to carry this trunk away and inter his remains." He paused to walk up to the hall, where he knelt and pleaded: "My son lost his life because of that peach. If you take pity on me and help with the burial, I swear that I will repay you even after death." Each of the stunned officials had a sum of gold for him. The magician put it into his waist pouch, then knocked on the trunk and called, "Dear son, won't you come out and thank these men for their presents? What are you waiting for?" Suddenly a tousle-haired boy pushed open the lid with his head, came out and kowtowed toward the north where the officials were seated. And who should it have been but the magician's son!

I remember this even now because it was such an amazing feat of magic. Later I heard that the White Lotus cult[1] was capable of such wizardry. Could these two have perhaps been among its latter-day adherents?

1. A peasants' society dating back to the Song dynasty (960-1279), which made it its aim to fight against the tyrannical rulers.

4. PLANTING PEARS

A VILLAGER was once vending pears in a marketplace. The pears were sweet and luscious, but the price was high out of all proportion. A Taoist wearing a tattered bandana and frayed clothes stopped before the cart and begged for a pear. When his shouts failed to turn the Taoist away, the vendor was so incensed that he loosed a torrent of abuse on him. The Taoist said, "There are several hundred pears in your cart. I ask for no more than one of them, which surely could not put you out too much. Why get angry?" The onlookers recommended getting rid of him by giving up a mushy pear, but the vendor held stubbornly to his position.

Finding the annoying jabber unbearable, a shop-boy used his own money to buy a pear, which he gave to the Taoist. The Taoist bowed in gratitude, then spoke to the crowd: "We who have renounced lay life do not understand miserliness. I have a fine pear which I would like to offer to my guests."

Someone said, "now that you've got it, why not eat it yourself?"

"I only needed the core for its seeds," he answered. Whereupon he raised the pear to his lips and started chomping away. When he finished, he had the core in his palm. Then he took down a mattock he had been carrying on his shoulder and dug a hole several inches deep in the ground. He put the core inside, covered it over with soil, and asked people who worked in the market for hot water to wet down the soil. A certain busybody procured boiling water from a roadside shop. The Taoist took it and poured it on the hoed-over spot. A multitude of eyes jostled for a view. They saw a curly sprout appear, get gradually bigger and, in no time at all, become a tree with luxuriant leaves and branches. Flowers quickly appeared and just as quickly turned to huge, fragrant fruits strung over every part of the tree. The Taoist reached for the top of the tree and picked pears for the onlookers. In a moment the pears were given out, whereupon he pitched into the tree with his mattock. The chopping sounds went on for a long time before the trunk was cut through. He raised the trunk to his shoulder, leaves and all, then ambled nonchalantly away.

When the Taoist began performing magic the vendor had mingled with the crowd, craning his neck and staring with no thought of his wares. Only when the Taoist had gone did he turn to look into his cart, which was now emptied of pears, and realized what the Taoist had just handed out were his. Looking further, he found to his great consternation that a shaft was missing from his cart and that it had been freshly chopped off. Setting off in hot pursuit, he rounded the corner of a wall and found the broken cart shaft abandoned beside it. He knew that this was the trunk of the tree that had just been chopped down. The Taoist was nowhere to be found. The whole market was humming with laughter.

The Chronicler of the Tales comments: "The dullness of the thick-skulled villager is almost palpable. No wonder the people in the market laughed at him. It often happens that men who are known in the villages as prosperous become upset when good friends beg for rice. They figure

種梨
任教慳吝偏人衰天道原來
是好還頃刻花開頃刻實
神仙游戲警貪頑

what it will cost them, saying: 'This is worth several days' income.' If they are called upon to succor people in dire need or feed a lone, helpless soul they calculate resentfully, saying: 'You're asking for food enough to sustain five or ten persons.' In the worst cases fathers, sons, and brothers count every last dram and grain against each other, but when seized by gambling fever they upend their pouches freely. And when they sense instruments of execution hanging over their own necks, they waste no time buying their way out of trouble. Such evils defy enumeration. Is it any wonder that this story makes the villager look so foolish?"

5. THE TAOIST OF LAO MOUNTAIN[1]

IN our district lived scholar Wang, the seventh son of an old family. From youth onward he was attracted to Taoist arts. Hearing that immortals abounded on Lao Mountain, he packed his books on his back and set out there on an adventure. Climbing to the top of a peak, Wang came to a Taoist temple set in a wild, secluded spot. A Taoist with white hair hanging past his collar was sitting on a bast mat. He had about him an other-worldly air that was graceful and lofty. Scholar Wang made obeisance to him and struck up a conversation. The Taoist's talk impressed him as quite mysterious and subtle. Wang asked to be accepted as his disciple, to which he replied, "I am afraid you are too soft and lazy to work hard."

"Oh, but I can," answered Wang. The Taoist had a crowd of acolytes, all of whom came together at dusk. Having saluted each of them, Wang settled down in the hermitage.

At the crack of dawn the Taoist woke Wang, gave him an axe and made him go to gather firewood with the others. Wang did exactly as he was told. After more than a month of this, his hands and feet had calluses on top of calluses. Unable to bear the toil, he nursed secret intentions of returning home. One evening on his return he saw

[1] An old divine spot for taoists on the Shandong coast of Jiaozhou Bay.

two men drinking with his master. The sun had already set but no lamps or candles had yet been lit, so the master cut paper in the shape of a mirror and pasted it on the wall. Suddenly a light as bright as the moon's flooded the room, making even the tiniest hairs visible. The acolytes in attendance ran back and forth at the guests' bidding. One of the guests said, "It's a beautiful night for good times. We ought to share them with everyone here." The Taoist picked up a pitcher of wine from the table and began to pour some for each acolyte, urging them to drink their fill. Wang thought to himself: "How can a pitcher of wine suffice for seven or eight people?" Each of them hunted up a drinking vessel. They vied to see who would be first to drain his cup. Their only fear was that the pitcher was empty, but when they went to pour from it again they were astonished to find that the wine had not gone down in the slightest. Soon another guest said, "You have been nice enough to give us moonlight to drink by, but there is still no entertainment. Why don't you call the goddess of the moon to come?" At this the Taoist tossed a chopstick into the moon and a beautiful woman appeared out of the circle of light. At first she was not even a foot tall, but she grew to normal size as she descended to the floor. Her slender waist and graceful neck moved through the fluttering gyrations of the Dance of the Rainbow Skirt and Feathered Blouse[1]. To the tempo of the dance she sang,

Immortal of the mountains
Is it true you're bound for home
Will you leave me all alone
In this icy crystal dome?

[1] A famous dance which flourished in palaces during the Tang dynasty (618-907).

勞山道士
願學
神仙一
念癡推
薪蘇艸苦難
枯袱求棲得穿
裔術何此居心
乙可知

Her silvery voice was as piercing as a flute. At the end of the song she arose with a sweeping motion, jumped up on the table and, in the space of an astonished glance, was already a chopstick again. The three men laughed boisterously.

The other guest spoke up: "This evening has been wonderful, but the wine is getting the better of me. Would it be all right if we had a farewell drink in the palace of the moon?" The three men moved their mats and slowly floated into the moon. The acolytes saw the three seated in the moon drinking, their features distinct as reflections in a mirror. After a time the moon gradually dimmed. When the acolytes brought a lighted candle they found the Taoist sitting alone, his guests nowhere to be seen. The delicacies on the table were just as before, and the moon on the wall was nothing more than a disc of paper.

"Did you have enough to drink?" the Taoist asked the acolytes.

"Enough" they said.

"Then you ought to go right to bed. Don't let this interfere with gathering wood and kindling."

The acolytes said "yes" and retired.

Wang's intention of leaving subsided out of heartfelt admiration. But after another month had passed the grinding toil became too much for him, and the Taoist would not pass on even a single magical technique. Unable to wait any longer, Wang took his leave, saying: "I came a hundred miles to study under such an immortal master as yourself. Even though I cannot learn the art of everlasting life, there may perhaps be some small skill you could impart that would appease my wish for learning. For the past two or three months all I have done is go out to gather wood in the morning and return in the evening. When I was at home, I was not used to this kind of hard work."

The Taoist answered with a laugh: "I said from the start that you would not be able to stand hard work, and you have proven me right. I will send you off tomorrow morning."

"I have labored for many days. If you could just impart some insignificant part of your art, my coming would not be in vain." The Taoist asked what art he hoped to learn.

Wang answered, "I have often noticed that walls are no hindrance to your free motion. I would be satisfied to learn the method of such magic."

The Taoist gave his assent with a laugh. Then he taught Wang the words of a spell and told him to chant it through by himself, at which he cried, "Go through." Wang faced the wall, not daring to walk into it. Again the Taoist cried, "Try to go through it!" Doing as he was told, Wang gingerly approached the wall, but it proved unyielding to his forward movement.

"Lower your head and go through quickly. Don't hold back," instructed the Taoist. So Wang backed several steps away from the wall and ran toward it. When he came to the wall it seemed not to be there at all. Turning around to look, he found that he was already outside the building. Overjoyed, he went back in to thank his master. The Taoist said, "You must live chastely after your return, or the spell will not work." Then he gave Wang money for the trip home and sent him off.

Upon reaching home Wang boasted that he had met with an immortal and that now his power was such that no solid wall could stop him. His wife found this hard to believe. Wang stood several feet from a wall and ran headlong against it as he had done before, but this time his head smacked against the hard wall and he tumbled backward. His wife helped him up and looked at the goose egg rising mound-like on his forehead. Shamed but incited by her ridicule into a fury, he raved that the old Taoist was nothing but a reprobate.

The Chronicler of the Tales comments: "No one who hears of this incident can keep from laughing out loud, but those who laugh do not realize that the Scholar Wangs of this world are by no means few and far between. Take the case of a worthless official who would 'rather swallow poison than medicines.' A 'boil-sucking, hemorrhoid-licking' sort of person might cater to his wishes by advocating brutal, self-aggrandizing policies and inveigle him, saying: 'You need only adhere to such and such a policy--nothing will stand in your way.' The first time he tries, it might yield some small measure of success, thus giving him the idea that such policy can be applied to all cases under heaven. Those who are taken by this will not stop until they run headlong into a solid wall and topple over backward."

6. FOX-FAIRY JIAONUO

SCHOLAR Kong Xueli, a descendant of Confucius, was poised in manner and accomplished in poetry. A close friend who served as magistrate of Tiantai district[1] summoned him by letter. Kong arrived only to find that the magistrate had just died. This left him down-and-out and without the means to return, so he put up in Potala Monastery, where he was employed copying sutras for the monks. The residence of one Master Shan lay a hundred-some steps to the west of the monastery. Master Shan, the scion of a gentry family, had moved to the country with his reduced household, leaving the residence vacant, after being involved in a lawsuit which had brought on the decline of his fortunes. One day while walking through the swirling eddies of a heavy snowfall, Scholar Kong happened to pass by the gate. A young man, quite striking in manner, was issuing from the gate when he saw Scholar Kong, and hurried over to greet him. Having expressed concern for Kong's health in a few words, he begged to have the honor of receiving him as a visitor. Delighted at the young man's refreshing charm, Kong followed him in with alacrity. The rooms were hardly spacious, but brocade draperies hung everywhere. A number of paintings and works of calligraphy by ancient masters were on the walls.

[1] In Zhejiang province.

On the desk lay a volume bearing the title *Random Notes from the Land of Langhuan.*[1] A quick glance through showed it to be full of things never seen in other books.

Because the young man occupied the Shan residence, Kong assumed him to be master of the house and did not inquire about his family's social standing. The young man questioned Kong at length about the life he led and was moved to pity by what he heard. He suggested setting up a private schoolhouse and finding some pupils. Kong sighed and said, "Who would vouch for a wanderer like me?"

"I would like to study under you, if you still find some redeeming value in a worthless nag like myself."

Delighted as he was, Kong could not presume to act as the young man's tutor, so he asked that they be bound by friendship instead. Kong went on to ask: "Why has your house been boarded up all this time?"

"This is the Shan manor," replied the young man. "The owner moved to the country and left the place empty quite some time ago. I belong to the Huangfu clan, which has its ancestral home in Shaanxi. I am using this as a temporary resting place because my family dwelling was destroyed by wildfire." Only then did Scholar Kong realize that his friend was not one of the Shans.

That evening the two of them conversed merrily, after which they shared the young man's sleeping mat. Just before dawn, a servant boy lit a charcoal fire in the room. The young man got up first and went into inner quarters, while Kong sat huddled under the covers. The servant came in to say that the old gentleman was coming. Kong

[1] A collection of fairy tales by Yi Shizhen of the Yuan dynasty (1206-1341). Its first article on the list bears the title "The Blessed Land of Langhuan."

嬌娜
不愧人間公子名
為憐家室太多
情松攘袂免嬌
娘德只合青天
誓死生

got up in surprise. A silver-headed old man entered and graciously thanked Kong, saying: "You have been kind enough not to spurn my thick-headed son, and you have even offered him the benefit of your teaching. My boy is just now learning to scribble. Don't treat him as an equal just because you are friends." Saying this, he presented Kong with a figured gown, a mink cap, and a pair each of shoes and stockings. He watched until Kong finished washing his face and combing his hair, then called for wine and victuals to be set out before him. The furnishings of the room and the host's clothing were of unfamiliar materials that dazzled the eyes with their lustre. After several rounds of wine the old man rose, took his leave and walked out leaning on his cane.

At the end of the meal the young gentleman brought out his exercises, all of which were written in classic style. There was not one example of up-to-date examination writing[1] among them. When Kong questioned him on this he answered with a laugh: "I am not out to climb the ladder of success." As evening approached, he filled the winecups again and said, "Let's enjoy ourselves to the full tonight: starting tomorrow there will be no more of this." He called to the servant boy: "See whether the old gentleman is in bed yet. If he is, call Xiangnu in here, and keep it quiet." The boy left, then return with an embroidered bag containing a four-string lute. In a moment a maid entered, looking as stunning as could be in her colorful adornments. The young gentleman told her to play the piece called "Goddesses of the River Xiang." Strumming the strings with an ivory pick, she played an intense and

[1] Better known as eight-legged (or eight-paragraph) essay, a style of writing prescribed for civil examinations during the Ming and Qing dynasties (1368-1911).

passionate melody to a rhythm unlike anything Kong had ever heard. Then she was ordered to serve wine in huge beakers. Only when the third watch came did they call it a night.

The next day they rose early to study together. The young gentleman was exceptionally bright, with the ability to memorize a passage simply by running his eyes over it. After two or three months his command of the ink-brush was thoroughly remarkable. They agreed to drink together once every five days and did not fail to summon Xiangnu to each bout. One night Kong, feeling his desire kindled by the mellowness of wine, let his eyes linger on her. The young gentleman grasped what was on his mind immediately and said, "This maid was brought up as one of the family by my father. Seeing you forlorn and wifeless, I have turned the matter over in my mind day and night. Sooner or later I should arrange a beautiful mate for you."

"If you would be so kind, let it be someone like Xiangnu," blurted Kong.

The young gentleman answered laughingly: "You certainly bear out the old saying that 'the inexperienced are easily excited.' If this is your idea of beauty, your wishes are indeed easily satisfied."

A half-year had passed when one day, Kong wanted to go rambling about the environs of the city, but when he reached the gate, he found that its double leaves had been bolted from the outside. When asked about it, the young gentleman told him: "The master of the house fears that socializing will distract me from my studies, so he is turning away all guests." This was readily accepted by Kong. That was at the height of the summer season—a time of sweltering heat—so they set up their studio in a pavilion in the garden. Soon afterwards a peach-sized swelling appeared on

Kong's chest. After one night, it grew to the size of a bowl and made him cry out in anguish. The young gentleman looked after him constantly, neglecting to eat and sleep. In a few days the pain from the boil became increasingly grievous, so that eating and drinking were now out of the question. The old gentleman, too, came out for a look and heaved a great sigh at what he saw.

"The night before last I was worrying about my tutor's affliction," said the young gentleman. "It occurred to me that sister Jiaonuo could cure it, so I sent someone to granny's place to bring her. After all this time why hasn't she arrived?" At that moment the servant boy came in to say, "Miss Jiaonuo has arrived. Auntie and Miss Song are with her." Father and son rushed into the inner quarters. In a short while they ushered in a girl to have a look at the scholar. She was around thirteen or fourteen years of age, her eyes were coy pools darting with brilliance and her slender-willow frame figured forth loveliness in its every attitude. When he glimpsed her charms, the scholar abruptly left off his moaning and his spirits revived. Then the young gentleman spoke: "This is my good friend. We are closer than if we had been born of the same parents. Try your best to treat him, sister."

At this the girl dispensed with her look of bashfulness and walked toward the bed to make an examination, trailing her long sleeves through the air. As she probed with her fingers, Kong was aware of a fragrance that surpassed orchids. "No wonder he has this affliction," said the girl laughingly. "His pulse is unsteady. The illness is critical, but it can be cured. However, this area of tissue is already moribund. Our only choice is to remove the skin and cut away the flesh." Whereupon she removed a bracelet from her arm, placed it on the afflicted spot and pressed down gradually. The boil bulged more than an inch out of the bracelet, and the base of the swelling was completely contained within. No longer was it as wide in diameter as a bowl. Then the girl lifted the front of her gossamer gown with one hand and unfastened a knife with a razor-thin blade which hung at her waist. Holding the bracelet and grasping the knife firmly, she cut gently along the base. Purple blood spilled out in gouts, staining the bed mat. But the scholar, in his craving for proximity to her soft loveliness, was not only unaware of the pain but even apprehensive lest the operation end too soon and put a stop to their nearness. Before long a lump of putrefied flesh, resembling a gall cut from a tree, was sliced away. The girl then called for water, which she used to cleanse the incision. She expelled a red lozenge the size of a crossbow pellet from her mouth and placed it on the raw flesh, then pressed downward and rolled it around the wound. When it had made one circuit, the scholar felt heat darting like flame. When the lozenge had rolled around the second time, the spot pulsated with a comfortable itching sensation. At the end of the third circuit a refreshing coolness flooded through his body and penetrated to the very marrow of his bones. The girl put the lozenge back into her throat, announced "He is cured!" and walked away with rapid steps. The scholar leapt up and ran to thank her, as if he had never been stricken by a serious malady. After that her glorious countenance hovered before his mind's eye: his painful yearning was not to be dispelled. From this time on he neglected his books and sat in fond vapidity. Nothing further could engage his attention.

The young gentleman, who had seen into the root of his unease, said, "I did some judicious looking, and I've settled on the perfect mate for you."

"Who?" asked the scholar.

"She is also a member of my family."

The scholar absorbed himself in considering this for quite some time, but he firmly said, "No need." Turning his face to the wall he recited:

These streams seem nothing since I've crossed
the vastness of the sea;
None other than Witch Mountain mists
are truly clouds to me.[1]

The young gentleman knew what he was getting at and said, "My father has the highest regard for your great abilities and has long wished to attach himself to you through marriage. But I have only this one younger sister: she is too tender in years. I do have a cousin named A Song who is eighteen years old and by no means of coarse mold. If you don't believe me, wait in the front chamber. Cousin Song takes a stroll through the garden every day, so you can get a look at her." The scholar did as he was told. Sure enough, he saw Jiaonuo come by in the company of another beautiful girl, whose jet eyebrows arched like moth antennae and whose lotus feet strode along in upturned phoenix slippers. She was every bit a match for Jiaonuo. The delighted scholar asked the young gentleman to help tie the knot.

On the next day the young gentleman came out to the garden and congratulated him, saying: "It's all arranged." The rooms around a side courtyard were then made ready, and the scholar's wedding ceremony was performed. That evening the place resounded to the beating of drums and the blaring of horns till the air rolled with dust. Now that

[1] Lines of a poem by the Tang poet, Yuan Zhen (779-831), lamenting his deceased wife.

the fairy maid of his dreams was about to share his canopy and quilt, he suspected that the Palace of Vast Coldness, where dwelt the goddess of the moon, was not necessarily beyond the clouds. After they had drunk together from the paired goblet of matrimony, they reveled deeply in the joy that answered to their longing.

One night the young gentleman said to the scholar: "I can never forget the kindness you showed by instructing me. But recently young Master Shan returned, following the resolution of his lawsuit, and now he insists on taking up residence here again. I think I'll leave this place and go west. Things being as they are, it will be difficult for us to remain together: You must know how the sorrow of parting tugs at my heart." The scholar wished to leave with him, but the young gentleman urged him to return to his home district. The scholar shrank back from the difficulty of doing so.

"Don't worry," said the young gentleman. "I'll see you off at once." Before long, the old gentleman led out Mistress Song and presented the scholar with one hundred taels of gold. The young gentleman clasped the couple with both his arms and cautioned them to close their eyes, and keep them closed. They went driftingly airborne, aware only of the wind rushing in their ears. "We've arrived," said the young gentleman after a long while. They opened their eyes and found that they had indeed come to the scholar's old neighborhood. It was plain by now that the young gentleman was no ordinary mortal. The scholar knocked delightedly on the door of his house. When his mother came out she could not believe her eyes. Then she met the scholar's beautiful wife, and the three of them rejoiced together. When they thought to turn and look behind them, the young gentleman was already gone.

Mistress Song proved filial to her mother-in-law. She was renowned for her ravishing good looks and wifely virtue. Afterwards the scholar took the doctorate of letters and was assigned the judgeship at Yenan[1]. He took his household with him and went to assume his post, but his mother remained behind because of the great distance involved. Mistress Song gave birth to a son, whom they named Xiaohuan.

Then the scholar gave offence to the censor, which resulted in the loss of his position. Because there were some unresolved problems relating to his dismissal, he was unable to return home. It happened that he was hunting in the wilds outside the city when he came upon a handsome young man sitting on a black colt, who kept glancing at him. A careful look told him that this was the young gentleman of the Huangfu family. The young gentleman drew back on the reins and pulled up the three-horse team hitched to his chariot, overcome by the mixture of sorrow and gladness that welled up within him. He asked the scholar to follow along to a village, where the shade cast by many trees cut off sun and sky and created a dense twilight. The door leading into the house had bronze bosses and studs in the style of a landowner's mansion. In response to the scholar's questions the young gentleman said that his younger sister had gotten married and his mother had passed away. The scholar expressed heartfelt condolences. After staying the night he left, then returned with his wife.

Jiaonuo also showed up. She hugged the scholar's son, dandled him in her arms and poked fun at him, saying, "Look how my cousin has diluted our bloodline!" The

[1] In Shaanxi.

scholar bowed down to thank her for past kindness. "Brother-in-law, you are an exalted personage now," she answered with a laugh. "Your wound is long healed: haven't you forgotten the pain by now?" Master Wu, the younger sister's husband, also came to pay his respects, then departed after a two-night stay.

One day the young gentleman came to the scholar with a troubled expression on his face and said, "Heaven is about to inflict grave calamity upon us. Can you find it in yourself to save us?" The scholar had no knowledge of what he had to deal with, nevertheless, he believed himself equal to the attempt. The young gentleman hurried out and summoned his whole family into the hall, where they lined up to make obeisance to him. The dismayed scholar anxiously asked for an explanation.

"I am a fox spirit, not a human being," said the young gentleman. "We are now faced with a cataclysm of thunder and lightning. If you consent to take the risk of rescuing us, my family has a hope of surviving. Otherwise, please take your child and leave; we will not involve you." The scholar vowed to live or die with them. The young gentleman had him stand with sword in hand at the gate and warned him: "When lightning strikes, do not move!" The scholar took his assigned position. Soon storm-clouds as dusky black as basalt turned day into night. Turning to look at the house where he had been staying, he saw that the gate was no longer there. Instead, there stood a great mound rearing upward, pierced by the gaping mouth of a huge cave. He was standing in astonished dread when —"CRACK"—the air was split by a peal of thunder that shook the very mountains. Demented winds driving torrents of rain uprooted ancient trees. The scholar was blinded and deafened, but he planted his feet and stood firm. Suddenly a sharp-beaked, taloned monster appeared out of the wind-whipped convolutions of a smoky black cloud. It dragged a person out of the cave, then rose directly with the dense vapor. In the one flashing glimpse that the scholar caught of the person's shoes and clothes, he was struck by the thought that this was Jiaonuo. He leapt into the air and thrust with his sword, bringing the monster down to the ground. At that instant the sky tore open with crashing thunder. The scholar fell over and expired. In a short time the sky cleared, and Jiaonuo regained conciousness. Seeing the scholar dead beside her she sobbed, "What is life to me if Master Kong dies for me?" Mistress Song, too, came out, and they carried him back together. Jiaonuo made Mistress Song hold up his head and her brother pry apart his jaws with a metal hairclasp, while she herself pulled his mouth open by pinching his cheeks. She used her tongue to put the red elixir-lozenge in his mouth, and then, placing her lips against his, she blew it further in. When the red lozenge had been blown into his throat, he began to make a gurgling sound. In a while he came to himself. Seeing all his relatives before him made him realize that he had now awakened from a dream.

Once they had gotten over the shock of these events, everyone in the house rejoiced in their renewed togetherness. But the scholar decided that he could not stay long in such a cave, so he proposed that the others return with him to his home district. The hall echoed with exclamations of approval: only Jiaonuo was unhappy. The scholar suggested that she and Master Wu go along, but she worried that her in-laws would not want to be separated from their young son. They discussed the matter most of the day without result. Just then a servant of the Wu family arrived, sweating profusely and gasping for breath. Everyone loosed a barrage of astonished questions. It turned out that calamity had struck Master Wu's house on the same day, and that the entire family had perished. Jiaonuo stamped her feet in grief and cried ceaselessly, while everyone tried to console her.

And so the plan to return together was agreed upon. The scholar went into the city for several days to attend to his affairs, then returned and stayed up into the night hurriedly packing for the trip. When they reached scholar's home, he set up rooms for the young gentleman in an unfrequented garden, which he always locked from the outside. The bolt was only removed when he and Mistress Song arrived for a visit. The scholar played chess, wined and dined, and conversed with the young gentleman and his sister as if they all belonged to one family. The child Xiaohuan grew up to be splendidly good-looking, but there was something vulpine about him. People who saw him rambling about the city knew he was a fox spirit's child.

The Chronicler of the Tales comments: "I envy Scholar Kong not because he found a ravishing wife but because he found a bosom friend. Looking at the face of such a friend can make one forget hunger; listening to his voice can bring a smile. Simply having such a good friend and visiting him sometimes for a meal and conversation brings greater 'communion between souls' than does love's 'sweet disorder in the dress.'"

7. BLACK MAGIC

A CERTAIN Master Yu was devoted to chivalry in his youth. He delighted in the might of his fists and was strong enough to do the whirlwind dance with a huge water clock. During the reign of Emperor Chong Zhen (1628-1644), he was in the capital for the palace examination when his servant was laid low by a pestilence. This brought sorrow to his heart.

At that time there was a skilled diviner in the market-place who could foresee life or death. Yu decided to inquire into his servant's fate. Before he had said a word about his reason for coming, the diviner said, "You want to ask about your servant's illness, don't you?" Yu confirmed this in astonishment. "No harm will come to the sick man," said the diviner. "But you, sir, are liable to grave danger." Yu cast the yarrow stalks of divination for himself. The diviner drew up a hexagram, then said in shock: "You will be dead in three days!" The diviner gave this bewildering revelation time to sink in, then went on nonchalantly: "However, I do have mastery of a trifling little spell. If you reward me with ten taels of gold, I will perform invocations for you to exorcise the evil." Yu thought to himself that since his time of death was already fixed, there would be little that magical arts could do to forestall it. He got up without answering to walk out of the booth. The diviner called after him: "Don't cling to such a measly sum, or you'll

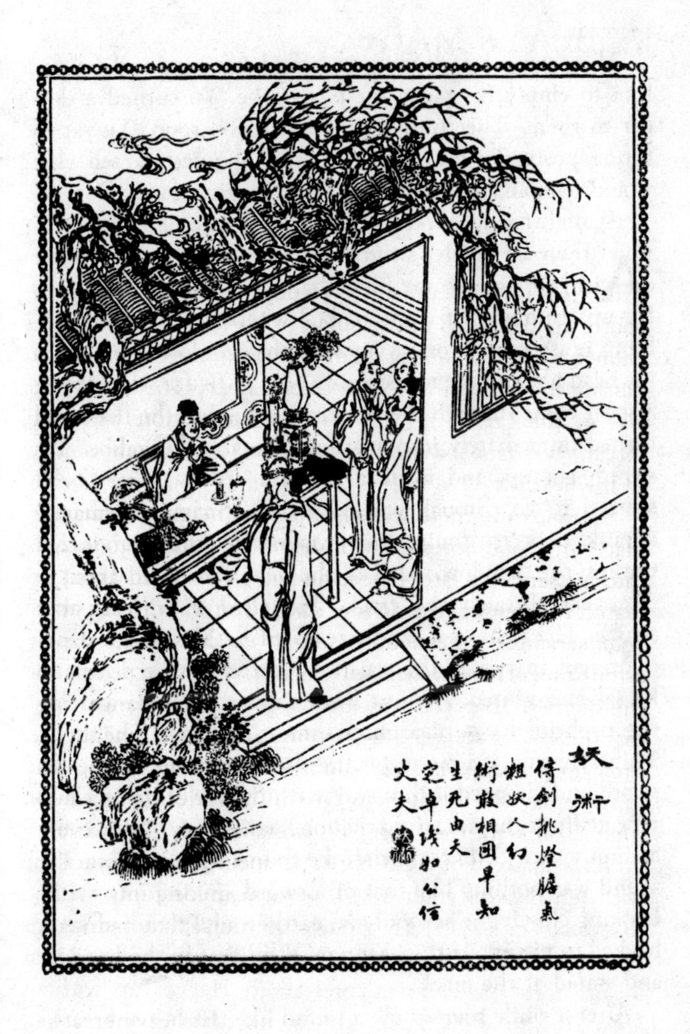
妖術
倚劍挑燈膽氣
粗妖人幻
術鼓相圖早知
生死由天
定卓殘如公信
丈夫

regret it!"

Those who loved Yu were afraid for him and begged him to empty his purse for pity's sake. Yu turned a deaf ear to them. The third day came all too soon. Yu sat in formal posture at his lodgings, watching quietly to see what would happen. The day passed without incident.

At nightfall he locked the door and trimmed the lamp-wick, then sat stiffly, sword at hip. Almost a watch wore on with no sign of anything that would bring his death. He was thinking of going to bed when suddenly a scrabbling noise came from a crack in the window. He turned his head just in time to see a tiny human figure shouldering a spear come through the crack. It jumped to the floor and turned immediately into a full-sized man. Yu grabbed his sword, got up, and made a lightning thrust. The sword seemed to go through empty air. The man immediately shrank back to diminutive proportions, then scrambled toward the window. Just as the manikin was about to disappear through the crack, Yu felled it with a swift stroke. The light of a candle revealed nothing but a paper figure cut in two at the waist. Yu dared not lie down, so he sat and waited. A short while later a creature wearing the frightful looks of a ghost came through the window. Yu barely gave it time to hit the floor before he swung his sword and chopped it into two writhing halves. He slashed repeatedly at them, fearing that one would get up and come at him again. Stroke after stroke found its mark, but the sound was nothing like that of a sword sinking into flesh. Looking closely, he saw only an earthen idol that had been hacked to pieces. At this, Yu moved his seat to the window and stared at the crack.

After a while there came a sound like the heavy breathing of a cow from outside the window. A creature pushed against the window frame with such force that the walls of the room shook and threatened to collapse. Fearing that he would be crushed inside, Yu figured that it would be better to go out and fight. He slid the bolt aside with a clatter and ran out. There stood a huge demon, its head even with the eaves. In the dim moonlight he saw its face dark as coal and its eyes glittering with yellow light. It wore no coat or shoes but carried a bow in its hand and a quiver of arrows fastened at its waist. As Yu stood stunned by fright the demon drew its bow. Yu deflected the arrow with his sword, making it glance onto the ground. He raised his sword to attack, but the demon drew its bow again. He leapt aside just in time: the arrow buried its head in the wall with a quivering hum. The enraged demon drew its sword, whirled it like the wind and brought it down on Yu with a forceful blow. However, Yu advanced with a nimble monkey leap to get inside the sword's path. The sword hit a decorative rock and cleaved it through. Yu ran past the demon's legs and slashed an ankle so hard that his sword clanged. Roaring like thunder with insane rage, the demon turned and chopped downward as before. Again Yu ducked inside the blow, which came so close that it cut through his robe. Yu was directly below the demon's underarm. He hacked fiercely. Again his sword clanged. The demon toppled over and lay stiff on the ground. Yu hacked at the body wildly, producing a sound like a watchman's clapper. By the light of a candle he discovered that he had been chopping at the body of a life-sized wooden puppet. Quiver and bow holder were still fastened at its waist. It had been carved and painted to look fierce and repulsive. Blood was flowing from the sword cuts.

Yu stayed up, candle in hand, until morning, when it finally dawned on him that the monsters had been sent after him by the diviner, who made an attempt on his life to verify his prognostications. The next day Yu told this to all his friends and acquaintances, who gathered together and went with him to the diviner's booth. The diviner saw them coming. Yu, too, spotted him for an instant, but then he was nowhere to be seen. "He's using an invisibility spell. The blood of a dog will break it," someone said. Following this advice, Yu went to make the necessary preparations and then went back to the booth. The diviner vanished as before, but Yu quickly drenched the spot where he had been standing with dog's blood. There the diviner stood, his head all splattered with dog's blood and, floating ghostlike in midair with eyes ablaze. They caught hold of him and turned him over to the authorities for execution.

The Chronicler of the Tales comments: "I have observed that paying for the services of a diviner is one type of folly. How many people pursue this trade without making false predictions of life and death? A false divination is the same as no divination at all. Even if someone tells me plainly when death is to come, what of it? And how much more horrible it is when a man uses another's death to impress people with the accuracy of his predictions!"

8. FOX-GIRL QINGFENG

THE Gengs of Taiyuan were an aristocratic family of long standing who lived in an enormous manor. Eventually their fortunes declined and half of the rambling complex of storied buildings and living quarters was left desolate. This gave rise to hauntings: the door to the main hall often opened and closed by itself, and the household members repeatedly broke the night stillness with terrified cries. Geng found this so disturbing that he moved to a country residence, leaving an old caretaker to watch the gate. From then on the place became even more negelected and overgrown. Laughter and music could sometimes be heard within. Geng had a nephew named Sickness-Free, who was a wild, uninhibited youth. The nephew instructed the caretaker to report anything he saw or heard without delay. One night lamplight was seen flickering in one of the storied buildings. When the caretaker rushed to inform him of this, the scholar wanted to enter the building and observe the disturbances. Attempts to dissuade him were in vain.

He had long been familiar with the layout of the buildings, but this time he had to push a circuitous way through thick mugworts and brambles. He climbed to the upper story of one building without seeing anything suspicious. Passing through the building, his ears caught the sibilance of human speech. Peeking into a room lighted in daylike brilliance by a pair of large candles, he saw a man in a scholar's cap seated facing a woman at the south of the room. Both were in their forties. On the east side was a young man, probably in his twenties, and on his right was a young woman who had just reached the hairpin age of fifteen. They sat talking jovially around a table laden with meat and wine. The scholar barged in and cried out laughingly: "An uninvited guest had arrived." The frightened group ran to hide. The old man alone came out and asked in rebuking tones: "Who are you that you dare to enter other people's private chambers?"

"These are my family's chambers," said the scholar. "You have taken them over. You drink exquisite wine by yourselves, without so much as asking the master of the house to join you. Aren't you pushing your stinginess too far?"

"You are not the master of the house," said the old man, inspecting him with a sidelong glance.

"I am the wayward scholar Geng Sickness-Free, nephew of the master of this house."

The old man uttered a respectful greeting: "I've long looked up to your luminosity!"

After bowing the scholar into the room, he called on his servants to replace the food on the table. The scholar stopped him, so the old man poured wine for his guest. The scholar said, "There is friendship between our families, so the guests who were just at table need not remain separate. I earnestly hope you will call them back to have a drink."

"Xiao-er!" called the man. A young man came quickly from outside. The older man said, "This is my humble child." The youth bowed and sat down. The conversation opened with inquiries into each other's family backgrounds. The older man volunteered: "My foster-father is

青鳳

surnamed Fox."

The scholar had always been outgoing, and his conversation sparkled with wit. Xiao-er, too, had an easy, charming manner. In the course of a forthright conversation, each felt attached to the other. The scholar, being twenty-one years old, was two years older than his friend, so he addressed Xiao-er as a younger brother.

The old man spoke up: "I've heard that your grandfather compiled *The Legends of Tushan.*[1] Do you know about it?"

"Yes I do."

"I am descended from the Tushan line," said the old man. "I can remember my family tree to as far back as the Tang dynasty (618-906), but there are no records of our lineage from the Five dynasties[2] period and before. I would feel fortunate if you could impart some of what you know."

The scholar gave a brief account of the assistance which the maid of Tushan had rendered to Emperor Yu. He embellished the new story with many fine phrases, and his flow of captivating thoughts gushed forth like a spring. The old man said to his son in great delight: "This is a chance to hear what we've never heard before. The young gentleman is not an outsider: go ahead and ask your mother and Qingfeng to listen with us, so they too will know of my ancestor's glory." Xiao-er went behind a curtain. In a moment the woman appeared with the girl. Geng took a good long look at her. Her dainty poise breathed loveliness, and her eyes rippled with brilliance like autumn pools. Nowhere in the world of men was such beauty to be seen.

[1] Based on the mythological marriage of an ancient ruler Yu with a nine-tailed vixen from Tushan of Anhui province.

[2] Not the Five dynasties period usually referred to (907-960), but the one (420-618) before the Tang dynasty.

The old man pointed first to his wife and then to the girl: "This is my old wife, and this is my niece, Qingfeng. She has quite a head on her shoulders. She always remembers everything she hears and sees, so I called her here to listen."

After the scholar finished telling his tale the drinking began. He turned his eyes to the young woman and let his gaze rest upon her. Sensing his glance she did nothing but lower her head. The scholar furtively placed his foot on her lotus-like slipper. She drew her foot quickly away, but gave no sign of displeasure. The scholar's roving thoughts robbed him of self-command. With a slap on the table he blurted: "If I had a wife like this, I would not trade places with a king facing south on his throne!"

Seeing the scholar become even more boisterous as he succumbed to the wine, the woman and the girl rose, hurriedly parted the curtain and left the room. The disappointed scholar took leave of the old man and departed, but the threads of affection tugged at his heart, and he could not rid his thought of Qingfeng.

At nightfall the next day he went back to the manor. Her orchid-musk remained in the air. He passed the night absorbed in waiting, but not so much as a cough of hers was heard. Returning home, he broached to his wife his plan to take the family there and stay, in hopes of having an encounter. Since his wife did not assent, he went alone. That night, as he sat reading at a desk in the lower story of the mansion, a wild-haired ghost with a lacquer-black face entered and stared wide-eyed at him. He laughingly dipped his fingers in freshly-rubbed ink, smeared it on his face and looked back at the ghost with a burning gaze. The ghost left in shame.

Late the following night he had blown out his candle

and was about to retire when he heard a bolt sliding open in the rear of the mansion, followed by the thud of an opening door. He rushed to take a look. A doorleaf was standing ajar. There was a sudden pattering of slippers, and the light of a candle shone from inside. He saw that it was Qingfeng. Frightened at the unexpected sight of the scholar, she backed away and slammed the double-leaved door. The scholar knelt upright before her door and delivered his plea: "It was for your sake that I did not shrink from danger. By good fortune no one else is here. If you were to grant me just once the joy of a touch of your hand, I would face death itself without regret."

The girl spoke through the intervening door: "Do not suppose that I know nothing of the heart-gripping longing you fell, but my uncle raised me by a stern code of womanly conduct: I dare not obey your wish."

The scholar kept pleading, nevertheless: "I do not presume to hope for bodily intimacy: it would be enough just to see your face." The girl seemed amenable to this. She opened the door and came out. In a paroxysm of delight the scholar took her arm and drew her into the mansion, where he sat her on his lap and embraced her.

"It is fortunate that fate has brought us together," said the girl. "But no matter how much we yearn for each other, it will do us no good after tonight."

"Why is that?" asked the scholar.

"Your wildness frightened my uncle, so he disguised himself as a fierce ghost to frighten you, but you were not fazed. Now he has already found another place to live. The whole family has taken our belongings and moved to our new home. They left me here to watch the place, but I have to leave tomorrow." Then she rose to leave, saying: "I'm afraid my uncle will come back." The scholar, who wanted to enjoy himself with her, did his utmost to detain her. The matter was still under discussion when her uncle entered stealthily. The shamed, frightened girl would have crawled into a hole had there been one handy. She bowed her head and leaned against the bed, wordlessly fingering her sash.

"You are a disgrace to my family, you cheap chambermaid!" roared the uncle. "If you don't get out of here now, I'll speed you on your way with a whip." The girl rushed from the room, her head lowered abjectly, and her uncle followed. As the scholar trailed behind them listening, the old man's raving curses and Qingfeng's muffled sobs pierced him to the heart.

"I am the guilty one," he shouted after them. "This is not Qingfeng's fault. If you'll be lenient with her, I'll gladly bear any punishment, be it by sword, saw, hatchet or axe." All sounds died down into prolonged silence. The scholar went back to bed. From this time on not a breath of noise was heard in the manor. The scholar's uncle, amazed by the news of these events, agreed to sell the manor to his nephew without haggling over the price. The scholar was delighted: he moved into the manor with his family. They lived there quite comfortably for more than a year, but the scholar never forgot Qingfeng.

Then, while returning from the family graves on Tomb Sweeping Day, he happened to see two small foxes closely pursued by hounds. One of them ducked into the brush, but the other was so frightened it kept running on the road. Seeing the scholar, it clung to his side whining pathetically, ears folded back and head hanging, as if to beg for help. The scholar's pity was aroused. He loosened his robe, picked up the fox and carried it home in his arms. When he closed the door to his room and put it onto the bed, it turned into Qingfeng. What joy he felt! He consoled her and asked how she had come to this pass.

"Just now I was out frolicking with a maid servant, when this terrible calamity threatened us. If it had not been for you, I would be buried now in a dog's stomach. I hope you don't hate me for not being one of your kind."

The scholar replied, "My constant yearning for you intrudes into the dreams of my soul. Seeing you is like discovering a precious treasure. How can you say 'hate'?"

"This meeting was fixed by the workings of fate. If it had not been for that near calamity, how could I be able to serve you? Fortunately for us, the maidservant will surely think I am dead. Now we can hold fast to our eternal vow."

With joy in his heart the scholar set the girl up in rooms separate from his family. Two years passed. One night the scholar was in the middle of his reading when Xiao-er came into his room. The startled scholar put down his book and asked the reason for his coming.

Xiao-er prostrated himself and said woefully: "My father is facing an unexpected disaster. Only you can save him.. He would have come to plead with you himself, but he feared you would not grant his request, so he sent me."

"Well, what is it?" asked the scholar.

"Do you know Mo the Third Son?"

"He is the son of a man who took examinations the year I did," said the scholar.

Xiao-er said, "He will pass by here tomorrow . If he is carrying a fox taken in the hunt, please ask him to leave it here."

"The shame your father subjected me to in the mansion still burns in my heart. Let me hear no more of what does not concern me. If you insist on my doing what little I can, I will do only if Qingfeng comes to me first!"

"Cousin Qingfeng died in the fields three years ago!" Xiao-er sniffled as he spoke.

The scholar retorted with a sweep of his sleeve, "If so, my resentment is so much the greater!" He picked up his book and loudly intoned a poem, without lifting his gaze in the slightest. Xiao-er rose and cried himself hoarse, then walked out, hiding his face in his hands. The scholar went to Qingfeng's room to let her know.

"Will you save him or not?" she asked, her face gone pale.

"I'll save him all right. My refusal just now was my way of repaying his past spitefulness."

At this the girl brightened: "I was orphaned at an early age, but my uncle took me in and raised me. Though he once offended you, that was only because of the family discipline he had demanded of me."

"True," said the scholar. "But one can't help holding it against him. If you were really dead, I wouldn't lift a finger for him."

"You really are hard-hearted!" she said with a laugh.

Sure enough, Mo the Third Son showed up the next day sporting engraved harness ornaments, a bowcase of tiger skin and an impressive entourage. Meeting him at the gate, the scholar saw that he had bagged a fair amount of game. Among it was a black fox, still warm to the touch, its fur matted with dark red blood. The scholar asked to have it, claiming that he needed the pelt to patch his worn fur coat. Mo parted with it magnanimously. The scholar turned it over to Qingfeng and drank wine with his guest. When the guest had gone, the girl held the fox in her arms. After three days it came back to life. Then, through several stages, it changed back into her uncle. Qingfeng was the first to meet his eyes when he looked up, which led him to suspect that he was no longer in the world of men. When the girl had gone through the true story, he bowed down and stammered an apology for his past offence. That done, he turned beamingly to the girl and said, "I kept saying that you weren't dead: now it turns out that I was right!"

The girl said to the scholar: "I also beg you, if you care for me, to give us the use of a building, so that I can care for the one who has cared for me." The scholar assented. The old man then excused himself blushingly and left. That night he returned with his whole family. From then on they lived like one big family, all ill feelings left in the past. The scholar lived a secluded life in his studio, but Xiao-er frequently joined him for wine and conversation. As the son born to the scholar's wife grew older, Xiao-er was asked to act as tutor, because he taught with skill and patience and conducted himself as a teacher should.

9. PAINTED SKIN

SCHOLAR Wang of Taiyuan went out for a morning walk and came upon a lone young woman with a bundle in her arms, hurrying along and faltering at every step. Running up behind, he found her to be in the bloom of youthful beauty, and his heart loved and delighted in her.

"Why are you walking all by yourself before the break of day?" he asked.

The girl answered, "Why should a passerby who can do nothing for my misery bother to ask?"

"What is your misery?" asked the scholar. "If there is anything I can do to help, I won't refuse."

The girl answered moodily: "My parents sold me to a rich family as a concubine, thinking of nothing but the marriage gift they would receive. The wife was terribly jealous: mornings she reviled me and evenings she insulted me with beatings. It was too much for me to bear. I must escape to someplace far away."

"Where will you go?" he asked.

"A fugitive does not choose a destination."

"My house is not far. Can I trouble you to pay me a visit?"

The girl followed him, delighted. The scholar picked up her bundle of possessions and showed her the way home. Seeing that the house was empty, she asked, "Why isn't anyone in your family here?"

"It's only my studio," was the answer.

"This is a wonderful place. If you pity me and wish to save me, my presence here must be a well-guarded secret." Having agreed to this, the scholar took her to bed with him.

He concealed her in a secret room, and several days passed without anyone being the wiser. The scholar revealed something of this to his wife Chen, who suspected that she was a dowry-maid or concubine from some important family and urged him to send her away. The scholar did not listen.

One day he went to the market, where he came upon a Taoist who turned and looked at him in astonishment, asking: "What have you come up against?"

"Nothing," he answered.

"An aura of evil surrounds you," said the Taoist. "Why do you say *nothing*?" The scholar denied this vigorously, whereupon the Taoist walked away muttering: "Such delusion! It only goes to show there are people in this world who don't even wake up when death is around the corner." The strangeness of these words stirred suspicion of the girl in the scholar's mind. But then he wondered how such an obviously beautiful girl could be a monster. He concluded that the Taoist probably made use of exorcism to make a living.

Soon he came to his studio gate, but it was blocked from inside and he could not enter. Suspicious that something had gone wrong, he leapt over a place where the wall had crumbled. The studio door would not open either. He tiptoed to a window and peeped in to see a frightful demon with green face and jagged, sawlike teeth. It spread a human skin on the bed, and painted the skin with color-dipped brushes. That done, the demon threw the brushes

畫皮
驀看羅刹
變西施只
要蛾眉様
入時如此

aside, lifted the skin and shook the wrinkles out as if it were a piece of clothing. The demon pulled the skin over its body and changed instantly into a young woman.

The scholar slunk away from the studio on all fours, greatly frightened at what he had seen. He ran to see the Taoist, who was nowhere to be found. He went searching everywhere and finally came upon him in a field. There he knelt upright and begged to be saved.

The Taoist said: "With your leave I will drive the monster away. But it has to suffer greatly before it can find someone to take its place. I really can't bear to kill it." With this he handed the scholar a fly-whisk, instructing him to hang it above the door to his bedroom. Before parting, they arranged to meet at the Blue Emperor Temple.

When he returned, the scholar did not dare to enter the studio, so he slept in an inner chamber and hung the whisk over the door. A short time into the second watch of the night, muted sounds could be heard outside. Not daring to look himself, the scholar had his wife Chen peek out. She saw the girl come toward the door and then stop short at the sight of the whisk. She stood there grinding her teeth for quite some time and then left. In a short while she returned and stormed: "That Taoist is trying to scare me off. But don't tell me I should spit out what has come into my mouth!"

She pulled down the whisk and tore it to pieces, battered down the door and came into the room. Jumping right onto the scholar's bed, she tore a gash into his chest, ripped out his heart and ran away with it. Chen wailed. A maid came in and held up a candle: the scholar was already dead. Blood from his chest cavity was splattered everywhere. Chen sniveled in terror, not daring to sob out loud.

The next day she had the scholar's second brother run to tell the Taoist.

The Taoist exploded: "I took pity on that ghost, but still it had the gall to do such a thing!" He followed the scholar's brother home, but the girl had disappeared. The Taoist lifted his head and looked upwards in all directions. "Luckily she isn't hiding far from here," he exclaimed, and then asked, "Whose house is that in the south courtyard?"

"I live there," said the second brother.

"She's in your place now," said the Taoist.

This startled the second brother, but he was not convinced.

The Taoist asked, "Has anyone you don't know been here?"

"I went to the Blue Emperor Temple this morning, so I have no idea. I'll go back and ask." The young man left and returned in a short while to say: "There was someone. An old woman came this morning asking for work as a household servant. My wife discouraged her, but she is still there."

"It's her all right," said the Taoist. He and the second brother went to the latter's house. He stood in the middle of the courtyard holding a wooden sword and cried, "Pay me back for my whisk, you hideous fiend!" The old woman's face blanched with panic when she heard his voice. She ran through the gate, trying to escape. The Taoist caught up with her and struck. The old woman fell flat, her human skin peeled away, and she changed into a fearsome demon that lay there bellowing like a pig. The Taoist dealt a death blow, skewered its head with his wooden sword and held it up in the air. The body changed into dense vapor that whirled into a single mass on the ground. The Taoist brought out his bottle gourd, uncorked it, and placed it in the smoke. There was the sound of a mouth sucking in breath, and in the wink of an eye the smoke was gone. The Taoist corked the gourd and put it in his pouch. Everyone stared at the human skin, which was complete with arms, legs and finely detailed eyes. The Taoist rolled it up with a sound like rolling up a scroll painting, then put it too into his pouch, after which he said good-bye and started to leave. The scholar's wife Chen bowed before him at the gate, begging in tears for a spell that would bring her husband to life. The Taoist apologized that it was beyond him. She was even more stricken and laid on the ground, refusing to get up. The Taoist pondered this and said, "My powers are insufficient to raise the dead. But I will recommend a man who may be able to. Go and ask him, and maybe things will work out."

"Who is he?"

"There is a madman in the market who often lies on piles of refuse. Try asking his advice and imploring his help. Do not be angry if he insults you in his madness." The second-brother, too, had heard of the madman. Thereupon he took leave of the Taoist and went to the market with his sister-in-law. They found the beggar singing loonily in the street. Snot dangled in a long string from his nose, and he was unapproachably filthy. Chen approached him on her knees.

The beggar laughed: "So the beauty loves me, does she?" Chen told him what had happened. He howled again with laughter, saying: "Any man could be your husband. Why bring *him* to life?" Chen would not give up her entreaties. "How strange! Her man dies, and she begs *me* to give back his life. Am I Yama, king of the underworld?" In a fit of anger he struck Chen with his staff. Chen steeled herself against the pain and took the beating. The crowd in the street gathered round so closely that the two were walled in. The beggar hacked up phlegm until it filled his cupped hand, then held it up to Chen's face, saying: "Eat it."

Chen's face flushed and grimaced with reluctance, but thinking of the Taoist's instructions, she forced it down. As it entered her throat, it felt hard like compacted fuzz. It slid slowly down into her chest and clotted firm.

The beggar howled with laughter: "Oh, the beauty loves me!" He rose and walked away without looking back. She trailed him till he went into a temple and went right in after him, but could not see where he had gone. Though she searched everywhere in the gloom, there was no sign of him. There was nothing to do but walk through the crowd in embarrassment and return home. Grieving at her husband's horrible death and burning with the humiliation of eating phlegm, she was racked by such sobs of misery she wanted to die then and there.

The time came to drain the blood and put the corpse in its coffin. The servants looked on stock still, not daring to approach. Chen embraced the corpse and put its vitals back into the abdomen, wailing as she got them tidy. When her wails reached their highest pitch her voice gave way: suddenly she felt like vomiting. The clotted thing that had settled on her diaphragm churned suddenly upwards and out. Before she could turn her head it had landed in the corpse's chest cavity. There before her amazed eyes was a human heart, jumping with rythmic beats and giving off a warm, steamy vapor. She was awestruck. She quickly closed the cavity with her hands and squeezed the body with all her strength. When she relaxed her embrace slightly, a breath of warmth issued from the opening. At this she tore plain silk into strips and hastily wrapped them around the torso. The corpse gradually became warm to the touch of her caressing hand. She put a cover over it. In the middle of the night she lifted the cover for a look: breath was coming from her husband's nostrils. In the morning he came to life.

"I was senseless, as if in a dream," he told them. "All I could feel was a burning pain in my chest." They looked for the gash but saw only a coin-sized scab. Even this soon healed.

The Chronicler of the Tales comments: "How foolish are the people of this world! That which is clearly bewitching they think beautiful. How deluded are the fools of this world! What is clearly trustworthy they think absurd. And as for those who net the beauties they adore, their wives must bear the shame of eating what others have disgorged. The way of heaven is reciprocity, but foolish, deluded people do not wake up. Is this not a pity?!"

10. JUDGE LU

ZHU Erdan, of Lingyang,[1] whose courtesy name was Xiaoming, was bold and outgoing by nature, though tending to be gullible. He studied industriously but had not yet made a name for himself. One day his literary club gathered for a drinking party, and one member taunted him: "We all know how daring you are. If you can go to the Hall of the Ten Kings of Hell in the middle of the night and bring back the judge in the left gallery, all of us will contribute to a feast in your honor." He was referring to Lingyang's Hall of Ten Kings, where there were lifelike images of gods and demons carved in wood. In the east corridor was a standing judge with green face and red beard, quite frightful in appearance. Sounds of torture and interrogation had been heard in the corridors at night, making the hair of those who entered stand chillingly on end. Zhu's compamions were only using this to embarrass him. But Zhu got up laughing and went straight out.

Not much time passed before a loud yell was heard outside the door: "The bearded master is here by my invitation! Everyone stood up. Presently Zhu came in carrying the judge, set him on a table and poured a libation of three cupfuls of wine. Everyone watched apprehensively, fidgeting in their seats. They asked him to carry the image

1. In Anhui province.

away as well. Again Zhu poured wine on the floor as he made this prayer: "Your disciple is willful and uncultivated. May your Honor not take offense. My humble quarters are not far. Please feel free to come for a drink with me anytime you choose. Let there be no barriers between us." Whereupon Zhu carried the image away.

Next day the club members kept their word and invited Zhu to a drinking party. At sundown he went home feeling halfway tipsy. Still being in a party mood, he trimmed the lampwick and poured himself a measure. Suddenly someone parted the curtain and entered. He looked up to see the judge before him.

Zhu stood up and said: "I suppose I'm about to die! Last night I committed sacrilege. Have you come to execute me?"

The judge smiled under his thick beard as he said, "You're wrong. Yesterday I was honored by your kind invitation. Since I happen to have leisure tonight, I am glad to accept an invitation from such a liberal-minded man as yourself." Zhu was overjoyed. He urged the judge to take a seat by tugging at his robe, then went to wash wine vessels and light a fire.

"The weather is pleasantly warm: we can drink it cold," said the judge. Zhu did as directed, putting the pitcher of wine on the table. He ran to tell his servants to prepare a light meal and fruit. His wife, greatly distraught at hearing of their guest, warned him not to leave the inner rooms. Zhu did not listen. He stood waiting for the dishes to be prepared so he could serve them. Having done so, he and his guest toasted back and forth. Only then did he ask his guest's name.

"Lu is my family name. I have no given name. When Zhu brought up subjects from the classics, the guest's

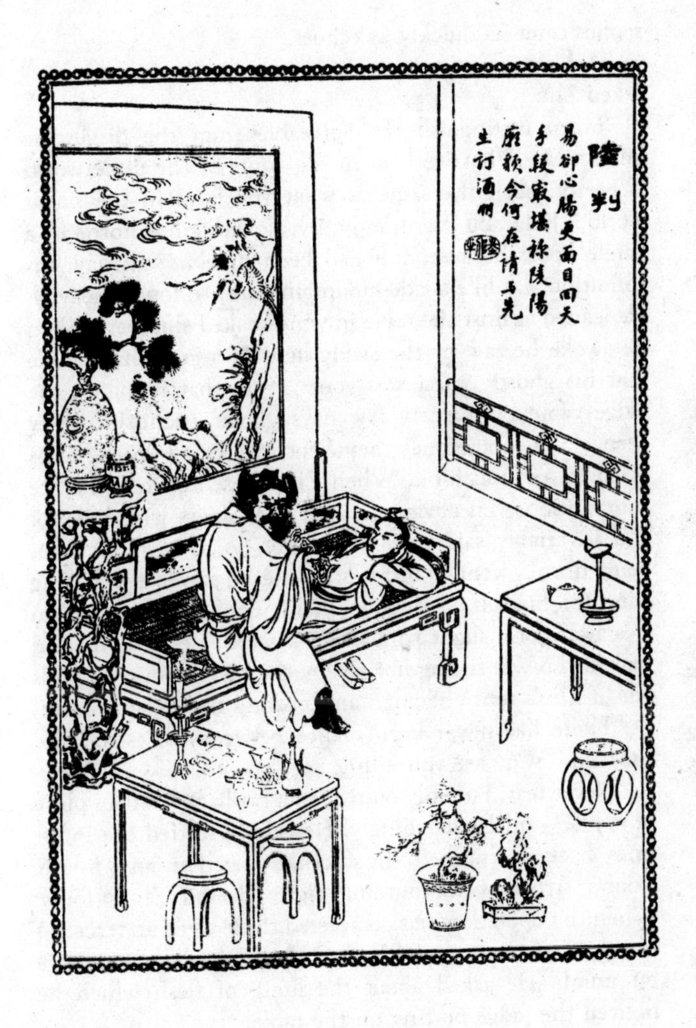
陸判
易卻心腸更面目回天
手段最堪稱陵陽
鹿穎今何在請与先
生訂酒朋

replies came as quickly as echoes.

"Are you conversant with the examination essay style?" asked Zhu.

"I can distinguish the agreeable from the disgusting fairly well. What we read in the court of the underworld is pretty much the same as what you have in the sunlit world." Judge Lu drank mightily, downing ten horns in a single bout. Because Zhu had been drinking all day, his condition was like a jade mountain ready to topple heavily. He leaned against the table in wine-soaked slumber. When he awoke he saw by the sickly light of a guttering candle that his ghostly guest was gone. From that night on the judge came once every few days. Their friendship grew even closer. Sometimes they slept together with the soles of their feet touching. When Zhu presented his practice compositions, Lu always covered the papers with red ink and invariably said they would not do. One night Zhu, being drunk, went to bed first, while Lu stayed up pouring wine for himself. Suddenly, in his drunken dream, Zhu was aware of a slight pain in his viscera. He woke up and looked: Lu was sitting upright by the bed drawing entrails out of Zhu's rent abdomen and putting the coils in order.

"There has never been malice between us," said Zhu, shocked. "Why are you killing me?"

"Never fear. I'm only putting in a brilliant heart in place of yours," said Lu laughingly. He calmly stuffed the intestines back in, pushed the incision together and finally wound strips of footbinding cloth around Zhu's loins. When the operation was completed there were no traces of blood to be seen on the bed. Only Zhu's abdomen felt a bit numb. He asked about the lump of flesh which he noticed the judge putting on the table.

"This is your own heart. From your slowness at writing

I knew your heart's apertures were blocked. Just now in the nether regions I picked out one excellent heart among tens of thousands. Now I have exchanged it for yours, which I'll keep to make up for the missing one." He rose and left, closing the door softly behind him. At dawn Zhu undid the bandage to have a look: the incision had already closed, leaving only a thin red line. From then on he showed great improvement in his ability to express thought in writing. When he passed his eyes over a page, he never forgot it. After a few days he brought out another composition and showed it to Lu.

"It will do," said Lu. "But your blessings are meager. You cannot win any great honors. The prefectural and provincial examinations are as far as you'll go."

"When will that be?" asked Zhu.

"You will take top honors in this year's provincial exam."

Not long afterwards he came out first in the prefectural examination and went on to win an honorable title in the provincial examinations. His friends in the literary club who had always poked fun at him looked at one another in amazement when they read copies of his examination papers. Finally, after thorough questioning, they learned of the marvel that lay behind this. They all pleaded with Zhu to say a word on their behalf, so that they might strike up an acquaintance with Lu. Lu consented. The group made elaborate preparations to entertain him. Lu arrived at the beginning of the first watch, his red beard wagging and his eyes glinting like lightning. The group members were pale and dazed; their teeth were on the point of chattering. Gradually they all withdrew.

Zhu, for his part, took Lu by the hand and went home to drink wine. When they were soaked, Zhu said, "By opening my stomach and washing my intestines, you have already given me a great deal. There is one more favor I'd like to ask of you, but I don't know if I should." Without hesitation, Lu offered to do his bidding. Zhu said, "If vitals can be exchanged, I suppose that facial features can be replaced too. My wife and I got married when we came of age. The lower part of her body is not bad at all, but her head and face are not very appealing. I would like to trouble you to put your blade to use once again. What do you say?"

Lu answered with a laugh: "As you wish. Give me time to work out the details." After several days he came knocking on the gate in the middle of the night. Zhu got up quickly and invited him in. The light of a candle revealed an object bulging beneath his coat. Zhu demanded to know what it was.

"What you asked for a while ago has been hard to select, but I just obtained the head of a beautiful woman, which I am now bringing you as you requested. Zhu pulled his lapel aside to look: the neck was still wet with blood. Lu immediately urged him to go inside in order not to arouse dogs and fowl. Zhu was concerned because the doors to the inner rooms had been locked for the night, but when Lu walked up and touched the double-leafed door with one hand, the door opened by itself. Zhu led him to the bedroom, where his wife lay sleeping on her side. Lu had Zhu hold the head in his arms, while he pulled a sharp daggerlike blade from his boot. He pressed it down on the neck of Zhu's wife as delicately as if he were slicing a piece of curd. The flesh parted before the blade, and the head fell beside the pillow. He quickly took the beautiful woman's head from the scholar's cradled arms and fitted it on the neck. After checking carefully to be sure it was correctly aligned, he pressed down. When that was done he slid a pillow under her shoulders. He ordered Zhu to bury the head in a quiet place and then left.

Zhu's wife awoke with a slight tingling in her neck and a crust on her cheeks. Rubbing them she discovered flakes of dried blood. Horrified, she called for a maid to draw a basin of water. The maid was thoroughly shocked when she saw her mistress's blood-spattered visage. Washing it clean made the whole basinful of water red. Looking up, the maid saw a set of features that in no way resembled those of her mistress. Nothing could have given her a greater shock. The wife reached for a mirror and was thrown into consternation by what she saw. She had no idea what had happened to herself. Zhu came in and told her all about it. Meanwhile he looked from every possible angles at her long eyebrows that lost themselves beneath the hair at her temples and the dimples on her cheeks when she smiled. She was, in short, a beauty right out of a painting. Zhu loosened her collar for a closer look and found a red line encircling her neck. The skin above and below her neck was of two distinct colors.

Prior to this, a certain Provincial Censor Wu had a very beautiful daughter who was still unwed at nineteen because her two prospective busbands had died before she could marry them. On the day of the Lantern Festival she went for a visit to the Hall of Ten Kings, at a time when all sorts of sightseers were there. Among them was a scoundrel who stared at her, aroused by her beauty. Unbeknownst to her, he found out which neighborhood she lived in. He went there under cover of night, climbed over the wall with a ladder and cut a hole in the bedroom door. He killed a maid beside the bed, then tried to make love to the young woman by force. She screamed and put up vigorous resistance, which so infuriated the rapist he killed her too. Lady Wu, faintly hearing the commotion, told a maid to go look. The maid fainted at the sight of the body. After the whole family had been roused up, they laid the girl's body in the hall, and her head was laid beside the neck. The entire household was in a screeching, wailing uproar all night. In the morning they lifted the quilt only to find the body there but the head gone. They beat all the waiting maids for not being attentive enough while watching over their mistress and so allowing her head to be buried in the stomachs of dogs.

The Censor reported this to the prefectural government. Though the district imposed a strict time limit for capture of the killer, he was still at large after three months. Eventually Master Wu was apprized of the wondrous head substitution in Zhu's house. His suspicions aroused, Wu sent an old woman there to sound out the family on this matter. She went in and saw the lady of the house, then ran back in fear to tell Master Wu. When he learned that his daughter's body was still intact, the master could not get over his astonishment and suspicion. He surmised that Zhu had used black arts to kill his daughter and went to him to demand the truth.

Zhu said, "My wife's head was changed in a dream, but I have no idea how it came about. It would be unjust to say that I killed your daughter."

Wu was not convinced. He brought charges against Zhu, and the members of his household were summoned for questioning. Everything they said corroborated Zhu's story. The prefectural magistrate could not reach a decision. Zhu went to home and asked Lu for a plan.

"This is not difficult," said Lu. "I'll simply have his daughter tell the truth."

That night Wu dreamed of his daughter, who said, "I was murdered by Yang Danian of Su Creek. Bachelor Zhu had nothing to do with it. He found his wife unattractive, so Judge Lu exchanged my head for hers. This way my head lives on, even though my body is dead. I hope you will bear no grudge against him." Wu awoke and told his wife of the dream. It was identical to what she had dreamed. They notified the authorities of this. Inquiries proved that there was indeed a Yang Danian, who later confessed his guilt after being arrested and shackled. Wu paid Zhu a visit and asked to see the lady of the house. From then on Wu and Zhu were as father and son-in-law. Zhu's wife's head was put together with Wu's daughter's corpse and buried.

Zhu entered the capital examination three times, but was thrown out each time for breaking rules of deportment. At this the goal of official advancement soured on him.

Thirty years passed. One evening Lu told him: "You do not have much longer to live. Zhu asked him when his time would come, and Lu answered that he had five days.

"Can you save me?"

"What good are personal wishes in the face of heaven's decree? And anyway life and death are one in the eyes of a man of broad perspective. Why should you rejoice at life and grieve at death?"

This made sense to Zhu. He readied a suit of burial clothes, a shroud, a coffin, and an outer coffin. That being done, he dressed himself impeccably and died. The next day, just as his wife was leaning against the coffin in tears, Zhu suddenly floated in from outside. His wife was terrified. Zhu spoke to her: "Yes, I am a ghost, but no different from when I lived. I worry about you two, a widowed mother and an orphaned boy; I simply can't bear parting with you." His wife was so overcome with the grief that snivel dripped onto her chest. Zhu consoled her tenderly. His wife said, "In ancient times men told of souls returning to their bodies. Since your spirit is not extinguished, why not live again?"

Zhu replied, "The workings of fate cannot be defied."

"What do you do in the court of the underworld?"

"Judge Lu recommended me for a position overseeing case records. I have an official title, but it is not too demanding." His wife wanted to say more, but Zhu cut her off: "Master Lu came here with me. Would you set out wine and food?" He walked out with rapid steps. His wife made preparations according to his wishes, and the room was soon filled with laughing toasts and loud, convivial talk, just as when her husband had been alive. Then she peeked into the room in the middle of night: both of them had departed without a trace. From then on Zhu came once every few days. Now and then he spent an intimate night with her. While there he advised her on the handling of household matters, and he always hugged his son Wei, who was five years old at the time of his death. When the boy was about seven he taught him to read by lamplight. The boy, too, was brilliant. At nine he could write a composition; at fifteen he entered the local academy, never realizing that he was fatherless. Then Zhu's visits tapered off, until he came only once or so a month. One evening he came and said to his wife: "The time has come for me to say goodbye to you forever."

"Where will you go?" she asked.

"Jade Emperor of Heaven has made me Governor of Hua Mountain. I must go a great distance to assume my post. My duties are many and the road is hard, so I cannot return. His wife and son cried and held him fast. "Don't take it so hard! Our son's position in life is assured, and the family fortune will be enough for you to live on. When has there ever been a pair of phoenixes that stayed together for a century?" Turning to his son, he said, "Be a man of character, and don't squander what I've left you. We'll get to see each other ten years from now." He walked straight out the door and was gone.

At the age of twenty-five, Wei was awarded a Master of Letters degree and given the position of inspecting commissioner. He was ordered to perform ceremonies at Hua Mountain, the Western Sacred Peak, and his route took him through Huayin County. To his surprise there suddenly appeared a carriage with attendants bearing plumed canopies, galloping toward the ranks of his escort. On closer inspection, the man in the carriage proved to be his father. He dismounted and threw himself down, sobbing, at the side of the road. His father stopped the carriage and said, "You have a good reputation as an official. Now I can rest easy." Wei did not rise from his prone position. Without turning his head, Zhu ordered his carriage to leave quickly. When he had gone several paces he turned, unfastened a sword from his waist and had an attendant hand it to his son.

"Wear it and you will prosper," he cried from afar. Wei was about to run after him, but, as he watched, the carriage with its horses and attendants floated airily over the ground and disappeared in the blinking of an eye. For a long time he gave himself up to disappointment and regret. Then he drew the sword and saw that it was a piece of extremely fine workmanship. A line of words was engraved upon it: "Be long on courage and short on foolhardiness; be round in wisdom and square in conduct." Wei later attained the rank of sub-prefect. He had five sons: Chen,

Qian, Mi, Hun and Shen. One night he dreamed his father said, "The sword should go to Hun." He acted accordingly. Hun later became a commissioner-general with a high reputation.

The Chronicler of the Tales comments: "To chop short the crane's legs and stretch the duck's[1] is the folly of artificiality, but grafting a flower to a tree is a marvel of creativity. How true these two statements are when vitals are to be hacked up and knives are to be wielded against necks! This Master Lu was repulsive on the outside but attractive on the inside. It has not been all that many years from the end of the Ming dynasty to the present. Is Master Lu of Lingyang still around? Does his supernatural power still work as of old? I would like nothing more than to serve, whip in hand, as his charioteer."

[1] From the *Zhuang-zi*.

11. YINGNING

WANG Zifu from Luo Bazaar in Ju County lost his father at an early age. An absolutely brilliant student, he received the baccalaureate at thirteen. His mother held him so dear that she seldom permitted him to go on outings in the country. He had been engaged to a girl of the Xiao family, but she passed away before they could be married, so his phoenix-mate was as yet unfound. On the Lantern Festival, the son of his maternal uncle, a scholar named Wu, invited him to do some sightseeing together. When they got outside the village a servant from his uncle's house came and called Wu home. Seeing that young women were out walking in droves, Scholar Wang gave in to the impulse to stroll by himself. There was a young woman walking arm-in-arm with a maid and toying with a twig of plum blossoms. Her flower-features topped the age, and the smiles playing across her face had a beauty that invited touching. The scholar riveted his gaze upon her, heedless of all scruples. The girl walked several dainty steps away, turned to her maid and said, "That fellow has a roguish glint in his eyes!" She dropped the flowers on the ground and moved off, talking gaily as she went. The scholar picked up the flowers wistfully. The spirit had gone out of him, and he walked pensively home.

At home he hid the flowers under his pillow. He spent his time moping and sleeping, refusing to eat or speak. His worried mother set up an alter and said prayers to drive out evil influences, but his condition only worsened. He soon grew emaciated. A doctor examined him and had him take medicines to draw the disease out, but he remained in a heartsick daze. His mother caressed him and asked the reason for his malady, but he would not break his silence.

Just then Scholar Wu showed up. He was instructed to get to the root of the matter without letting Wang know what he was about. Seeing Wu at his bedside made tears roll down Wang's cheeks. Wu set on his bed and comforted him, then gradually brought the conversation around to pointed questions. Wang spat out the whole truth and asked Wu to recommend a course of action.

"You are being downright silly!" laughed Wu. "Nothing stands in the way of fulfilling your wish! I will make inquiries for you. Since she was out in the wilds on foot, she could not belong to a noble family. If she is not yet engaged, then everything is fine. Otherwise, a substantial gratuity will very likely win acceptance. All you have to do is recover: leave the rest to me."

When he heard this the scholar grinned broadly in spite of himself. Wu came out and told Wang's mother everything. He checked into the girl's place of residence, but exhausted every avenue of inquiry without turning up a single trace or thread. The mother could do nothing but eat her heart out. However, Wang started smiling and began to show some interest in food after Wu's visit.

A few days later Wu came again. The scholar asked how the matter was progressing.

Wu deceived him saying: "I've found her already. I never would have thought that she is the daughter of my paternal aunt, which makes her your cousin on your mother's side. She is not engaged as yet. Though marriage

嬰甯
拈花微笑欲傾
城情到濃時轉
不情一味天真
何爛漫只宜
呼作太憨生

between maternal relatives is frowned upon, everything should work out if we tell them the truth."

Joy shone from the scholar's brow as he asked, "Where does she live?"

Wu concocted another reply: "A little more than ten miles away in the mountains southwest of here." The scholar entrusted him repeatedly with the task. Wu insisted he would take it upon himself. From then on the scholar's intake of food and liquids gradually increased, and he made daily progress toward recovery. Checking under his pillow he saw that the flowers, though dry, had not yet withered away. He toyed with them in rapt absorption, as if he were looking at the one who had left them. He wondered why Wu did not come, so he sent a letter summoning him. Wu procrastinated and would not go to him. The scholar was enraged and despondent. Fearing that he would take sick again, his mother hastened to arrange for him to marry another girl, but he shook his head whenever she tried to discuss it.

Day after day he did nothing but await Wu's coming. Much to his vexation, there was no word from Wu after all this time. Then it occurred to him that ten miles was not far. Why should he depend on anyone else? Putting the twig of plum blossoms in his sleeve, he sullenly set out by himself, without so much as a word to his family. With nobody to ask for directions, he turned toward the mountain to the south and went his solitary way on foot. When he had gone something more than ten miles, jumbled mountains closed in upon him. The great expanse of verdure sent a tingle through his body. No one was abroad in the stillness. Only steep trails could be seen traversing the mountains.

Looking toward the bottom of a valley in the distance

he could make out a small settlement almost hidden among flowering thickets and dense trees. He descended the mountain and entered the village. The few buildings he saw were all thatched huts, but they were elegantly constructed. One house to the north had weeping willows before the gate. Within the walls grew especially luxuriant peach and apricot trees, interspersed with tall bamboos. Wild birds went clucking here and there among them. Surmising that this was someone's garden, he dared not enter abruptly. A look around revealed a clean, smooth boulder in front of the facing house, so he sat there to make himself comfortable for a spell.

Suddenly from inside the wall he heard a girl's delicate voice calling in drawn-out tones: "Gloria." As he stood listening, a young woman walked past from east to west, holding an almond blossom and lowering her head to fasten it in her hair. Raising her head, she saw the scholar and ceased fastening the flower; she toyed smilingly with the flower and walked into the house. To his sudden joy he recognized that she was the very girl he had met along the road during the Lantern Festival, but then he reflected that this gave him no pretext for presenting himself. He wanted to call at the house as if it were his aunt's, but considering that the two families had never kept in touch, he was afraid there might be some mistake. What was more, there was no one within the gate whom he could ask. Oblivious to hunger and thirst, he sat, reclined, then paced back and forth from morning into the afternoon, till his eager eyes ached with watching. Now and then he caught a glimpse of the girl's face peeking around a corner, as if she was surprised that he had not left.

Suddenly an old matron came out leaning on a cane, took a look at the scholar and said, "I was told that a young man from who knows where came early this morning and has been here ever since. What are you here for? Aren't you hungry?"

The scholar quickly got up, raised his folded hands in greeting and replied, "I intended to look up my relatives." The old woman, being hard of hearing, did not catch what he had said. He repeated his words loudly.

"What is the family name of your relations?" she asked. The scholar was unable to answer. The old woman laughed: "How strange! If you don't even know their names, what relatives are there for you to visit? From the look of you, you're nothing but a book-addled scholar. I suppose you'd better come with me. I'll feed you husked millet, and there's a settee inside you can lie on. You can go back tomorrow morning. Once you've gotten the name straight, you'll have plenty of chances to pay a visit." His famished stomach had put him in the mood to wolf down a meal, and this was a chance to approach the beautiful girl, so the scholar was overjoyed. Following the old woman through the gate, he saw a path of white flagstones lined with red flowers. The steps were strewn with fallen petals. The winding path took them westward to another gate, which opened into a courtyard covered by a bean arbor supported on trellises. The woman invited the guest into the house. The whitewashed walls were dazzling white. Branches from a flowering crabapple outside the window reached into the room. Cushions, table, and settee—everything glistened with cleanliness.

As they moved to their seats a face could indistinctly be seen peeking through the window. The old woman called, "Gloria, make some millet right away." The maid's answering cry was heard outside. When they were seated, they both made known their family histories. The old woman asked, "Was your maternal grandfather by any chance named Wu?"

"Yes, he was."

"Then you're my nephew!" she said in wonderment. "Your mother is my little sister. For years now we've been destitute, and there's not even a three-foot manchild in the house, so our connection has been broken off. Look how grown up you are, nephew: I didn't even recognize you."

The scholar said, "I came just to see you, Aunt, but things happened so quickly that I forgot your name."

"My married name is Qin," said the old woman. I have no descendants. I do have a tender young thing, but she was born to a concubine. Her mother remarried and left her upbringing to me. She is not dull, by any means, but she has had little guidance. She is fun-loving and free of care. In a little while I'll have her come to meet you."

Soon the maid served a meal. On the table was a dish of young chickens small enough to fit in the palm of one's hand. When the old woman had finished urging him to eat, the maid came to clear off the dishes. "Call Miss Yingning here," said the old woman. The maid nodded and left.

After a long wait, a muted laugh was heard from outside. The old woman called again: "Yingning, your cousin is here." There was a drawn-out, chortling laugh from outside the door. As the maid pushed her in, Yingning was still covering her mouth and laughing uncontrollably.

The old woman glared at her and said, "There is a guest here. What sort of impression will you make with all this snorting and spluttering?" The girl mastered her laughter and stood still. The scholar joined his hands before his chest in greeting.

"This is Mister Wang, your aunt's son," said the old woman. "It is laughable that members of the same family don't know each other."

"How old is my cousin here?" asked the scholar. The old woman did not hear him clearly, so the scholar had to repeat his question, which made the girl double up with laughter.

The old woman said to him: "I said that she has had little guidance, and now you see what I mean. She's already sixteen, but still as silly as a child."

"She is a year younger than I," said the scholar.

"So you're already seventeen, nephew. You were born in the year of the horse, weren't you?"

The scholar answered with a nod.

"And who is your wife?"

"I have none," he replied.

"How could someone with your ability and good looks still be unengaged at seventeen? Yingning has no in-laws yet either. You two would make a wonderful match. Unfortunately, there remains the objection that you are close kin."

The scholar gave no answer. He was too busy staring wordlessly at Yingning to glance at anything else. The maid whispered to the girl: "See how his eyes gleam: he's still a rogue inside!"

The girl burst out laughing again. "Let's go see if the peach blossoms are out yet," she said, turning to the maid. She rose abruptly, hid her mouth with a sleeve and walked out with dainty, pattering steps. Once outside the gate she loosed a peal of laughter. The old woman also rose and called the maid to make the scholar's bed.

"Your coming was not easy, nephew. I hope you stay for a few days before we get around to sending you home. If you feel restless, there is a small garden behind the house to amuse yourself in, and there are books to read."

On the next day, he went behind the house where a small plot had been given over to a garden carpeted with fine grass. The walks were strewn with poplar catkins. Flowers and trees surrounded three rows of thatched huts. Threading his way among the flowers, he heard a tittering coming from the top of a tree. Looking up, he saw Yingning above him. The scholar's coming had sent her into gales of laughter that threatened to tumble her from the tree.

"Don't act like that: you're going to fall," said the scholar. As she climbed down the girl kept laughing, unable to contain herself. When she almost reached the ground she lost her grip and fell, whereupon she finally stopped laughing. Helping her, the scholar gave her wrist a slight pinch. Her laugh started up again. She leaned against the tree for a long time, unable to walk, before it stopped. The scholar gave her laughter time to die down, then pulled the flowers from his sleeve to show her.

She took them in her hand saying: "They are withered. Why do you keep them?"

"These are the ones you left behind on Lantern Festival day, so I kept them."

"What's the point in keeping them?"

"To show that my love for you is not forgotten. Since I met you on Lantern Festival day, I pined for you till I grew ill: I thought that I would surely end up a dead man. Now unexpectedly I have this chance to gaze at your beautiful face. Please take pity on me."

The girl said, "This is a mere trifle. Close relatives should never be stingy to one another. When you leave I'll tell the old servant to pick a giant bundle of flowers from the garden and send them along with you."

"Are you being silly?" asked the scholar.

"What's so silly about that?"

"I don't love the flowers; I love the one who was holding the flowers in her fingers."

Between relatives love goes without saying.

"What I mean by love is not the love between gourds on the same vine, but the love between husband and wife."

"What makes that different?"

"They share pillow and mat at night."

The girl lowered her head in thought for a long while, then said, "I'm not used to sleeping with people I don't know well." The maid stole up in the middle of the conversation, frightening the scholar away. A little later they met in the mother's room.

"Where did you go?" asked the mother. The girl replied that they had been talking together in the garden. "The meal has been ready for quite some time. What subject kept you gabbing so long?" asked the old woman.

"Cousin wants to sleep with me," said the girl. She would have kept talking, but the mortified scholar gave her an anxious look. She smiled and stopped. Luckily the old woman was still prattling along with her longwinded question and did not hear what the girl said. The scholar covered up by speaking of something else. In a low voice he reproved the girl.

"Shouldn't I have said what I did just now?" she asked.

"That should only be talked about behind people's backs."

"I might hide things from other people, but I would never do anything behind my mother's back? Besides, sleeping is an everyday matter: why treat it like a taboo?" Irritated as he was with her simple-mindedness, he had no way to make her grasp his meaning.

Some days earlier, the scholar's mother had grown worried when he failed to return after a long wait. She searched nearly everywhere in the village without finding a sign of him, so she went to ask Wu. Recalling what he had said in the past, Wu told her to look for him in a mountain village to the southwest. The servant had passed through several villages before reaching this one.

When the scholar finished his meal he went to the gate, and there he met the servant from home, leading a pair of donkeys in search of him. He returned to tell the old woman and ask if he could take the girl back with him.

The old woman replied happily: "That has been my intention for a long time. But my weak old bones cannot venture far. It's wonderful, nephew, that we have you to take her back and let her get to know her aunt." She called for Yingning, who came laughing. "What makes you so happy that you can't stop laughing?" asked the old woman. "You would be perfect if you didn't laugh." Anger showed in her eyes. "Your cousin wants to take you with him. Go ahead and pack." Then, after she had served food and wine to the servant, she saw the girl out the gate, saying: "Your aunt's family has ample landholdings and can support extra people. Once you're there you don't have to come back. Learn something of poetry and rites, so you'll be able to serve your in-laws well. Trouble your aunt to choose a good mate for you."

The two of them set out. They went down into a glen, from which, looking back, they could make out the shape of the old woman leaning against the gate and looking northward. When they reached home his mother, surprised at the sight of the beautiful young woman, asked who she might be. The scholar answered that this was her niece.

The mother said, "What Master Wu told you before was false. I don't have a sister: how can I have a niece?"

When questioned, the girl replied, "I am not my mother's child by birth. My father's family name was Qin, and he died when I was still in swaddling clothes. I don't remember him."

The mother said, "True, my older sister did marry a Qin, but she passed away long ago. How could she be alive now?" She questioned the girl closely about her mother's facial features and the location of warts and moles. Everything the girl said tallied perfectly. But the mother was still suspicious: "That may well be, but she's been dead for many years. How could she be alive now?"

Scholar Wu came, at which the girl retreated to her room. When he learned her story, he seemed lost in thought for quite some time. Suddenly he asked, "Is the girl's name Yingning?" The scholar nodded. Wu declared that this was indeed a strange matter.

When asked how he knew, Wu said, "After my aunt who married into the Qin family died, uncle remained single. He was beset by a werefox until he wasted away and died. The fox spirit gave birth to a daughter named Yingning. Everyone in my family used to see her lying in a crib in her baby clothes. The werefox kept coming after uncle died. Then we procured a Heavenly Preceptor[1] charm, which we pasted to the wall, and the werefox spirit fled with the girl. Could this be her?" The three discussed each of their suspicions. All this time the snorting sounds of Yingning's laughter could be heard from the inner room.

[1] Title given to a Taoist dignitary during the Yuan dynasty (1277-1368).

"That girl is just too mindless," said the mother. Wu asked to see her. The mother went into the inner room, but the girl was laughing so hard she paid no attention. When the mother prevailed on her to go out, she finally did her best to stifle her chuckles by turning her face to the wall for some time before making an appearance. No sooner had she made gestures of greeting than she turned right back into the inner rooms and loosed a loud peal of laughter, much to the amusement of all the women in the room.

Wu offered to go to her village to look into the mystery and, while he was at it, to act as go-between. He found the spot where the village had been, but not a building was there, only a scattering of mountain flowers. Wu remembered that his aunt's burial spot was somewhere nearby, but the grave was overgrown beyond recognition. With a sigh of bewilderment, he headed back.

Thereafter, Wang's mother suspected the girl was a ghost. When she went in to relay the news that Wu had brought, the girl did not betray the slightest astonishment. The mother consoled her for having no family, but she, without showing a sign of grief, only persisted in laughing giddily. No one could fathom her.

The mother made her stay with the other young women. She always presented herself at the break of day to ask after the mother's health. She surpassed all her peers in cleverness at sewing. The only thing wrong was her predisposition to laughter, which she could not stop even when forbidden. But there was a winning beauty in her laugh, an abandon that did not detract from her charm. Everyone found it delightful. The girls and young wives in the neighborhood vied in making overtures to her. The mother, in spite of her persistent fear that the girl was a ghostly being, selected an auspicious day for toasting with nuptial winecups. She observed the girl stealthily when the sun was behind her, but there was nothing abnormal about the shadow cast by her body. When the day came they tried to make her perform the bridal ceremony in her wedding finery, but they had to give it up because she laughed so hard she could not go through the motions.

Thinking that she was mindless and silly, the scholar feared she would reveal private, bedroom matters, but she proved to be close-mouthed and would not say a word.

Whenever the mother was depressed or angry the girl would come and lift her spirits with a single laugh. Servants and maids who feared beatings for minor mistakes would beg her to go with them to intercede with the mistress. Guilty maids who threw themselves on her mercy were always excused. She loved flowers to the point of mania and made rounds of every relative and family friend to search for what would catch her eye. She secretly pawned her jewelry to buy fine varieties. In a few months there was not a step, path, fence or outhouse that did not have flowers growing on or around it.

At the rear of the courtyard was an arbor of banksia roses adjoining the yard of the neighbor on the west. The girl often climbed onto it and amused herself by picking flowers to fasten in her hair. The mother reprimanded her every time she found her doing this, but the girl would not give it up. One day the son of the neighbor was staring fixedly at her, infatuated with her beauty. She laughed and made no attempt to get out of sight. The neighbor's son thought that the girl was showing an interest in him, and his heart began to churn. The girl pointed to a spot beneath the wall and climbed down laughing. He was overjoyed, thinking that she was making an assignation.

When dusk came he went to the place, and she was waiting. He went to her and entered her. At that moment something in her private parts pierced him like an awl: the pain of it shot through him to his heart. With a loud wail he stumbled back and fell. He peered at her but saw, instead of the girl, a dead log lying beside the wall. What he had joined with was a water-moistened knothole.

Hearing the scream, the neighbor dashed to the spot and asked what had happened. His son moaned and would not answer. When the neighbor's wife came he finally told them the truth. They lit a torch and held it to the knothole: inside was a huge scorpion, the size of a small crab. The father chopped the log apart, caught the scorpion and killed it. He carried his son home, and the young man died suddenly in the middle of the night.

The neighbor brought charges against Scholar Wang and exposed Yingning as a witch. The district magistrate, having long admired the scholar's genius, knew well that he was a gentleman of irreproachable conduct. Concluding that the neighbor was making false accusations, he would have punished him with a beating had the scholar not begged to have him pardoned. The neighbor was released and driven from the courthouse.

The mother said to the girl: "As mindless and brash as you are, I knew that your silliness would cause a tragedy. Because of the magistrate's wise judgment, you were lucky enough not to be entangled. If he had been a muddle-headed official, you would surely have been arrested and interrogated in court. How could my son have faced our relatives and neighbors after that?" The girl made a sober face, promising not to laugh again.

"There is no one who doesn't laugh, but it has its proper time," said the mother.

The girl never laughed again, even when she was teased on purpose, but not even once did she make a grim face.

Then one night she cried and sniveled before the scholar. This was something strange to him.

"I did not say this earlier, when I had not been with you long, for fear you would be shaken," she sobbed. "Now I see how sincerely you and your mother lavish affection on me. There can't be any harm in being honest, can there? I am a werefox's child. Before mother died she entrusted me to my ghost mother, who gave me a home for over ten years. That is why I am here today. What is more, I have no brothers: you are the one I rely on. My mother lies in forlorn stillness on the slope of a mountain, with no one to take pity on her and bury her in a grave beside her husband. This is the constant grief she bears there in the underworld. If you don't grudge the trouble and expense of easing the unjust suffering of the departed, then those who rear daughters will perhaps not be so hard-hearted as to drown or abandon them.

The scholar gave his consent, but worried that the burial mound might be lost under wild grasses. The girl simply told him not to worry. On the arranged day husband and wife loaded a coffin on a cart and set out. The girl pointed out the burial place among the mists of a dense thicket. There they found the old woman's body, flesh still on the bones. The girl bent over it and cried dolefully. After transporting it back, they located the Qin family graves and buried her with her husband. That night the scholar dreamed the old woman came to express thanks. Upon awakening he told the dream.

The girl said, "I saw her during the night, but she told me not to rouse you." The scholar regretted that Yingning had not invited her to stay. The girl said, "She is a ghost.

There are many living people about and vital forces are overpowering here. How could she stay long?" The scholar asked about Gloria. "She too is a fox, and quite a clever one," was the answer. "My werefox mother left her to watch over me. She often fed me choice morsels with her own hands, so I will always be grateful to her. When I asked about her last night, mother said she has already found her a husband."

From then on, every year when the Cold Food Festival rolled around, husband and wife never failed to visit the Qins' grave, sweeping and paying respects to the dead. When a year had passed the girl gave birth to a son. While still in his mother's arms, he was unafraid of strangers. He laughed at anyone he saw, much in the manner of his mother.

The Chronicler of the Tales comments: "Judging from her persistent mindless laughter, she seemed wholly lacking in sensibility, and what could be more deviously cunning than her wicked prank beneath the wall? But her sorrowful yearning for her ghostly mother and her switch from laughter to tears lead one to think that laughter was merely a mask for the real Yingning. I have heard of a mountain herb called Laugharia which, when smelled, makes men laugh without stopping. If some of these were planted in a room, then herbs like Forget-Your-Sorrow and Joy of Union would not make much of an impression, while the 'flower that understands speech'[1] would seem to be putting on air.

[1] First used by the Tang emperor Xuanzong in reference to his beloved concubine Yang Yuhuan.

12. NIE XIAOQIAN

NING Caichen, a native of Zhejiang, was bold and forthright by nature. He disciplined himself to uprightness and valued his own integrity. He often told people that there was only one woman in his life.

It happened that he went to Jinhua.[1] Arriving at the north wall, he set down his baggage in a monastery. The shrine-hall and pagoda within were magnificent, but tangled grasses grew head high and no traces of human presence were seen. The double-leaved doors of the monks' quarters to the east and west were closed but left unlatched. Only a small apartment to the south had a knocker and latch that looked new. At the eastern corner of the shrine-hall were tall bamboos one or two hands in circumference. Below the steps was a large pond blooming with wild lotuses. The hidden, faraway quality of the place pleased Ning greatly. At that time high rents were being charged for rooms in the city, because the Commissioner of Education was there to preside over examinations. These considerations made Ning decide to stay in the monastery, so he strolled about to pass the time until the monks return. At sundown a gentleman came in and opened the south door. Ning went to greet him with rapid steps and told him of his plans.

1. Name of a town in Zhejiang province.

聶小倩
䟽具光明磊
落腸不逢
劍俠亦何傷
良宵自說
奇緣者多
半青燐
注墓楊

"There is no landlord here," said the gentleman. "I am a squater too. If you can put up with the desolation and be kind enough to share your knowledge when time permits, I will be fortunate." Ning was delighted. Anticipating a long stay, he bound up sheaves of straw for a mattress and put up boards to do duty for a desk. That night the moon was high and bright, and its clear light was like water. The two men sat face to face on the shrine-hall gallery, telling each other their names and courtesy titles. The gentleman gave the family name Yan and the soubriquet Chixia. Ning thought he might be one of the scholars who had come for the examination, but he certainly did not speak with a Zhejiang accent. Ning asked him. Yan told him in a plain, forthright manner that he hailed from Shaanxi. When they had finished what they had to say to each other, each joined his hands before his chest by way of leavetaking and retired.

Ning did not fall asleep for a long time because of the unfamiliar surroundings. He heard an undertone of voices north of his quarters, as if a family lived there. He got out of bed and, crouching beneath the stone windowsill at the north wall, peeked outside. There in a small courtyard beyond a low wall he saw a woman in her forties talking in the moonlight with an old decrepit stoop-backed lady dressed in faded red silk and a large decorative comb stuck in her hair.

"What's keeping Xiaoqian?" asked the woman.

"She'll be here any minute," said the old lady.

"Don't tell me she has grumbled to you?"

"Not to my face, but she looks down in the mouth."

"We shouldn't show too much of a friendship toward that little maid."

A girl of sixteen or seventeen arrived while the woman

was talking. From what Ning could see she was utterly ravishing.

The old lady said laughingly: "It only goes to show we shouldn't speak of others behind their backs. You sneaked up on us without a sound, just when we were talking about you, little witchmaid. Fortunately, we weren't backbiting you." She went on, "Young lady, you sure do look like you're right out of a painting. If I were a man you'd even steal my soul away."

The girl said, "If Granny didn't praise me, who else would say a good word for me?"

The women and the girl went on talking about something or other. Ning lay down and stopped listening, assuming they belonged to a family in the neighborhood. After a while the voices died away. As he was about to fall asleep, he became aware that someone was in his room. He jumped up and took a close look: it was the girl from the north courtyard. Startled, he asked what brought her there.

The girl said with a laugh: "The moonlight tonight is keeping me awake: I'd like to enter into an intimate friendship."

"You should guard against scandal," said Ning, giving her a stern look. "I fear what others will say. If you take one false step, you will stray from the path of virtue and modesty."

"It is night: no one will be the wiser," said the girl.

Again Ning rebuked her. The girl shilly-shallied as if she had more to say. "Leave quickly," snapped Ning. "Or I'll shout loud enough for the scholar in the south apartment to know." At this the frightened girl withdrew. She got outside the door, but came back in and placed a gold ingot on his cover. Ning grabbed the ingot and hurled it onto the courtyard steps, saying: "This ill-gotten stuff would soil my pouch!"

The girl picked up the gold in shame and went out, saying to herself: "This man must be made of iron or stone."

In the morning a student from Lanxi[1] came in the company of a servant and put up in the east chamber to await the examination. That night he died suddenly. Blood trickled from small punctures in the soles of his feet that seemed to have been made by an awl. Nobody knew what had happened. The next night the servant also died in a similar condition. Toward evening Scholar Yan returned. In answer to Ning's queries, he gave the opinion that it was a banshee. Ning, bold in his uprightness, did not let the matter weigh on his mind.

At nighttime the girl came again and said to him: "I've had experience with many men, but never was there anyone with your moral integrity. You are truly a saint: I dare not deceive you. My name is Xiaoqian, my family name Nie. I died prematurely at eighteen and was buried beside the monastery. Since then I have been forced by a demon to do one low-down deed after another. I have to force myself on people immodestly. I certainly did it against my will. Now there is nobody in the monastery to kill: I fear he will take the form of a *yakṣa* demon and come here." In dismay, Ning begged her to recommend a course of action. The girl said, "You can escape harm if you are in the same room with Scholar Yan."

"Why haven't you tried to tempt Scholar Yan?" he asked.

"He is an extraordinary man: I dare not go near him."

"What happens to the deluded ones?" he asked.

[1] Name of another town in Zhejiang province.

"When someone has relations with me I catch them unawares and puncture their feet with an awl. Then they go into a delirium, and I draw their blood for the demon to drink. Or I tempt them with gold which really isn't gold —it is the demon bone of a *yakṣa*. He who keeps it will have his heart and liver cut out. Of the two methods, I use whichever happens to have the greater appeal at the time."

Ning thanked her and asked when he should prepare himself. She answered that tomorrow night was the time. While taking her leave she sobbed, "I have fallen into a dark sea. Though I cast about for the shore, I fail to reach it. Your sense of honor, sir, towers to the very clouds: you can surely rescue me from my misery. If you would wrap up my remains, take them back with you and give them a resting place, this would be a clemency greater than resurrection."

Ning gave his forthright consent and asked where she was buried.

"Just remember that it is under a white poplar—the one with a birds' nest." With these words she went out the gate and vanished in a whirl. The next day, fearing that Yan would go elsewhere, Ning paid an early visit to invite him over. At midmorning he set out wine and victuals while observing Yan attentively. When he got around to inviting Yan to stay overnight, Yan declined, claiming to be eccentric and found of solitude. Ning refused to listen and insisted on bringing Yan's bedding. Yan had no choice but to follow, bearing his cot.

"I know you are an upstanding man," Yan cautioned his host. "And I have the highest admiration for you. But there is a trifling personal matter which cannot be revealed just now. Please do not open or peek into my chest and bundle. If you go against this, the consequences will be unfavorable for both of us."

Ning solemnly acquiesced to these instructions, whereupon they went to bed. Yan placed the chest above the window. Not long after laying head to pillow, he commenced snoring thunderously. Ning could not sleep.

Shortly after the first watch a dim human shape appeared outside the window. Suddenly it came close to the window and peered inside with glittering eyes. In his fright, Ning was about to call out to Yan when an object suddenly split the side of the chest and flew out, flashing like a jet of water in instantaneous arc; it broke through the stone cornice above the window, then flicked abruptly back into the chest like a vanishing bolt of lightning. Yan awoke and got out of bed as Ning watched, pretending to be asleep. Yan picked up the chest and examined it, then pulled out a gleaming crystalline object, about two inches long and hardly broader than the stalk of a scallion, which he sniffed and stared at in the moonlight. After wrapping it tightly in several layers of cloth he placed it back in the broken chest and muttered, "The nerve of that banshee! My wooden chest is ruined on account of him." He laid back down again. Ning was greatly amazed, so he rose and asked about it, telling Yan what he had seen.

Yan said, "Since you have shown your understanding and affection, why should I hide the fact that I am a swordsman. If it had not been for that stone cornice, the demon would have died instantly. He was wounded as it was."

"What was that you wrapped up?"

"A sword. I smelled a demon aura about it just now." Ning wanted to have a look. Yan generously showed it to him. It was a gleaming, miniature sword. Ning found himself admiring Yan all the more. The next day Ning looked outside the window and saw traces of blood. He went to the north of the monastery, where untended graves were crowded one against the other. Sure enough there was a poplar with birds nesting at its tip.

When Ning had discharged his business, he hurriedly packed his bags for the return trip. Scholar Yan gave him a send-off dinner and showered him with friendliness. He presented Ning with a torn leather pouch, saying: "The sword was kept in this bag. If you guard it like a treasure, it will keep banshees and goblins away."

Ning wished to learn swordsmanship from him, but Yan demurred: "A person of your firm integrity would be capable of it, but you are ultimately a man of worldly prospects, not a man of the Way."

On the pretext that this was his sister's burial place, Ning dug up the girl's remains, laid them out in new burial gown and shroud, and then rented a boat for the trip home. Ning's studio looked out over the wilds, so he had a grave dug and buried her outside his studio. He made a burial offering and said an invocation: "Out of pity for your solitary soul I have buried you near my humble dwelling, within hearing of your songs and wails, in hopes that you will not be tortured by vicious demons. I offer you a jarful of wine to drink. The flavor is certainly not pure and sweet: I hope you will not frown on it." The invocation over, he was heading homeward when someone called him from behind: "Slow down and wait for me to walk along!" He turned to look: it was Xiaoqian.

She thanked him joyfully: "Ten deaths would not be enough to repay your integrity. I wish to go back with you and make the acquaintance of my in-laws. I will have no regrets, even if I am treated like a concubine or dowry maid." Ning scrutinized her carefully. Her face shone as with the hues of a dawn sky; her feet in their upturned slippers were like tapering shoots of bamboo. Now that he could look at her closely in the daylight, she was even more matchless in grace and allure. So they went together into his studio, where he had her sit and wait while he went in to let his mother know. His mother was dumbfounded. She warned him not to say anything to his wife, who had long been sick, for fear of giving her a fright. As they were talking, the girl whisked in and prostrated herself on the floor. Ning said, "This is Xiaoqian." The mother was too surprised to do anything but stare.

The girl said to the mother: "I was adrift all alone, far from my parents and brothers, but now that I have bathed in the dew of this young man's kindness, I am willing to serve him as a slave to repay his chivalry."

Seeing how etherial and lovely she was, the mother found the courage to speak to her: "I am delighted by the gracious favor you have shown my son, young lady, but I have only this one son to carry on the offering of ancestral sacrifices, and I dare not let him have a ghost mate."

"Rest assured there is no other aim in my heart. Since you, venerable mother, cannot give your trust to a person from the nether world, I beg leave to treat him as an elder brother. I will place myself in your hands and serve you day and night. May I?"

The mother, moved to pity by her earnestness, gave approval. The girl wished to make a call on her sister-in-law, Ning's wife, but when the mother declined by reason of the woman's illness, she gave up the idea. Then the girl entered the kitchen and presided over preparation of meals in the mother's stead. She threaded her way in and out of rooms and around the furniture like a longtime resident. At sundown the mother, frightened by her presence, bid her goodnight without setting out a bed and covers. Seeing what the mother had in mind, the girl finally left the house. When she passed the studio, she was about to enter but backed away. She walked back and forth before the door, as if something were frightening her.

The scholar called to her. She said, "There is a fearsome sword-aura in this room: that is why I did not come to see you on the way home." Ning realized she was speaking of the leather pouch, so he got it down and hung it up in another room. At this the girl entered and sat down by the candle. For a while she did not utter a word. At last she asked, "Do you read at night? In my childhood I could recite the *Śūrangama Sūtras*. I've forgotten most of it now. If you could get hold of a copy, I could have you correct me when you are free at night." Ning said he would. Again they sat in silence, until the second watch was almost at an end, and still she said nothing of leaving. Ning urged her to go.

"A barren grave in a strange place is mighty frightening to a solitary soul," she said glumly.

"I have no other bed in my studio," said Ning. "And even brother and sister should keep themselves above suspicion." The girl rose, knitting her brows as if she were on the verge of weeping. Her feet shuffled lingeringly, carrying her slowly through the gate. She walked onto the steps and descended out of sight. Deep in his heart Ning pitied her. He wanted to let her stay the night on another bed, but he feared his mother's anger. The girl went to serve the mother every morning, bringing a basin and helping her wash. When she left the main hall to do chores, she always accommodated herself to the mother's wishes. At dusk she would leave off her work, pass by the studio and read aloud from sutras by candlelight. Only when she noticed that Ning was ready for bed did she go out dejectedly.

Prior to this, when Ning's wife had fallen ill, the mother had been unbearably overworked. Since the girl's coming she had been quite at ease. In her heart she appreciated the girl and, as she came to know her better every day, loved her like a daughter and even forgot she was a ghost. She could not bear to send the girl out late at night, so she let her stay and sleep in her room. The girl never ate or drank when she first came, but after half a year she began to sip thin rice gruel. Mother and son showered her with affection. They avoided mentioning that she was a ghost, nor could other people tell by looking at her. Before long Ning's wife died. His mother was secretly inclined to bring the girl into the family, but she feared harm would come to her son. The girl, divining this, took advantage of an available moment to tell her: "After living with me for a year, you should know my innermost feelings. I did not wish to keep harming travellers and that's why I followed your son here. The young master is a man of shining openheartedness. He looked on admiringly both in Heaven and among men. And so I have no other intention but to stay close to him and do my part for a few years; this way I can gain a title of nobility that will bring glory on me in the nether world."

The mother knew she harbored no evil intent. Nevertheless, she feared that the girl would be unable to continue the clan's line of descent. The girl said, "Children are given according to the will of heaven. The entry under your son's name in the *Register of Fated Blessings* lists three sons who will be a credit to their clan. This cannot be taken from him on account of a ghost wife." Believing what she said, the mother discussed it with her son. Delighted,

Ning laid out a banquet and broke the news to his relatives. Someone asked to have a look at the bride. The girl agreed cheerfully and came out in formal dress. The whole hall stared in amazement, not because they suspected she was a ghost, but because they thought she was a fairy. After this, all the female relatives came with get-acquainted gifts to congratulate her, vying with one another to become her friend. The girl painted excellent orchids and plum blossoms, so she repaid them with picture scrolls. Those who got them treasured them proudly.

One day Ning found her before the window, hanging her head and lost in moody thought. Suddenly she asked: "Where is the leather pouch?"

"I wrapped it up and put it somewhere else, because you're afraid of it," said Ning.

"I've been absorbing the breath of life for some time now, so I shouldn't be afraid any more. You had better bring it and hang it above the bed." Ning asked what she had in mind. "For three days my heart has not stopped fluttering," she said. "I think the demon from Jinhua hates me for escaping. I fear he'll find this place any time now." Ning brought the leather pouch. The girl turned it over in her hands as she examined it and said, "This is what the sword-immortal put men's heads in. See how worn it is. Who knows the number of men he has killed! Even now when I look at it my flesh crawls." At this they hung it over the bed. The next day she told him to hang it above the door instead. That night they sat beside the lamp, the girl having arranged with Ning not to sleep. In an instant something swooped out of the sky like a bird. The startled girl hid among the curtains. Ning watched as a *yakṣa*-like figure with sparking eyes and blood-red tongue came toward him, its arms flailing out and its eyes glittering. At the gate it stepped back, hesitated for a time, then sidled up to the leather pouch. It snatched at the pouch with its claws, as if to tear it apart. Suddenly the pouch went "pfft" and grew to the size of a hod basket. In a barely visible flash, a creature stuck its body halfway out and pulled the *yakṣa* inside. Then there was silence, and the pouch shrank back to its original size. Ning was stunned. The girl came out from her hiding place and joyfully exclaimed, "No need to worry any more!" Together they looked into the pouch, which contained nothing but a few dipperfuls of clear water.

Several years later Ning did indeed receive a Doctorate of Letters. The girl gave birth to a son. A concubine was brought into the family, and she and the girl each bore a son. All three became well-known in their official careers.

13. EARTHQUAKE

ON the seventeenth day of the sixth lunar month in the seventh year of the Kangxi reign period (1668) between seven and nine in the evening, there was a great earthquake. I was staying at Jixia[1] and drinking by candlelight with my cousin Li Duzhi, when suddenly we heard a sound like thunder coming from the southeast and going northwest. Everyone was shocked and amazed, puzzling about the sound. Soon the table started heaving and winecups fell over. The rafters, beams, and pillars of the room twisted and creaked. We looked at each other, each face turning pale. It took us awhile to realize it was an earthquake. Each of us hastened outside. Storied buildings and houses were tottering and righting themselves again. The sound of falling walls and collapsing houses, with the cries of children and the wails of women, blended into a seething uproar. People were too dazed and dizzy to stand, so they sat on the ground and were tossed about with the bucklings of the earth. The water in the river was flung over ten feet high in the air. The crowing of cocks and barking of dogs resounded through the streets. Something like two hours passed before the tremors quieted down slightly. We looked at the street, where unclad men and women were gathered talking frantically to one another, forgetting that

[1] In Shandong province, not far from Pu Songling's hometown.

they had not gotten dressed. Later I heard that the well at such-and-such a place had caved in and water could not be drawn; the north end of a certain family's pavilion was now pointing south; Qixia Mountain had split open; and the Yi river had disappeared into a crater an acre across. This was a truly incredible anomaly in the order of nature.

The wife of a man in my district arose one night to urinate. She returned to the house: there was a wolf holding her son in its jaws. The woman immediately fought with the wolf for the child. When the wolf relaxed its jaws for an instant, the woman pulled the child away and held it in her arms. The wolf squatted down and would not leave. The woman let out a great screech, which brought the neighbors running, whereupon the wolf went away. The woman was happy when she got over the shock. She pointed and gesticulated as she described how the wolf had held her child in its jaws and how she pulled it away. This continued for quite a while before she suddenly realized she was not wearing a thread on her body. Off she ran. This situation was the same as after the earthquake, when men and women forgot themselves. How laughable is the heedlessness of panic-stricken people.

地震
井傾山裂處
非常稷下停
驚散拳鶴絕
仙々史官書地震
編年紀有事尤詳

14. A CHIVALROUS WOMAN

SCHOLAR Gu of Jinling[1] was a man of diverse accomplishments. His mother's age, combined with their straitened circumstances, made him reluctant to leave her side. Instead he spent his days painting and doing calligraphy on request, supporting the family with the gifts he received. In his twenty-fifth year, his marital plans were still undecided. Then the vacant house across the lane was rented by an old lady and a young woman. Since there were no men in the house, he did not ask who they were. One day he happened to be returning home when he saw the young woman come out of his mother's room. She was eighteen or nineteen years of age, with graceful charm and elegance that are seldom rivalled in this world. Seeing the scholar, she made no move to turn away, but there was an icy aloofness about her.

The scholar went in to ask his mother, who said, "That was the young woman from across the lane. She was here to borrow scissors and a ruler from me. Just now she said that she has only a mother in her family too. She doesn't strike me as the product of a poor family. When I asked why she isn't engaged, she gave her mother's age as the reason. I will go visit her mother tomorrow and drop a hint about what I'm thinking. If her sights aren't set too high, you can support her mother for her."

[1] An old name for Nanjing.

俠女
恩仇了、飄然
去玉貌衣冠
何處尋香後
尋常兒女態
隱娘肝胆
小娥心

In the morning she paid a call at their house. The mother turned out to be hard of hearing. A look around the house showed that there were no provisions for the next day. Asked how they made a living, the old woman replied that they relied on her daughter's skilled fingers. Gu's mother gradually sounded out her feelings toward a joint dining arrangement. The old woman seemed willing, but when she turned to discuss it with her daughter, the girl kept silent and looked displeased. At this Gu's mother went home.

Gu asked his mother for all the details, then said in bewilderment: "Don't tell me she objects to my poverty. She is quiet and never laughs, as beautiful as peaches and plums but cold as frost and snow. What a strange person!" Mother and son sighed as they tried to figure her out, then let the matter drop.

One day as the scholar sat in his studio a young man came and asked for a painting. He had striking good looks and gave the impression of being rather frivolous. Asked where he was from, he replied "a neighboring village." Afterwards he came once every two or three days. As they got to know each other a bit, they began to banter back and forth. When the scholar embraced him familiarly, he did little to resist, and the two of them became intimate. From then on their relationship was quite close. Once the young woman walked past them. The young man followed her with his eyes and asked who she was. Gu replied that she was a "neighbor girl."

The young man said, "Such a stunning girl, but how forbidding her manner is!"

In a little while the scholar went inside. His mother said, "Just now the girl came to borrow rice. She said they haven't lit a fire for days. She treats her mother remarkably well. It's pity they are in such desperate straits. We should give them a little relief." In accordance with his mother's words, the scholar carried a peck of rice to their door and communicated her feelings. The girl took the rice without giving thanks. Every day thereafter she went to the scholar's house, and when she saw his mother making clothes or shoes, she did the sewing for her. She bustled in and out of the hall, doing housework like a wife. The scholar appreciated her even more. Whenever he was given a gift of choice food, he would share it with her mother, but she never bothered to say a word of acknowledgement for this either.

Then the scholar's mother developed boils on her private parts, which had her sobbing and wailing night and day. The girl frequently went to her bed to look after her by washing the affected place and applying salve three or four times a day. This made the mother quite ill at ease, but the girl was not revolted by her foulness.

"Ai!" sighed the mother. "Where can I find a daughter-in-law like you to care for my old body until the end!" This was said with such sorrow that the last words stuck in her throat.

The girl comforted her: "You have a highly filial son. That is a hundred times better than being a widowed mother with an orphan."

"A filial son could not have nursed me as tirelessly as you have," said the mother. "Anyway, I am in the sunset of my life: any time now my body will be left out in the mist and dew. I am deeply worried that there will be no one to continue to making offerings to our family's ancestors." The scholar came in as she was talking.

"You owe the little Miss an awful lot," sobbed his mother. "Don't you forget to repay for kindness!" The scholar went down on his knees before the girl.

"You showed respect for my mother, but I would not thank you," she protested. "Why should you be grateful to me?" The scholar revered and loved her all the more for this, but her bearing was hard and distant. She was completely unapproachable.

One day the scholar was gazing at the girl as she went out the door, when suddenly she turned her head and smiled alluringly. The scholar had never thought such happiness would be his. He hurried after her to her house. He made advances and she put up no resistance. They merged joyfully.

When it was over she warned him: "It happened once, but it won't happen again."

The scholar went home without answering. The next day he tried to set up a rendezvous. A furious look came over her face, and she walked away without looking back. They encountered each other frequently during her daily visits, but she would not spare him a word or a warm look. When he tried a little good-humored teasing, she froze him with icy replies.

Once in an unoccupied moment she suddenly asked him: "Who is the young man who comes every day?" The scholar told her.

"He has affronted me many times, both in behavior and attitude. I have let it pass because of your intimacy with him. But tell him for me that if he behaves that way again, he will not live long."

That night the scholar gave the message to the young man and said, "You'd better watch out. She is not to be toyed with!"

The young man said, "If she is not to be toyed with, why did you toy with her?" The scholar protested that he had not.

"If you haven't, then how did you hear those malicious remarks about me?" The scholar was unable to answer.

"Well, let me trouble you to give her this message," said the young man. "Don't give yourself airs, or I'll let everyone know about you!" The scholar made no attempt to hide his fury, whereupon the young man left.

One night the girl came suddenly while the scholar was sitting alone and said with a laugh: "The affinity between us is not yet broken. It must be the workings of fate!" He embraced her in wild joy. Just then they heard footsteps clattering. They stood up in surprise: it was the young man who pushed open the door and entered.

"What are you doing here?" asked the startled scholar.

"I came to have a look at a chaste woman," laughed the young man. He looked at the girl and said, "Doesn't this make a person wonder?" The girl's brows arched and her cheeks reddened, but she was silent. She turned up her blouse with a quick movement, revealing a leather bag, and deftly drew out a long glistening dagger. At the sight of this the young man backed up in fright. They chased him out the door: he was nowhere to be seen. The girl hurled the dagger upward. It screamed through the air, tracing a brilliant arc. Suddenly an object plopped down on the ground. The scholar hurried over with a candle: it was a white fox, its head severed from its body. What a shock!

"This is your pleasure-boy," said the girl. "I did my best to forgive him, but what could I do when he insisted on parting with his life?" She put the knife back in its bag. The scholar pulled her toward the house, but she said, "That creature put me out of the mood. Could we make it tomorrow night?" She went straight out the gate.

The girl did indeed come the next night and intertwine

her body with his. Afterwards he asked about her knife-craft, but she said, "That is not for you to know. It is a secret that must be carefully guarded. It would not, I fear, be in your best interests for me to divulge it." He made a proposal of marriage, to which she replied. "I've slept with you and carried water for you. If that isn't being a wife, then what is? We are already husband and wife: why must we talk of marriage?"

"Is it because you hate my lack of wealth?"

"You are poor, all right, but am I wealthy? I have joined with you tonight precisely because I was moved to pity by your poverty. Before they parted she warned him: "Indulgent acts should not be repeated. If it is necessary for me to come, I will come on my own. If it is not, trying to force it will do no good."

Later when they met he often tried to tempt her into a private conversation, but she always avoided him. Nevertheless, she was as good as a wife in the way she tended to clothes mending, cooking, and all the other household chores. After several months her mother died. The scholar buried her as well as his means permitted. From then on the girl lived alone. The scholar, thinking that it would be possible to have his way with her now that she slept alone, climbed over the wall. He called several times through the window without getting an answer. He found that the gate was bolted on an empty house. He suspected the girl of having made a rendezvous with someone else. He went again during the night and found things the same way, so he left his jade waist-pendant on the windowsill and left.

A day later he met the girl in his mother's room. When he went out the girl trailed behind and said, "Do you doubt me? Everyone has something that can't be told to others. Now, even though I try to lay your suspicions to rest, it is no use. But there is one thing I would like you to arrange for me, quickly." He asked what it was.

"I am already eight months pregnant. I am likely to give birth any time now. Since 'my identity as wife is not clear,'[1] I can bear you a child but cannot raise it. Please tell your mother to find a wet nurse secretly. Make it seem that you are adopting an orphan, and don't say anything about me." The scholar consented, then told this to his mother.

"What a strange girl!" said his mother with a laugh. "She refuses an offer of marriage, and yet goes ahead and has relations with my son." She was glad to prepare for the event in accordance with the girl's plan.

Over a month went by. When the girl did not show up for several days the mother, thinking that something was amiss, went to her house to check. She found the closed-up house deserted and still. She knocked for quite some time before the girl came out, her hair hanging untidily and her face smudged. The girl opened the door to admit her, then closed it again. They went to her bedroom, where a bawling infant was lying on the bed.

"When was it born?" asked the surprised mother.

"Three days ago," was the reply.

Gu's mother lifted the wrapping-cloth for a look: it was a boy with full cheeks and broad forehead. She exclaimed happily: "Now you have given me a grandson. You are unattached and alone: who will you look to for support?"

The girl said, "I dare not expose my paltry inner motive to you, mother. Wait till night when no one is around; then you can carry the child away."

The mother returned and told this to her son, and neither of them knew what to make of it. That night they

[1] Line from a poem by Du Fu (712-770).

went and carried the child home.

Several evenings later the girl rapped on the door in the middle of the night and entered, carrying a leather bag in her hand. "I have accomplished an enormous task. Now I beg leave to part forever." He immediately asked the reason.

"Your kindness to my mother has never been out of my mind for a moment. Earlier I told you that it could happen once, but it would not happen again, because going to bed together was not my way of repaying you. Since you are poor and unable to marry, I thought to give you a thread to carry on your family line. At first I planned to get it at one attempt, but my period came again, which is why I broke my vow and let it happen a second time. Now your kindness has been repaid and my goal has been realized: I have no more regrets."

"What is that in the bag?" he asked.

"Only the head of my mortal enemy."

He hefted the bag and peeked inside: the head's hair and beard were matted and the face was smeared with blood. Thoroughly shocked, he questioned her further.

"I did not tell you before for fear that you would fail to preserve secrecy, and word of my undertaking would get out. Now the task is accomplished, so it will not hurt to tell you. I am from Zhejiang. My father held the position of Department Magistrate, but he was implicated in crimes by an enemy, who confiscated our family property. I carried my old mother away. I have been laying low and living under an assumed name for three years. First I did not take immediate revenge because my mother was alive. My mother left this world, but then I still had an encumberence of flesh in my belly, so again there was a long delay. I used to leave home at night, not for any other reason, but because I was not yet sure of the roads and the appearance of his house. I might have made a dreadful mistake." With that she went through the gate, then stopped to give him parting instructions: "Take good care of the son I bore. Your blessings are scanty and your life will not be long, but the child will win glory for your family. We must not rouse mother at this late hour. I'm off!"

Before the sorrowful scholar could ask where to, the girl was off in a lightning-like flash. In the space of a glance she was gone. The scholar sighed at his loss and stood woodenly, like one bereft of spirit. In the morning he told his mother. They sighed and marveled without end. After three years the scholar died, just as expected. At eighteen his son attained the Doctorate of Letters, and he continued to care for his grandmother to the end of her years, or so the story goes.

The Chronicler of the Tales comments: "In order to keep a pleasure-boy, it is necessary that one's wife be a chivalrous woman. Otherwise, while you are loving your fine young boar, he will be loving your brood-sow!"

15. PRECIOUS

SUN Zichu, a celebrated man of letters of Guangxi, had a sixth finger growing on one of his hands. He was unrealistic by nature, halting in speech and inclined to accept the deceitful words of others at face value. If singing girls or courtesans happened to be present at a gathering, he would invariably run off as soon as he caught sight of them. When those who knew of his peculiarity tricked him into coming and had prostitutes press themselves upon him, he would redden to the base of his neck, and sweat would trickle down his face. He was made the butt of everyone's laughter. People wrote descriptions of his witless antics, circulated them as items of abusive gossip and nicknamed him Sun the Fool.

Old Man Jia, a big merchant in the district, had wealth enough to rival a prince, and his relations were all of noble blood. His daughter Precious was incomparably beautiful. When the time came to choose her a suitable mate, sons of major families rushed to offer marriage presents, but none measured up to the old man's wishes. The scholar had been bereaved of his wife sometime before, and someone tricked him into sending a go-between. The scholar, singularly unmindful of his own limitations, went ahead and followed this suggestion. The old man had long heard of the scholar's reputation but considered him too poor. As the go-between left the house she came upon Precious, who asked the purpose of her coming. When the go-between

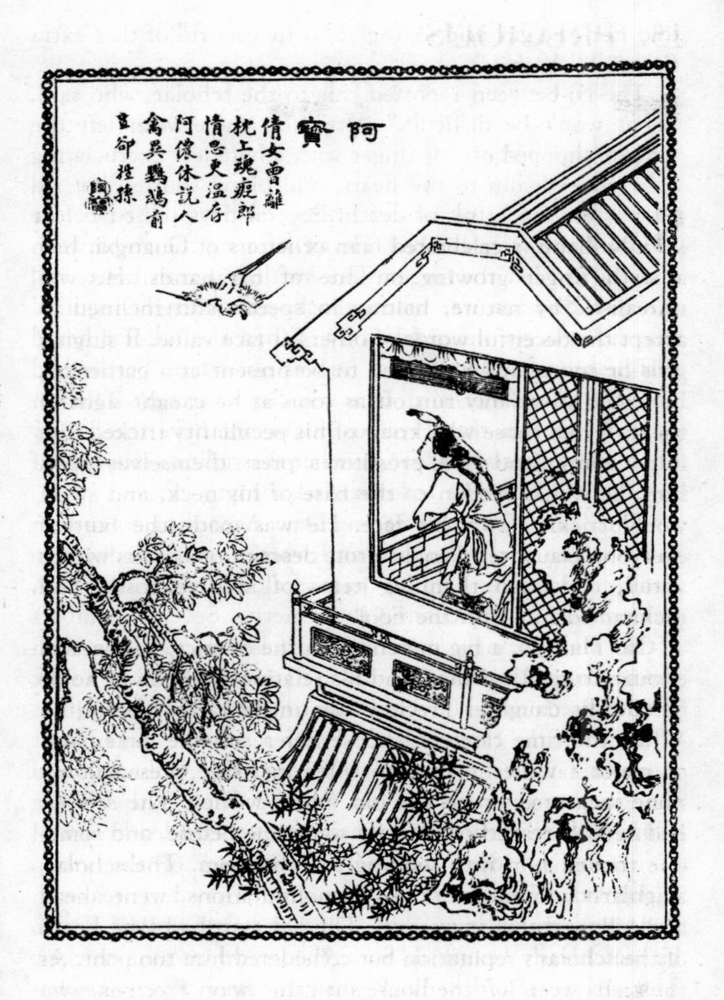

阿寶
倩女曾離
枕上魂癡郎
情思更温存
阿儂休説人
禽異鸚鵡前
身卻姓孫

told her, the girl said jokingly: "If he gets rid of that extra finger, I'll be his."

The go-between reported this to the scholar, who said, "That won't be difficult." After the go-between left the scholar chopped off his finger with a hatchet. Excruciating pain pierced him to the heart, and blood spurted out till he was on the brink of death. Several days passed before he could rise from his bed. He went to see the go-between and showed her the finger. The startled woman ran to tell the girl. She too was taken aback. She jokingly required that he also get rid of his folly. When the scholar heard this he protested loudly that he was not a fool, but he had no way to see her and bare his heart to her. Then it occurred to him that Precious might not have the beauty of an angel after all. What gave her the right to rate herself so highly? His earlier ardor cooled abruptly.

Then came Tomb-Sweeping Day. According to custom this was the day when girls and women went outdoors to stroll, and frivolus young men followed after them in groups, brazenly discussing their merits. Several members of his club strongly urged the scholar to go along with them. One said mockingly: "Don't you want to have a look at your Precious?" The scholar knew they were making fun of him, but the ridicule he had suffered at the girl's hands made him want to see her in person. He gladly followed the group to get a look at her. From a distance they saw a young woman resting beneath a tree, surrounded by a wall of obnoxious young men. The members of the group exclaimed, "That must be Precious." They hurried over, and sure enough it was she. Close scrutiny proved her to be matchlessly beautiful. Soon the crowd became thicker. The girl rose and walked abruptly away. Everyone was bowled over. They set up a wild hubbub of appraisals of her face and comments on her legs. Only the scholar kept silent. When the group went elsewhere, they looked back and saw the scholar, still standing numbly in the same spot. They called to him, but there was no response. They pulled at his arm, saying: "Has your soul left you to follow after Precious?" Still he did not answer. No one thought this strange, because they knew him to be slow of speech. Some pushed and some pulled until they got him back. Once home he climbed straight into bed and lay there all day without rising. He was in stupor, as if drunk, and could not be roused. His family suspected that his soul had left his body. They went to deserted fields and prayed for his soul's return without success. When they slapped him and forced him to respond to their questions, he answered indistinctly: "I am at Precious' house." They asked specific questions, but he would say no more. His family was dismayed and baffled.

Earlier, when watching the girl walk away, the scholar could not bear to see her go, and felt his body walking behind her. He gradually moved toward her and leaned against her sash, without anyone reprimanding him. He followed her home and stayed beside her every moment. At night he made love to her, to the great delight of both. Then he felt a tremendous hollowness in his stomach. He wanted to make the trip back to his home gate, but he did not know the way. The girl herself dreamed repeatedly of copulating with a man. When she asked his name he said "I am Sun Zichu." She was unable to confide her amazement to anyone.

The scholar lay at home for three days, drawing each halting breath as if it might be his last. Deeply frightened, his family sent someone to communicate the matter to the old man in a roundabout way and ask if they could say soul-summoning prayers in his house, at which he laughed and said "Our two families have never visited back and forth: how could he have left his soul in my house?" Sun's family would not give up their pleading, so the old man finally assented. The shaman went to his house, carrying Sun's sleeping mat and a suit of his clothes. The girl was greatly shocked to learn his reason for coming. She led him straight to her chamber, not letting him go anywhere else, and instructed him to leave after summoning Sun's soul. By the time the shaman returned to the Sun family gate, the scholar was moaning on his bed. Upon waking, he unerringly named and described all the toiletries and possessions in the girl's chamber. Hearing of this, the girl was amazed and secretly moved by the depth of his affection.

Upon leaving the bed the scholar spent his waking hours absorbed in thought and lost in forgetfulness. He constantly watched for Precious, in hopes that fortune would favor him with another encounter. He learned that she would offer incense at the Moon-in-the-Water Monastery on Buddha-Bathing Festival,[1] so he went early in the morning and stationed himself beside the road to wait. He watched the crowd until his eyes blurred and ached in their sockets. The sun had passed its zenith before the girl arrived. Glimpsing the scholar from within her carriage, she pulled aside the curtain with slender fingers and redoubled his excitement by fixing her gaze upon him. He fell in line behind her. Unexpectedly, she sent a servant to ask his name and courtesy title. He eagerly identified himself, losing what little composure he still had left. He

[1] The Buddha's birthday (eighth day of the fourth month in the lunar calendar) when images of the Buddha are bathed with fragrant water.

did not return until the carriage left. At home he fell ill again. He lapsed into a fog and stopped eating. He kept calling out Precious' name in his dreams, and cursed his soul for failing to do what it could before.

A parrot which the family had kept for a long time suddenly died. As his young son sat on the bed, holding and stroking it, the scholar thought to himself that if only he were a parrot he could arrive at the girl's room with a few flaps of his wings. As his mind immersed itself in these thoughts, his body turned into a parrot with fluttering suddenness. In an instant he was off and flying straight to Precious' place.

The delighted girl embraced the parrot, chained its leg to a perch and fed it with hempseeds. She was taken aback when it cried, "Don't chain me, sister. I am Sun Zichu!" She untied its bond, but it did not fly away. The girl offered a prayer, saying "Your deep affection is engraved upon my heart, but now we are different in kind--a human being and a bird. How can we ever join in marriage?"

"All I wish for is to be near your fragrance," said the bird. He would not eat when others fed him, but only when the girl fed him herself. When she sat he roosted on her knees; when she lay down he moved next to her bed. This went on for three days. The girl pitied him sorely and secretly sent someone to have a look at the scholar. He had lain stiff and unbreathing for three days, but the area around his heart was not yet cold. Once more the girl prayed to the parrot: "If you can turn back into a man, I vow to remain with you until death."

"You are fooling me," said the bird, but the girl swore she was not. The bird cocked its head thougtfully. Soon the girl removed the slippers from her bound feet and put them under her bed. The parrot leapt down all of a sudden, sized a shoe in its beak, and flew away. The girl anxiously called after it, but it had already flown far. An old servant-woman she sent to probe for news of the scholar found on her arrival that he had already awakened.

Moments before, his family had been thrown into consternation by a parrot which had flown in holding an embroidered shoe in its beak and dropped dead on the floor. Immediately afterwards the scholar awoke and immediately asked for the shoe. No one knew what lay behind his strange request. The servant-woman who had just arrived went in to see the scholar, and asked where the shoe was.

"I am keeping it as a token of Precious promise," said the scholar. "Give her this reply: 'I will not forget your golden vow.' "

When the servant woman reported back, the girl was doubly impressed and so had a maid reveal these events to her mother. After confirming the truth of this, the mother said, "This young man has quite a reputation for literary talent, but he is as poor as Xiangru.[1] If we don't do any better than this after all those years of trying to choose you a husband, I fear that people of good families will langh at us." But because of the shoe, the girl vowed she would have no one else. Her parents gave in and sent a messenger running to notify the scholar, whose malady was instantly cured by joy. When the old man suggested that he be brought into the family as a live-in son-in-law, the girl said, "It is not good for a man to remain long in the home of his in-laws. What is more, he is poor and such a step would eventually cause people to look down on him all the more.

[1] Sima Xiangru (179-117 B.C.), an eminent man of letters of the Western Han period, was extremely poor as a youth.

Now that I have given him my hand, I will gladly live under a thatched roof and eat wild greens without complaint."

The scholar then went to escort her home, and the wedding ceremony was completed. They came together like lovers from a past lifetime. With the help of the girl's dowry his family became moderately prosperous and acquired sizeable new assets. The scholar, however, was book-addled and did not know enough to handle the family enterprises. The girl was skilled in management and did not embroil the scholar in extraneous matters. Within three years the family was wealthy.

Then the scholar fell abruptly ill and succumbed to diabetes. The girl mourned him so grievously that she ceased eating and sleeping. She refused to be consoled, and under cover of night she hung herself. A maid discovered her and rushed to her rescue. She came to her senses, but refused to eat. Three days later when the scholar's relatives gathered for the funeral, they heard moaning and gasping in the coffin. Lifting the lid, they found that he had come back to life.

"I was called before the king of the underworld," he told them. "Because of my lifelong honesty, I was appointed to serve on an official board. Suddenly a man came and informed the king: 'The wife of Board Official Sun is about to arrive.' The king checked the ghost register and said, 'It is not yet her time to die.'

" 'She didn't eat for three days,' the man explained.

"Turning to look at me, the king said, 'In consideration of your wife's sense of honor. I will allow you to live again for the time being.' Then he ordered a driver to hitch up horses and escort me back here."

After this, his health gradually returned to normal.

Then came the annual provincial examinations. As the time for entering the examination cells drew near, some young men played a joke on Sun by making up seven obscure composition topics. They dragged the scholar off to an out-of-the-way spot and said, "We got hold of these through certain family connections. To show our respect, we are giving them to you secretly."

The scholar believed them and turned the questions over in his mind night and day until he succeeded in writing seven practice compositions. The group laughed at him behind his back. At that time the officiating examiner, concerned lest the familiar topics encourage plagiarism, made efforts to go against the convention. When the list of topics was handed out, all seven tallied with the ones Sun had prepared, and so the scholar took top honors. The year after that he was awarded the Doctorate of Letters and given a position in the Imperial Academy. The emperor, hearing of his wondrous story, summoned him and asked if it were true. The scholar informed the throne of everything, winning considerable favor from the emperor. Later he summoned Precious to an audience and bestowed presents of even greater munificence.

The Chronicler of the Tales comments: " 'Foolishness' or fixation in a man's character makes for dedication. Thus one who is fixated on books will surely write proficiently and one who is fixated on a craft will have consummate skill. The down-and-out losers of this world are all people who claim to be free of fixation. Look at those who throw money away on powdered ladies and ruin their families for gambling! Are they not playing the fool's part? From this we can see that the worst foolishness is cleverness and cunning carried to extremes. What was so foolish about Master Sun?"

16. VENTRILOQUISM

A WOMAN in her mid-twenties came to our village, carrying a medicine bag on her arm and offering medical treatment. Someone went to her to have an illness treated. The woman could not make up a prescription herself: she had to wait till nightfall and take counsel with spirits. In the evening she swept her cubbyhole of a room clean and closed herself inside. A hushed crowd gathered around the window and the door, straining to eavesdrop. They exchanged whispers, but no one dared cough. Sound and movement were stilled both inside and out. When night came they suddenly heard the sound of a curtain being drawn. Inside the room the woman said "Is that you, Ninth Mistress?"

"It is me," answered another woman's voice.

"Did Winter-Plum come with you?"

A voice that seemed to belong to a maid answered: "Here I am."

The three women chattered ceaselessly about odds and ends. Before long the crowd heard curtain hooks sliding again. The woman's voice said "Sixth Mistress has come."

Stray voices said, "Has Spring-Plum come with the young master in her arms?"

"You naughty little boy," came a woman's voice. "Bawling and refusing to sleep. You had to come with your mother. It feels like you weigh three thousand catties.

Carrying you is enough to tire a person to death!"

They soon heard the woman's words of greeting, Ninth Mistress' questions about health, Sixth Mistress' formalities, the maids' sympathetic remarks, the happy laughter of the child—all blended into a cacophony of voices.

Then they heard the woman laugh: "The little master certainly is a funloving kid: he came all this way holding a kitty-cat."

Gradually the voices came few and far between. Again there was the sound of the curtain being drawn, and the whole room rang with voices saying: "Why have you come so late, Fourth Mistress?"

A dainty voice answered: "The way here was more than three hundred miles long. Mother-in-law and I have been hurrying along all this time and we've only gotten here now. She's such a slow walker." Then each of them made some perfunctory remarks about the weather by way of salutation. The room rang with mingled sounds of scraping chairs and cries for more chairs. This went on for the duration of a meal. Then the crowd heard the woman ask about her patient's illness. Ninth Mistress said ginseng was indicated; Sixth-Mistress, yellow vetch; and Fourth Mistress, atractylis. This was discussed for a while. Then Ninth Mistress was heard calling for brush and inkstone. Soon came the crinkling of paper, the tinkling of the inkbrush cap being pulled off and thrown on the table, and the grating of an ink-stick being rubbed on a slab. Then there was the click of the inkbrush being dropped on the desk, and the tiny sounds of herbs being measured out and wrapped.

Soon the woman pushed aside the curtain at the entrance of the room and told her patient to come and get the medicine and prescription. She turned back into the

口技
紗窗月
上夜迢
迢嘈雜珠
喉勝管
簫是幻之
真且莫辨
但聞嬌語
亦魂銷

room. The farewells of the three mistresses and the three maids, the burbling of the child, and the mewing of the cat all rang out at once. Ninth Mistress' voice was clear and piercing; Sixth Mistress' halting and flat; and Fourth Mistress' coy and appealing. These, along with the voices of the three maids, each had its own clearly distinguishable intonation. The amazed crowd thought these were truly spirit visitors. But the prescription was tried without much effect. This was what is known as ventriloquism, employed to sell medical art, but amazing nonetheless!

Wang Xinyi[1] once said he was passing through a marketplace in the capital when he heard a song accompanied by a string instrument. Onlookers were packed together as densely as a wall. He moved closer for a look and saw a young man performing an aria in rich voice. He had no instrument. Instead, he pressed a finger against his cheek as he sang, producing a twanging sound just like one made by a string instrument. He too was an adept in the skill of ventriloquism that has been handed down from long ago.

1. A Shandong contemporary (Doctorate of Letters) of the author.

17. LIANCHENG

SCHOLAR Qiao of Jinning[1] was hailed as a genius at an early age, but was still frustrated and unrecognized in his twenties. He was a man of chivalrous qualities. He was close to a scholar named Gu, and when Gu died he gave frequent aid to his wife and children. When the district magistrate, who had prized his talent, died in office, leaving the members of his household stranded far from home, the scholar liquidated his holdings to escort the coffin of the deceased to his hometown, which entailed a round trip of nearly a thousand miles. This gave the scholarly community an even higher opinion of him, but it also furthered the decline of his family's fortunes.

Master of Letters Shi had a daughter with the soubriquet Liancheng who was skilled at embroidery and well-read in books. Her father pampered her with affection. He brought forth a tapestry done by her needle entitled "Weary With Embroidery" and invited young men to write poems about it, intended as a means to select a son-in-law. Scholar Qiao presented a poem which read:

The languid coils of her chignon
Are tumbled waves of darkest shade
By morning's orchid window light
Lily pads of green thread are made

[1] Name of a district in Yunnan province.

But a linking lovebird pattern
Disturbs the calm that time allows
Her needle pausing furtively
She pouts and knits her mothwing brows
With nimble stitch of colored thread,
She turns to life for her designs;
The scene is filled with birds and blooms
And all are formed to nature's lines.
No special skill was used to make
The brocade legends tell us of
T'was the palindromic poem thereon
That won the monarch's love.[1]

The girl was delighted with the poems and praised them to her father, but he objected to the scholar's poverty. The girl spoke highly of the scholar to everyone she met and even sent an old woman with money to help him buy lamp oil for reading, ostensibly upon instructions from her father. The scholar sighed, "Liancheng is the one person who truly knows me!" His heart inclined toward her, and his thoughts were tied to her as those of a starving man are to food.

But soon the girl was betrothed to Wang Huacheng, the son of a salt merchant. The scholar finally lost hope, but his dreaming soul still attached to her. Before long the girl was stricken so badly with consumption that she could not rise. An ascetic from the Western Regions claimed that he could heal her, if only he had a tenth of a tael of flesh from a man's chest to grind up and mix with other medicinal powders. Master Shi sent a man to the Wang

[1] The last two lines of this poem contain allusions, respectively, to a famous palindromic embroidery of the Jin period (265-420), and to an admiring preface written for it by the Tang empress Wu Zetian (624-705).

連
吟將新句獻妝臺博得傾
城笑靨開靨由區、何足
娥
情多情遂肯殉身來

house to notify his son-in-law, who laughed and said, "Foolish old man! He wants me to slice away the flesh that covers my heart."

After the messenger returned, Shi announced: "I will give my daughter's hand in marriage to the man who can part with this bit of flesh." Hearing of this, the scholar went to Shi's house. He drew out a keen blade, sliced his chest and handed the flesh to the monk. Blood soaked his robe and trousers, but finally stopped when the monk applied a compress. The monk compounded three pills. After three days, when she had taken all the pills, the girl's disease was healed in an instant.

Shi let Wang know that he intended to keep his promise. Wang was infuriated and threatened to take his case to the authorities, so Shi invited the scholar to a feast and, spreading one thousand taels of gold out on the table, said, "Please accept this as payment for the great debt of gratitude I owe you." Then he explained his reason for going back on his word.

The scholar replied indignantly: "I did not grudge the flesh from my chest, because I wanted to show appreciation for one who truly knows me. Do you think I want to sell my flesh?" He walked out with a disdainful flourish of his sleeves.

Hearing of this, the girl felt unbearably sorry for him, so she entrusted the old woman to go comfort him and let him know her feelings.

"With his genius he will not be frustrated for long," the girl added. "Why should he worry that there is no beautiful woman for him in this wide world? My ill-omened dreams foretell that I will die within three years. He need not fight for someone who already has one foot in the grave."

The scholar told the old woman: " 'A man of honor

gives his life for the one who knows him'[1], not because of sexual attraction. My real fear is that Liancheng may not recognize my worth. If only she does, our union could fail to work out and I still would not care."

The old woman conveyed the girl's soul-baring vows of faithfulness.

"If she truly feels that way," said the scholar, "She should smile at me next time we meet. Then I could die without regrets!"

The old woman left. Several days later the scholar happened to go out and meet the girl as she returned from her uncle's house. He looked at her intently. Her limpid eyes turned in his direction, and her mouth parted winningly. The scholar exclaimed joyfully: "Liancheng is the one who truly knows me!"

Just when the Wang family came to discuss an auspicious day for the wedding, the girl had a relapse. Within a few months she was dead. The scholar went to mourn her and collapsed in anguish. As Shi was having him carried home, the scholar was well aware of his own death but did not feel upset. He walked out of the village, but still hoped to see Liancheng again. In the distance he saw an antlike line of people walking on a north-south road, so he mingled in among them. Soon he came to an office building, where he encountered Scholar Gu, who asked in surprise: "What brought you here?" He grabbed Scholar Qiao's arm and started to escort him back.

With a heavy sigh Qiao said, "What has been weighing on my mind is far from resolved."

"Quite a lot of responsibility has been delegated to me since I began handling documents here," said Gu, "I will

[1] From the *Records of the Grand Historian*.

not hesitate to do anything within my power for you."

When Qiao asked about Liancheng, Scholar Gu led him around from place to place until they saw Liancheng and a white-robed young woman sitting in the corner of a veranda, their eyes forlorn and wet with tears. Seeing Scholar Qiao arrive, Liancheng leapt up with apparent pleasure and inquired into the manner of his coming.

"Now that you have died, how can I go on living?" answered the scholar.

The tears rolled down as she said, "I behaved like such an ingrate and still you did not spurn me. Why should you sacrifice your life for me? It is impossible to give myself to you in this life: I want nothing more than to promise my next life to you."

The scholar told Gu: "You can go on about your business. I am glad for death and have no wish to live. But I would like to bother you to look up the locality of Liancheng's next incarnation, so I can go there with her." Gu left after promising to do so. The white-robed woman asked who the scholar was, so Liancheng told her the whole story. The sadness of it seemed to overwhelm her as she listened.

"She and I share the same family name," Liancheng told the scholar. "Her youth-name is Binniang. She is the daughter of the prefect Shi of Changsha. We became close as we walked together on the road here."

The scholar took a good look and found her to have a charming manner. He was about to ask more about her when Gu returned and congratulated the scholar, saying: "I already have everything worked out for you. I'm going to have the young lady follow your soul back to the world of the living. How would you like that?"

The two were overjoyed. They were about to take their

leave when Binniang broke into loud sobs and said, "When you go, sister, where am I to turn to? If you are generous enough to come to my rescue, I will wait on you hand and foot." Liancheng was distressed and at a loss, so she turned to ask for the scholar's advice. The scholar begged Gu to give them further help, but Gu considered this too difficult and protested strongly that it could not be done. At last, worn down by the scholar's pleading, he said, "I'll give it my best, for what that's worth." He went out for the time it takes to eat a meal and returned, waving his hands and saying: "I told you so! I simply cannot do anything for you."

Hearing this made Binniang break into plaintive, drawn-out sobs. She held fast to Liancheng's arm, fearful of being left behind that very moment. They could do nothing but look at one another in silent despair. To see her wretched, forlorn countenance was enough to make a person's heart ache. "Take Binniang away with you," Scholar Gu said hotly. "Should any blame be incurred, I will accept it, even if it costs me my life!" Binniang happily followed Scholar Qiao out. The scholar worried about her going on such a long journey home without any companion. Binniang said, "I'll go with you. I don't want to go back to Hunan."

"You are carrying your foolishness too far," said the scholar. "If you don't go back, how can you be reincarnated? I'll be going to Hunan someday, and will be pleased if you don't run away from me then." At that moment two old women walked by, carrying travelling papers for Changsha. The scholar commended Binniang to their care. They parted tearfully and left. Liancheng was hampered by lameness on the trip and had to take a rest after walking a little more than a third of a mile. They made more than ten stops before they saw the gate to their residential quarter.

Liancheng said, "I'm afraid complications may crop up after we come back to life. Please ask for my remains and bring them here. If I come to life in your house, nothing will happen that we might regret later." This made sense to the scholar. Both of them headed toward his house. The girl shrank back timidly with fear and seemed unable to go forward, so the scholar stood waiting for her. "I've come a long way, and my arms and legs are shaking," said the girl. "They won't do what I tell them to. I'm afraid our intentions may not be realized. We should talk it over further. Otherwise, after we have regained our lives, how can we carry out our wishes?" She tugged him into a side chamber. There were a few moments of quiet and then Liancheng said laughingly: "Do you hate me?" The bewildered scholar asked the reason for this question. Blushingly, she replied: "I'm afraid our plans won't work out and I'll end up betraying you again. First let me repay your love with my ghostly body." The scholar was overjoyed. They abandoned themselves to tender ecstasy. Since they were afraid to come to life right away, they dallied in the chamber for three days.

Then Liancheng said, "As the saying goes—'Even an ugly bride must eventually meet her in-laws.' Staying here on pins and needles is not a long-term plan." With this she urged the scholar to go in. The moment he reached the bier he revived suddenly. The stunned members of his family poured warm water down his throat. The scholar then sent for Shi. He asked to have Liancheng's remains, claiming that he could bring them to life. Shi was glad to do as he asked. As soon as the girl's body was carried into the room, she was seen to waken.

"I've already given myself to Master Qiao," the girl told her father. "There is no reason for me to go home again. If anything happens to thwart me in this, my only alternative will be to die again!" Shi returned home and sent a maid to wait upon her.

When Wang heard of this, he drew up a statement presenting his position and bribed the magistrate, who then determined that Wang was the rightful husband. The scholar was close to expiring from indignation, but there was no help for it. When she arrived at the Wang house, Liancheng's resentment was such that she would not eat or drink, but only begged that they allow her to die quickly. When she was left alone in her room, she tried to hang herself from a rafter with her sash. In a few days she had wasted away to the point of imminent death. Wang was frightened and sent her back to her father, who then had her carried back to the scholar's house. Wang knew of this, but there was nothing he could do, so he let the matter rest.

After her recovery Liancheng often thought of Binniang and, owing to the difficulty of making such a long trip, she hesitated to send a messenger to inquire after her. One day a servant ran in to say: "There is a horse and carriage at the gate." Husband and wife went out to look and found that Binniang was already there in their courtyard. It was a tearful, happy reunion. The scholar invited the prefect, who had escorted his daughter there personally, to come in.

"My daughter owes her renewed life to you, sir," said the prefect. "She swears that she will marry no one else, so I have decided to go along with her wishes." The scholar touched his head to the floor in gratitude as etiquette demanded. Shi, the Master of Letters, came too, and the two gentlemen confirmed their clan ties.

By the way, Scholar Qiao's name was Nian and his soubriquet, Danian.

The Chronicler of the Tales comments: "Some may call it foolish for a man to commit himself to a woman when no more recognition than a smile has passed between them. But could the five hundred followers of Tian Heng[1] have all been fools? From them we learn how highly men value those who recognize their worth,[2] and what makes able, outstanding men rally around a leader without thinking of themselves. And yet, it would surely be tragic if a young man in all the splendor of his gifts could find nothing more in this vast world on which to pin his hopes for recognition than the smiles of a young beauty!"

1. An opponent of the first emperor of the Han dynasty, he committed suicide rather than submit. Five hundred of his followers did likewise out of loyalty.

2. Based on a passage from the *Dao-de-jing*:
Few are who appreciate me;
Honor to those who follow in my footsteps.

18. THE RÁKṢASAS AND THE OCEAN BAZAAR

MA Jun, also known as Dragon Messenger, was a merchant's son. He had striking good looks and in his untrammeled youth gave himself up to the pleasures of singing and dancing. He frequented the Pear Garden, where he amused himself in the company of the actors. Wrapping his head in a brocade turban he had all the charm of an attractive woman, and hence was given the nickname "Stunner." He also made a name for himself by being admitted to the prefectural academy at fourteen.

When age and declining health made the young scholar's father give up business and go into retirement, he said these words to his son: "Those books you have read cannot feed you when you are hungry and cannot keep you warm when you are cold. You should take over my business, son." From then on Ma devoted part of his attention to matters of investment and profit.

Ma embarked on an ocean voyage with a party of other passengers, but it happened that they were blown off course by a typhoon. After several days the ship came to a city in which all the inhabitants were freakishly ugly. They ran off in an uproar as Ma approached, taking him for a monster. When Ma first saw this he was greatly frightened, but once he realized they were afraid of him, he used their fear to gain the upper hand. Finding a group of them sitting at table, he rushed toward them and, after they dashed away in fright, gulped down the food they left. After a time he went into a mountain village, where some of the inhabitants looked almost human, though they wore the tattered rags of beggars. Ma sat down to rest beneath a tree. The villagers watched him from a distance, not daring to approach. After a while, when they realized that Ma was not a man-eating monster, they finally edged toward him. Ma smiled and talked with them. Although their speech was strange, it was halfway comprehensible. Without being asked, Ma told where he had come from. The delighted villagers told everyone in the neighborhood that the stranger was not violent. Still the freakishly ugly ones stole furtive looks at him and ran off, never daring to come near. Those who did come close had mouths and noses in just about the same places as we do here in China. Together they hunted up wine and served it to Ma.

Ma asked why they had been afraid of him. "I once heard my grandfather say," one of them replied, "that 8,500 miles to the west lies a land called the Middle Kingdom, and the people there are all grotesque in appearance. I knew it only by hearsay, but now I believe it."

Ma asked why they were so poor. Someone answered, "In our country what is valued is appearance rather than literary ability. The most handsome among us become high ministers at court; the fairly handsome are given posts in local administrative offices; and the somewhat handsome can support their wives and children in style by winning the favor of some nobleman. As for people like us, we are thought to be bearers of evil fortune, and our parents often abandon us at birth. All the people who cannot bear to abandon their offspring straightaway are thinking about

羅刹海市
妍媸倒置亦奇聞
海市遙開萬里
雲畢竟文章
幹富貴水晶
宮裏琴龍天

the continuity of their family line.

"What is the name of this kingdom?" asked Ma.

"The Great Kingdom of the Rákṣasas," was the answer. "The capital is ten miles north of here." Ma asked them to lead him there for a look. And so they arose at cock's crow the next day and took him there. They reached the capital after daybreak. The walls of the city were built of stone as black as ink, and the storied buildings were nearly a hundred feet high. There were few rooftiles to be seen. Instead, the buildings were covered with shingles of red stone. Ma picked up a loose piece and rubbed it against his armor; it was exactly like cinnabar.

Just then came the time for dismissal of the morning court session at the palace. The villagers pointed to one of the dignitaries who were coming out of the palace gate: "That is the prime minister." Ma saw that his ears were attached to the back of his head, his nose had three nostrils and his eyelashes covered his eyes like curtains. Then several men came out on horseback. "Those are privy counselors," said the villagers. As the officials came out in succession, the villagers pointed out their ranks. All of them had grotesque, monstrous faces, but as the lower ranks came out the degree of ugliness gradually abated. Before long Ma started back toward the village. People in the streets who saw him screamed and fell over one another trying to run away, as if they had met with a monster. Only when the villagers had gone to great lengths to reassure them did the city dwellers dare to stand and watch from a distance.

After they returned to the village, everyone in the kingdom, regardless of rank, knew there was an unusual person there. Members of the gentry and court officials, eager to broaden their horizons, told the villagers to invite

Ma to visit them, but whenever he showed up at someone's house, the gatekeeper would close the door, and the men and women alike would only venture to peer at him and speak with him through cracks in the door. This would go on all day without anyone asking him in for a visit.

One villager said, "There is an officer of the guard living in this district who was sent abroad as emissary by our former king. He has had experience with many sorts of people, so he may not be frightened of you."

They went to the officer's house and, as the villager had foreseen, he was delighted at their visit and received Ma as an honored guest. Apparently between eighty and ninety years of age, he had goggle eyes and hair that stood out like a hedgehog's.

"In my youth I went on more diplomatic missions for the king than anyone else, but the Middle Kingdom of China is the one place I have never been. Now I am over a hundred and twenty years old, and at last I have the chance to see someone from your esteemed country. The king simply must be informed of this. Though I have been leading a life of retirement and have not set foot upon the palace steps these past ten years or more, I will make the trip for your sake in the morning."

Observing all the formalities of a host to his guest, he then had wine and victuals set out. After they had drunk several rounds, he brought out ten or so female entertainers with faces like *yaksa* monsters, who took turns singing and dancing. All of them wore white brocade turbans on their heads and flowing red robes that dragged on the ground. Ma could not make out the lyrics, but he found the tune and rhythm oddly fascinating. The host watched them with immense enjoyment.

"Do you have entertainment like this in the Middle

Kingdom?" he asked.

"Oh yes," answered Ma.

The host asked him to imitate the music for them, so Ma drummed on the table and performed a song.

"Well if that isn't most extraordinary!" exclaimed the delighted host. "The melody makes me think of phoenixes calling and dragons roaring. It is unlike anything I have ever heard." The next day he went to court and recommended Ma to the king. The king gladly commanded that Ma be brought before him, but when a few high counselors claimed that Ma's monstrous appearance might result in a shock injurious to His Majesty's health, the order was rescinded. The old officer of the guard came out and gave Ma the news of this crushing disappointment.

Ma stayed with the officer for a long while. One day, when he and his host were in their cups, he smeared his face with soot to look like Zhang Fei[1] and began to dance with sword in hand. The host thought he was attractive and said, "Why don't you make yourself up as Zhang Fei and go to see the prime minister. I am sure he will be delighted to find a place for you. An ample salary is within your grasp."

"Hah! It is one thing to play games, but why should I put on a new face to chase after honor and fame?" But when the host insisted, Ma gave in. The host invited the ranking officials to a feast and told Ma to wait on them with his face painted. Before long the guests arrived, and Ma was called out to meet them.

"Isn't that strange!" said the guests in surprise. "How could someone who was once so ugly turn into such a good

[1] A famous general of The Three Kingdoms period (220-265). In popular lore he is always protrayed with a very dark face.

looking fellow? Whereupon they all drank together with exceeding joy. Ma swayed with the rhythm as he sang the Yiyang Melody,[1] and every person at the table was positively bowled over. The next day a number of petitions recommending Ma were sent to the throne. The king was so delighted he summoned Ma with a big fanfare. During their first audience the king asked how law and order were maintained in the Middle Kingdom. Ma gave a detailed explanation which met with sighs of admiring approval. The king granted him the favor of dining with him in the royal hostel. When both were mellow with wine, the king said, "I have heard that you are skilled in fine music. Might I be so fortunate as to hear you perform?" So Ma got up to dance. He sang softly and languidly, in the style of the white-turbaned entertainers. The king was overjoyed. On that every day he gave Ma the title of deputy minister. He often dined privately with Ma and showered him with exceptional generosity and favor. After a time the other officials and administrators were fairly certain of the falseness of Ma's countenance. Wherever he went, he would see people whispering to one another instead of greeting him cordially. Being thus ostracized made Ma ill at ease, so he submitted a request for retirement, but this was not granted. Again he requested official leave, and was given a vacation of three months.

Ma lost no time loading his gold and jewels onto a stage coach and returning to the mountain village. The villagers came out to greet him on their knees. Joyful cries rang through the air when Ma divided gold coins among his old friends.

[1] A loud, sonorous style of singing that originated in the county of the same name (Jiangxi province) during the Yuan and Ming dynasties.

The villagers said, "Since we lowly folk have been honored by your gifts, we will set out for the ocean bazaar tomorrow and seek precious gems to repay you."

"Where is the ocean bazaar?" asked Ma.

"Mermen from the four seas gather at the ocean bazaar to trade in pearls and jewels. People from four directions and twelve kingdoms all come to trade with them. Many deities are engaged in pleasurable pastimes there. The sky is filled with clouds, and great waves roll ashore from time to time. People of rank are too concerned for their personal stafety to expose themselves to these dangers, so they entrust us with their gold and silk in order to purchase rare treasures for them. Now the date of the bazaar is not distant.

Ma asked how they knew it.

"When red birds are seen flying back and forth over the sea, the opening of the bazaar is seven days away."

Ma asked their time of departure and expressed a desire to make the trip with them and do some sightseeing. The villagers begged him to consider his personal safety.

"But I am a seafarer. Do you suppose I fear rough weather? Before long there were people at the gate bringing valuables to invest in the voyage. Ma helped the crew stow the valuables on board the ship. It was a flat-bottomed craft with high gunwales and room for several dozen men. With ten men at the oars it churned up a seething wake and skimmed along like an arrow. After three days they glimpsed buildings and towers one behind the other through the shifting clouds that hung over the water. Trading ships converged on the place like ants. In no time they drew up beneath the city wall, which was made of bricks as long as a man's body. The battlements towered into the clouds above. Having moored their ship and entered the city, they saw displayed in the bazaar strange treasures and rare gems of dazzling brilliance, many never seen in the world of men.

Just then a young man mounted on a splendid stallion rode up to them. The shopkeepers and buyers scattered before him, saying that he was the "third crown prince of the Eastern Ocean." As the crown prince rode by he eyed the scholar and said, "Isn't this man from a faraway country?" A runner came over to Ma and wanted to know his native land. Ma greeted him from the side of the road and made known the land and people of his birth.

"Since you've honored us by coming here, it is plain that there is a deep bond of fate between us!" exclaimed the prince happily. He gave the scholar a mount and invited him to ride alongside. Riding beyond the western wall, they came to the shore of the island, where their mounts neighed and plunged into the water. The scholar was struck dumb with terror, but he soon saw that they were in an open space, with walls of seawater arching above them. Suddenly a palace appeared ahead, its beams made of tortoise shell and its roof tiled with scales of bream. The crystalline walls mirrored the shapes around them with blinding brilliance. Dismounting, the prince motioned Ma inside. At the head of the hall before them was the Dragon Lord. The crown prince informed the throne: "While riding through the bazaar I found this worthy scholar from the Middle Kingdom whom I have brought for an audience with Your Highness." The scholar stepped forward and made an elaborate bow.

"I see sir, that you are a man of literary accomplishment," said the Dragon Lord. "I am sure you are good enough to lord it over famous poets of antiquity like Qu Yuan and Song Yu. Might I trouble you to brandish your rafter-sized inkbrush to write a rhapsody on the ocean bazaar? Please do not grudge us your precious words."

The scholar touched his forehead to the floor in acknowledgement. He was given a crystal inkstone, a dragon-bristle inkbrush, paper with the bright smoothness of snow and an inkstick exuding the fragrance of orchids. Without stopping to think, he completed a piece of over a thousand words and offered it to the throne. The dragon lord beat time while reciting the rhymed prose.

"Sir, your great talent has brought much glory to my acquatic kingdom!" he said.

So it was that the hosts of dragondom were assembled for a feast in Glowing-Cloud Palace. After several rounds of wine and several courses of roast meat, the dragon lord raised his cup and said to his guest: "I have not yet found a good match for my beloved daughter. Sir, I would like to inflict her upon you. Would this be in accordance with your wishes?"

The scholar rose to his knees from the mat, so overcome with gratitude that he could only stammer, "Yes, yes." The Dragon Lord turned and spoke to his attendants. Before long a group of court maids led forth a young woman, Jade rings tinkling at her waist as she moved. A sudden fanfare rang out. When he had finished bowing the scholar gave her an appraising glance: She was a veritable fairy maiden. She bowed and withdrew.

Soon the drinking ceased. Maids with hair done up in double buns bearing painted candles led the scholar into a side palace. The girl sat there waiting in her finest adornments. The coral bed was studded with a galaxy of gems, and shining pearls the size of spoons were knotted into the tassels that hung outside the canopy. The quilts were fragrant and yielding.

At the crack of dawn, budding young girls and bewitching maids ran in and stood in a row around the bed. The scholar rose, hurried to court and thanked the king. He was given the title of royal son-in-law. Because his rhapsody was rapidly disseminated throughout the four seas, the dragon lords from all quarters sent special envoys to congratulate him and deliver invitations to banquets. The scholar dressed in brocades and rode about on a green, horned dragon. He set forth from the palace with warning shouts to clear his way. An entourage of several dozen mounted knights bearing carved bows and white staffs clustered about him, their armor flashing. There were mounted musicians strumming zithers and others in a carriage playing jade flutes. Within three days the scholar had journeyed to all the oceans. From then on the name Dragon Messenger resounded throughout the four seas.

A jade tree as big in girth as a man's embrace grew in the palace. The trunk was shimmeringly transparent, like clear glass, with a pale yellow center slightly thinner than an arm. The leaves resembled green jade and were a bit thicker than copper coins. This profuse foliage cast dense shade, in which the scholar and his bride often sang and chanted poetry. The whole tree was blooming with flowers that looked like gardenias. Each time a petal fell a distinct tinkle could be heard. Upon closer inspection each gleaming, delicate petal seemed to be sculpted of red agate.

Rare birds with feathers of iridescent blue and tails longer than their bodies often alighted on the tree and sang strains every bit as heart-rending as notes from a plaintive jade flute. Everytime the scholar heard them, he thought of his homeland. One day he spoke of this to his wife: "Three years have passed since I lost touch with my family. Everytime I think of separation from my parents, snivel drips onto my chest and sweat drenches my back. Would you go back with me?"

"Faerie and earth have separate roads," she said. "They cannot remain together. I cannot bear, for the sake of our marital love, to deny you the happiness of being at your parents' side. Give me time to think of a way." The scholar could not help but cry to hear her. His wife, too, heaved a sigh and said, "You cannot have it both ways!"

The next day when the scholar came back to the palace the dragon lord said to him: "I am told that you are homesick. How will it be if we have your baggage ready the first thing tomorrow morning?"

The scholar thanked him: "I was a solitary wanderer far from home until you made me your subject and lavished your favor and concern upon me. From the depths of my heart I feel a sincere wish to repay you. Let me go home to visit for a time: I will try to meet with you again."

When evening came, the girl had set out wine for a farewell. The scholar wanted to set a time to meet again, but she said, "The affinity that bound us together has run out." The scholar was deeply grieved.

"Go back and care for your parents," she said. "Show them what a filial son you are. The hundred years of a human life, with its meetings and partings, is like a single day. What is the good of whining like a child? From this day on I shall remain chaste for your sake, and you will be true to me in your thoughts. Though we will be in different places, our hearts will be as one, so we will still be husband and wife. We can grow old together without having to remain side by side day and night. If either of us transgresses this vow, heaven will not bless our marriage. If you worry that there is no one to do the housekeeping, you can take a maid. I have one more thing to tell you. After serving you all this time, I have noticed signs of a joyous event to come. Would you please give this child a name?"

"If the baby is a girl, name her Dragon-Palace; if it is a boy, name him Blessing-Sea," said the scholar.

His wife begged for a token of their vow. The scholar brought out a pair of red jade lotuses he had gotten in the Kingdom of Rákṣasas and gave them to her.

"Three years from now on the eighth day of the fourth month make sure to sail around South Island," she said. "I will return your flesh and blood to you." She filled a fish-skin pouch with pearls and gems, gave it to him and said, "Keep this well. Your family can live off it for generations."

At the first faint light of dawn the king had a farewell party set up for the departure, and there bounteous gifts were heaped before the scholar. With a parting bow the scholar left the palace. The girl, riding in a cart drawn by white rams, saw him to the shore. He rode onto the beach and dismounted. She bid him farewell, then turned the cart around and left. In a few short moments, she was far away. The waters of the sea closed back together, hiding her from view.

Then the scholar started homeward. His voyage had lasted so long that everyone assumed him dead, but now, to his family's amazement, he turned up at home. Fortunately his parents were in good health, but his wife had married again. The meaning of the dragon girl's words "be true to me" finally became clear to him. She must have known of this already. The father wanted to arrange another marriage, but the scholar would not allow it and took a maid instead.

With the appointed time engraved in his mind, the scholar sailed to the island three years later. There he saw two children sitting afloat on the surface of the water. They were amusing themselves by splashing with their hands, yet this neither caused them to move nor to sink. He drew up to them and held out his hands. One child grabbed his wrist and jumped giggling into his arms. The other wailed as if vexed at the scholar for not lending a helping hand. This one too was lifted aboard. A closer look showed that one was a girl and the other a boy. Both had fair, appealing features. On their heads were coronets studded with jade; in the middle of each was one of the red lotuses. One of them bore a brocade pouch. The scholar opened it and found a letter which read:

"I trust that father and mother are in good health. Three years have gone by in a flash: the world of red dust is forever out of reach. The messenger is hard put to cross this great expanse water. Longing has taken shape as dreams: my neck is weary with gazing into the boundless blue. What good are my regrets? My thoughts now turn to Chang'e, who ran away to the moon only to spend a lone life of loneness in Cassia Mansion, and Weaving Maid, who once threw down her shuttle but to this day ruefully watches her lover from across the Milky Way. Who am I, that I should have everlasting love? Once this thought arises, tears give way to laughter. Two months after we parted, I was blessed, to my amazement, with twins. Now they are babbling in arms, and understand something of speech and laughter. They grab whatever fruits they see and can live without their mother's milk. Now I worshipfully return them to you. I have decorated their coronets with the red jade lotus flowers you gave me, as a token of the fulfillment of my vow. When you lift the children to your knees and embrace them, it will be like having me at your side. I felt comforted to hear that you are conscientiously observing your vow of yesteryear. I will be faithful to you all my life: unto death there will be no change. I no longer keep perfumed unguents within my trousseau, and the reflection in my mirror has long ago said farewell to powder and mascara. You are like a wayfarer, and I am the wayfarer's wife. But yet, though the lute and harp are left long unplayed, no one can say they do not harmonize. Now, I trust, my in-laws can be with their grandchildren, though they have never met their daughter-in-law. Thinking of my duty to them, I cannot help feeling much regret. When the time comes for mother's interment, I will perform my duty by going to mourn at her tomb. Here's hoping that Dragon-Palace will henceforth remain in good health, and that I will not miss the chance to hold her in my arms. May Blessing-Sea live long and travel back and forth between us. Not having finished all that I wished to say, I entreat you to take good care of yourself." The scholar pored repeatedly over the letter, wiping tears from his eyes. His two children threw their arms around his neck, saying: "Oh please, let's go back!"

This only added to the scholar's misery. He caressed them and asked, "Do you children know how to find your home?" Their only answer was to burst into sobs and wail that they wanted to go home.

The scholar looked out over the boundless sea; as far as the eye could see stretched a ravelling mist devoid of human presence, a road leading nowhere through the foggy waves. He held his children close as he made for the ship, and returned in discouragement.

The scholar, knowing that his mother's days were numbered, made ready her burial accoutrements beforehand and planted over a hundred pine and catalpa trees in the enclosure around her tomb. Sure enough, after a year passed, the old woman died. When the hearse reached the final resting place, a woman in hempen mourning clothes stood before the tomb. Suddenly, as the mourners stared in surprise, a fierce wind began to blow and thunder rumbled. This was followed by heavy rain. In the blink of an eye she was gone. Many of the pines and catalpas had died from being transplanted, but after this they all came to life.

As Blessing-Sea grew a little older he thought often of his mother. One day he was seen to throw himself into the sea, and he did not return till several days later. Dragon-Palace, being a girl, could not go, and so she cried in her room day after day. One day the light of the sun dimmed; in an instant the dragon lord's daughter appeared and calmed her: "Someday you will have a family of your own. What good will crying do?" She gave her daughter a dowry consisting of an eight-foot tree of coral, a packet of borneol camphor, one hundred gleaming pearls and a pair of small gold boxes set with eight sorts of gems. Hearing her voice, the scholar burst into the room and took her by the hand, sobbing. In a moment a sharp clap of thunder shook the room, and she was gone.

The Chronicler of the Tales comments: "The ways of the world are no different from the ways of goblins: both would have us paint our faces to curry favor. When it comes to proclivities for eating scabs and such, the whole world is in the same rut. Moderately embarrassing actions receive moderate praise; greatly embarrassing actions receive great praise.[1] If a person were to amble through a city with his true face exposed for all to see, few must be the

[1] From a letter by the famous Tang dyansty poet and prose stylist Han Yu (768-824), in which he confesses his shame at having written some perfunctory pieces because of social obligations.

ones who would not take to their heels in fright. Whose shoulder can the Fool of Lingyang[1] cry on with his fabled jade worth fifteen cities? Alas! Glory and wealth can only be found in castles in the air and ocean bazaars."

1. An allusion to Bian He of the state of Chu during the Spring and Antumn period (722-484 B.C.), who presented two kings successively with a jade enclosed in an uncut stone, and each time was accused of trying to pass off sham jade as genuine and punished by the loss of one of his feet. When the third king came to the throne, he summoned Bian He, had the stone carved up and found the jade inside. The jade was later claimed by a king to be worth the price of fifteen cities.

19. THE CRICKET

DURING the Xuande reign period (1426-1435) of the Ming dynasty cricket keeping was a popular amusement in the palace. The insects were levied annually from the populace. Live crickets were not originally a Shaanxi product until a magistrate in Huayin county who was anxious to win favor with his superiors presented one, which was tried in the ring and found to be an outstanding fighter. From then on Huayin County was charged with providing crickets to the court regularly. The magistrate delegated the responsibility to the headman in each ward. Young idlers in the marketplace kept the best of them in cages, forcing prices up by cornering the market. Cunning ward administrators used this as an excuse to impose a head tax on the peasants. For every cricket that was requisitioned, several families were driven into bankruptcy.

In the district there was a man named Cheng Ming, a long unsuccessful candidate for the Bachelor of Letters dagree. The crafty ward administrator, seeing that Cheng was impractical and slow of speech, recommended him for the position of headman. Cheng made numerous futile attempts to free himself from the obligations of this office. Before a year had passed his meager resources were used up. Then came the cricket levy. Cheng did not dare collect money from the households, nor could he fulfil the duty out of his own funds. He was so despondent he wanted to

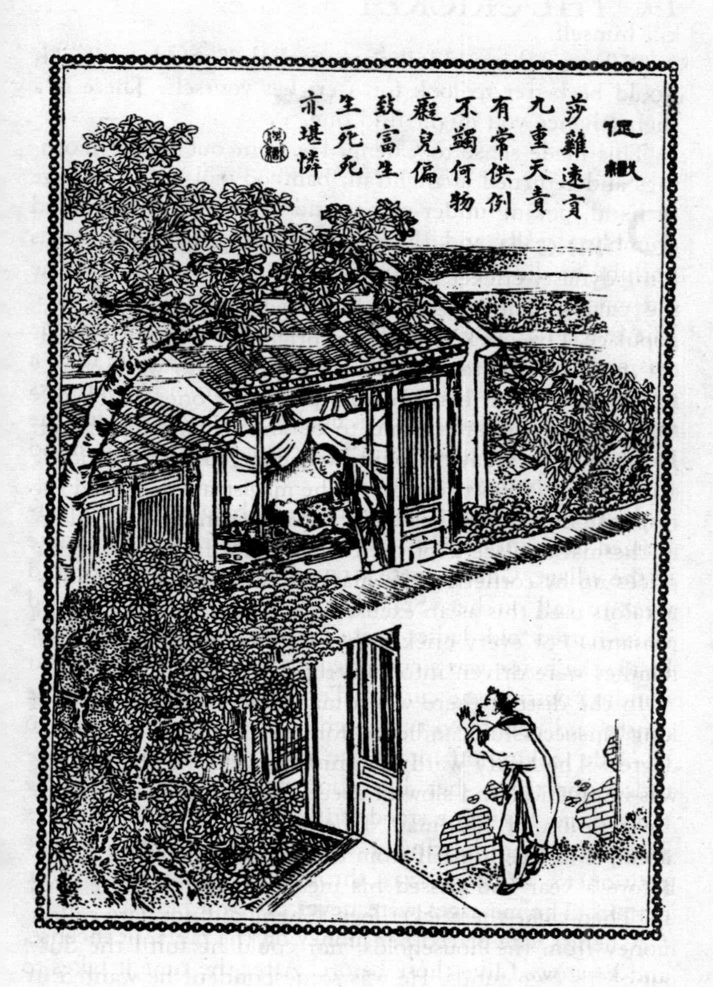

促織
莎雞遠貢
九重天責
有常供例
不蠲何物
癡兒偏
致富生
生死死
亦堪憐
促織

kill himself.

"What good would killing yourself do?" said his wife. "It would be better to look for a cricket yourself. There is a slight chance you might find one."

This made sense to Cheng. He went out in the mornings and returned at nightfall, bamboo pail and wire cage in hand, poking under stones and opening burrows amid crumbling walls and thick growths of grass. There was nothing he did not try, but it was no use. The few that he did manage to catch were too puny to fit the regulations. The magistrate's deadline was rigorously enforced, and he was given a total of a hundred strokes with a cane over a period of ten days. Blood and puss oozed from his buttocks and, what was worse, he was unable to go looking for the insects at all. He tossed and turned on his bed, his mind filled with thoughts of suicide.

It was then that a hunchbacked shamaness who performed divinations with the help of a spirit-familiar came to the village. Cheng's wife scraped up a sum of money and went to call on her. Smartly dressed young women and white-haired old ladies were milling around the door. Inside the house was a curtained-off sanctum, with an altar standing outside the curtain. Petitioners lit incense in the censer and kowtowed twice, while the shamaness stood to one side looking off into space and pronouncing an invocation for them, her lips contorted with unintelligible mutterings. Everyone stood stiffly listening until shortly a piece of paper, bearing a message that dealt with the petitioner's troubles, was thrown out from within the curtain. The messages were never off by a hair.

Cheng's wife placed her money on the table, lit incense, and kowtowed like those before. After the time it takes to eat a meal passed by, the curtain moved and a slip of paper was tossed out onto the ground. Picking it up, she saw not words but a drawing depicting a group of buildings, apparently those of a monastery. Behind it at the foot of a hill was a jumble of odd-looking boulders. There, at the edge of a dense bramble thicket, crouched a shiny black cricket. Beside it was a toad that seemed to be on the point of leaping. She spread the drawing out and pored over it, unable to make out its meaning. Still the cricket was just what she had been looking for. She folded the paper up, tucked it away and took it back to show Cheng who, after much reflection, wondered if the picture were not telling him where to hunt for a cricket. Careful scrutiny of the scene in the drawing revealed a close resemblance to the Great Buddha Abbey east of the village.

Cheng dragged himself out of bed, propped himself up with a cane and proceeded, drawing in hand, to the rear of the monastery. The overgrown ruins of an ancient tomb stood before him. Following the edge of the tomb, he saw boulders squatting one on top of the other like fish scales, precisely as in the drawing. He walked slowly through a jungle of weeds, cocking his head to catch the slightest sound and looking for all the world as if he were searching for a needle or a mustard seed. He could no longer maintain the intentness of eyes, ears and mind, but he had not yet seen or heard a cricket. He was still groping about, when suddenly to his great amazement a wart-headed toad leapt from underfoot. He stayed close behind it as it ducked into a dense growth of grass. He stepped gingerly into the grass, spreading the blades apart with his hands to get a better look. There, crouching at the base of a bramble-bush was an insect. He hurriedly grabbed for it, but it ducked into a hole in the stones. He poked at it with a sharp blade of grass, but it would not come out. Finally, by pouring water from his bucket into the hole, he was able to flush the robust-looking cricket out. He gave chase and caught it. A closer look showed it to have a thick torso, a long tail, a blue-green neck and metallic wings. Great was Cheng's joy as he put it in the cage and returned home.

The whole family rejoiced as if he had found a treasure more precious than the legendary piece of jade to the worth of fifteen cities.[1] They put it in a basin and nourished it on crab meat and chestnuts, going to every extreme to give it the best of care. They planned to keep it until the deadline, when Cheng would use it to discharge his official duty.

But one day Cheng's nine-year-old son, seeing that his father was out, furtively lifted the lid off the basin. The cricket hopped straight out, so quickly that the boy could not grab it. He jumped and caught it in his hand, breaking off a leg and cracking its abdomen. In a few short moments it was dead. The terrified boy ran crying to tell his mother. Her face paled to the hue of ashes at what she heard.

"A bad seed, that's what you are!" she cursed him loudly, "Your day of doom will not be long now! When your father comes home he'll settle accounts with you." The boy ran out sniveling. Cheng soon returned. When his wife told him what had happened, it was as if a heap of freezing snow had been dumped on his head. He called angrily for his son but the boy was nowhere to be seen. Soon afterwards, they found his body in a well. Cheng's rage turned to sorrow. Stricken half-dead with grief, he struck his head on the ground and cried out to heaven. Husband and wife went inside and each turned their sobbing faces toward separate corners. No cooking fire was lit in their thatched hut that night. They had come to their wit's end and could

[1] See "The Rákṣasas and the Ocean Bazaar," Note 4.

only stare dumbly at one another. As the day drew to an end, they prepared to wrap their son in a grass mat for burial. Touching him, they found that he was now breathing haltingly. Joyfully they placed him on the bed. In the middle of the night he regained consciousness, which relieved his parents somewhat, but his breath came in gasps and he had the vacant look of a sleepwalker. Looking at the empty cricket cage was enough to rob them of breath and make their voices die in their throats, but they dared not question their son again. Their eyes did not close for the whole night. When the sun in the east began its course through the heavens they lay down stiffly, brooding sleeplessly.

Suddenly there was a chirping outside their door. They got up in amazement to observe: there was the cricket looking as sound as ever. Jumping for joy, they ran to catch it, but it gave a chirp and hopped rapidly away. Cheng covered it with a cupped hand, but he seemed to have grasped nothing but thin air. As soon as he lifted his hand the cricket leapt swiftly out from under it. He followed it closely, but lost it when it rounded the corner of a wall. As he walked about distractedly, looking all around him, he saw a cricket crouching on the wall. A careful look showed that it was short, small and reddish-black in color—certainly not the one he had been chasing. It was worthless to him because of its small size. He went on walking aimlessly and staring in all directions for the one he had been chasing. All of a sudden the little cricket jumped off the wall and landed on the side of his robe. It was built like a mole cricket, with finely veined wings, a square head and long neck. It impressed him as a good specimen, so he was glad to keep it. His plan was to present it at the yamen, but the thought that it might not meet the magistrate's expectations made him shudder, so he decided to observe how it would perform in a fight.

A young man known as a busybody in the village was keeping a cricket which he had named Crabshell Blue. He matched it daily with the crickets of other young men, and it was always emerged victorious. He was holding onto it until he could turn a nice profit, but nobody would pay the high price he asked. One day this young man went to Cheng's house for a visit. Seeing the cricket Cheng was keeping, he had to stifle a laugh with his hand. He took out his cricket and put it into the cage. Cheng was discomfited at the sight of its huge build. He dared not pick up the gauntlet, but the young man insisted. It occurred to Cheng that keeping an inferior specimen would be useless anyway, and that he might as well set his cricket against the other for a laugh. Both insects were placed in a fighting basin. The small one crouched motionless, looking as foolish as a wooden chicken.[1] The young man guffawed once more as he used a boar bristle to poke at the cricket's antennae. Still it did not move, provoking the young man into another burst of laughter. He prodded it repeatedly. The insect exploded with rage and ran at its opponent. They attacked one another with flying leaps, rousing themselves to battle with defiant chirps. In an instant the small cricket jumped up, its antennae and tail stiffly erect, and bit down on its opponent's neck. The frightened young man pulled them apart and put an end to the fight. The small cricket drew itself up and chirped proudly, as if it were reporting victory to its master.

Cheng was overjoyed. As he and his guests were admir-

[1] A fable in the *Zhuang-zi*, a work of the Warring States period (475-221 B.C.), describes a superb gamecock as having such a placid exterior that it seemed to be made of wood.

ing the winner, a chicken caught sight of it, ran over and delivered a peck at the small cricket. Cheng stood there numb with dread and cried out in alarm. Luckily the chicken's beak had missed its mark; the cricket leaped a foot and some inches away. The chicken lunged forward and bore down upon it. Before Cheng could come to its rescue, the insect was under the chicken's claws; he turned pale and stamped his feet helplessly. But in the next moment he saw the chicken stretching its neck and fluttering about. Much to his amazed delight upon closer inspection, he found the cricket hanging tenaciously onto the fowl's comb. He picked it up, put it in its cage and presented it to the magistrate the next day.

The magistrate berated Cheng angrily for bringing such a puny cricket, nor was he convinced by Cheng's account of the cricket's extraordinary prowess. The cricket was tried in the ring against others of its kind: all were vanquished. When it was tried against a chicken the outcome confirmed Cheng's story. The magistrate thereupon rewarded him and presented the cricket to the provincial governor. The governor, greatly delighted, presented it to the emperor in a golden cage along with a memorial detailing its abilities.

After the champion was taken into the palace, all sorts of unusual crickets, such as "butterflies," "mantises," "oily beaters" and "silky green foreheads" were tried against it, but none could get the better of it. When it heard the music of lutes and zithers it hopped to the beat, which made people marvel at it all the more. The emperor was so pleased that he called for the provincial governor and gave him thoroughbred horses and satins for clothing. The governor did not forget the source of his good fortune: before long word was going around that the magistrate was an "outstanding" official. The delighted magistrate released

Cheng from his duties as headman and instructed the civil examiner to grant him admission to the district academy.

A little more than a year later Cheng's son regained his faculties, claiming that he had been transformed into an agile, combative cricket and that today his soul had finally re-entered his body. The provincial governor rewarded Cheng generously. Within a few years Cheng possessed 1,500 acres of fields; pavilions and storied buildings in such number that thousands of rafters had been used to roof them over; and sheep and horses numbering in the hundreds. The furs he wore and the horses he rode when he went out could not have been equalled by an aristocratic family.

The Chronicler of the Tales comments: "The emperor may use something once on a whim and give it no more thought, but for the people who carry out his wishes it becomes a fixed article of tribute. With the greed of officials and the cruelty of administrators on top of this, there is no end to hardships which make peasants give up their wives and sell their children. Thus every time the emperor takes a step the lives of the people are affected. There is no room for carelessness. Cheng's case was unique: after being reduced to poverty by the depradations of corrupt officials, a cricket brought him wealth enough to go about flaunting furs and fine horses. Back in the days when he was beaten for failing to fulfill his duties as headman, how could he have foreseen that such a fortune was in store for him? Heaven made the provincial governor and magistrate enjoy the benefits of the cricket's favor as a means of rewarding one man's honesty. When the Taoist master in the old story perfected the elixir and rose to heaven, immortality redounded even to his dogs and chickens. There is much truth in this!"

20. SISTERS SWITCH PLACES

MASTER Mao,[1] the prime minister from Ye county, was born of a humble family. His father often tended cows for other people. At one time the Zhangs, a noble family of the district, had a new family gravesite south of East Mountain. Someone passing by the grounds heard a scolding voice from inside the grave say, "Clear out now, all of you. Don't keep defiling a nobleman's house!" Zhang learned of this and did not give it much credence, but then he had recurring dreams of a voice that warned, "Your family cemetery was intended to be Master Mao's graveyard. Why do you keep using it?" After this the Zhang family's fortunes declined. A retainer urged them to move the body to a more auspicious site. Zhang complied with his suggestion and had the body reburied.

One day the father of the future prime minister was tending cows beside the Zhangs' vacant gravesite when he was caught in a sudden rain and took shelter in the empty vault. Soon the rain became a steady downpour. The crashing torrent of a flash flood poured into the vault and drowned the unfortunate man. The prime minister was still a child at the time. His mother called on Zhang and begged for a few feet of ground in which to bury the boy's father. Zhang was greatly amazed to learn that their family

[1] Mao Ji, first on the pass hit of provincial graduates under the reign of the Ming Emperor Xianzong (1465-1487).

name was Mao. He was even more shocked when he went to examine the spot of the drowning and found it was precisely where one of his family coffins had previously been situated. He gave permission for the man to be buried in the old vault and told the woman to bring her son to his house.

After the burial mother and son called on Zhang to thank him. Zhang took an immediate liking to the boy and invited him to stay at his house. The boy was taught to read and treated as one of the family. Later Zhang offered to give the young man his elder daughter's hand in marriage, but the mother was too intimidated to accept.

"Now that we have made the offer, why should we go back on it?" said Zhang's wife.

The betrothal was thus settled. The bride-to-be, however, despised Mao's family. Chagrin and disdain were evident in her every word and expression. When anyone spoke to her of the marriage, she would cover her ears with her hands. She invariably told people: "I would rather die than be the wife of a cowherd's son."

The day came for the groom to receive the bride. The groom went in to the Zhangs' banquet, leaving the bridal carriage at the gate, but the girl hid her face in her sleeves and turned weeping toward a corner. Her relatives pressed her to dress, but she would not. None of their appeals could move her. Soon the groom announced that it was time to go. A loud fanfare was sounded. The girl's face was wet with tears and her hair as disorderly as a tumbleweed. The father kept his son-in-law from leaving and went in to urge his daughter. She went on crying as if his words did not register. In his anger he tried to force her, but she cried until her voice grew hoarse. There was nothing father could do about it. Just then a servant came in and informed

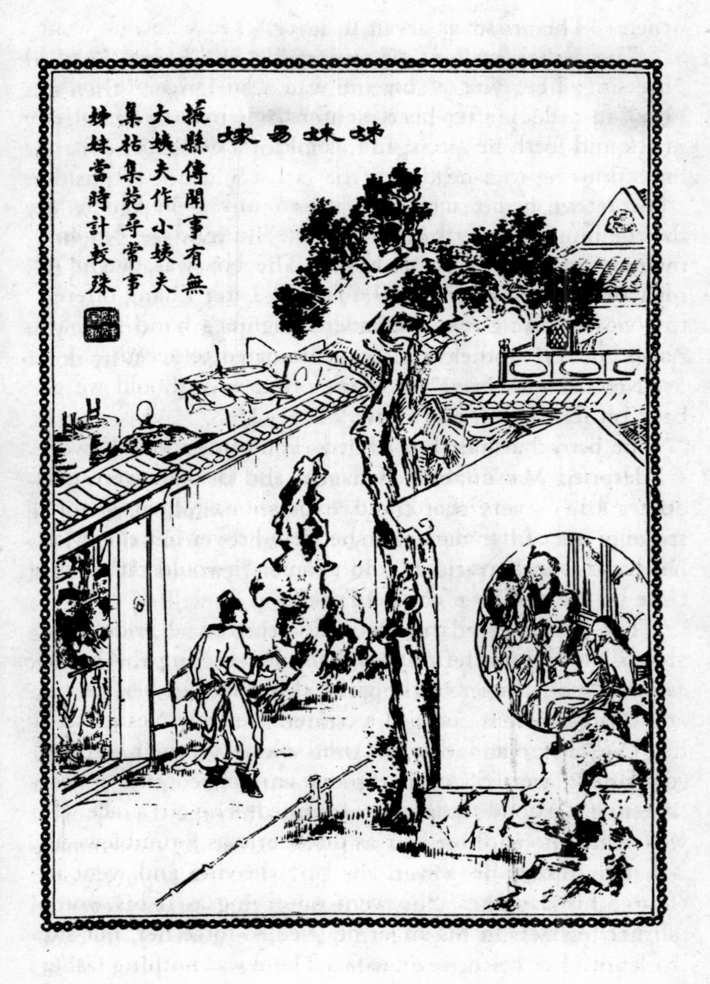

姊妹易嫁
掖縣傳聞事有無
大姨夫作小姨夫
集枯集菀尋常事
姊妹當時計較殊

them: "The groom is about to leave."

The father rushed out and said, "She hasn't finished dressing: I beg you to stay and wait a bit longer," then ran back in to look after his daughter. By scurrying ceaselessly back and forth he managed to stall for a while. The matter was drawing to a head, but the girl would not reconsider. The father had reached his wit's end: he looked wildly about him, wishing he were dead. His younger daughter, who stood beside him, spoke critically to her sister and did her best to pressure and persuade her.

"So now you are mouthing other people's drivel, you little flunky!" the elder sister spat out angrily. "Why don't you go off with him?"

"Father did not give me to Master Mao," said her sister. "If he had, I wouldn't need any urging from you."

Hearing her unabashed words, the father quietly proposed to his wife that the two sisters switch places. The mother turned to her younger daughter and said, "This insolent chambermaid will not obey her parents. We would like you to take her place. Would you be willing?"

The girl accepted readily: "Now that you have told me to go, I would not refuse even if he were a beggar. Anyway, what reason is there to suppose that the young master of the Mao family is doomed to starve to death?"

The father and mother were overjoyed to hear their daughter's words. After they dressed her in her elder sister's finery, she hurriedly climbed into the carriage and left. Once home, husband and wife gracefully consummated their union. However, the girl suffered from chronic *favus* of the scalp, a disfigurement that preyed ever so slightly on Master Mao's mind. As time went by, he came to learn that his present wife had taken the place of his intended bride which made him appreciate her all the more for recognizing his true worth.

Before long Mao was entered on the roll of Attending Scholars which qualified him to take part in the autumn provincial examinations. His road there took him past the Master Wang Inn, where the innkeeper had dreamt the night before of a spirit that said to him, "Tomorrow a Head Master of Letters Mao will come: someday he will deliver you from calamity." And so the host rose with the sun and watched for a traveller from the east. Great was his delight when he saw Master Mao at last. He received his guest with generous fare and services without asking for payment. Instead, he threw himself upon Master Mao's willingness to do as the dream had foretold. The latter, for his part, began to have a rather high opinion of himself.

Concerned that his wife, with her straggly hair, might be laughed at by people of high society, he decided to abandon her for another woman when his fortune was made. Later, the examination results were posted, but his name was nowhere on the list. He stumbled away moaning and cursing in frustration, his strength of will obliterated by remorse. The mere thought of his onetime host made his face turn crimson, so he went home by a different route, not daring to pass by the Master Wang Inn.

Three years later when he went to take part in the examinations a second time, the innkeeper extended the same hospitality as before.

"Your hospitality is especially embarrassing because the truth of your words has not yet been borne out," said Master Mao.

"You had a secret wish to change your wife for another." replied the innkeeper. "That is why the officials of the unseen world struck your name from the rolls. Do not think for a minute that my prophetic dream was false. The amazed Mao asked for an explanation and learned that after their last parting the innkeeper had had another dream in which this revelation was made. Upon hearing this Mao was shot through with dread and grief: he stood in numb immobility, like a puppet.

"It behooves you, Bachelor of Letters, to maintain your self-respect: then you will eventually take top honors."

Before long Mao did indeed win first place among the successful provincial candidates. His wife's hair, too grew out rapidly. Her cloudlike tresses, coiled and gleaming, added much to her charms.

Her elder sister married the son of a wealthy family in the neighborhood—a match over which she became puffed up with self-importance. But her husband was a wastrel and a no-account who brought his family by degrees to ruin. They soon found themselves living in an empty house with no fire in the hearth. News that her younger sister was now the wife of a Master of Letters only intensified her humiliation. She took pains to avoid meeting her younger sister on the street. Not long afterwards her husband died, leaving his family destitute. After a time, when she learned that Master Mao had taken the Doctorate of Letter, she was shot through to the very bones with such self-loathing that she bitterly parted with secular life and became a nun.

Master Mao returned home holding the rank of prime minister, whereupon the elder sister ordered one of her disciples to pay a call at his mansion, hoping for a present. When she got there, the lady of the house presented as gifts a few bolts each of twilled silk, crepe, gauze and raw silk. Unbeknownst to the messenger she slipped gold in among them. The messenger carried them back to her mistress, whose high hopes were dashed.

"If they had given me money, I could have spent it on wood and rice," she said in disappointment. "What good are presents like these?" She had them taken back. The prime minister and his wife wondered why their gifts had been turned down until they unrolled the cloth and found the gold still there.

Mao uncovered the gold and said laughingly: "Even a hundred or so taels of gold was too much for your mistress: no wonder she did not have the good fortune to pair up with an old minister like myself!" Then he sent off the messenger with fifty taels of gold, saying: "Taken this back to use for your mistress' living expenses. I am afraid that more gold would be too much of a burden for a person of her scant blessings."

After the messenger returned, she told all of this to her mistress, who gave a quiet sign and reflected that throughout her life the results of her actions had been the opposite of her intentions. Alas—people may attempt to seek the blessings and avoid evils, can they be sure it is up to them?

Later the innkeeper was arrested in connection with a murder case and thrown in jail. Master Mao used his influence to gain his release and have the charges against him dropped.

The Chronicler of the Tales comments: "The old burial grounds of Master Zhang became a final resting place for the Mao family: this in itself is already strange. As the current saying has it: "The elder sister's bridegroom marries the younger sister: This year's top examinee has to wait another three years. Such twists of fortune cannot be traced even by the clever-witted, can they? Ah well! The blue heaven above has long held itself aloof from men's pleas. Why, when Master Mao came along, did it respond with as unfailingly as an echo?"

21. SEQUEL TO THE "YELLOW MILLET DREAM"[1]

WHEN Master of Letters Zeng of Fujian placed highly in the doctoral examination held at South Palace, he and a few other newly successful examinees went on an excursion to the outskirts of the city. Rumor had it that an astrologer was staying at the Contemplative Priory of Vairocana, so they rode there together to ask their fortunes. They bowed with folded hands on entering and then took their seats. The astrologer took note of their smugness and proceeded to flatter them with what they wished to hear. Zeng waved his fan and grinned as he listened and then asked, "Does my future hold a python robe and jade sash pendants?" The diviner assured him with a straight face that he would hold the prime ministership for twenty peaceful years. Zeng was overjoyed and ever more pleased with himself.

Just then a small rainstorm came along, so Zeng and his companions took shelter in the monk's quarters. There on a rush mat sat an old monk with deep-set eyes and aquiline nose, indifferent to their presence. The group raised their

[1] A well-known Tang period classical tale in which, with the aid of a magic pillow offered by a Taoist, the poverty-stricken hero experienced a lifetime of wealth and fame during a dream. He fell asleep as an innkeeper on the road to Handan after setting a pot of yellow millet on the fire, and awoke to find that it was still cooking.

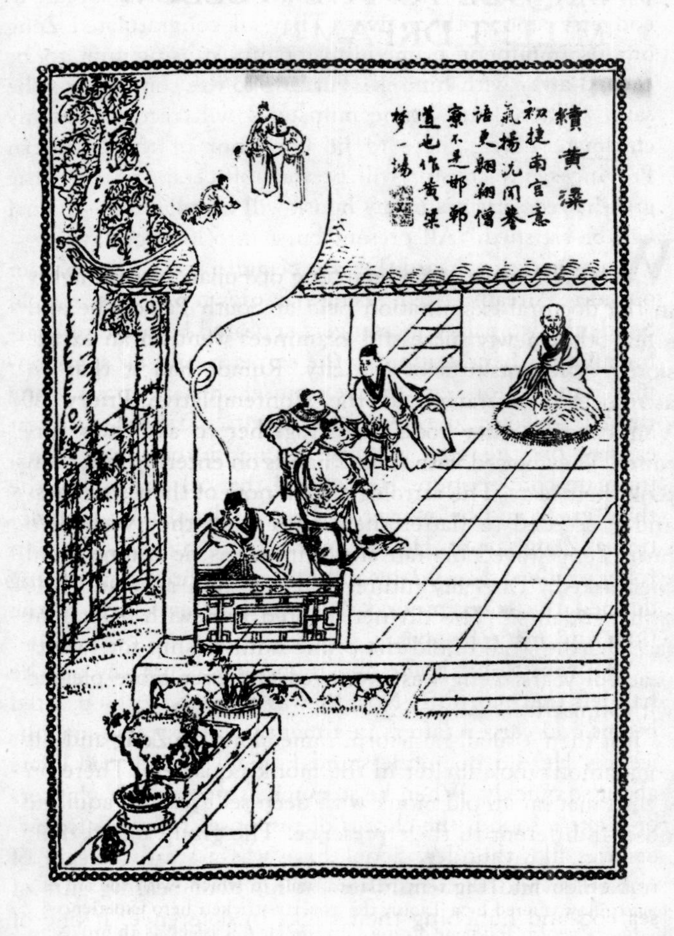
續黃粱
初捷南宮意
氣揚沈閑巷
語更翱翔僧
寮不是邯鄲
道也作黃粱
夢一場

hands in greeting, then sat on the couches and began to converse among themselves. They all congratulated Zeng on his imminent prime-ministership, causing him to be carried away with himself. Turning to the companions, he said, "When I am prime minister I will recommend my classmate Zhang, here to be Governor of the Southern Provinces; my cousins will be staff officers; and even the grey-haired servants in my house will be adjutants—then I will be satisfied." All present burst into loud guffaws.

Just then they heard the rain begin to pour down harder outside. Already tired, Zeng lay down on the couch. Suddenly two palace messengers appeared before him bearing an edict handwritten by the emperor himself summoning Grand Tutor Zeng to give counsel on state affairs. Zeng rushed to court in great high spirits. The emperor sat eagerly on the edge of his throne during their long, intimate conversation. He decreed that all officials of the third grade and below were subject to dismissal or promotion as Zeng saw fit. He then presented Zeng with a python robe, a jade sash-pendant and a thoroughbred horse. Zeng donned the robe, pressed his forehead reverently to the floor and made his exit.

He went to his house and found it was not the one he had left that morning. Now he was surrounded by painted beams and carved rafters in a mansion of extreme magnificence. He did not understand how all of this had come about so quickly. When he so much as stroked his whiskers or make a sound, the chorus of responses from his followers was like thunder. Soon there was a steady stream of noblemen and high ministers at his door bearing gifts of seafood and hunching their backs in deference. If one of the six high ministers came, Zeng would rise so hastily to greet them that he could barely put his slippers on straight;

to vice ministers he bowed with folded hands and made conversation; but to anyone lower than that he gave nothing more than a nod. The governor of Shanxi presented him with ten female entertainers, all fine women. The best among them were Willowette and Flutter, both of whom he favored with special regard. On days when he lounged bareheaded at home, bathing or relaxing, the two of them stayed at his side singing songs.

One day Zeng recalled how he had been helped through a difficult period by Wang Ziliang, one of the gentry in his district. "Now I am up here in the clouds," thought Zeng, "while he is still mired down along the road to advancement. Why don't I give him a hand?" The first thing next morning Zeng handed up a memorial recommending Wang as a counselor. An edict was then issued for Wang's immediate promotion.

Again Zeng recalled that Master-Steward Guo had once given him a dirty look. He lost no time in calling Imperial Advisor Lu, Censor Chen Chang and a few others before him and communicating his wish to them. The next day letters of accusation flooded in from all quarters. An edict was issued by the emperor ordering that the culprit be stripped of official rank and sent out of the capital.

Zeng found it quite pleasurable to pay off his old grudges and debts of gratitude. Once, as he made his way along a thoroughfare on the outskirts of the city, a drunk was found in the way of his retinue procession. Zeng ordered his underlings to bind the man and hand him over to the metropolitan prefect, where summary execution was carried out by beating the man to death. People who owned land adjacent to Zeng's houses and fields offered him fertile acreage and property out of fear of his power. Henceforth he had wealth enough to rival the resources of a kingdom.

Later Willowette and Flutter passed away, one after another, and Zeng's mind was filled morning and night with straying thoughts. Suddenly he remembered the time, years ago, when he had seen the daughter of his neighbors to the east and found her beautiful beyond compare. He had often thought of buying her as a concubine, but his wish had been denied because of his meagre wealth. Now that he was fortunate enough to have the wherewithal for realizing his aim, he sent several capable servants to force a marriage payment on the family. Before long they returned bearing a wicker sedan chair. The girl was even more stunning than when he had caught sight of her in the past. Looking back over his life thus far, he was sure that the girl marked the complete fulfillment of his wishes.

As the years passed, courtiers began to whisper among themselves: some seemed inwardly opposed to Zeng, but all were like palace horses trained to stand stock-still on guard. Zeng was too wrapped up in his arrogance and sense of power to let it bother him.

Then a scholar from the Hall of Dragon Symbols sent up a memorial that went something like this:

> It is this writer's humble opinion that Zeng was originally no more than a gambler and a drunk—a rascal straight out of the marketplace. Owing to a single agreeable conversation, he was honored with Your Majesty's sagely regard. His father was clothed in ministerial purple and his son in official crimson: such were the extremes of generosity and favor Your Majesty showered on him. But he gives no thought to sacrificing himself in weary toil to repay even one ten-thousandth of Your Majesty's kindness. On the contrary he indulges his whims and tyranically a

buses the powers he has arrogated to himself. All the hairs on a person's head are hardly enough to count his capital offenses! He monopolizes the offices of the Imperial Court as if they were commodities for speculation, assessing vacancies according to their potential for gain and fixing their prices accordingly. That is why dukes, ministers, generals, and scholars flock to his door and scheme to establish connections with him in such blatantly mercenary fashion. Innumerable are the people who wait in suspense for his every breath and gaze after the dust trail he leaves behind. Some outstanding scholars and worthy counselors will not toady to him: in mild cases they are relegated to positions of obscurity, and in serious cases they are stripped of their titles and reduced to commoners. Failure to stand on his side of the fence may provoke him so far as to condemn his victims for alleged treachery; even one word that displeases him is cause for banishment to a region of bobcats and wolves. Hence courtiers have no stomach for involvement, and the court has become isolated.

To make matters worse, he indiscriminately gobbles up the fertile lands of the common people and forces marriage payments upon girls of decent families. A miasma of injustice has shrouded the sun and sky in darkness. His slaves and servants are greeted wherever they go by the ingratiating smiles of prefects and magistrates. A letter from him is sufficient to make judges and procurators bend the law. His domestic familiars and distant relatives raise thunderous and stormy commotions where they go about in official carriages. When locals are late forwarding supplies, they immediately receive a thorough whipping from his mounted henchmen. Common people are savagely tormented and officials treated like slaves. Wherever his entourage passes the fields are left desolate.

Despite all this, the flames of the accused's ascendancy continue to blaze hotly: he relies on Your Majesty's favor and acts without scruple. Whenever Zeng is summoned to the palace explaining himself, then he presents Your Majesty with an elaborately overdrawn account of the peccadillos of his rivals. Moments after he smugly withdraws from court to his own house, music and singing can be heard from his rear garden. His days and nights are dissipated in sensual indulgence, horsemanship, and dog racing. The people's livelihood and affairs of the empire mean nothing to him. What sort of prime minister is this? There are alarms and vague rumors within and outside of the capital: public sentiment has become threateningly restless. Unless this man is immediately turned over to the excutioner, a usurpation of imperial authority on the scale of that committed by the traitors Cao Cao (155-220) and Wang Mang (45 B.C.-A.D. 23) will surely develop. It is impossible for me to sit calmly by while such fears preoccupy me day and night, and so I risk my life to list this man's offenses and offer them for Your Majesty's perusal. I humbly beseech Your Majasty to have this wicked traitor beheaded and his ill-gotten property confiscated, to appease the anger of Heaven above and gratify public opinion here below. If my words prove to be false or misleading, may my body be consigned to the axe or the oil cauldron. (And so forth.)

The news of this memorial had as chilling an effect on Zeng's spirits as a drink of icewater has on a man's internal warmth. Luckily for him the emperor was lenient, leniency and the document was shelved. But then section heads, government inspectors and the nine high ministers sent up one accusation after another. Even those who had bowed at Zeng's gate and called him godfather now faced him defiantly. An imperial command was issued to confiscate his home and exile him to Yunnan. A special commissioner had already been assigned to try his son, who was the prefect of Pingyang in Shanxi. Zeng was in a state of shock and dread, having just heard the command, when several dozen soldiers, bearing swords and spears, precipitately barged into his inner chamber, stripped him of his robe and official headpiece and bound both him and his wife. Soon he saw several porters carrying his valuables into the courtyard. There were gold, silver, coins and notes worth millions of taels; hundreds of bushels of pearls, jadeite, agate and nephrite; and netting, canopies, curtains and beds to the sum of several thousand articles. Nothing was left unturned; even baby clothes and women's shoes were scattered here and there on the courtyard steps. Zeng looked at the remnants one by one with aching heart and stinging eyes. Suddenly he heard a plaintive cry: someone was dragging out his beautiful concubine, her hair now dishevelled and her jade countenance forlorn. Flames of anguish seared his heart, but he dared not give vent to his outrage.

No sooner had the doors to his mansion and storehouse been sealed with notices of confiscation than Zeng was gruffly told to leave the premises. Guards tied a rope to him and dragged him away. Husband and wife swallowed their resentment and set out on foot. Now they could not even get a team of nags or a broken-down cart as a conveyance to spare them a few steps. When they had gone four miles his wife's legs were ready to give out. Zeng braced her from time to time and helped her along with his arm, but after another four miles he too was exhausted. Soon they saw a huge mountain towering into the clouds ahead. Fearing what would happen if they could not make the climb, the couple joined hands repeatedly and looked at each other with tear-filled eyes, but each time the guards approached them and leered threateningly, not allowing them to stop for a moment. They looked up and saw the slanting rays of the setting sun, but there was no place to take shelter for the night. They had no choice but to hobble onward falteringly. Halfway up the mountain his wife's strength gave out, and she sat down sobbing at the side of the road. Zeng too ignored the curses and shouts of the guards and stopped for a rest. Suddenly they heard a hundred voices whooping and shouting all at once. A party of bandits brandishing sharp swords approached, sending the guards fleeing in terror.

Zeng knelt before the bandits saying: "I am being exiled to a faraway place. There is nothing of value in my bag." He begged them to let him free.

The bandits glowered at him and announced, "All of us here have suffered from injustice. Your head is the only thing we want, you bootlicker. We don't care about anything else!"

"Even though charges have been pressed against me, I am an appointed court official," Zeng bellowed angrily. "How dare you petty thieves treat me this way?" The bandits, too, lost their tempers. One of them swung a huge axe at Zeng's neck. He felt his head hitting the ground with a thud, to the terror and bewilderment of his soul.

Then two ghosts came to him at once, tied his hands behind his back and prodded him forward. He walked for several notches[1] until he entered a metropolis. Moments later he found himself in a palace hall, at the head of which a hideous looking king leaned against a desk passing judgement. Zeng went forward and prostrated himself to beg for his life.

The king read only a few lines from Zeng's file and exploded with anger: "For deceiving your lord and betraying your country, you must be thrown into the oil cauldron!" Ten thousand ghosts applauded the decision with a thunderous roar. A giant demon dragged him to the foot of the stairs. There stood a cauldron at least seven feet high, with blazing charcoal around its base, its three legs glowing red. Zeng shuddered and wailed, but there was no escape. A ghost grabbed Zeng's hair with its left hand and his ankles in its right, then hurled him into the cauldron. Zeng felt his body dragged under the surface and then lifted by the currents of boiling oil. The pain from his scorching flesh pierced through him. The seething oil flowed into his mouth and fried his vital organs. He wished himself dead at that every moment, but he could think of nothing to make death come. This went on for the time it takes to eat a meal before a ghost lifted him out with a huge pitchfork and deposited him prone at the foot of the hall.

The king examined the file again and raged, "For using your power to mistreat others, you must be tortured on the mountain of knives!" The demon dragged him out again to a mountain. It was not very broad, but its sides were sheer,

[1] Name of a unit of time, refers to carved notches on a water clock. Approximately one quarter of an hour.

wall-like cliffs. Keen blades were everywhere on its surface like a dense growth of bamboo shoots. Several people were already on its slopes, their abdomens pierced and their intestines hanging on the blades. The ghastliness of their wails and screams was heart rending. The demon drove Zeng forward and, when he sobbed loudly and cringed, it raised a poison-tipped awl and punctured his skull. Overcome by pain, Zeng begged for mercy. The infuriated demon lifted him and hurled him in the air. He felt himself flying up through the clouds, and then came a dizzying fall onto knives that pierced his ribcage from all sides, causing an agony beyond the power of words to describe. After a time the wounds in his sagging body gaped larger and larger until he slid off the blades, his limbs clenched as though he were an inchworm. Again the ghosts drove him before the king, who ordered his officials to calculate the amount of money he had made while alive by selling official posts and titles, twisting the law, and seizing property. A man with a tangled beard manipulated his tally chips and reported: "3,210,000 taels' worth."

The king roared, "As much as he has hoarded, let him devour!"

Within moments, gold coins had been laid out in piles on the steps. They were moved load by load into iron pots and melted over blazing fires. Several ghosts poured ladlefuls of the molten metal down Zeng's mouth. Some ran down his chin, sending up an odor of charred flesh. The rest went down his throat and made his guts seethe. While alive he had worried that he would never get enough of the stuff, but now he worried that there was too much. Half a day passed before it was gone.

The king ordered that Zeng be taken to Ganzhou[1] for rebirth as a woman. A few steps brought him to a frame supporting an iron beam several feet in circumference, around which turned a wheel of fire uncountable *li* in diameter. Five colors glowed in its flames and its light flickered against the clouds. The ghosts beat him, forcing him to climb onto the wheel. No sooner had he closed his eyes and jumped on than the wheel turned beneath his feet. He seemed to be hurtling downward, and a cool feeling spread through his body. He opened his eyes to find himself in an infant's body, and a female one at that. The girl's parents were dressed in as tattered as a quail tail; a beggar's staff and gourd leaned against the wall of the earthen room. He knew that he had been reborn as a beggar's daughter.

Every day she went along with the other beggars, holding out an almsbowl. Her rumbling stomach was hardly ever filled. The wind pierced her to the bone through her tattered clothes. At fourteen she was sold to Bachelor of Letters Gu as a concubine. Her food and clothing were barely sufficient, and the mistress of the house was a terrible shrew. She served the girl every day with whip or bamboo rod and branded her breast with a red hot iron. Luckily the girl could take comfort in the loving regard shown by her husband. One day a no-good youth who lived east of them climbed the wall and forced himself upon her. She thought of how the ghosts had punished her for the sins of her past life: No, it must not happen again! She screamed and hollered until her husband and the mistress were aroused and the no-good youth slunk away. Soon afterward her husband was spending the

[1] In the remote western province of Gansu.

night in her room. She was rattling along with her head next to his on the pillow, complaining of her troubles and the wrongs done to her, when two knife-wielding robbers burst through the door with a fierce shout. They cut off the scholar's head, and bagged all clothes and other articles. The girl huddled under the covers, not daring to make a sound. When the robbers had gone, she ran screaming to the mistress' room. The mistress leapt up in fright. Both of them broke out in sobs when they found him truly dead. The mistress, suspecting that the concubine had conspired with a lover to kill her husband, accused the girl before the district magistrate. The magistrate subjected her to severe interrogation and finally used torture to establish her guilt. The sentence prescribed by law was death by dismemberment. She was bound and taken to the execution ground. Outrage at this injustice swelled within her chest till she could no longer contain it. She stamped frenziedly and screamed that she had been wronged. There could be no darkness worse than this, she thought, not even in the nine dungeons and eighteen levels of hell. In the midst of her wailing the voices of Zeng's fellow sightseers were heard calling: "Are you having a nightmare, brother?"

Zeng came back to himself with a start: he saw the old monk still sitting in lotus posture on the mat. Zeng's companions all spoke at the same time: "The sun is going down and we haven't had a thing to eat. What made you sleep so deeply all this time?" Zeng gave them a grim look and rose.

"Did the prediction that you would be prime minister turn out to be true?" asked the monk with a smile. This amazed Zeng all the more. He bowed to the monk and asked to be instructed.

"If you cultivate virtue and act with benevolence, you

can make a blue lotus grow out of a pit of fire," said the monk. But you can't expect a mountain monk like me to know about it?"

Zeng's spirits had been high when he set out that morning, but on his return they were unexpectedly low. Henceforth, his ardor for the prime ministership waned. He went into the mountains, and no one knows what became of him.

The Chronicler of the Tales comments: "Blessings are given to the good and calamity is visited upon the decadent: this has always been the way of Heaven. A man who takes secret delight at predictions that he will be prime minister is obviously not glad for the chance to work himself to the bone for his country. Palaces, houses, wives, and concubines all appeared within the small space of Zeng's imagination—nothing was lacking. But dreams are reducible to delusion, and wishes are unreal. When a man acts with hypocrisy, the spirits counter with illusion. When yellow millet is on the fire and nearly finished cooking, the time for this dream is bound to come. It deserves to be appended as a sequel to what another young man dreamt along the road to Handan."

22. PRINCESS LOTUS

DOU Xu of Jiaozhou,[1] also known as Xiaohui, was lying in bed one day when he noticed a man in a robe of coarse cloth standing hesitantly at the foot of his bed and looking about nervously as if he had something to say. Scholar Dou asked his business, and he answered, "The prime minister awaits your pleasure."

"What prime minister?"

"He is here in the vicinity," said the man. Dou followed him out and around the corner of his house. The man led the way to a place with row upon row of pavilions and mansions supported by thousands of parallel beams. The scholar found himself in a maze of gates opening onto doors and doors opening onto gates—a scene totally unlike anything in this world. Numerous palace attendants and ladies-in-waiting bustling back and forth all asked the cloth-robed man: "Is this Master Dou?" Each time the man answered yes.

Soon a distinguished looking official came out and welcomed the scholar with great civility. When they had climbed a staircase into a hall, Dou opened with a question: "Not having enjoyed your acquaintance, I have never gotten around to paying you a visit. I cannot help but entertain some misgivings at the undue regard you have

[1] A district in Shandong province.

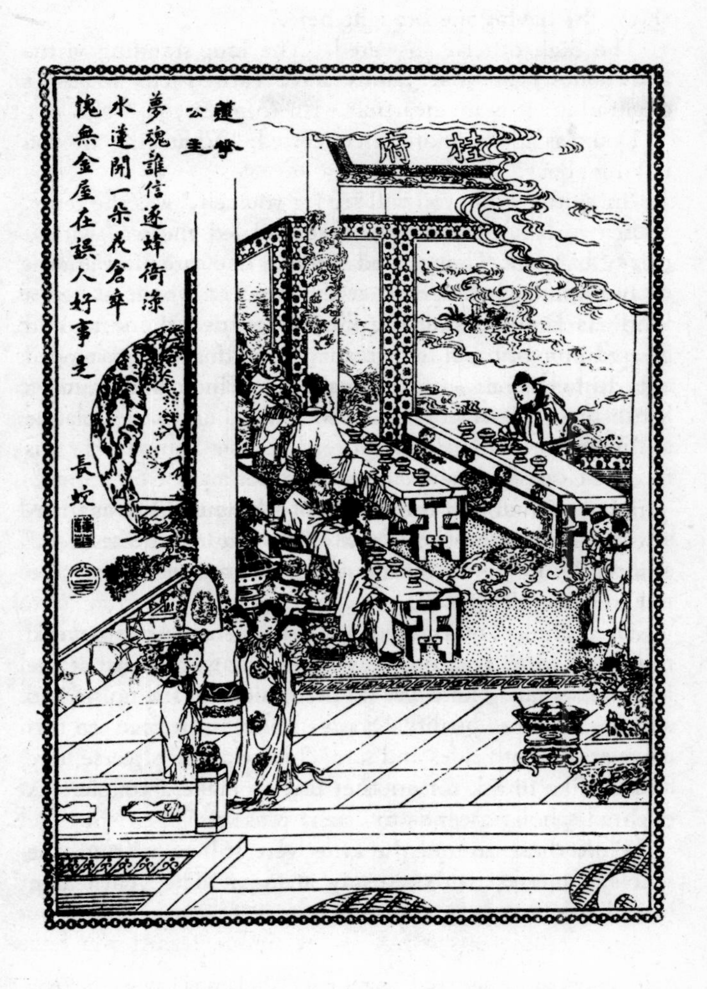

蓮花公主
夢魂誰信逐蜂衙涤
水蓬開一朵花倉卒
愧無金屋在誤人好事是
長蛟
桂府

shown by having me brought here."

The high official answered, "The long-standing virtue and honesty of your family have earned His Majesty's admiration; it is his heartfelt wish to meet you."

Dou was all the more disconcerted. "What king are you talking about?" he demanded.

"In a little while you will see for yourself," was the reply. Soon two ladies-in-waiting came and led the way with a pair of banners. They passed through one gate after another and approached a hall, at the head of which waited a king. As Dou entered, the king descended the steps and greeted him with polite formality. That done, they stepped over to take their seats at a table on which was spread a lavish feast. The scholar glanced upward and saw a plaque at the head of the hall which read "Cassia Manor." He was too ill at ease to begin the conversation.

"My proximity to such an honorable neighbor as yourself proves that the bond of fate between us is quite deep," said the king. "So it is fitting for us to open our hearts and not to show mistrust."

The scholar murmured in agreement. After several rounds of wine, reed organs and singing were heard at the foot of the hall. There was no percussion, so the music had an airy, serene quality. Soon the king turned to his courtiers on both sides and said, "I have a line of verse here and I'd like to ask for another line to make a couplet: 'A talented scholar ascends to Cassia Manor!' "

While those around the king were still pondering, the scholar came up with a ready answer: "The gentheman loves lotus flowers."[1]

[1] This sentence is adapted from the essay "On Loving Lotuses" by Zhou Dunyi, a Neo-Confucian of the Song dynasty (960-1278).

"Marvelous!" said the king delightedly. "Lotus is the princess' nickname. How did you hit on it like that? Could there be a tie between you and her from former life? Send word to the princess that she absolutely must come out and make the acquaintance of this young gentleman."

After a time the tinkle of sash pendants was heard approaching, fragrance of orchid and musk filled the air, and the princess appeared. She was sixteen or seventeen years of age and graced with matchless beauty. The king ordered her to bow to the scholar and introduced her: "This is my daughter Princess Lotus." Having made an obeisance, she withdrew.

The scholar's self-possession was much shaken at the sight of her: he sat there woodenly, immersed in thought and oblivious even to the toast offered by the king. The king seemed to perceive what preoccupied him, for he said, "My daughter would be a good match for you, but I am ashamed that we are not of your kind. What do you say?"

Again the scholar, in heartsick befuddlement, was oblivious to his words. The man sitting beside him nudged his foot and said, "The king greeted you politely, but you didn't respond. Don't tell me you didn't hear what the king just said to you!"

The scholar was lost in a daze and greatly ashamed of himself. He rose from his seat and said, "Your Majesty has entertained me with such hospitality that, without my knowing it, the wine has gone to my head and I have behaved improperly, for which I beg your forgiveness. But now the day is late and you are busy, so I must ask leave to depart."

"Meeting with you is truly the fulfillment of my heart's wishes. Why must you speak so abruptly of leaving? But since you are not inclined to stay, I dare not force you. If you would be so kind as to remember us, I should like to invite you again." With this the king ordered a lady-in-waiting to lead him out.

On the way she said to the scholar, "Just now the king said that his daughter would be a good match for you. He seems willing to connect himself to you through marriage. Why didn't you speak up?"

The scholar stamped his feet in remorse. He agonized over his mistake with each step he took until he arrived at home. Suddenly he was awake, his eyes open to the last rays of the setting sun. He sat quietly letting the images from his dream pass one by one before his mind's eye. Later that night he blew out the candles in his studio, hoping to find his way back to the same dream, but the road was lost in haze. All he could do was heave a sigh of regret.

One night as he lay in bed with a friend, the same lady-in-waiting suddenly came to him to relay a summons from the king. The scholar gladly followed. When he came before the king he knelt down and announced himself. The king pulled him to his feet, showed him to a seat in a private corner, and said, "I know that since our parting you have devoted a great deal of thought to us. Would it be brash to suppose that you will not mind to having my daughter wait on you?"

The scholar bowed in gratitude. The king ordered his councillors and ministers to be present at the wedding banquet. When the wine had gone the rounds a palace attendant came forward to say: "The princess has finished dressing."

Soon several dozen palace maids emerged, clustered about the princess, who wore on her head a bridal veil of red brocade. She walked forward with steps delicate enough to skim over waves and was led onto a felt rug.

There she performed, with the scholar, the mutual kowtow by which the wedding ceremony was completed. Then they were escorted to their residence. In the comfortable warmth of the nuptial chamber, he was treated to all the rich fragrance that human senses can absorb.

"Having you before my eyes is such a joy that I can forget death," he said to his bride. "But I fear that what happened today is only a dream."

"Here we are, you and I, as clear as day. How could it be a dream?" asked the princess, covering her mouth to hold back a laugh.

As soon as he rose early the next morning he playfully applied cream to the princess' face and kohl to her eyebrows. When that was done, he encircled her waist with a sash and measured her feet with his fingers.

"Are you losing your mind?" she asked.

"I have been misled by dreams many times before, so now I am making a detailed record. Even if it turns out to be a dream, this will be enough to refresh my memory."

They were still poking fun at each other when a palace maid ran in and said, "A monster has entered the palace gate, and the king has fled to a side hall. An evil calamity is upon us!"

Greatly shocked, the scholar hurried to see the king, who took the scholar's hand in his own and said in a voice broken by sobs: "Since you did not spurn us, I was looking forward to a long friendship. Who could have foreseen that Heaven would send this great evil down upon us? My kingdom is on the brink of collapse: what can I do?"

In reply to the bewildered scholar's questions, the king took a memorial from the desk and gave it to him to read. The memorial was as follows:

"Your subject Black-Wing, Grand Councillor of

Incense-Redolent Hall, prays that you will quickly move the capital, so that the heart of our kingdom may continue beating. According to a report by the privy council, a giant python ten thousand feet in length appeared on the sixth day of the fifth month, coiled itself outside the palace, then proceeded to devour 13,800 of your subjects and courtiers. All the palace halls and mansions the snake crawled over were reduced to rubble. I mustered up the courage to observe the disaster, and did indeed see a monstrous python—its head as massive as a mountain and its eyes like bodies of water—gulp down halls and pavilions with a toss of its head and flatten towers and walls by flexing its waist. It is truly a disaster unparalleled throughout history and a calamity of a scope never met with in past ages! The danger to our state and ancestral temple is imminent. I beg Your Majesty to lead the royal family to a safe place immediately. Would that I could say more." By the time the scholar had finished reading his face was like the shade of ashes.

At that point a palace servant ran in and reported, "The monster has come!" All through the palace people set up such a wretched howling that the sky and sun seemed blotted out by their misery. The king, immobilized by panic, simply stared at the scholar and sobbed as he said, "I must entrust my daughter to you."

The scholar gasped at the news and went back to where the princess was huddled wailing with her servants. She grasped the front of his robe when she saw him enter and said, "What will you do with me, husband?"

The scholar was nearly overcome with grief, but he grasped her wrist as he thought aloud, "I am only a poor student. It shames me that I have no room of gold to accommodate you. What I do have is a thatched hut with several rooms. We can hide away there for a time, can't we?"

"What choice do we have?" sniffed the princess. "Please give me your arm and take me there right away!" So the scholar wrapped his arm around her and led her out. Soon they reached his house.

"This is a great, invulnerable house—much better than our palace. But who will my parents rely on now that I have come here with you? Please construct another house; then I can have the whole kingdom move in." The scholar expressed qualms at this.

"People are in danger, but you have no sympathy for them," wailed the princess. "What good are you?"

The scholar made an effort to comfort her, but she ignored him and ran to his room, where she threw herself on the bed and sobbed uncontrollably. Just as he was racking his brains for a way to calm her, he suddenly awoke and realized he had been dreaming. But still the sound of her sobbing hummed in his ear. Turning to look, he found that it was not a human voice at all but the buzzing of a few bees that flew around his pillow. The strangeness of this brought a loud exclamation to his lips. When his friend questioned him, he told him the dream. His amazed friend, too, knew that this was no ordinary dream. They got up and looked at the bees, which were hovering close to the scholar's sleeve and would not let themselves be brushed away. The friend urged him to build a hive. The scholar accepted his suggestion and directed a workman to construct it. No sooner were two of the walls been in place than a swarm of bees from over the wall flew into it in a steady stream. Before the roof was on a peck basketful of them had come. Tracing the direction of their flight, he found that they came from an old garden kept by an elderly man next door. For the past thirty years there had been a highly prolific hive of bees in the garden. After hearing of the scholar's dream, the old man examined the hive and found no sign of activity. Removing a wall, he found the hive occupied by a snake over ten feet long, which he pulled out and killed. Now it was plain that this snake was the giant python in the dream. After the bees swarmed into the hive built against the scholar's house, they were more productive than ever, and there were no more strange occurrences.

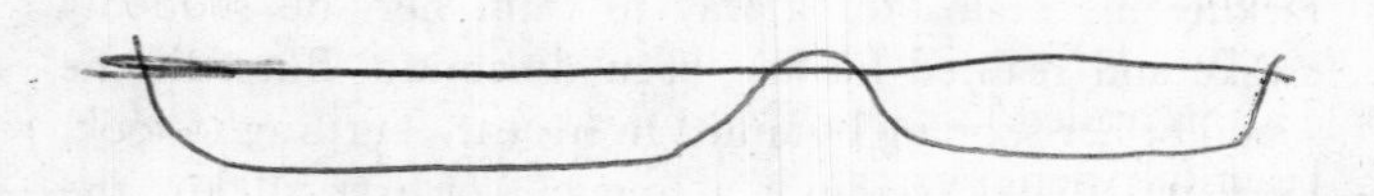

23. YUN CUIXIAN

LIANG Youcai was originally from Shanxi, but his wanderings took him to the area around Jinan in Shandong, where he worked as a peddler. He had neither wife, children, nor land. On the first day of summer he climbed Mt. Tai along with some villagers. On that day Mt. Tai is crowded with pilgrims, as lay Buddhists, both male and female, lead groups of men numbering about a hundred before the image of a deity, where both sexes kneel together for the length of time a stick of incense burns. This is called "kneeling to incense." Youcai spotted a beautiful young woman, seventeen or eighteen years old, in the crowd and felt a liking for her. He knelt beside her, pretending to be a pilgrim. Then, acting as if his knees had given out, he put his hand on her leg. She turned her head to give him an exasperated look, then moved away from him on her knees. Youcai moved over to her also on his knees, and after a moment, touched her again. Realizing what he was up to, the young woman rose abruptly, gave up trying to kneel and went out the gate.

Youcai stood up and followed on her trail, but he did not know which way she had gone. Giving up hope, he walked along dejectedly. Then, seeing the young woman walking with an old woman, apparently her mother, on the road ahead, he hurried toward them and heard them talking as they walked.

"I'm so glad you went to worship the Goddess! You don't have any brothers or sisters, but the Goddess will be your Guardian Angel and secretly arrange for you to find a fine husband. As long as he can treat me with respect and deference, he need not be a noble young gentleman or the son of a rich family."

Youcai was relieved to hear these words. He started a conversation and bit by bit began to ply the old woman with questions. The old woman said that her surname was Yun, that the girl, named Cuixian, was her daughter and that their house was in the mountains forty *li* to the west.

"This is a steep mountain road," said Youcai. "With your feet dragging the way they are, and Sister being as delicate as she is, do you really think you can make it?"

"It's getting late," said Cuixian. "We're going to stay the night at my uncle's house."

Youcai said, "Just now you were saying that when you look for a son-in-law you won't turn a person away because of his poverty or low station. I am still single. Do you think I might meet your wishes, Mother?"

The old woman asked her daughter but received no answer. After she asked several times the girl said, "He is a man of scant blessings: besides, he is loose and immoral. He has a wanton heart and is liable to grow restless. I will not be the wife of a wild, dissipated man."

Upon hearing this, Youcai insisted that he was perfectly sincere and swore by the sun above. The old woman, who found this to her liking, finally gave her approval. The girl could only show her disapproval with a scowl. The mother patted her and spoke reassuringly to make her give in. Youcai graciously reached into his pouch and hired two mountain sedan chairs to carry the woman and the girl. He himself followed on foot like their servant. As they passed

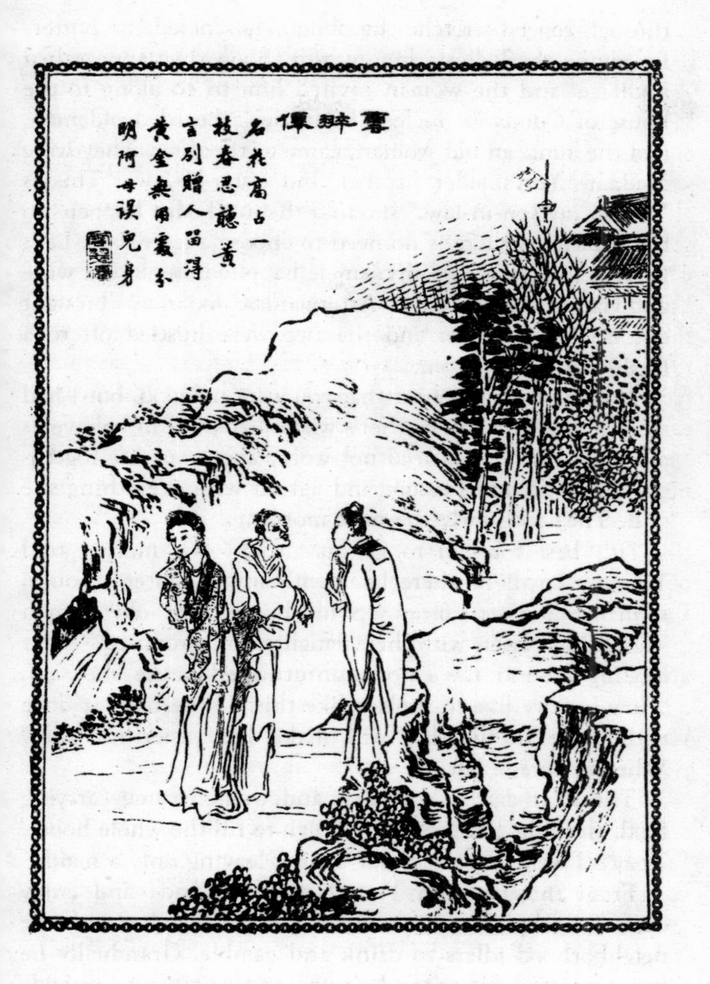
雲翠僊
名花高占一
枝春忍聽黃
言別贈人留得
黃金無用處分
明阿母误兒身

through rugged stretches he obligingly scolded the porters for giving the ladies a bumpy ride. Soon they approached a village, and the woman invited him to go along to the house of Cuixian's uncle. The uncle, a bearded old man, and the aunt, an old woman, came to the door. They were Madame Yun's elder brother and sister-in-law. "This is Youcai, my son-in-law," she told them. "Today happens to be auspicious; there is no need to choose a later date. Let's make it tonight." The girl's uncle happily brought out wine and viands to feed Youcai. Afterwards Cuixian was brought out in formal dress, and the two were hustled off to a freshly swept bedroom.

"I knew from the start that you were no good, but I had to go along with my mother's wishes. If you can behave as a human being, you need not worry about our life together." Youcai heard her out and agreed with everything she said. They rose early the next morning.

"It's best for you to go on ahead," the mother told Youcai. "I will be there later with my daughter." Youcai returned home to clean up his house. The old woman showed up later with her daughter as promised. After looking around the empty, unfurnished house she said, "How can we live in a place like this? I'll be back at once with some things that will make life easier for you." Whereupon she left.

The next day several men and women came carrying food, clothing, and utensils enough to fill the whole house. They all went away without eating, leaving only a maid.

From this time on Youcai could sit back and enjoy comfort and plenty, but every day he got together with the neighborhood idlers to drink and gamble. Grandually he began to steal his wife's hairpins and earrings to provide himself with gambling funds. She tried to reason with him, but he would not listen. She was exasperated by his behavior and took precautions to guard her hope chest closely, as if she were warding off a bandit. One day when one of Youcai's cronies knocked at his gate for a visit he caught a glimpse of the girl and was stunned by her beauty.

"You are a rich man," he told Youcai jokingly. "You will never have to worry about being poor."

When Youcai asked what he meant he answered, "I just saw your wife. No doubt about it, she is a fairy maiden. You and she were simply not made for each other. If you sell her as a concubine, you can get a hundred taels of gold; as a courtesan she would go for one thousand taels. With a thousand taels of gold to your name, you would ever have to cramp your style for lack of money?"

Youcai said nothing, but in his heart he agreed. Back home he sighed heavily in front of his wife and said over and over that they were too poor to get by. When she ignored him he slammed the table repeatedly with his fist, threw down his soup spoon and chopsticks, raged at the maid and did everything else he could to be obnoxious.

One night his wife bought wine to drink with him and, without leading up to the subject, said, "You fret day in and day out over being poor. I feel guilty for not being able to end our poverty or share the burden of worry. But I own nothing worthy of mention except this maid. Selling her will help our finances a bit."

Youcai shook his head and said, "We couldn't get much for her!"

After they had been drinking a while longer she said, "There is nothing I would not do to help you, but I am powerless. I was willing to spend my life with you, even in poverty like this, but if staying with you means nothing more than sharing a lifetime of despair, what is the good of it? You might as well sell me to a rich family. It would be a good deal for both sides, and you would probably get more for me than for the maid."

Youcai looked shocked and said, "How can I let that happen?" The girl repeated what she said, this time insistently and seriously.

"Let me think it over," said Youcai delightedly. So he offered to sell her, through the good offices of a eunuch at court, to the Registry of Entertainers. The eunuch visited Youcai and was overjoyed when he saw her. Fearing that he might not get her after all, he made a down payment of 800 strings of a thousand cash each, and the deal was virtually closed.

"Our poverty has been a matter of constant concern for my mother," said the girl. "Now that it is over between us, I will go home and visit my mother for a while. It would hardly be right not to tell her we are parting."

When Youcai voiced his fear that her mother would interfere, she said, "I am going through with this because it pleases me. I guarantee you nothing will go wrong."

Youcai went along with her. They did not reach her mother's house until almost midnight. They knocked on the gate and were admitted to a magnificient manor house with servants running about ceaselessly. During their days together Youcai had often asked if they could visit her mother's, but she had always refused. So he had been a son-in-law for over a year without ever visiting his in-laws' house. What he now saw filled him with dread: he feared that a family of such a magnitude would not tolerate one of its daughters being sold as a concubine or courtesan.

Cuixian led Youcai to the upper floor of a storied building. The old woman was startled to see them and asked why they had come. "I told you he was no good, and that's just how he turned out," said the girl reproachfully. She pulled two ingots from underneath her clothes and placed them on the table, saying: "Fortunately the low-down snake did not trick these away from me. Now I am returning them to you." Her shocked mother asked for an explanation.

"He is going to sell me, so there is no use keeping this gold in reserve." She pointed to Youcai and reviled him: "You son of a rat and a lynx! A while ago you were carrying a shoulder pole, and your face was so streaked with grime you looked like a demon. The first time you came near me you reeked of stale sweat, and your skin was so crusty with filth it was ready to peel off. The calluses on your hands and feet were an inch thick. It was enough to make a person feel like retching the whole night through. After I went to live with you and you could sit back in comfort and eat your fill, you finally showed your true colors. My mother is here, so speak out if what I say is false!" Youcai hung his head, hardly daring to breathe.

She went on: "I took a good look at myself and realized I was not the sort of beauty that men destroy cities for. I was not fit to serve a nobleman, but I dare say I was a good enough match for the likes of you. In what way did I let you down that you gave up all thought of our family ties? Do you think I couldn't have built a manor and bought rich land if I had wanted to? I knew you did not have a steadfast bone in your body: you were cut out to be a beggar in the end, not my lifetime mate."

As she spoke, maids and women servants linked arms tightly and circled about him. Hearing the girl's accusations, they spat on him and reviled him, saying: "What the use of talking? We might as well do away with him!" Youcai sank to the floor in great fright and threw himself on their mercy, saying again and again that he repented of his mistakes.

"The enormity of selling your wife was not bad enough for you," said Cuixian in a fresh surge of anger. "But how could you bear to sell the woman who shared your bed into prostitution?" Before she was finished the servants had closed in, eyes wide with anger, jabbing him in the ribs with sharp hairpins and scissor blades. Youcai howled pitifully and begged for his life. The girl stopped them, saying: "Let him go for the moment. Even though he is a rotten ingrate, I can't bear to see him quivering."

Thereupon she went downstairs, leading her mother and the servants. Youcai sat listening for a while, until all their voices had died down. As he thought of escape, he raised his head and saw the starry skies above with the pale light of dawn already showing in the east. The fields around were just emerging from the gloom. Not a lamp was in sight, nor were there any buildings. He was seated at the edge of a cliff overlooking an abyss so deep no bottom could be seen. His blood froze at the thought of himself plunging headlong into nothingness. As he made a move to slide back, the edge gave out from under him with a sound of crumbling stone. His fall was stopped by a dead tree projecting from the cliff face which caught him in the stomach, leaving his arms and legs hanging in mid-air. Below was untold hundreds of feet of blackness. Not daring to shift his position, he hung there shrieking himself hoarse with terror. His body was swollen all over, his senses were numb and his strength was gone. The sun climbed high in the heavens before a woodcutter spotted him and hunted up a rope, on which he climbed down and raised Youcai to the top of the cliff half-dead.

The woodcutter carried Youcai back to his own house.

The door was standing wide open, and the house was as bare as a broken-down temple. Beds, chests, and furnishings had all vanished. Only a rope cot and broken desk —possessions from before his marriage—remained. He lay dejectedly on the cot. Every day after that he went out to beg food from the neighbors when he was hungry. Before long he was a swollen, ulcerous leper. His neighbors, despising him for the life he had led, rejected him scornfully. Coming to the end of his rope, Youcai sold his house and lived in a cave. He begged in the streets, always with a knife at his belt. When someone urged him to trade the knife for food, he refused, saying: "I need it for self-defense, to protect myself from tigers and wolves where I live out in the wilds."

Later he and the man who had once urged him to sell his wife met in the street. He walked up close to the man, complaining of his troubles, then suddenly pulled out his knife and stabbed the man to death, for which he was put under arrest. The magistrate, having made a careful investigation and gotten to the bottom of the case, could not bear to punish him with torture, so he sent him straight to prison, where he soon died of illness.

The Chronicler of the Tales comments: "A man who finds a hibiscus of a woman from across the mountains and shares his room with her would not change places with a king on his throne. But what happens when someone who is himself a beast of a man lays blame for his misfortune on the friend who plays along with his evil wishes? Anyone who has a friend must beware of this. If a person is enticed by men of low character into gambling recklessly or committing other evils, even if the outcome is not disastrous, he may not resent them, but he will feel no gratitude. But when the man gambles away his shirt and his wife's panties, when everyone points at him derisively and he feels like dying for shame, when thoughts of failure constantly weigh on his mind and complaints of failure constantly escape his lips, he will lie awake in the still night, tossing and turning in his burlap clothes. At such a time vivid recollections will pass through his mind of the days before his fall, of the events leading up to his fall, of the reasons for his fall and, inevitably, of the instigator who brought about his fall. When this happens, the weak man will sit up, huddled in his threadbare clothes, and rave impotently. The strong man, on the other hand, will go out poorly-clothed in spite of the cold and, shading the light of his lamp with a basket, get his hands on a knife. He will whet it to a fine edge and use it before the night is through.

That is why I say, advising a man to do good is like giving him an olive—bitter at first but gradually tasty—while tempting a man with evil is like giving him putrid meat. Naturally those who listen to advice should be on their guard, nor can those who give it afford to be unscrupulous!"

24. MISS YAN

A STUDENT from a poor family of Shuntian prefecture[1] moved to Luoyang in Henan province with his father during a year of famine. He was slow to develop and could not write a complete composition until the age of seventeen. On the other hand, he had fine, handsome features; he was a witty conversationalist and an excellent letter writer. These gifts drew people's attention away from his deficiencies. Before long his father and mother died in quick succession. Alone in the world, he began tutoring at a village school near where the Luo River flows into the Yellow River. At that time there lived in the village an orphaned girl from the Yan family, who was the daughter of a renowned scholar. She had shown considerable intellectual powers in childhood. When her father was alive he taught her to read, and she could retain in her memory anything that passed before her eyes. In her early teens she learned poetry from her father, who once remarked, "We have a female scholar in my family: if only she wore scholar's hat!"

Owing to his deep fondness for her, he hoped to find her a husband from a noble family. After his death the girl's mother held to this aim without success for three years, until she also died. Some people advised the girl to

[1] Beijing (Peking).

marry a promising student. The girl concurred, but the right man had not yet come along.

Then one day the woman who lived next door climbed over the wall to talk with her. She showed the girl a paper parcel enclosing silk threads for embroidery. The girl opened it and found the paper to be a letter in the young student's hand to the scholar who lived next door. Reading it over and over, she began to feel attracted to the youth who had written it. The woman saw what was on her mind and said in a low voice: "This was written by a lively, handsome young man who is an orphan like yourself and close to you in age. If you are favorably disposed, I will have my husband bring the two of you together."

The girl responded with a meaningful silence. The woman went home and communicated her plan to her husband, who was on good terms with the young man. The young man was overjoyed to hear the news brought by his friend. He had a gold sun-ring left him by his mother, which he asked his friend to give to Miss Yan. A date was set and the wedding was held, whereupon the two of them were as happy as fish finding their way to water. But the girl laughed when she read the young man's compositions and said, "I can't help thinking that you and the writer of these had to be two different people. With writing like this, how are you ever going to make it?"

Morning and evening, with the strictness of a teacher or well-meaning friend, she urged him to pore over his books. When daylight was fading she would bring out a candle and sit at the desk reciting passages until the third watch—an example for her husband to follow. After a year of this the young man had a fair mastery of examination writing, but then he failed two examinations in a row. His fortunes and reputation were mired in decline, and he

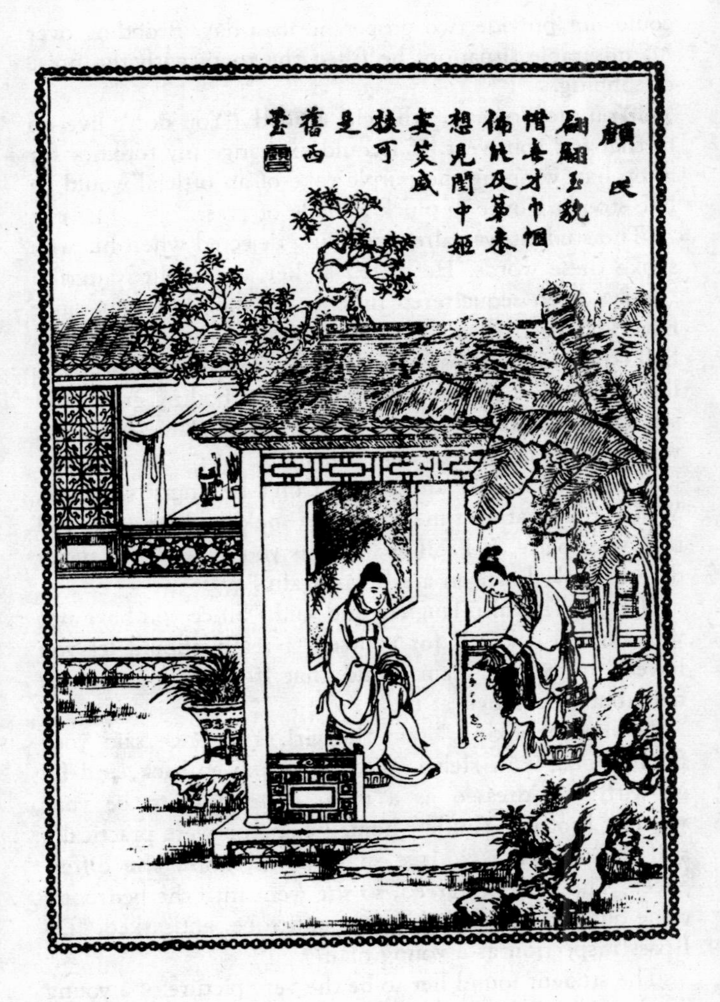

顧氏
翩翩玉貌
惜春才巾幗
佈能及第春
想見閨中姬
妻笑戚
妹可
是
舊西
雲

could not provide two proper meals a day. Brooding over his miserable situation, he filled the room with the noise of sobbing.

"You are no man," the girl chided. "You don't live up to that hat you wear. If I could exchange my topknot for a top hat, winning the purple robe of an official would be like stooping over to pluck a blade of grass."

The student was already feeling dejected when his wife spoke these words. He glared at her and replied angrily: "You've been sequestered indoors all your life—not once have you been in an isolation booth at the examination hall—but you suppose that winning fame and fortune is like fetching water for the kitchen and boiling gruel. If a scholar's hat were placed on your head, I'm afraid you wouldn't do any better than a man."

The girl laughed and said, "Don't be angry with me. When examination time comes, let me disguise myself and take your place. If I fail as badly as you have, I will never dare to look down on a scholar again."

The student also laughed and said, "Since you have not yet sampled oak gall for yourself, I really should let you have a taste, but I am afraid that if this slips out our neighbors will laugh at us."

"I am not joking," said the girl. You once said your family home is in Hebei. Why don't you go back, and I'll go with you dressed as a man, pretending to be your younger brother. You left home when you were practically still in swaddling clothes, so who will know the difference?" The student agreed, so she went into the bedroom, came out in a scholar's kerchief and robe, and asked, "Do I pass inspection as a young man?"

The student found her to be the very picture of a young dandy. He delightedly went around taking leave of all his neighbors. Using the meager gifts of his young friends, he bought a bony ass, mounted his wife on it and returned to his family home. His elder cousin on his father's side, who had remained there, was delighted to see two cousins as fine as jade hatpins, and he looked after them day and night. His esteem for them doubled when he saw them slaving over their books from early in the morning until late at night. He engaged a short-haired young slave to provide for their needs, but when night came they sent him away. Whenever there was a funeral or happy occasion in the area, the elder brother went out to socialize, but the younger drew his curtains and went on studying. Half a year passed, but seldom had anyone seen his face. If guests asked to see him, the elder brother would make excuses for him. When people read his essays, their eyes bulged with amazement. A few tried to force their acquaintance on him by breaking into his room, but he simply greeted them with a bow and turned away. Everyone who glimpsed his fine features became an admirer. So it was that his reputation was spread over a wide area, and noblemen vied to have him marry into their families. When his cousin brought up the subject, he responded with a bemused smile. When urged further he replied, "I have vowed to attain to the height of honors. Until my name is posted on the notice board, there will be no marriage for me."

At that time the civil examiner came to preside over an examination, and the two went up for it. The elder brother failed again, but the younger took top honors in the qualifying examination and placed fourth in Shuntian prefecture. The year after he took the Doctorate and was given the magistracy of Tongcheng in Anhui province, where he had a good record as an administrator. He was soon promoted to censor with imperial credentials of the

Henan circuit. He possessed the wealth of a prince or marquis.

On the pretext of ill health, he asked to be allowed to resign and was given permission to return to his family lands. Guests milled about his door, but all were turned away. Everyone thought it strange that from his student days right up to this time of prosperity and renown, he had never spoken of marriage. Upon his return he gradually staffed his household with maids. Some surmised that he was having relations with them, but investigations by his cousin's wife proved that there were no licentious goings-on.

Before long came the widespread disorder following the fall of the Ming dynasty. The younger brother finally confessed to his cousin's wife: "To tell the truth, I am the young gentleman's wife, not his brother. He is a nobody who cannot stand on his own feet, so I insisted on doing it myself. I fear that if this gets out I'll be summoned for questioning by the emperor, and my husband and I will be the laughingstocks of the empire." The cousin's wife could not believe this. He removed 'his' boots to expose 'his' feet: much to her amazement, the boots were stuffed with old cotton.

From then on the woman had her husband assume her title, while she withdrew behind closed doors as most females do. She had never gotten pregnant, so she put up the money to buy a concubine and said to the student: "Any man who makes a success of himself buys a concubine to serve him. After ten years as an official I still have only one partner. What makes you so fortunate, that you can sit back and have a pretty woman come to you."

"Go ahead and provide yourself with a stable of thirty male concubines," said the student. People often retell this witty exchange for amusement.

During this period the student's deceased parents were frequently honored on occasions of imperial bounty granting. The gentry came to pay their respects to the student and honored him as though he were censor. The student was ashamed to accept the title his wife had earned. He felt comfortable only when treated as a scholar and lived out his days without riding in a carriage under an official canopy.

The Chronicler of the Tales comments: "For parents to receive posthumous titles because of a daughter-in-law is remarkable, but when have we ever been without people who become censors and proceed to act like women? The rare thing is a woman who becomes a censor. That would be enough to make everyone in this world who wears a scholar's hat and calls himself a man die of shame!"

25. GHOST-GIRL XIAOXIE

THE mansion of Ministry Secretary Jiang in Weinan[1] was haunted by a large number of supernatural beings that misled people. Because of this the Jiang family moved away, leaving an old man to watch the gate. This man died, as did several others that were sent to take his place, so the house was deserted. In the same neighborhood lived a scholar named Tao Wangsan, a carefree, self-assured sort, who enjoyed the companionship of courtesans but always left them when the drinking was over. Some friends had a courtesan follow him to his place. He let her in with a smile but did not lay a hand on her all night. Once while staying overnight at the secretary's mansion, he earned a high place in his host's estimation by firmly refusing the advances of a maid who went to him at night.

Tao lived in dire poverty. Moreover, he had just been bereaved of his wife, and his tiny thatched hut was unbearably hot in sweltering summer. For these reasons he asked the secretary if he might make use of the vacant mansion. The secretary refused because of the hauntings. This inspired the scholar to write an essay entitled "Further Arguments on the Non-Existence of Ghosts"[2] and present it to the secretary with the comment: "What can a ghost

[1] A district in Shaanxi.

[2] Several earlier writers had already tackled the same subject.

小謝
香葯双珠合道士何
亦術小奇

do to me?"

At last the secretary gave in to his determined requests, and the scholar went there to clean up and move into one of the rooms. At dusk he set down a book and went out to bring in some other things. When he came back the book was gone. Baffled by this turn of events, he lay quietly on his bed looking at the ceiling and waiting for what would happen next. After the duration of a meal he heard footsteps. Looking out of the corner of his eyes, he saw two young women coming from an inner chamber and replacing the missing book on the desk. One was about twenty and the other seventeen or eighteen. Both of them were beautiful. They walked hesitantly to the side of his bed and exchanged grins. The scholar kept quiet and did not stir. The older girl raised her foot and planted it on the scholar's belly: the younger one covered her mouth with her hand to stifle a giggle. The scholar felt himself wavering: he made a sober effort to straighten his thoughts and succeeded in turning his eyes away. The girl came closer and stroked his whiskers with her left hand as she patted his cheek with her right, which caused the younger to laugh all the more. The scholar leapt up and shouted, "How dare you ghosts behave this way?"

The two girls ran off in fright. The scholar feared they would bother him at night and wanted to move back home, but he felt ashamed not to back up his words with deeds, so he lit a lamp and stayed up reading. Spectral forms flitted about in the dark, but he did not ever glance at them. When it was almost the middle of the night, he went to bed with a candle burning. The minute his eyelids shut he felt someone poking a fine object into his nose. The exceedingly itching sensation was too much for him: he let loose with a mighty sneeze, which was answered by muffled laughter from a dark corner. Saying nothing, he pretended to be asleep and waited for them to try again. Soon he saw the younger girl roll a slip of paper into the shape of a toothpick and then come toward him, placing each foot carefully like crane and crouching like an egret. He leapt up and railed at her. She floated into hiding. Again he lay down, and this time she stuck something in his ear. He had to put up with these torments the whole night.

At cockcrow the sounds finally died down, and the scholar slept soundly. He saw and heard nothing of the girls all day, but at sundown they were there before he knew it. That night he started a cooking fire, intending to stay up until morning. The older girl gradually approached, leaned her forearm against the table and watched him read. Without warning she reached over and closed his book. He grabbed angrily at her, but she had already floated out of reach. A little while passed, and again she flipped it shut, so he pressed down on the book with his hands as he read. Before long the younger girl stole up behind him, put her hands over his eyes, darted away and stood at a distance giggling.

The scholar shook his finger at her and scolded, "You little imp! It will be all over for you when I catch you."

This did nothing to deter them, so he said playfully: "I don't know the first thing about riding young fillies in bed, so what's the use of pestering me?" The two girls grinned and turned toward the stove, where they set to work splitting firewood, rinsing rice and doing the cooking for him. He looked up and praised them: "Now isn't this better than the idiotic way you were acting?"

Soon the rice gruel was done, and they raced to set chopsticks, a spoon and earthenware bowl on the desk. "How can I show my gratitude for your helpfulness?"

"No need. We mixed arsenic and essence of falcon feathers with your rice."

"There has never been any ill-will between us," he said. "I don't think you would do that to me?" When his bowl was empty, they filled it again: they ran back and forth trying to outdo one another in helpfulness. He enjoyed their attentions and grew accustomed to them. As time passed they became more familiar, until one day he invited them to sit down for a talk and asked their names.

"My name is Qiurong and my surname is Qiao: she is Xiaoxie of the Ruan family," said the older.

When he inquired into their backgrounds, Xiaoxie said laughingly: "Silly man. Why should you ask about our families when you haven't shown your true feelings toward us. Are you thinking about marriage?"

"Do you think I am so unfeeling as to be unmoved by your beauty?" he asked earnestly. "But any man who is touched by dark, supernatural forces must die. If you don't like living with me, you can leave. If you like living with me, it's all right to stay. If you don't care for me, why should two nice girls like you lower yourselves? If you do have love in your heart, why would you wish to cause the death of a book-crazed scholar?"

Visibly moved, the two girls exchanged glances. From then on they were less forward in their playfulness. Still they sometimes slipped their hands under his shirt or pulled down his pants, but he did not let it bother him. One day he got up from a book he was in the middle of copying and went out. On his return he found Xiaoxie hunch over the desk, writing brush in hand, copying for him. Seeing him, she threw down the brush and laughed, looking at him with sidelong glances. He took a close look: her characters were too ill-formed to be called calligraphy, but the lines were evenly spaced.

"You are a woman of refinement," he praised her. "If you enjoy this, I'll teach you." He took her on his lap and guided her hand to show her how to make the strokes. When Qiurong came into the room her face fell abruptly, obviously out of jealousy.

Xiaoxie laughed and said, "I learned calligraphy from my father when I was little, but I haven't practiced for ages, so it feels like it's coming back to me in a dream." Qiurong said nothing. The scholar sensed what she felt but, pretending not to notice, he set her on his lap, handed her a brush and said, "Let me see if you can do it."

She wrote several characters and got up. "Miss Qiurong wields a mighty pen!" was his comment, which brightened Qiurong's face.

The scholar thereupon folded a piece of paper, tore it into halves and wrote model characters on each one for them to copy while he went to read under another lamp, secretly relieved that they would stop bothering him now they had something to keep them busy. When they were done copying, they stood respectfully before the desk waiting for his comments. Qiurong had never learned to recognize characters, and her scribbling was undecipherable. When he finished making a few offhand corrections, a humiliated look came over her face as she realized she was not Xiaoxie's rival, but the scholar's praise and reassurance finally cleared the clouds on her brow.

From then on the two girls treated the scholar as their teacher. When he sat they scratched his back; when he lay down they massaged his thighs. Far from affronting him, they vied to please. After a month Xiaoxie was writing in an unexpectedly neat and elegant hand, for which he occasionly praised her. Qiurong was sorely abashed: her rouge and mascara were streaked with trickling tears that would not stop until the scholar went to great lengths to reassure her. To make her feel better, he taught her to read and found her to possess remarkable powers of comprehension. Once he had pointed something out, she never needed to ask a second time. Often she stayed up all night trying to outread the scholar.

Xiaoxie also brought her third brother to bow before the scholar and become his student. He was fifteen or sixteen years old and well-favored in face and bearing. His gift to his teacher was an as-you-will sceptre of gold. The scholar assigned him the same classic that Qiurong was studying. Soon the hall was filled with reciting voices: the scholar had founded a private school for ghosts. The ministry secretary was delighted by the news of this and began to pay him a regular salary. After several months Qiurong and third brother were accomplished in poetry and frequently presented poems to each other. Xiaoxie secretly told the scholar not to teach Qiurong: he agreed not to. When Qiurong told him to stop teaching Xiaoxie, he assented to her too.

The day came when the scholar left to take part in an examination. The girls sniffed and tears ran down their cheeks as they said their farewells.

"Maybe you should ask to be excused from this examination on grounds of illness," said third brother. "Otherwise, I'm afraid you will land in an unfortunate predicament."

The scholar considered it degrading to ask for leave on account of illness, so he went anyway. Prior to this the scholar, who was fond of writing topical poems in a satirical vein, had offended a nobleman in the district, who brooded daily over how he could retaliate. He secretly bribed the civil examiner to have Tao thrown in prison on a trumped-up charge of misconduct. The scholar ran out of pocket money and was forced to beg for food from other prisoners. He had already resigned himself to death when suddenly a person appeared out of nowhere in his cell. It was Qiurong. She set dishes of food before him, gave him a long sorrowful look and quavered: "Third brother's fear that you would come to harm was well-founded. He and I came together: now he is going to the governor's *yamen* to lodge an appeal." She slipped out unnoticed after speaking only these few words.

The next day when the governor went out, third brother stopped him in the street crying "Injustice!" The governor agreed to read his appeal.

After appearing in the prison to let the scholar know of third brother's plan, Qiurong had gone back to watch the outcome. Three days went by without her showing up again. For the scholar, helplessness and the misery of hunger made each day pass like a year. Suddenly Xiaoxie appeared in his cell in great anguish and said, "On her way back Qiurong passed through shrine to the City-God. The Black Judge of the Western Corridor abducted her and tried to force her to be his chambermaid, but she would not give in, so now she too is in captivity. I ran the hundred *li* here so fast I nearly dropped. When I reached the northern wall the sole of my foot was punctured by a nasty thorn. The pain went right through to the marrow of my bones. I'm afraid I won't be able to come again." She showed him her foot covered with crimson blood, then pulled out three taels of gold, hobbled away, and disappeared.

Meanwhile the governor, having ascertained that third brother lacked even a tenuous relationship with the accused and was making an appeal for no good reason, ordered his men to beat him with staffs only to see him dive to the ground and disappear. The amazed governor read the written appeal which the strange visitant had just given him and was touched by the content and the manner of writing. He had the scholar brought out for questioning and asked "Who is this third brother?" The scholar pretended not to know. The governor realized the injustice of the sentence and released him.

The whole evening of the scholar's return passed without anyone coming. It was late in the night before Xiaoxie finally came and reported gloomily: "Third brother was seized by a corridor spirit in the governor's *yamen* and taken to the underworld court. The king of the underworld sent him to be reborn into a rich family in consideration of his commendable deeds. I submitted a statement to the city god speaking out against Qiurong's undue detainment, but the case was pigeonholed and I was not given an audience. Now what can I do?"

The scholar flew into a rage and spluttered, "Who does that black fiend think he is, taking liberties like this? Tomorrow I'm going to knock his image over and grind it to mud under my feet. While I'm at it I'll give that city god a piece of my mind for letting his underlings get out of hand like this. Is he off in some drunken dream or what?"

The two of them sat there sharing their indignation and sorrow. Before they knew it the fourth watch was nearly at an end. Suddenly Qiurong appeared out of thin air. When they had gotten over their joyful surprise, they pressed her to tell them all that had happened.

Tears ran down Qiurong's face as she said, "I suffered terribly because of you! The judge threatened me with knives and clubs every day, but today he suddenly let me go. He said, 'I only behaved as I did out of my tender feelings for you. But you were unwilling, and anyway I did not molest you. Please convey that fact to Tao, who is foreordained to be minister of punishments, and ask him not to reproach me.' "

The scholar was elated by this and found himself wishing he could sleep with her. "Today I want to die in your arms," he said.

The two women answered glumly: "Now that you have opened our eyes for us, we known a little something about right and wrong. We could not bear it if what we did to show our love caused you to die."

They persisted in refusing, but they submissively bowed their heads with wifelike tenderness. The difficulties they had gone through had completely done away with their feelings of jealousy.

One day as the scholar walked along the road he met a Taoist priest who turned to him and said, "You are giving off a ghost aura."

Because the Taoist's manner of speaking was so extraordinary, the scholar told him everything. The Taoist said, "These ghosts are too good to let down."

With this he wrote out two paper charms and gave them to the scholar, saying: "When you get home give one to each ghost, and let fate decide who will be the lucky one. The moment you hear a funeral procession for a young woman outside your gate, have the ghosts swallow the charms and run out. The one who gets there first will come to life."

The scholar took the charms with a bow, returned home and relayed the instructions to the girls. Sure enough, a little more than a month later they heard the sound of people mourning the death of a young woman in their family. The two girls raced to the spot. Xiaoxie was so flustered that she forgot to swallow her charm. As the hearse passed by, Qiurong ran straight to it, jumped into the coffin and disappeared. Xiaoxie, who was unable to find away in, sobbed miserably and turned back. The scholar went out for a look and found that it was a funeral procession for a daughter of the wealthy Hao family. Everyone present had seen a girl jump through the top of the coffin and disappear. Now, while they gaped in bewilderment, a voice was heard from within the coffin. The bearers took the coffin off their shoulders and opened it for a look. The girl had come back to life. They put her down outside the scholar's studio and formed a circle around her. The girl opened her eyes with a start and asked for the scholar. In response to Mr. Hao's questions she answered, "I am not your daughter."

Then she told him the truth, but this was not enough to convince Hao, who wanted to have her carried back to his house. The girl refused to go: instead, she darted into the scholar's studio, lay down, and would not rise. Whereupon Hao acknowledged the scholar as his son-in-law and left. The scholar went to her and took a good look: her features were different, but this face was a no less radiantly beautiful than Qiurong's own. This was a joyful blessing beyond his expectations. He was making an earnest declaration of his everlasting affection when they were interrupted by a muffled ghostly sobbing—it was Xiaoxie crying in a dark corner. Pitying her from the depths of his heart he picked up the lamp, walked over to her and spoke eloquent words of consolation. Still the sleeves and front of her blouse were soaked with tears, and nothing he said could relieve her misery. She did not leave until near dawn.

At daybreak Hao, every bit the new father-in-law, sent maids and serving women with dowry chests. That night when the scholar walked through the bedroom curtain, Xiaoxie started crying again. This went on every night for a week. Husband and wife were so affected by her dismal presence that they could not consummate their marriage. The scholar worried over the matter, but he could not come up with a solution.

"That Taoist priest is surely an immortal," said Qiurong. "If you go and plead with him, he might take pity on her and save her."

This seemed sensible to the scholar. He trailed the Taoist to where he was staying, kowtowed to him and stated his reason for coming. The Taoist protested that he had "no magical abilities," but the scholar would not give up his distraught pleading.

"This foolheaded scholar won't give a person a moment's peace. I suppose there is a bond of fate between us. All right, I'll do whatever lies within my power."

He went home with the scholar, asked for a quiet room and warned that he was not to be disturbed. Then he closed the door behind him and assumed a sitting position. For over ten days he did not eat or drink. Peeking in on him, they saw that he was deep in a trance. One morning as they were getting up a young woman parted the curtains and entered. The radiance of her bright eyes and gleaming teeth shone into their eyes.

"I've been trudging the whole night through," she said with a little laugh, "and now I am utterly worn out! You would not leave me alone, so I had to run myself ragged: I was a hundred *li* from here before I found a nice bodily dwelling. She is coming with the Taoist. When she shows up, he will turn her over to you."

As dusk closed in that evening, Xiaoxie appeared. The strange girl jumped up and ran to embrace her. Their outlines overlapped and then merged into a single body which fell stiffly on the floor. The Taoist came out of his room, joined his hands before his chest, and turned to leave. The scholar bowed to him and saw him off. When he came back in, the girl had regained consciousness. He helped her onto the bed. As she rested the circulation of vital energy through her body was gradually restored, but she clutched at her legs and moaned of sharp muscular pain in her feet and thighs. Several days passed before she was on her feet.

Later the scholar went up for examinations and won a place on the roster of prospective officials. A fellow examinee named Cai Zijing visited him on some matter or other and stayed several days. When Cai caught sight of Xiaoxie returning from next door, he ran over to her and practically trod on her heels. Xiaoxie turned away and ran from the room, seething inwardly at his rashness. Cai turned and unburdened himself to the scholar: "There is something on my mind which could be a shock to people who hear of it. Can I confide in you?"

The scholar questioned him until he let it out: "Three years ago my little sister died young. Two nights later her body disappeared. To this day this remains a mystery to me. I saw your wife just now, and I wonder how she came to bear such a startling resemblance to my sister?"

The scholar answered jokingly, "My wife is homely, how can she compare with your sister? But since you are my fellow candidate and my close friend, there could not be any harm in introducing my wife to you."

With this he entered the inner chamber and had Xiaoxie dress in her burial clothes to greet the guest.

"She really is my sister," Cai exclaimed in great astonishment. Tears began to run down his face. The scholar then told him the whole story. Cai howled gleefully: "My sister is still alive! I must hurry home and give my parents the comfort of knowing she is alive." And so he left. After a few days the whole family came, and afterward they exchanged visits with the scholar just as the Hao family did.

The Chronicler of the Tales comments: "To find one matchless beauty is no easy matter, not to speak of two at once! This is something that only happens once every few thousand years, and then only to a man who can keep himself from running off with whatever woman is available. Was the Taoist priest an immortal? What made his magic so powerful? With the right magic, hideous ghouls can be worth befriending."

26. THE INSPECTORATE OF MISDEEDS

WEN Rensheng of Henan had been laid up with an illness for days when a bachelor of letters appeared and kowtowed a deferential greeting at the foot of his bed. That done, he invited the scholar to go on a stroll. He took the scholar by the arm and chattered ceaselessly as they walked, but made no mention of leaving him even after they had gone a couple of *li*. The scholar stopped, joined his hands before his chest and said farewell.

"I must trouble you to keep walking," said the bachelor of letters. "I would like you to do a favor for me." The scholar asked what it was, and he answered, "People of my rank are all under the authority of the Inspectorate of Misdeeds. Its chief is called the Empty-Bellied Ghoul-King. When new subordinates have a first audience with him, the rules require that we offer him pieces of flesh cut form our thighs. May I impose on you to put in a good word for me."

"What crime have you committed that you must suffer this?" asked the scholar.

"One need not be guilty of a crime. This is an established precedent. Anyone who gives a generous bribe can buy his way out of it, but I am penniless."

"But I have never been connected in any way with the

考弊司
鬼名虚肚未前闻
考弊如何不考文
割肉竟容堂睹贖
不知可许肤抽筋
弊司
上中士下士一堂礼乐鬼门生
禮義廉恥
孝弟忠信

Ghoul-King. How can I help you?"

"In a former life you were of the same generation as his grandfather. He is likely to listen to you on that account."

What with all their talking, they were inside the walls of a city before they knew it. They came to a *yamen* housed in a none-too-spacious building, only the central hall of which was highroofed and roomy. At the foot of the raised hall, to the east and the west stood two stone tablets bearing green characters, each a square foot in size. One tablet read: "Filiality, fraternity, loyalty, faithfulness" and the other "Propriety, justice, honesty, honor." Walking up the entrance steps, they saw a plaque with the words "Inspectorate of Misdeeds" at the head of the hall. A couplet in malachite-tinted characters was carved on two opposing pillars: "Be they institutes, academies or schools, the essence of subterranean teaching is 'virtuous behavior': Be they superior, mediocre or inferior, the hall of music and etiquette educates ghostly disciples." Before they had finished looking the place over, an official whose frizzy hair and hunched back made him look hundreds of years old came toward them. His nostrils were turned up to the sky and his lips protruded, unable to contain his teeth. Behind him trailed a clerk in charge of files, who had a tiger's head and human body. Last of all came ten or so men who lined up in attendence, half of whom had the fierce ugliness of trolls.

"That is the Ghoul-King," said the bachelor of letters. The scholar recoiled in terror, but before he could get away the Ghoul-King caught sight of him, descended the steps, invited him into the hall with hands clasped obsequiously and inquired after his health. The scholar merely grunted in acknowledgement, whereupon the king asked, "To what do I owe the honor of this visit?"

The scholar answered by telling him exactly what the bachelor of letters had asked him to say. A displeased look came over the Ghoul-King's face as he said, "In a case like this, when there is a fixed rule to go by, I could not change things if my father ordered me to." He delivered these words with an icy finality that made pursuing the matter seem futile. Not daring to say another word, the scholar rose abruptly and asked to be excused. The Ghoul-King saw him all the way to the door, walking sideways.

Instead of going home, the scholar slipped back in to watch what happened. From the foot of the hall he saw the bachelor of letters and his fellows with their arms tied behind their backs and their fingers held tightly between torture clamps: obviously they had already been bound and trussed. A hideous man came out carrying a knife and proceeded to strip their thighs bare and slice off chunks of flesh three fingers in breadth. The bachelor of letter's shrieks trailed off into hoarse gurgling.

The scholar, being a young man with a sense of justice, could not help but shout in indignation: "What sort of world are you trying to create with such brutality?"

The Ghoul-King got up with a start, ordered a short halt to the slicing and strode menacingly in the scholar's direction. But the scholar stormed out, telling every townsman he met that he would bring an accusation before the Lord on High.

People jeered at him: "What a deluded fool! Where in the deep blue sky can you find a Lord on High to complain of injustice to? Officials like these are subject to no spirit but Yama. If you call upon him you may get a response."

With this they pointed out the road. The scholar hurried along it until he came to the steps of an imposing hall. He crouched on the steps before Yama's throne and cried out that a great wrong had been committed. Yama called the scholar forward and, after questioning him, immediately dispatched a number of ghosts carrying ropes and iron-tipped clubs. Before long the Ghoul-King and the bachelor of letters appeared. When Yama ascertained the truth of the case, he roared at the Ghoul king: "Out of consideration of your studiousness in your former life, I temporarily assigned you this post while you were on call for rebirth into a wealthy family. How dare you behave so shamelessly! It is my judgement that your sinews of goodness be removed and your bones of wickedness be increased. You are condemned to being a nonentity for endless lives to come!"

The ghosts caned the Ghoul-King until he toppled to the ground, knocking out a tooth. They cut off the tips of his fingers and pulled out white sinews that gleamed like silk. The Ghoul-King howled like a pig being butchered. When the strands had been drawn from his hands and feet, two ghosts led him away.

The scholar touched his forehead to the ground and went out, followed by the bachelor of letters, who was eager for a chance to show his gratitude. The latter took the scholar's arm and led him through a busy district, where they glimpsed a face of matchless beauty peeking from behind the crimson curtains of one of the buildings.

"Whose home is this?" asked the scholar.

"This is one of those 'back alley houses,'" said the bachelor of letters.

As they walked past the scholar, unable to tear himself away, insisted that the bachelor of letters leave him to himself.

"You came here for my sake," said the bachelor of letters. "I cannot bear to make you go back all by yourself."

He finally left when the scholar firmly refused his offer to accompany him farther. The scholar watched till he was out of sight, then lost no time going through the door curtain. The girl received him with obvious pleasure on her face. They entered a parlour and she sat down next to him, after which they introduced themselves.

"My surname is Liu, and I go by the name Qiuhua," offered the girl.

An old woman came to set out viands and wine. When they had drunk their fill they went behind bed curtains. Their lovemaking was of rare intensity, and they fervently vowed to become man and wife. The next morning the old woman came in and said, "I have nothing left to pay for household expenses. As much as I hate to speak out, I must ask the young gentleman for some money."

The sudden recollection that his pouch was empty plunged the scholar into guilty silence for an awkward interval before he answered, "To tell the truth, I didn't bring a single along. What I can do is write out a note of credit, which I will make good as soon as I get back home."

An ominous look came over the old woman's face as she snarled: "Have you ever heard of an overnight girl going to collect a debt?"

Qiuhua knit her brows in silence. The scholar stripped off his robe to serve for the time being as a guarantee of payment. The old woman held it up and jeered, "Ha! This doesn't even cover the wine!" She continued to gibber disappointedly as she led the girl from the room.

The scholar was mortified. Hours passed but still he waited, hoping that the girl would come back to bid him farewell and reaffirm her vow. More time went by without a sign of her. He stole toward the inner chamber and peered through a doorway: there were the woman and

Qiuhua, but from the shoulders up they had transformed into ox-demons. They stood there looking right at him, their eyes flashing fire. He ran outside in terror. He wanted to go home, but a hundred roads branched out in all directions. Which one should he take? He asked the people in the market, but nobody knew the name of his village. He wandered aimlessly among the stalls and shops for two days and two nights, his heart aching with loss and his hungry stomach rumbling complainingly. He could not make up his mind to go one way or another. It was then that the bachelor of letters passed by and happened to see him.

"Why haven't you gone home yet, and why are you dressed so scantily?" he asked in amazement. The scholar was too embarrassed to reply.

"I know!" exclaimed the bachelor of letters. "You got trapped by that seductive she-devil, didn't you?" With that he stormed off indignantly, shouting: "Qiuhua and Madame! Why don't you show regard for my friends any more?" He left for a little while, came back with the robe and gave it to the scholar, saying: "That sex-hungry chambermaid won't behave herself. I just gave her a piece of my mind." He accompanied the scholar home, then said goodbye and left. The scholar, who had died suddenly three days before, came back to life and told of these events in detail.

27. WEIRD DOVES

DOVES come in all shapes and sizes. Shanxi has its Earthstar, Shandong its Crane-Prime, Guizhou its Butterfly-in-Arms, Henan its Somerhop, Zhejiang its Tip-top: all are extraordinary varieties. Beyond that there are Boot-Heads, Specklets, Bigwhites, Blackrocks, Couplebirds, and Dappled-Dog-Eyes. There are more names than you can count on your fingers: it would take a trivia buff to keep track of them all. Zhang Youliang, son of a wealthy family in Zouping,[1] was inordinately fond of the birds. In collecting them he went by the *Book of Doves*: he was determined to exhaust the list of breeds therein. He nursed them as carefully as human infants. When they had colds he treated them with a powder made from dried grasses; if they became feverish he dosed them with salt pellets. Doves like to sleep, but if they sleep too much there is danger of death by paralysis. Zhang paid ten taels of gold in Guangling[2] for a dove of diminutive proportions that was a congenital 'walker.' Placed on the ground, it walked constantly in circles and, if it was not stopped, would walk itself to death. For this reason it often needed Someone to hold it. At night it was put in with the flock in order to rouse the other doves and keep them from catching numb-

1. In Shandong.
2. Yangzhou on north bank of the Yangtse.

leg disease, so it was named Night Walker. Nobody in all of Shandong rivalled young master Zhang in the art of keeping doves, and he was not adverse to telling people so.

One night as he sat in his study, a white-robed young man whom he had never seen in his life knocked and entered. When asked for his name, the young man answered, "A drifter's name would mean nothing to you even if you knew it. Word has reached me that your dove flock is the finest anywhere. This has been my lifelong pursuit too, and I would be glad for the chance to feast my eyes on your flock."

Zhang brought out every dove he had, and he had them in all the varied hues of clouds and satin. The young man laughed and said, "What I heard was not a lot of empty talk after all. I think it is fair to say that in dove-keeping you have left nothing undone. I too have brought along a couple of birds. Would you care to see them?"

Delighted, Zhang followed the young man outside. The shapes of things were indistinct in the shadowy moonlight, and the fields bare and desolate. Dread mounted in Zhang's heart. The young man pointed and said, "Please keep walking, my lodging is not far."

Several more steps brought them to a Taoist abbey, a building supported by only two front pillars. The young man took Zhang's hand and led him into the lampless gloom. He stood in the courtyard and made a cooing sound. Soon two doves appeared. They looked like normal doves with pure white feathers. They flew along the eaves, cooing and fighting, but with every swoop they turned a somersault. When the young man motioned to them with his arm, they flew away wing to wing. Then he puckered his lips and made a strange sound. Two more doves appeared. One was as big as a mallard, the other no bigger

鴿異
撮口何人作異穀
連翩双鴿鬬飛鳴
雁门貪雁真堪羡
不惜珍禽付鼎烹

than a fist. They perched on the steps and did a "crane dance." The large one stood with neck outstretched and wings spread to form a backdrop, making an elaborate series of sounds and hopping movements as if cueing the small one, which flew singing up and down the steps. Sometimes it perched on the large one's head, fluttering its wings like a swallow that has landed on a cat-tail leaf and making a sound as delicate and distinct as the ratatatat of a miniature drum, while the large one held out its neck without moving a feather. Their calls grew in intensity and took on the tones of chimes. The two of them sang together harmoniously, their rhythms in perfect counterpoint. At the end the small one flew into the air, and the large one turned over on its back and cooed to it.

Zhang kept sighing admiringly, humbled like a proud river as it first flows into the vast sea. He bowed with clasped hands and implored the young man to part with his treasures, but the young man refused. Zhang would not leave off his pleading. Finally the young man shooed the doves away and made the same cooing sound he had earlier. The two white doves came to his call. He caught them on his arm and said, "I guess these two will be a sort of gift, if you don't think too little of them."

Zhang took the doves and admired them closely. It seemed that the moonlight was shining into one perfectly transparent eye and out the other, changing to an amber color, as if there were nothing to obstruct its rays. In the center were black pupils as round as peppercorns. Lifting their wings, he found that the tissues beneath were translucent, making the entrails plainly visible. Zhang was tremendously impressed but, thinking that greater wonders might be in store for him, he went on devising ingenious pleas.

"There are still two varieties that I have not brought out for you. Now I'm afraid to let you look at them," said the young man.

Right in the middle of their vociferous discussion, Zhang's servants came in with hempstalk torches looking for their master. Turning back toward the young man, Zhang saw him change into a chicken-sized dove that flew straight into the clouds. Then he saw that the abbey and courtyard that had been there moments ago were gone. In their place was only a small tomb and two cypress trees. He and the servants gathered the doves into their arms and, started home, whewing with fright.

Zhang tried them on the wing, and they performed the same exotic maneuvers they had earlier. Though they were not the ultimate pair, they were, for this world, exceedingly rare, and so Zhang's love for them could not have been greater. After two years they had given birth to three females and three males. Not even the pleas of a relative could make him give one away.

But then a gentleman who was a high official and a close friend of his father's saw young Zhang one day and said, "How many doves do you have?"

Zhang mumbled evasively and withdrew. He suspected that the gentleman fancied his doves and thought of showing gratitude for the man's interest, but could not bring himself to part with one of his treasures. Then he thought that he must not rudely ignore the request of an elder. Not daring to respond with a normal dove, he chose two of the rare white doves and presented them in a cage, sure that this was a gift worth no less than a thousand taels of gold.

Later when he saw the gentleman he fairly glowed with pride, but the gentleman did not say so much as a word of thanks. Impatient for the compliment he expected, Zhang asked, "Weren't those fine little birds I sent you?"

"They were pretty juicy," was the answer.

"You had them cooked?"

"Yes."

Zhang could hardly believe it. "Those weren't normal doves. They were what is commonly called 'Tartar Doves'!"

The gentleman thought back for a moment and said, "There was nothing out of the ordinary about the flavor."

Zhang moaned in remorse as he went home. That night the white-robed young man came in a dream and berated him: "I entrusted my descendants to you because I thought you would take care of them. How could you throw such shining pearls into the darkness and let their lives come to a cruel end in a stewpot? Now I am going to lead my children away."

As soon as the words were out of his mouth he transformed into a dove. All of the white doves Zhang had raised followed it and flew chirping out of sight. In the morning he went to look: sure enough, all of them were gone. The remorse he felt was too great to bear: he began to give away his doves to his bosom friends. A few days later there was nothing left.

The Chronicler of the Tales comments: "Things always gravitate to where they are welcome. Thus Duke Xie liked dragons, so a real dragon came to his house. How much more true this is for scholars who like virtuous friends, and enlightened rulers who like virtuous ministers. But in the case of the 'stuff' which lines our pockets we find that the more eager we are for it, the less it gravitates toward us. From this we can see that it is greed, not foolishness, that arouses the wrath of ghosts and spirits."

A friend once presented some golden-red carp to the

young master Sun Yunian.[1] His family did not have any clever servants, so he had an old hired hand carry the fish over. When the old man reached the gate, he poured out the water and put the fish on a platter so that he could present it. By the time he reached sin's house, the fish had already breathed its last.

Seeing this, the young master Sun laughed but said nothing. He tipped the hired hand with some wine and immediately had the fish cooked and served to him. When the hired hand returned, his master asked, "Was young Sun happy to get the fish?"

"Very happy," was the answer.

"How do you know?" asked the master.

"As soon as he saw the fish, he broke into a pleased smile. He ordered wine to be served and had several of the fish cooked up as a reward for my services."

The master was astonished. He reflected that his gift was not at all bad, so why would young Sun have cooked it as a reward for an underling? He scolded the hired hand, saying, "You must have behaved stupidly and impolitely or the young master would not have taken out his anger on the fish."

"I may be uncouth," the hired hand vigorously defended himself with animated gestures, "but I'm not thoughtless. When I got to the young master's gate, I was as careful as could be. I worried that a nobody like me would not be elegant enough to do the job, so I respectfully sought out a platter and, after lining the fish up neatly on it, I sent them in. What did I leave out? Being less than circumspect?"

[1] From the same town as Pu Songling, he later became a district magistrate in Hebei. See the following story.

The master cursed the hired hand and dismissed him.

A monk at the Temple of Hidden Mystery was famous for his tea. All the equipment he used to process the tea was of the highest quality, but the tea that he grew was of several grades. He would always judge the rank of his guests when brewing tea for them. His best was reserved solely for the most esteemed guests and connoisseurs.

One day a high official came. The monk treated him with utmost deference and respect. He brought out fine tea which he steeped and served to the guest by himself. Though he eagerly waited for some commendation, the honored official remained silent. The monk was deeply puzzled so he proceeded to steep and serve his top quality product. When the guest had nearly finished the tea, he still had not uttered a word of praise. The monk was so agitated that he could wait no longer. "How was the tea?" he asked with a bow. Raising the cup in his hands, the honored official replied, "Very hot!"

Just like the story of young master Zhang's gift of doves, these two incidents are good for a laugh.

28. THE CITY ON THE MOUNTAIN

THE "city on the mountain" at Mt. Huan is one of the eight scenic wonders of my district, but it is usually not seen for years at a time. Young master Sun Yunian and his companions were drinking in a pavilion when they suddenly noticed a lone pagoda standing high on the mountain and towering into the deep blue sky. They looked at one another in bewilderment. They knew there was no such monastery anywhere in the area. Before long scores of palace buildings with green-glazed tiles and high roof ridges appeared: at last they realized that it was the "city on the mountain." Soon they saw a high wall with battlements extending for six or seven *li*—the city wall, obviously. Inside it the shapes of what appeared to be storied buildings, halls, and lanes by the tens of thousands could be discerned. Suddenly a great wind blew up clouds of dust that hid the city in obscurity. After the wind settled down and the sky cleared, all was gone but the single lofty tower that touched the very clouds. Five shuttered windows were wide open on each story, and the light of the sky shining through from the other side made lines of five bright spots. By counting the lines, one could count the stories. The farther up the tower, the less light shone through. By the eighth story they were no bigger than stars: above that they were there and yet not there in the twilight, going an uncountable number of stories farther up. People were coming and going busily on the tower, while some leaned or stood, all in different poses. After a while, the tower grew lower and the top became invisible. Gradually it diminished into a regular storied building, then to the size of a tall house, and then quickly into something the size of a fist, then a bean, till finally it dwindled to nothing. I have also heard that an early morning wayfarer once saw habitations and market shops on the mountain that were no different from those of this world, for which reason the apparition was also named the "city of ghosts."

山市
山市將無海市同
蜄垣宮闕望玲瓏
大風吹後危樓在
笑指煙雲縹緲中

29. FAIRY QING-E

HUO Huan, alias Kuangjiu, was a native of Shanxi. His father, a onetime district garrison commander, had died young. Huo Huan, the youngest survivor, possessed intellectual powers that outshone his peers. His precocity gained him admission to the government academy at the age of eleven. However, his mother was excessively protective and would not allow him to leave the house. At thirteen he still could not distinguish between his paternal and maternal uncles and nephews. In the same neighborhood lived Assessor Wu, a man with a penchant for Taoism, who went into the mountains and never came back. His fourteen-year-old daughter Qing-E was beautiful beyond compare. As a child she had secretly read her father's books and come to admire the deeds of Fairy-Mistress He. After her father left to be a hermit, she resolved not to marry. Her mother was forced to respect her wishes.

One day Huo Huan caught sight of her outside her door. Though he was an adolescent with no understanding of these matters, he was sure of one thing, and that was the surge of longing he felt for her, which he could not express in words. He went straight to his mother and asked her to send gifts of betrothal to the Wus. His mother, knowing it was hopeless, was reluctant. The student could no longer feel at peace within himself and lapsed into frustration. His mother, afraid to cross his wishes, asked a frequent visitor

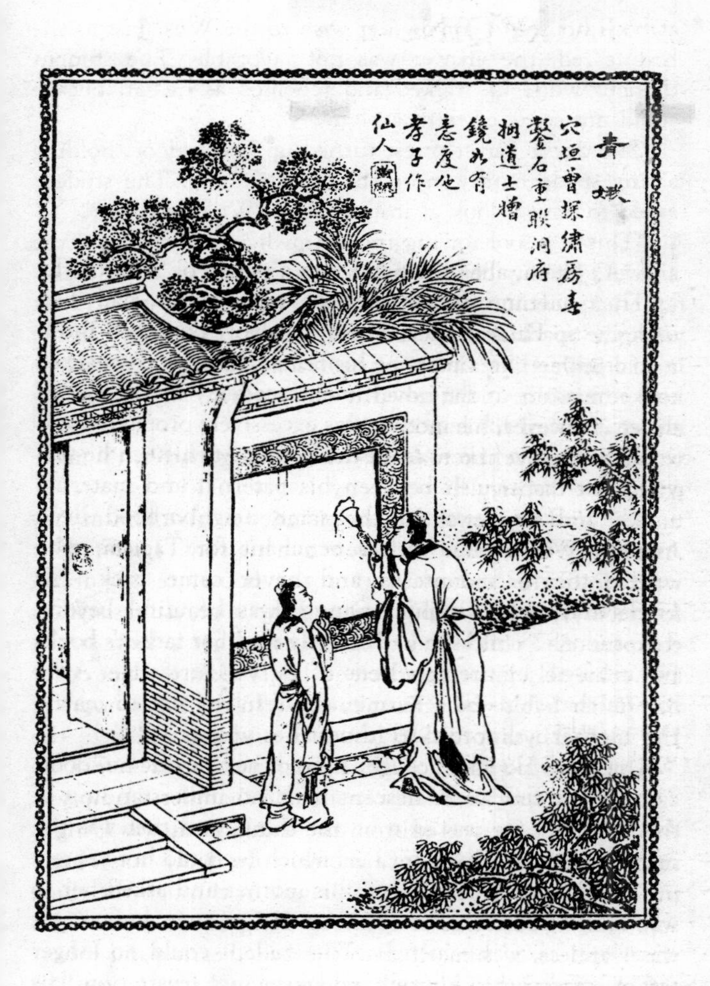
青娥
穴垣曾探綉房春
鑿石重聯洞府
擲道士贈
鑱原有
意度他
孝子作
仙人

at both houses to convey her wish to the Wus. Just as she had feared, the answer was not favorable. The student thought while he walked and schemed as he sat, but he could not come up with a plan.

One day a Taoist priest turned up at the door, holding a tiny spade hardly more than a foot long. The student asked to have a look at it and asked "What is it for?"

"This is a tool for digging up medicinal roots," was the answer. "It may be small, but it can penetrate solid rock."

The student was incredulous, whereupon the Taoist took the spade and hacked at a stone in the wall, causing it to crumble like a piece of curd. The dumbstruck student took the spade and fondled it every which way, unwilling to let it out of his hands.

"Since you've taken a fancy to it, young master, I'll make you a present of it."

The student was overjoyed and tried to give him money for it, but he refused and went on his way. The student carried the spade back toward the house, testing it on bricks and rocks without meeting the slightest resistance. The thought struck him that he could get a look at the beautiful girl by boring a hole in her wall: it did not occur to him that this was against the law. In the quiet hours of the night he slipped over the wall and proceeded to the Wu manor. He had to dig through two walls before he came to the courtyard. In a small side chamber a lamp was still burning. He peered from the shadows: it was Qing-E getting ready for bed. In a moment the lamp was blown out and all was still. He dug his way in through the thick wall and found the girl fast asleep. He gingerly took off his shoes and eased himself onto the bed. Fearing the inhospitable reception the young woman would surely give him if she were roused, he slid over only as far as the edge of her embroidered coverlet. Faint inhalations of her aroma were enough to soothe the pangs in his heart. Utterly worn out from half a night of exertions, he let his eyelids droop a bit and, before he knew it, he was asleep.

The girl awoke to the measured sounds of air being expelled through someone else's nostrils. Opening her eyes, she saw light coming through a hole in the wall. This frightened her greatly: she jumped up, fumbled for the bolt in the dark and quietly went out. She knocked at a window and called to the women servants. Torches were lit and staffs were taken up as she and the servants went back to her room. There they saw a young student in a topknot sleeping soundly on the embroidered bedspread. Closer inspection proved him to be Huo Huan. When pushed he awoke and jumped up with a crazed gleam in his eyes. He gave little sign of being apprehensive, but remained awkardly silent. The servants called him a burglar and shouted threats at him. Finally he began sniffling and said, "I am no burglar. Honestly, it was because I love the young lady and wanted to be next to her fragrance."

The servants did not believe that a boy could have tunneled through several walls. The student pulled out the spade and told them of its marvelous power. They tried it and were so shocked by what they saw they believed it must have been the gift of a supernatural being. They were about to go to tell the mistress of the house, but the girl lowered her head pensively, as if she wished otherwise. The servants, surmising what was on her mind, said, "This boy's reputation and family background certainly would not dishonor you. Better to let him go and have him send another go-between. In the morning we'll tell the Missus it was a burglar. What do you think?"

The girl did not answer. The servants told the student

to be on his way. He asked to have his spade. Everyone laughed: "You little fool! You don't want to leave the tool of your trade behind, do you?"

The student glanced down beside the pillow and saw a phoenix hairpin, which he slipped into his sleeve, but not before a maid saw what he was doing. She told the girl, who said nothing, and showed no anger. One serving old woman patted him on the neck and said, "Don't let that silly look on his face fool you: he knows well enough what he's up to."

They led him away, and he went out through the holes in the walls where he had come from. Back home, he dared not tell his mother everything, so he merely asked her to send another go-between. His mother, who could not bear to refuse him bluntly, merely asked all the local go-betweens to find some other likely prospect quickly.

Learning of this made Qing-E chafe with anxiety. She sent her confidante to drop a hint to Huo's mother. The old woman, glad for the new development, sent a go-between to the Wus. But right about that time a serving maid let out word of the previous incident. Madame Wu was enraged at the news of this dishonor. The coming of a go-between at such a time goaded her into even greater fits of anger. Striking her staff on the ground, she reviled the student and even threw in a few curses at his mother. The frightened go-between slunk back to the Huos and told of the reception she had met. The student's mother, too, flew into a passion: "I don't have the slightest idea what that idiotic son of mine has done. But why does she have to add insult to injury? Why didn't she have my debauched son and that little tart of hers killed together while they were in the act?"

From then on she told her relatives the whole story

every chance she got. The girl felt like dying for shame when she heard of this. Madame Wu terribly regretted causing this to happen, but she could not stop Mrs. Huo from talking. The girl secretly sent someone to convey her wish to the student's mother, along with her own vow never to love another. It was a soul-stirring message, and the mother was touched by it. She left off spreading vicious stories, but by this time neither side wanted to pursue plans for the marriage.

At that time a certain Master Ou of Shaanxi, who was serving as district magistrate, read the student's essays. He had a high opinion of the boy's potential, often invited him to his private chambers, and did all he could to see the boy got the best of everything. One day he asked the student: "Are you married?"

"Not yet."

To more specific questions the boy replied, "At one time I had an understanding with the daughter of Assessor Wu, but owing to a slight discord it was left up in the air."

"Do you still want her?" asked the magistrate. The student was too embarrassed to reply.

"I'll fix everything for you," said the magistrate with a laugh. Then he told the district garrison commander and the superintendant of education to send silk and jade to the Wus as gifts of betrothel. This made Madame Wu happy, and soon the engagement was finalized.

A year later the girl was brought to her husband's home. As soon as she came in, she threw down the spade and said "Get this burglar's tool out of my sight!"

"Don't act so ungratefully toward our go-between," laughed the student. He wore it everyday dangling from his sash like a precious pendant.

The girl was good-hearted but quiet. Aside from paying

her respects to her mother-in-law three times a day, she spent her time sitting in silence behind closed doors and did not give much attention to household affairs. Once in a while the mother would go away to a funeral, wedding or birthday, in which case the girl would take charge and set everything in order. After little more than a year she gave birth to a son named Mengxian, whom she entrusted completely to the care of a nursemaid. She gave few signs of fondness for the child.

After four or five more years she said to the student one day out of the blue: "The bond of love has kept us together for eight years. Now I foresee a lifelong parting and only a short time of togetherness remaining. Ah well, there is nothing we can do!"

The student plied her with bewildered questions, but she lapsed into silence. She put on her finest clothes, went to kowtow to his mother, then turned and went back to her room. He chased after her, demanding to know what she meant, only to find her lying face up in bed, her breathing already stopped. Mother and son mourned her bitterly. A coffin of fine wood was bought for the burial.

As she held the baby and thought of its mother, the old woman, already burdened by advanced age, felt pain tearing through her vitals. She contracted an illness and became too feeble to rise. Food and drink tasted revolting to her, but she thought continually of fish broth. No fish were available in the vicinity: the closest place they were to be had was over a hundred *li* away, and all the servants who could ride happened to be off on errands. But the student's devotion to his mother made him too anxious to wait. Taking some money with him, he set out alone, making the whole trip without stopping day or night. On the way back he found himself in the middle of the mountains as the sun sank and twilight came. His legs ached too much to go another step. Then an old mountain man appeared and asked, "Do you have blisters on your feet?"

The student said yes. The old man took his arm and had him sit by the side of road. Then he struck two stones together to make a fire and fumigated the student's feet by heating a paper package of powder over the fire. He had the student try walking: not only was the pain gone, there was even an added springiness to his steps. He told the old man he was deeply grateful.

"And what makes you run about so frantically?" asked the old man. The student answered first by telling him of his mother's illness, and then with an account of everything that had led up to it.

"Why don't you marry again?" asked the old man.

"I haven't found the right woman," was the answer.

The old man pointed to a mountain village in the distance, saying, "There is a fine young woman over there. If you will follow me there, I'll put in a word for you."

The student refused, saying that his sick mother was waiting for fish and he had no time to spare just now. The old man saluted him and assured him that if he ever did go to that village, he need only ask for Old Wang. With that he said goodbye and walked off.

The student returned home, cooked the fish and served it to his mother. With this nourishment in her system she bounced back to health in a few days.

That settled, he called for his servant and horse and started out in search of the old man. He came to the place they had met, but now he could not find a trace of the village. Time passed as they combed the area, until the evening sun began to drop over the horizon. The valley was so thickly grown it was impossible to see the length of it, so he and his servant separated to climb different peaks and see whether they could spot any settlements. The mountain path was too rugged to negotiate on horseback, so the student climbed to the top on foot. By this time the valley was veiled in the mists of twilight. Pacing back and forth, he looked in all directions: there was no village to be seen. He was ready to go down the mountain, but the road back was lost in gloom. Agitation burned like a fire within him. He began thrashing about, and blindly fell over the edge of a sheer cliff. Luckily, the merest sliver of a ledge covered with thick weeds broke his fall a few feet below. The ledge was only wide enough to hold his body: below was bottomless blackness. The student was so frightened of another fall that he dared not stir. By luck there were saplings growing up from the face of the cliff that held him like a railing. After a time he discovered, to his heartfelt joy, the mouth of a small cave next to his feet. Keeping his back pressed against the rock, he shifted position and wormed his way in. As his mood grew calm, he began to hope that the sound of his calls would bring help in the morning. Peering into the cave, he soon made out sparks of light in its depths. He proceeded three or four *li* inward, gradually approaching them. Suddenly he saw covered walkways and buildings before him. There were no lamps or candles, yet the place was bright as day. a beautiful woman came out of one of the houses: one look told him it was Qing-E.

She was shocked to see him: "How did you get here?"

The student wasted no time on explanations. He took hold of her sleeve and sobbed miserably. The girl consoled him till he was calm, and then asked of his mother and their son. The student told her how they had suffered, and the girl herself grew sad.

"You died over a year ago," he said. "This is the underworld, isn't it?"

"No, it isn't. This is the grotto of the immortals. I did not die then. What you buried was only a transformed bamboo pole. Your coming means we are fated to be immortal together." Then she led him away to pay a visit to her father--a long-bearded old man who sat at the head of a hall. The student hurried forward and kowtowed to him.

"Master Huo has come," the girl informed her father.

The old man rose in surprise, took the student's hand and spoke briefly of his past. "It's wonderful that you've come, son, you deserve to stay here."

The student declined, saying that he could not stay long because his mother was waiting. "I thought as much," said the old man. "But there won't be any harm in your lingering here a couple of days.

He treated the student to wine and dishes of food, then ordered a maid to get a bed ready in the west hall and cover it with a satin quilt. When they withdrew, the student asked the girl to sleep with him.

She refused, saying: "What makes you think you can behave lecherously in a place like this?" The student grabbed her arm and would not let her go. The snorting giggles of a maid outside the window perturbed the girl even more. She was struggling to free herself when the old man walked in and spat out: "Your vulgar carcass is soiling my grotto! Get out now!"

The hot-tempered student could not bear to be shamed. A scowl came over his face, and he retorted: "Love between husband and wife is only natural. Why should an elder like you make it your business to peep at us? I'm going all right, but you must let your daughter go with me." The father had nothing to say against it: he instructed his daughter to go along, then opened the back door to see them out. When he had fooled the student into walking out first, father and daughter slammed the door behind them.

The student turned to see jagged rocks and a sheer cliff-face without the tiniest crack. There was nothing before him but his own forlorn shadow; he had nowhere to go. The crescent moon had climbed high in the sky, and the stars were few and far between. For a long while he was plunged in despair, until his brooding changed to anger. He turned to the wall and howled, but there was no response. In a fit of rage, he grabbed the spade that hung at his waist and laid into the rock, cursing with every stroke. In a flash he had made an opening three or four feet deep. He could hear a muffled voice saying "Damn him!" This roused him to dig even more frantically. Suddenly the inside of the tunnel sprung open like a two-leaved door, and Qing-E was pushed out with the words: "Go ahead!" The cliff-face closed back together.

"If you love me as a wife, how could you treat your father-in-law this way?" said the girl accusingly. "I'd like to know where the old Taoist came from who gave you this burglar's tool so you could pester me to death!"

Now that he had found her, the student was content and offered no argument. He was wondering how they would find their way home over the rugged terrain. The girl broke a stick into two halves, and each of them straddled one. The sticks transformed into horses that skimmed over the ground. In a flash they were home.

By that time the student had been missing for seven days. At first the servant had gotten separated from him and, after an unsuccessful search, returned to tell his mother. She sent men to comb the entire valley, but they failed to find a trace of him. Just when she was beginning to fear the worst, she heard her son arriving and went joyfully out to greet him. When she took her eyes off him and looked up, the sight of her daughter-in-law gave her a rude shock, but this turned to delight and relief once the student had given a brief explanation.

Concerned that her strange actions might give rise to fearful rumors, the girl asked to move out of the area. This the mother granted. Before long they set out on their journey unknown to anyone, bound for an estate the family kept in another prefecture. There they lived together for eighteen years and gave birth to a daughter, who married into the Li family of that district.

After this the mother died of old age. Then Qing-E said to the student. "In the pasture on our land there is a pheasant's nest with eight eggs that marks a good burial site. You and Mengxian take the casket to the grave. Since he is already grown up now, it is all right for him to stay to mourn in the hut by the grave. There is no need for him to come back with you." The student followed her instructions by returning alone after the burial.

A little over a month later, Mengxian went to visit his parents, but they had disappeared. He asked an old servant and was told: "They never came back from the burial." Mengxian knew that something unnatural had happened, but all he could do was heave a long sigh.

Mengxian made quite a name for himself as a writer, but the examination cell was a barrier he could not break through. By age forty, he still was not successful. Finally he was admitted as a senior licentiate to the provincial examinations held in Peking prefecture. There he met and was attracted to seventeen-or-eighteen-year old scholar assigned to the same block as himself who was clever and carefree in manner. He looked at the young man's examination paper and found that it was marked Fellow Huo Zhongxian of Shuntian prefecture (Peking). His eyes grew wide in astonishment as he told the other his own name. Zhongxian too, thought this was strange and wanted to know his native place. Mengxian told him everything.

Zhongxian exclaimed delightedly: "When I left for the capital my father told me that if I were to meet someone named Huo from Shanxi he would be of my own clan and I should receive him accordingly. Now things have turned out just as he said! But how do you explain our names being so similar?"

Mengxian, after questioning the other on the family and given names of his great-grandparents, grandparents, and parents, exclaimed, "Those are my parents!" The disparity of age made Zhongxian dubious, but Mengxian said, "Our father and mother are both immortals. Their age cannot be taken at face value." Only when he had related all that had gone before was Zhongxian convinced. After the examination Zhongxian called for a carriage and they set out together for his home without a moment's delay. The servants met them at the gate with the news that the master and mistress had been missing since the night before. The two of them were dumbfounded. Zhongxian went in to get an explanation from his wife.

"I had a cup of wine with them just last night," said the wife. "Mother said 'You and my son are still not dry behind the ears, but I won't worry now that his older brother is coming here tomorrow.' I went to their room early this morning, but it was deserted." They brothers stamped their feet in disappointment when they heard this. Zhongxian was all in favor of going off in search of them, but was dissuaded by Mengxian, for it would do no good.

The outcome of the examination was a provincial recommendation to the palace examination for Zhongxian. Since his ancestor's tombs were in Shanxi, he returned there with his brother. Still hoping that his parents remained in the human world, he made inquiries wherever he went, all without turning up a sign of them.

The Chronicler of the Tales comments: Tunnelling into a bedroom was a bit of lover's foolishness. Drilling through a wall to curse a loved one's father was the act of a maniac. An immortal brought the two together nevertheless, so that a son's devotion to his mother could be rewarded with everlasting life. But seeing that Qing-E mingled her tracks with humans and lustfully gave birth to children, why not just stay on and come to a natural end? And how could she get away with abandoning her children repeatedly over a period of thirty years? Strange!"

30 HU FOURTH-MAIDEN

CHENG Xiaosi of Jiannan[1] was a precocious literary talent. His parents died when he was young, leaving him destitute. Having no means to provide himself with food and clothing, he applied for service under Commissioner Hu of the Memorial Screening Board. Master Hu gave him an essay topic to write on and was greatly pleased with result.

"This one won't be poor for long," he said. "He would make a good husband for my daughter."

Marriages with noble families had been arranged for all of Commissioner Hu's three sons and four daughters while they were still in swaddling clothes. Only the youngest daughter Fourth-Maiden, born by a concubine who had died when the girl was young, had reached hairpin age without anyone asking for her hand, so Hu brought Cheng into the family as a son-in-law. Some derided this as the brainless decision of a senile man, but Master Hu paid them no heed. He cleared a suite of rooms to accommodate the scholar and furnished it handsomely. All the commissioner's sons despised their new brother-in-law and would not eat at the same table with him. Every one of his servants and maids made fun of him. The student did not waste words on petty conflicts, but only read and studied

1. A district in Sichuan.

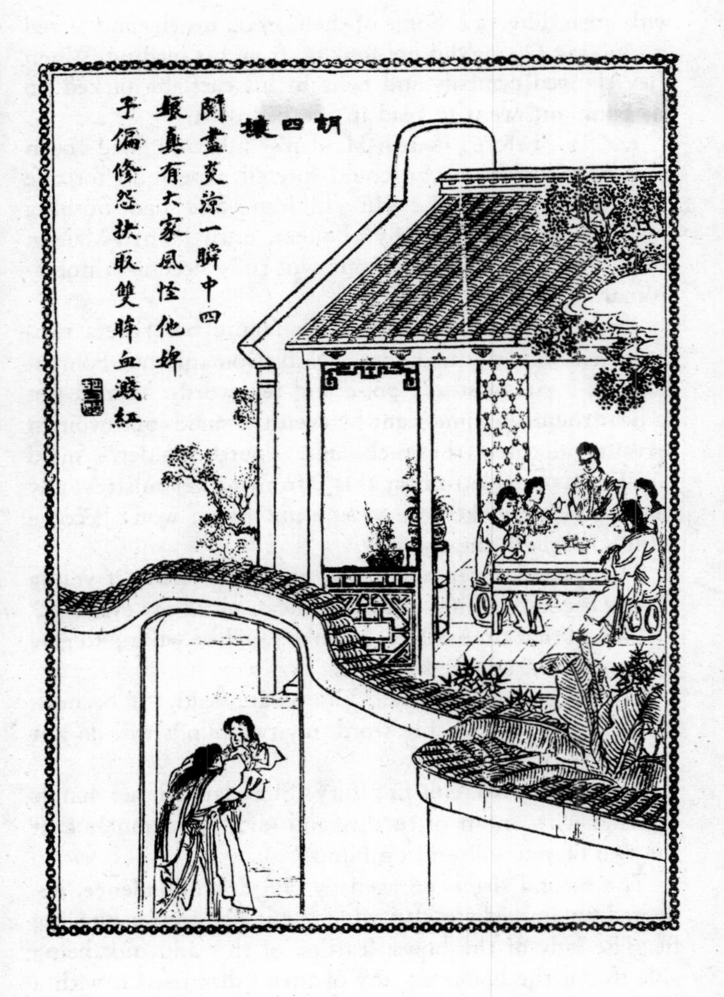
胡四娘
鬭盡炎涼一瞬中四
娘真有大家風怪他婢
子偏修怨抉取雙眸血濺紅

with great diligence. Some of them stood nearby and jeered at him, but Cheng did not look up from his reading. When they clanged cymbals and bells in his ears, he picked up his book and went to read in the bedroom.

Earlier, before Fourth-Maiden's husband had been chosen, a sorcerers who could foretell a person's fortune had looked at all the Hu children. She had nothing favorable to say about any of them, until Fourth-Maiden came, when she said "This one will truly become a noblewoman."

After Cheng married into the family her sisters ridiculed her with the nickname "Noblewoman," but Fourth-Maiden, a girl of steady poise and few words, seemed not to hear them. As time went by even the maids and woman servants all used the nickname. Fourth-Maiden's maid Gui-Er was unable to bear this affront to her mistress any longer. "What makes you so sure my master won't become a high official?" she shouted.

The second sister heard this and snickered: "If young Cheng becomes a high official, you can pluck my eyes out!"

"When that time comes, I doubt you'll be willing to give up your eyes," stormed Gui-Er.

The second sister's maid Chunxiang said, "If Second-Maiden goes back on her word, my two pupils will do just as well."

This redoubled Gui-Er's fury. She clapped her hands together with an air of finality and said, "I guarantee that the two of you will end up blind!"

The second sister, enraged by Gui-Er's impudence, delivered an immediate slap which sent her into a howling fit. The lady of the house learned of this and, not being able to put the blame on any of them, dismissed it with a chuckle. Gui-Er stridently aired her grievance to Fourth-

Maiden, who was busy weaving. Fourth-Maiden showed no anger and said nothing, but calmly went on weaving.

Then it came time for Master Hu's birthday jubilee. All his sons-in-law came, and their congratulatory gifts filled the courtyard. The wife of the eldest brother sneered at Fourth-Maiden, saying: "And what was the congratulatory gift from your branch of the family?"

"Two shoulders carrying a mouth!" said the second brother's wife. Fourth-Maiden remained unruffled and did not betray the slightest sign of embarrassment. Seeing that she responded to everything like a simpleton, they treated her with greater insolence. Only the master's beloved concubine Lady Li, the mother of the third sister, behaved respectfully toward Fourth-Maiden and offered her sympathy and affection.

She often said to the third sister: "Fourth-Maiden is unassuming on the outside and brilliant on the inside. Her intelligence enters into everything she does, so she doesn't make a show of it. All the maids are under her sway without even knowing it. What is more, young Cheng studies himself ragged night and day. Does he look like the sort to remain on the bottom for long? Don't you get caught up in the others' mistakes. Be nice to them, and someday they will look on you favorably."

And so every time the third sister came home on visits to her parents, she did her best to make her half-sister feel good.

This same year Cheng gained admission to the district academy on the strength of the commissioner's influence. The next year the old man died just when the civil examiner was evaluating candidates. Cheng mourned him like a son and was thus unable to take part in the examination. When the period of mourning was over,

Fourth-Maiden gave him money to have his name entered on the "Neglected Talent Examination" roll, and at the same time she warned him: "We were only able to stay here this long without being hounded out because my father was here. Now there is no way they will let us stay! If you can show the stuff you're made of, there is a good chance you will have a home to come back to."

Just before he left, Lady Li and the third sister invested in his future with generous presents of cash. Cheng racked his brains in the examination cell, determined to win at all costs, but the results posted afterward listed him among the eliminated candidates. He could hardly return home with his hopes dashed and spirits lagging. Fortunately there was a little left over in his purse, so he packed his books and headed for the capital. At that time many of his wife's relatives were holding office there. Fearing their ridicules, he adopted a new name, lied about his native place and sought shelter under some powerful figure. Grand Historian Li of Donghai[1] realized that he showed promise and so brought him into his personal office, provided him with lamp-oil and firewood and paid his entry fee for the Shuntian[2] prefectural examination. He emerged victorious from several tests in a row and was awarded the title of "scholar of promise." At long last he brought the truth out in the open. Master Li lent him a thousand taels of gold and sent his steward ahead to Jiannan to help him set up a household. It happened that Hu's eldest son, his coffers empty after his father's death, had put his best property up for sale, and this was the estate that the steward bought for Cheng. This accomplished, he arranged for a horse and

1. A district in the province of Jiangsu.
2. Former name of Beijing (Peking).

carriage to fetch Fourth-Maiden.

Somewhat earlier, after Cheng had passed his doctoral examination, the whole house heard with displeasure the announcement of this news by post messenger but, finding the name of the victorious examinee was none they knew, they hooted the messenger away.

Now the third brother was in the midst of celebrating his marriage with relatives gathering in the hall for the occasion. All the sisters and aunts were there: only Fourth-Maiden had received no invitation from her brother and sister-in-law. Suddenly a man ran in with a letter for Fourth-Maiden from Cheng. The brothers opened and read it, then stared at one another, their faces gone pale. Only then did the relatives at the banquet ask to see Fourth-Maiden. The sisters shuddered at the thought that Fourth-Maiden might not come because she bore them a grudge.

Before long she made her entrance, fine and fancy-free. The hall rang with congratulations, offers to be seated and ingratiating chatter. Everyone's ears were pricked up to Fourth-Maiden's words; all eyes were turned her way; and all mouths could talk of none but her. Yet Fourth-Maiden was as placid as always. Seeing that she was not in a mood to make trouble with anyone, they all felt somewhat relieved and vied with one another to drink her health. In the middle of their revelry a shrill scream was heard from outside. While everyone wondered what was happening, Chunxiang ran in suddenly, her face smeared with blood. They tried to pry the truth out of her, but her only answer was to keep crying. When the second sister roared angrily at her, she finally burst out sobbing: "Gui-Er came after me to get my eyes. If I hadn't gotten away, she would have plucked them out!"

The second sister was so mortified that her makeup ran down in beads of trickling sweat, but Fourth-Maiden did not betray any emotion. All around the table there was a wordless stillness, until the guests took their leave. Fourth-Maiden put on her best finery, made a parting bow to Madame Li and her third sister alone, went out the gate and climbed into a carriage that had come for her. Now it dawned on everyone that the man who had purchased the estate was Cheng.

When Fourth-Maiden first arrived at the estate, she was short of household articles. Madame Hu and her sons presented her with maids, servants, and furniture, all of which she refused, except for a maid from Lady Li.

Later, Cheng returned on tomb-visiting leave accompanied by a swarm of carriages and retainers. He called at his in-laws' house, bowed before his father-in-law's coffin and then visited Lady Li. By the time his brothers-in-law had donned their formal wear to greet him, he had already climbed into his carriage.

Following Master Hu's death, his sons had been too busy bickering over his assets to give a thought to his coffin. After a few years the shelter over the preburial resting place had given way to the elements; the once ornate structure turned into a burial mound.[1] Cheng was pained by the sight of this. Without so much as mentioning the matter to his brothers-in-law, he immediately made arrangements for a burial which would be proper in every respect. On the day of the funeral the continuous stream of distinguished guests drew admiring gasps from the neighborhood.

[1] Allusion to a line from a poem by Cao Zhi (192-232) lamenting the vicissitudes of life.

For more than ten years Cheng pursued an irreproachable political career, never failing to do his utmost for people from his home district who were in distress. Then the second brother was seized on a murder charge. The inspector appointed to handle the case had passed the examination the same year as Cheng. He was a man of strict principles. The eldest brother asked his father-in-law, Circuit Intendent Wang, to write a letter for him but, much to his dismay, it did not produce the slightest response. Wanting to ask Fourth-Maiden for help but realizing that he had no claim to her favor, he went to visit her with a letter from Lady Li in his hand. Once in the capital he was afraid to show himself right away. He watched until Cheng left for the audience, and then paid his call, hoping that Fourth-Maiden would be moved by blood ties to forget the disdain they had shown her. After the doorman had announced his arrival, an old serving woman came out and led him to a parlor where wine and food were perfunctorily set out for him. When he was finished Fourth-Maiden came into the room, her face bearing an expression of kindness and repose, and asked, "Your work keeps you very busy, Elder-Brother. Where did you find the time to come this far to honor us with a visit?"

The eldest brother threw himself at her feet and sobbingly recounted the reason for his coming. Fourth-Maiden helped him to his feet and laughed: "Is this matter so serious that a big strong man should work himself into such a state, Elder-Brother? I belong to the weaker sex, but how many times have you seen me bawling in front of people?"

At this the eldest brother pulled out Lady Li's letter.

"All of my sisters-in-law are high ranking enough to walk the streets of heaven. If each one had gone to her father and brothers for help, it would have been taken care of. Why did you have to run all this way?"

The eldest brother's only answer was more insistent pleading. Fourth-Maiden scowled and said, "I thought you trudged all this way to visit me, but maybe you're just looking for a high-ranking person to help you with a big court case." With a sweep of her sleeves, she walked straight into the inner rooms.

The eldest brother left in humiliation and anger. On his return he gave a complete account of the visit. There was no one, old or young, in the family who did not curse her name. Even Lady Li called her hardhearted. Several days later the second brother was released and came back to everyone's great joy. They were laughing at Fourth-Maiden for incurring their ill-will for nothing, when a servant sent by Fourth-Maiden came to see Madame Li.

When they called him in, the servant pulled out some gold coins, saying: "The mistress was so busy giving orders to people about Second Master's case that she had no time to reply. She thought that sending this little gift might make up for not writing a letter."

By this time the family understood that the second brother owed his release to Cheng's efforts. Later the family of the third sister fell on hard times, and Cheng treated them with more than normal generosity. As Lady Li had no son, he brought her into his house and cared for her as though she were his own mother.

31. GHOST-MAIDEN HUANNIANG

WEN As-Spring belonged to a noble Shaanxi family. When young he was inordinately fond of the lute, which he never put aside for a moment, even when staying at roadside inns. While traveling in Shaanxi he passed by an ancient temple and hitched his horse outside the gate to have a short rest. Inside, a Taoist priest dressed in homespun cloth sat cross-legged on the veranda, with a bamboo staff leaning against the wall next to him and a lute wrapped in gaily-patterned cloth.

Stumbling upon his favorite thing prompted Wen to ask: "Do you go in for this too?"

"I'm not accomplished," said the priest. "But I would like to study under a virtuoso." With that he removed the covering and handed it to Wen, who found the grain and texture of its surfaces exquisite. Moving his fingers lightly over the strings produced an extraordinarily clear, lilting sound. Wen gladly strummed a short piece to show what he could do. The priest smiled with something less than complete approval, which spurred Wen to play with his utmost skill.

The priest chuckled and said, "That's fine as far as it goes, but not good enough to teach me anything."

Wen, thinking that he spoke presumptuously, invited

him to play. The priest took the lute and put it on his knees. He had no more than run his fingers across the strings than a gentle breeze seemed to stir in the air around them. He had not played long before birds of all sorts gathered in flocks, till the courtyard trees were covered with them. Unable to contain his amazement, Wen bowed before him and asked to be his pupil. And so the priest repeated the tune three times for him.

Wen cocked his head and poured his heart into listening until he had gained a certain feel for his teacher's rhythms. The priest had Wen try the piece while he tapped out the beat and made comments. "Already there is no match for you in this world," he said.

After that Wen absorbed himself in honing his skills until he could lay claim to unrivalled mastery. Then he set out on the return trip to Shaanxi. While still scores of *li* from home, the sun went down and he was caught in a sudden storm with nowhere to stay the night. There was a small village off to the side of the road, and he hurried toward it. He was in too much of a hurry to be particular, so he dashed through the first gate he saw and climbed a flight of steps into a gloomy, deserted house. Suddenly a young woman of seventeen or eighteen with the face of a goddess appeared. She raised her head, saw the stranger and ran to an inner room in alarm. Wen, who was still single, was drawn to her by feelings of unusual depth. Soon an old woman came out to greet him. Wen gave his name and asked to be put up for the night.

"There is no harm in staying the night," said the old woman. "But we are short on beds, so you will have to make do with a mattress of straw." Soon she brought a candle and graciously spread the straw on the floor for him. He asked her family name and learned that it was Zhao.

宦孃
顧聆雅奏
拜门墻踏
衷良缘撮合
怅绪闲焚香
缠缦候分明一
曲凤求凰

He then asked who the young woman was.

"That was my niece Huanniang."

Wen said, "In spite of my poverty and ignorance, what would you think if I asked to marry her?"

"I don't think I could go along with your wishes in that respect," said the woman, knitting her brows. Wen wanted to know why, but she would only say that it was an embarrassing subject, so Wen reluctantly dropped it. When the old woman left, Wen, seeing that the bed straw was too damp and mouldy to lie on, sat erect playing his lute to pass the long night. When the rain let up he risked a wetting by starting out for home.

In his district lived the retired Ministerial Secretary Master Ge, a man who relished the company of scholars. Once Wen visited him and played the lute at his request. A female member of the family could be dimly discerned listening from behind the screen. A quick gust of wind blew the screen open, revealing a girl with newly pinned back hair whose beauty was unmatched by any woman alive. Wen had heard that the master had a daughter whose childhood name was Lianggong, who excelled at poetry, and was known for her beauty, and now his heart leapt at the sight of her. He returned and spoke of this to his mother, after which a go-between was sent to broach the subject. Ge refused because of the declining state of the Wen family fortune. But the girl, after hearing Wen's lute, was secretly attracted to him and was continually hoped to hear his exquisite playing once again. But Wen, whose hopes had been dashed by the refusal, was no longer seen at the gate of her house.

One day when the girl was in the garden, she found a piece of letter paper. On it was a lyric to the tune of "Cherish the Lingering Spring" which went as follows:

Regret is now a foolish daze
And longing to dreaming has given way,
As passion sets my days awry.
The crab trees totter drunkenly
And willow trees droop listlessly—
What we cherish is the same.
Worries old and new oppress me:
I mow them down but they grow back
Just like fresh green shoots of grass.
Since we had to part
I bide the passing nights and days
Beneath a resignation-colored sky.
My smooth, soft brow is worn with frowning
My limpid pools are strained with gazing.
Goodbye to hope, goodbye forever!
These cozy covers keep me from my dreams;
The dripping timepiece startles me awake.
I try to sleep, but sleep eludes me.
Some liken dreary nights to years;
To me it seems that one whole year
Flies faster than this midnight watch.
Three nights, no, three long years have gone.
Can anyone tie time's wings down?

The girl recited the lyric repeatedly and, finding it to her liking, went home with it inside her blouse. She took out some fancy stationery and carefully made a complete copy, which she left on her desk. A while later she was unable to find it, so she concluded that it had been blown away by the wind. Actually Master Ge had passed by the door of her room and picked it up, thinking she had written it, and had then thrown it in the fire, disgusted with the wantonness of the words but unwilling to face her with them. He decided to arrange a betrothal right away. It was then that the son of Provincial Governor Liu from Lin Yi district, sent a go-between to ask for her hand. Ge was pleased to have an offer from such a person, but he wanted to meet him face to face. The governor's son came in formal clothes, a model of manly grace. Overjoyed at what he saw, Ge treated him to a sumptuous dinner. After dinner, when Liu had taken his leave, a girl's upturned slipper was found under his seat. Disgusted by his cavalier approach to women, Ge called for the go-between and told her what had happened. The governor's son hotly protested that he was being maligned, but Ge did not listen and finally cut off relations with him.

Prior to this, Ge had gotten hold of a green variety of chrysanthemums which he niggardly kept to himself, and Lianggong planted some in her chamber. Later a couple of chrysanthemums growing in Wen's courtyard suddenly turned green. Word of them reached his colleagues, and they visited him for the pleasure of gazing on them. This made Wen treasure them all the more. He rushed out to see them by the first light of dawn and found next to the flower bed a sheet of letter paper bearing a lyric to the tune of "Cherish the Lingering Spring." He unfolded it and read it repeatedly, not knowing where it was from. He was especially puzzled by the lyric's apparent reference to the word "Spring" in his name. He took it to his desk, where he painstakingly made emphasis marks with bright-colored inks and wrote indecorous comments. Just then Ge, shocked by the news that Wen's chrysanthemums had turned green, paid a personal call to Wen's studio, where he saw the lyric and commenced reading it. Wen, who did not care to let him see the suggestive comments, snatched it away and crumpled it, but not before Ge was convinced by the first line or two that this was the same lyric he had found up at the door of his daughter's bedroom. The green chrysantemums, which he guessed were a gift from Lianggong, added to his suspicions. He returned home, told his wife and had her force the truth out of the girl. Lianggong sobbed herself into insensibility, but there was no proof of her involvement and no way of arriving at the truth.

Mrs. Ge figured that giving their daughter to Wen would be better than letting the matter be noised abroad, so they sent to tell him their plan. Wen was so overjoyed he invited friends to a dinner beside the green chrysanthemums. He lit incense and played the lute until well into the night. After he retired, his studio boy heard sounds coming from the lute. At first he thought that the other servants were playing a prank, but when he found no one there he reported it to Wen. Wen went there himself: the servant was not fooling him. The notes were a halting imitation of his own playing. Wen lit a torch and ran into the studio, but saw nobody there so he took the lute in his arm and left. The rest of the night was quiet. He guessed that it was a werefox and, since it had wanted to study under him, he played a piece every evening and left the lute out so the fox could imitate him. Every night he hid nearby to listen. In six or seven nights the disjointed notes surprisingly began to come together into a piece worth the attention of a cultivated ear.

Once their nuptial ceremonies had been performed, Wen and Lianggong exchanged recollections of the lyric and began to realize that it was what had brought them together, but they still did not understand where it had come from. When Lianggong heard the strange story of the nightly lute music, she listened and said, "This music is not being played by a werefox. The tone is mournful. There is a ghostly ring to it."

Since Wen was not convinced, Lianggong told him of an antique mirror belonging to her family that could show the true colors of a spectre or ghoul. The next day she sent someone for it. The moment the lute music started she rushed in with the mirror in her hand, and in the glare of the lamp they brought in a young woman could plainly be seen cowering in a corner of the room, unable to hide. Wen questioned her closely and found to his great amazement that she was Huanniang of the Zhao family. She broke down under the questioning and sobbed: "My services to you as go-between surely count for something. Why must you drive me into a corner?"

Wen offered to get rid of the mirror if she agreed not to run away. She gave her word. The mirror was put in a bag. She sat down at a distance and said: "I am the daughter of a prefect: I've been dead for a hundred years. As a girl I was fond of the lute and the zither. I was able to learn something about the zither, but I never found anyone to pass the skill of lute playing down to me. I carried my regret over this with me into the underworld. When you so kindly visited us, I had a chance listen to your excellent playing. My heart went out to you, but, unfortunately, I could not serve you intimately because I am not of your kind. I worked behind the scenes to bring you together with the right person, as a way of repaying the regard you showed for me. The girl's slipper that young master Liu supposedly left and the banal lyric "Cherish the Remaining Spring" were my work. You cannot say that I did not put a lot of effort into repaying my teacher." Husband and wife bowed to her in appreciation.

"I have thought through most of what you taught, but the spirit that moves your music still escapes me," she said.

"Would you please play for me again?" Wen did as she said, giving an elaborate demonstration of his fingering.

"Now I have it!" Huanniang exclaimed delightedly.

With this she excused herself and rose to leave. But Lianggong, herself an accomplished zither player, was fascinated to learn of the other's forte and wished to give ear to a sample piece. Huanniang did not refuse. The music and her rendering of it were unlike anything achievable in this world. Lianggong tapped along raptly as she listened, then asked if to learn something of her skill. Huanniang called for a brush and wrote down a score in eighteen sections, then rose and said goodbye. The couple held her back imploringly.

"You are like a matching lute and zither set," said Huanniang gloomily. "You can appreciate each other's music. Fate has been too unkind to allow me such blessings. If we are linked by the ties of destiny, we will meet again in the next life." With this she handed Wen a scroll, saying: "This is a little portrait of me. If you don't want to neglect your matchmaker, you can hang it in your bedroom. When you are in the mood, burn a stick of incense and play a piece in front of it. It will be just as if I am here to enjoy it." Then she went through the gate and vanished.

32. MONK JIN

MONK Jin came from Zhucheng district.[1] His father was a shiftless idler who sold him for a few hundred coppers to Five-Lotus-Mountain Monastery. As a boy he was too slow a learner to practice the "pure livelihood" of sutra reading, meditation, and the like. Instead, he drove pigs to market like an indentured servant. In time Monk Jin's master died, leaving behind a small amount of money. Jin absconded from the monastery with as much of the money as he could lay hands on and went off to be a peddler. He was skillful at getting the better of people with tricks like bloating his sheep with water or monopolizing commodities at market fairs. Within a few years he made a quick fortune and bought land and buildings in Water-slope Ward. His disciples, lined up in bristling rows, numbered a thousand at daily roll call. He had over a thousand *mu*[2] of rich land around the ward, and within it he built several dozen houses. The residents were monks, not laypersons. Even such laypersons as were there were poor men with no means of livelihood, who had brought their wives and children to live in rented rooms and work the land as tenants. Within every gate were quadrangles of dormitories where such people lived. The monk's residence

1. In the southeast part of Shandong province.
2. One *mu* is about 1/6 acre.

金和尚，
富貴叢中結
善緣不持經咒
不參禪粹迎來
語闍黎笑衣鉢
而今有別傳

was situated in the center of these dwellings and fronted by a reception parlor. Pillars, beams, and roof supports glittered with designs in gold leaf and enamel. The tables and folding screens at the head of the hall shone with such crystalline brilliance they could have been used as mirrors. Behind this was the sleeping chamber, with bead curtains and embroidered canopies. A dense odor of orchid and musk invaded the visitor's nostrils. The bed was of carved sandalwood inlaid with mother-of-pearl. The brocaded quilts on the bed were layered a foot and some inches thick. The walls were all but covered with landscapes and portraits of beautiful women by famous painters.

At a single drawn-out call, dozens of men outside the door rumbled in thunderous response. Men with tiny tassels on their caps and leather boots on their feet would flock in like crows and stand with their necks stretched out like swans. They took orders with their mouths pressed shut and their ears pricked up. Guests showed on a moment's notice; a banquet for ten or more tables was arranged at a shouted command. Rich meats, full-bodied wines, steamed dishes and smoked delectables were laid out in disorderly profusion.

Though he did not dare to keep singing girls, he had ten or more budding boys, all irresistibly charming. They wrapped their heads in bandanas of black gauze, sang seductive songs and were by no means unpleasant to hear and see. If Jin went out, he was escorted by thirty or forty horsemen whose waist-mounted bows and arrows touched and rattled against each other. Servants addressed him as "Sir." Even the common people of the district "Grandfather"-ed and "Uncle"-ed him. They never called him "Master" or "Abbot" or used his *dharma* name. His disciples were not quite as conspicuous as he when they went out, but even they were the equals of young noblemen with their horses' manes tossing in the wind and their cloud-patterned trappings. Jin also went in for social connections in a big way: the very breath he drew had an effect over thousands of *li*. This gave him leverage over local officials, who feared what would happen if they ever got on his bad side.

As for Jin's character, he was crude and illiterate. From crown to toes he did not have a refined bone in his body. Never in his life did he take up a sutra or hold a mantra in mind, nor did his feet ever leave their traces in monasteries and abbeys, nor did he keep a chanting bell or drum in his room. Such things were never seen or heard by his disciples.

Among his renters were loose, attractive women who looked as if they belonged in the capital. Their rouge and face powder were provided by the monks, who were never frugal with their money. Consequently, the ward had hundreds of residents who, in a manner of speaking, were farmers without farming. Occasionally a murderous tenant would chop off a monk's head and bury it under his bed. Later he would be sent away without much of an investigation. These were some of the things that went on there.

Jin also bought a child with a family name different from his own and made the boy his own son. He hired a tutor to teach him examination writing. The boy was intelligent and good at composition, so Jin had him admitted to the district academy. Soon he rose by predictable steps to the rank of Grand Academy scholar. Before long he travelled to Shuntian prefectual examinations and won the title of master of letters. From then on Jin was widely known as the Grand Sire. People who had once called him "Great" now prefaced that with "Great," and those who had knelt on mats before him now kept their hands at their sides and bowed to him like sons and grandsons.

Not long afterward the Grand Sire expired. The master of letters put on hempen mourning clothes, slept on a straw mat with a clod pillow, and faced north, toward the soul of the departed, as he bewailed his orphan's lot. The beggars' staffs of Jin's disciples covered a whole bed. Of course the delicate sobbing from behind the mourning curtain was made by the master of letter's wife and no one else. The wives of high-ranking officials came, all done up in their best finery, to part the curtain and offer their condolences. So the roads were congested with officials' carriages and horses. On the day of burial, awnings and pavilions merged into a cloud of colors. Pennants and banners blocked out the sun. Lifelike straw figures wrapped in gold foil and silk accompanied the deceased to his grave. The burial objects included several dozen canopied carriages with mounted escorts, a thousand horses, and one hundred beautiful women. They built a gigantic spirit guard and guide to the underworld out of papier maché, and outfitted them with black turbans and metal armor. They were supported by inner wooden frames and borne along by men inside. Each was provided with a mechanism that, when turned, caused the giants' beards and eyebrows to wave in the air. The flashing light of their eyes made them look as if they were about to bellow with rage. Those who looked upon them were dumbstruck, and small children who saw them from a distance ran away squealing. The paper mansion that was to be sent to the underworld had the grandeur of a palace. It was a complex of adjoining towers, pavilions, chambers, and galleries that covered several dozen *mu*. If anyone could have entered one of its thousands of gates and doors he would never have found his way out. The offerings and representational objects were too numerous to mention one by one. The canopies of the mourners' carriages rubbed against each other in the road. No one from the provincial officials—who approached with bent backs and bowed as if at the emperor's morning audience—down to senior licentiates, collegians of the Imperial Academy of Learning and office clerks —who lowered their hands to the ground and followed them with their foreheads—dared do anything to the young master or the deceased's disciples.

By now the whole district had turned out to view the spectacle. Men and women sweated and panted against one another in the street. There were husbands leading wives, mothers carrying babies and brothers calling their sisters. Blaring music, booming drums and the clanging of a hundred street operas mingled with their cries to make a bubbling cauldron of noise that drowned all human speech. Nothing of the onlookers could be seen below their shoulders: there were only thousands of milling heads. A pregnant woman was stricken with labor pains. Her friends fanned out about her and spread their skirts to make a curtain. As soon as the baby's squalling was heard it was wrapped up in a torn-off dress without anyone bothering to see if it were a boy or girl, and taken off in someone's arms. With some friends holding her up and some pulling her along, the mother managed to hobble away. What a sight!

After the burial, the money and property left by Jin were divided into two parts, one of which went to his son and one to his disciples. The master of letters got half and, in all four directions around his residence were none but the brotherhood of the cloth. The monks went on addressing each other as brothers, and it is said they went on looking out for one another's interests.

The Chronicler of the Tales comments: "This is a sect which was never included in the Northern or Southern schools of Buddhism and which did not come down from the Sixth Patriarch. One can say that this sect developed its own unique dharma. I have also heard that the man who knows the emptiness of the five aggregates[1] and stays undefiled by the six dusts[2] is called a monk, or follower of higher things. When a man speaks the dharma with his mouth and meditates on his cushion he is called a follower of posturings. One whose shoes are perfumed by the flowers of Chu and who has worn his umbrella hat beneath the sky of Wu is a man of many wanderings. One who noisily chimes bells of different sizes is called a chanter of songs, and one who grovels at other people's feet like a dog or buzzes like a carrion-fly around gamblers on a binge is called a follower of hellish wrongs. Now which was it in Jin's case? Was it "higher things," "posturings," "wanderings," "songs," or "hellish wrongs?"

1. Form, sensation, conception, action, and cognition.
2. Sight, sound, smell, taste, touch, and ideation.

33. THE HORSE IN THE PAINTING

SCHOLAR Cui of Linqing district[1] lived in dire poverty. Even the crumbling wall around his house was left unrepaired. Every morning when he rose he saw a horse lying in the dewy grass outside. Its coat was pure black with white markings: only its tail, which apparently had been burnt short in a fire, was ragged. He would chase it away, only to see it come back again at night from wherever it had gone.

Cui wanted to go to Shanxi and stay with a friend who was an official there, but his lack of a mount had held him back, so he caught the horse and bridled it, climbed on it and set out, leaving these instructions with his family: "If someone comes looking for the horse, they can go claim it in Shanxi."

Once he got out on the open road the horse fell into a gallop that covered a hundred *li* in a blink and a breath. That night it hardly touched its hay and bean mash, which made Cui suspect it was ill. The next day he drew in the bit and did not let it gallop, but the horse neighed and whickered, spraying flecks of foam, with the same healthy spirit it had shown yesterday. He gave it free rein, and by noon he had already reached Shanxi. He rode it through several marketplaces at a speed that made everyone who

1. In Shandong province.

saw it gasp. The Prince of Jin learned of this and offered to pay a hefty sum for the horse, but Cui did not sell it for fear that the owner would find him. Half a year passed with no news from home so Cui sold the horse to the House of Jin for eight hundred taels. Later he bought himself a sturdy mule for the trip home.

Afterward the prince, due to some urgent matter, dispatched a staff sergeant to Linqing on the horse. The horse got away from the sergeant, and he chased it up to the gate of the man who lived one door east of the Cui house. The horse disappeared inside so he demanded that the owner of the house return it to him. The owner, named Zeng, had truly not seen it. They went in the house, where the sergeant saw an equestrian painting by Zhao Meng-fu (1254-1322) hanging on the wall. One of the horses was exactly like the one he was after, both in the color and texture of its coat. The tail area had been burnt by a stick of incense. It was clear now that the horse was a painting come to life. It would have been difficult for the sergeant to report this back to the prince, so he brought charges against Zeng. By this time Cui had parlayed the capital gained from selling the horse into a small fortune and was perfectly willing to lend the amount he had gotten for the horse to Zeng, who paid the money to the sergeant and sent him on his way. Zeng was quite appreciative, little knowing that Cui was the man who had sold the horse years ago.

畫馬
千金不惜購驊
騮妙畫通靈何
家求漫道點睛
龍破壁子昂直
可繼僧繇

34. FRAUD (NUMBER THREE)

SCHOLAR Li of Jiaxiang[1] was an accomplished lutanist. One day he happened to be in the eastern suburbs when some laborers uncovered an ancient lute while making an excavation. It was his for a negligible sum. Rubbed clean, it gave off an unearthly gleam. He strung it and played: the sound was piercingly pure. His joy could not have been greater than if he had found a piece of jade too big to hold in one hand. He kept it in a brocade bag hidden in a secret room, never showing it even to his closest relatives.

The newly arrived district commissioner Cheng announced himself with a calling card and paid Li a visit. Though Li seldom socialized, he returned the visit because the other had taken the initiative. Several days later he was invited for a drink, and, since the host was insistent, he went. Cheng was a charming, unconventional character, and Li enjoyed the animated ease of his conversation. After some days passed, Li sent a return invitation. This time the two found even more pleasure in each other's company. From then on there was not a moonlit evening or flower bedecked morning that they did not share.

More than a year had gone by when Li happened to notice a lute in an embroidered bag on the desk in Cheng's office. Li took it out and turned it in his hands.

[1] In Shandong province.

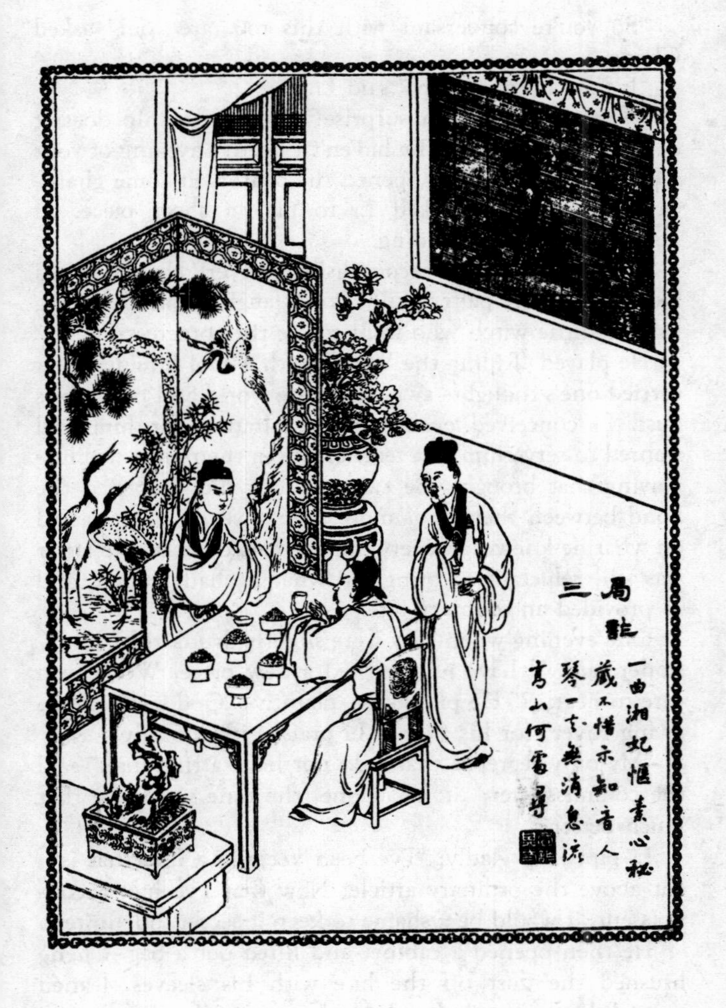

局詐
三
一曲湘妃愜素心秘
藏不惜示知音人
琴一去無清息流
高山何處尋

"So you're conversant with this too, are you?" asked Cheng.

"It's my life's passion," said Li.

Cheng exclaimed in surprise: "Our friendship doesn't date from yesterday. Why haven't I heard anything of your consummate skill?" He opened the censer, lit some gharu-wood incense and asked Li to play a short piece. Li respectfully did his bidding.

"You are quite an accomplished player! Now I would like to offer my paltry skill. Don't laugh at me for being like the little witch who went to see the sorceress."

He played "Riding the Wind" with a cool liquidity that carried one's thoughts away from the world and beyond its dust. Li conceived even more admiration for him and wanted to serve him as a teacher. From then on it was lute playing that brought the two together and deepened the bond between them. For more than a year Cheng passed on what he knew, but every time he called on Li, the latter was still reluctant to bring out what he had hidden, and so provided an ordinary lute.

One evening when they were slightly drunk the commisioner said, "I have just learned a new piece. Would you care to hear it?" He played the plaintive "Goddesses of the Xiang River" for his friend. Li praised it profusely.

"My only regret is that I do not have a fine lute," said the commissioner; "if I had one, the tone would be that much better."

Li piped up gladly: "I've been keeping a lute that is a cut above the ordinary article. Now that I've met a connoisseur, it would be a shame to keep it secret indefinitely.

He then opened a cabinet and lifted out a bag. Cheng brushed the dust off the lute with his sleeves, leaned toward the desk and played the piece again. It was a perfect interweaving of boldness and softness, played with virtuosity that was more than human. Li could not help but tap to the rhythm in appreciation.

"My limited and awkward skills have failed this fine instrument," said the commissioner. If my wife were allowed to play it, there would be a note or two worth hearing."

"You mean the lady of your house has mastered the lute too?" asked Li in shock.

"The exercise I just played was taught me by my wife," the commissioner chuckled.

"What a pity she is hidden away in your private chambers. I'll never be able to hear her," Li complained.

"We are such good friends that my family is your family," said the commissioner. "We should not let appearances restrict us. I wish you would take your lute to my house tomorrow. I'll have her play for you from behind the screen."

Li was delighted. The next day he went there, lute in arms. Cheng made preparations for a bout of convivial drinking. In a little while he took the lute inside, came right back and sat down. Then the faint shape of a beautifully dressed and coiffured woman appeared behind the screen, followed by a fragrance that wafted into the room. Before long the strings came delicately alive. Li did not know what piece it was, but the sound of it swept his thoughts away and thrilled him to the marrow, so that his soul took leave of his body. At the end of her piece he went to peek around the screen: there was a woman in her early twenties who was surely one of the beauties of the age.

The commissioner urged huge cups of wine on Li, while the woman within the screen switched to a "Rhapsody of Leisure," which drove Li's body and mind to greater distraction. Having poured more than his measure of wine down his throat, he rose from the seat, started to say his goodbyes and asked for his lute.

"In your condition we must guard against your taking a flop with it," said the commissioner. "Visit us again tomorrow; I'll have my wife perform all her best pieces."

Li went home. The next day he went back and found the office suite deserted except for an old servant who answered the door. When questioned the old man said, "He left with his family during the fifth watch this morning. I don't know what he plans to do, but he said it'll only take him three days to make the trip.

On the third day Li went to wait for them. He waited until sundown, but still there was no sign of them. The clerks and servants were mystified. They reported to the magistrate, who had the lock broken and the house searched. The house was completely empty: only desks and beds remained. The matter was communicated to higher authorities, but they too were unable to determine what had happened.

Li could not sleep or eat for grief over losing his lute. Disregarding the great distance, he set out on a few thousand-*li* search for the culprit's home—Cheng was a native of Chu who had paid for the post in Jiaxiang three years before. With a card bearing Cheng's name in his hand, Li made inquiries in the man's old neighborhood and learned that there was no such person in Chu. Someone told him: "There was a Taoist named Cheng who was good at the lute. Some say he possessed the golden touch. Three years ago he left and hasn't been here since."

Li suspected that this was the person. He asked detailed questions about the man's age and appearance: all the answers tallied perfectly with what he knew. He realized that the Taoist had procured an official title expressly for the sake of the lute. For the first year or more of their friendship, he had not said a word about music. Then slowly, but with well-timed certainty, he had left his lute out and then demonstrated his own skill and finally used the beautiful woman to distract Li. Three years of easing himself under Li's guard—then he had gotten the lute and left. The Taoist's obsession for the instrument was even greater than Li's. There are many angles from which to practice deception in this world. In the Taoist's case, there was a certain refinement in his trickery.

35. DREAM OF WOLVES

SQUIRE Bai was from Zhili.[1] Three years before our story, his eldest son Jia had left for an official post in the south, but Bai had heard no news of him since. One day a relative named Ding came to call, and the squire entertained him. Ding had long been a journeyer into the realm of the dead. In the course of their conversation, the squire asked him what went on in the dark world. Ding's answers verged on being phantasmagorical. The unconvinced squire only chuckled. A few days after this visit the squire, lying in bed, saw Ding come once again to invite him along on a trip. He followed Ding until they entered a walled city. After walking awhile Ding pointed to a gate and said: "Your nephew is here."

At that time a son of the squire's sister was a magistrate in Shanxi. "How could he be here?" asked the squire in surprise.

"If you don't believe me, go in: you'll find out soon enough," said Ding. The squire went in and, indeed saw his nephew sitting at the head of a hall wearing a locust-pattern headpiece and a robe embroidered with the figure of an evil-exorcising ram—the garb of a censor. Around him the standards and two-pronged spears of his guards

[1] Province under the "direct control" of the central administration, now called Hebei.

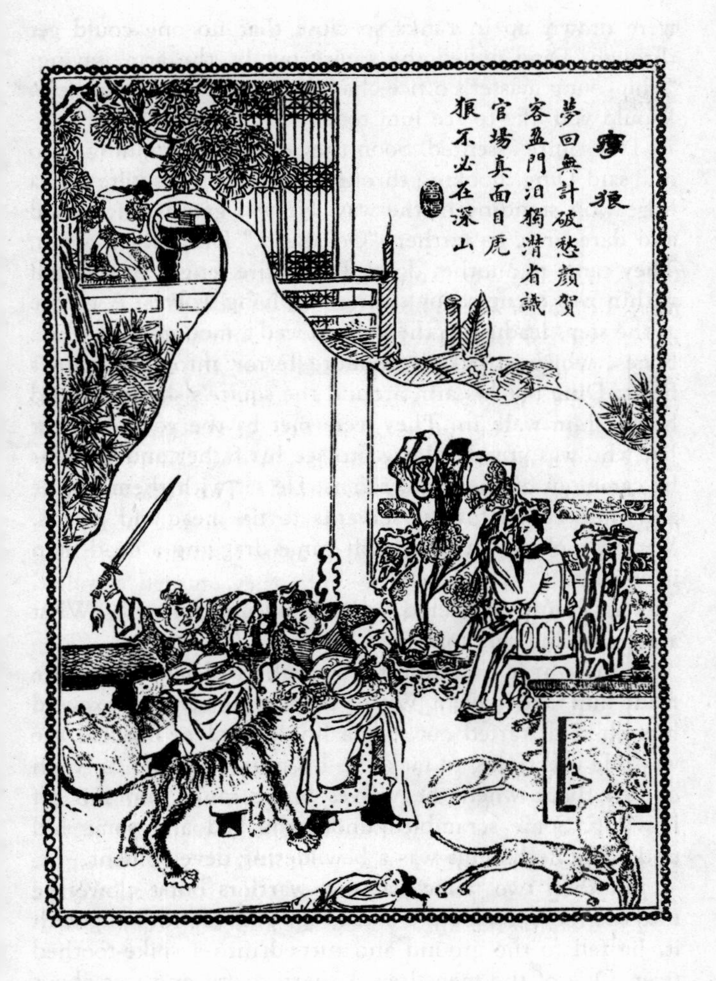
夢狼
夢回無計破愁顏賀
客盈門汨獨潸省識
官場真面目虎
狼不必在深山

were drawn up in ranks so close that no one could get through. Ding pulled the squire out by the arm, saying: "The young master's office chambers are not far from here. Would you like to see him too?"

The squire assented. Soon they came to a building. "Go in," said Ding. Looking through the gate, the squire saw a huge wolf standing in the way. He was greatly frightened and dared not go farther. "Go ahead," Ding urged again. They came to another door. The entire length of the hall within was occupied by sitting and lying wolves. A glance at the steps leading to the hall showed a mountain of white bones, which struck even more terror into the squire's heart. Ding put his arm around the squire's shoulders and helped him walk in. They were met by the young master Jia, who was greatly pleased to see his father and Ding as he came out of the inner rooms. He sat with them awhile and then called for his servants to fix meat and greens. Within moments a huge wolf came dragging a dead man in its jaws.

The squire shuddered as he stood up and said, "What are you doing this for?"

"I thought it would do for a meal," said Jia. The squire made him take it away. With a palpitating heart he excused himself and started out, but a line of wolves blocked the way. He was trying to make up his mind whether to go on or turn back when the wolves broke ranks and ran off howling. Some scrambled under the bed and some hid under the desk. This was a bewildering development.

Just then two fierce armored warriors burst glowering into the room, took out a black rope and bound Jia up with it. Jia fell to the ground and turned into a spike-toothed tiger. One of the men drew a sharp sword and was about to chop off its head.

"Wait! Don't!" said the other. "That will happen in the fourth month of next year. We had better content ourselves with smashing its teeth. They took out a huge mace and hammered its teeth until they fell in pieces on the ground. The tiger let loose an earthshaking roar. The squire was petrified, but suddenly he awoke and realized that it was a dream.

The squire could not get the strange dream out of his head. He sent someone to fetch Ding, but Ding refused to come. The squire wrote an account of the dream and sent his second son to visit Jia with a letter warning him of the purport of the dream. On his arrival the boy was shocked to see that his elder brother's front teeth were all missing and wanted to know why. He was told that they had been knocked out in a drunken fall from a horse. Then he asked what day this had happened: it had been on the very day of their father's dream. This came as an even greater shock. He pulled out their father's letter.

Jia's face turned livid as he read it. There was an interval of silence, and then he said, "So what if a deluded dream happened to coincide with the facts. What's so strange about that?" He had just bribed some power-wielding officials into giving him top priority for promotion, and the evil dream meant nothing to him. The younger brother stayed several days, watching the rapacious underlings who crowded the hall. He saw men offering bribes and seeking favors come and go continually, even into the wee hours. Sobbing messily, he counseled his brother to stop these dealings.

"You spend your days in a thatched hut, little brother: you don't know the key to officialdom. The power to promote or demote is in the hands of my superiors, not with the people. If the higher-ups are pleased with someone, he's good official. What good is love of the people for winning favor with the higher-ups?"

Realizing that he could not be persuaded to stop, the younger brother went home and told his father. The squire broke down crying at the news. There was no course open but to give money from his own pocket to relieve the poor and to pray to the gods every day not to implicate his wife and children in their retribution against his defiant son.

The year after that came news of Jia's recommendation for promotion to the Board of Civil Personnel. Well-wishers swarmed at the gate. The squire could only sob and sigh as he lay on his pillow and feigned illness so he would not have to show his face. Before long he learned that his son had met with bandits on the road back to the capital and that he and his servants had lost their lives. At last the squire got out of bed.

"The anger of the spirits stopped with him," he told people. "I have to admit they did their best to look out for my family." And so he lit incense to them in gratitude. People tried to console the squire by saying the news was unfounded; he alone believed it without a doubt and began looking for a burial plot immediately.

In truth, Jia had not died. Earlier, in the fourth month, Jia had been relieved of his duties. He had just crossed the county line when he encountered bandits. He upended his bags and offered them the contents, but the bandits said, "We came to avenge ourselves for your outrages against the people of this district. We don't care a pin about these trinkets!" With this they cut off his head. Then they asked his house servants: "Which one of you is called Si Dacheng?"

The servants pointed out Si, who had long been Jia's confidant and companion in wickedness. The bandits killed him as well. Four rapacious underlings—Jia's tax collectors—whom he intended to take along with him to the capital were also searched out and beheaded. After this the bandits divided the money, put it in their pouches and galloped away.

Jia's soul watched from the side of the road as a local official rode by and asked, "Who was murdered here?"

"Magistrate Bai of so-and-so district," said the escort who rode ahead of him.

"This man is the son of Bai so-and-so," said the official. "It wouldn't do for the old man to see him in this grisly state. We should sew the head onto the body."

Then someone picked up the head and placed it on the neck stump, saying "A crooked man should not be made to look straight. Let's line up his chin with his shoulder." With that they left.

After a while Jia revived. His wife, who had come to claim the corpse, detected a hint of breath and carried him back in a wagon. He began to take liquids poured into his mouth a few drops at a time. The trouble was that they were stranded in a roadside inn without the funds to return home. More than half a year went by before the squire got the true story. He sent his second son to bring Jia back. Even though Jia came back to life, he could look at his back with his own eyes. He no longer counted as a member of the human race.

The squire's nephew, well-known for his political abilities, was chosen to be a censor that year. Everything tallied with the squire's dream.

The Chronicler of the Tales comments: "Regretably one need not look far to find that many officials in this world are tigers, and their subordinates, wolves. Even if the officials are not tigers, their subordinates go ahead with their wolfish doings. What is more, some officials are fiercer than tigers! It is a failing for a man to be unable to look back on what he has done. But he might just wake up one day to find that he has been made to look backward. Such are the subtle lessons taught by ghosts!"

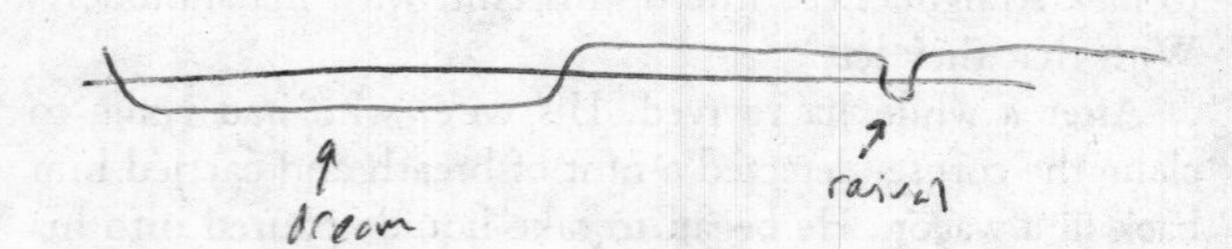

36. GHOST-SCHOLAR YU QU-E

TAO Shengyu of Beiping[1] was a renowned scholar. During the Shunzhi reign of the first Qing emperor (1644-1661) he went up for the provincial examination and took lodgings on the outskirts of the capital. One day he went out and met a man with a wicker pack of books on his back scurrying about and apparently looking for a place to live. Tao asked him a few questions. The man set his pack down on the road and entered into a conversation. His manner of speech marked him a singular man of learning. Tao took a strong liking to him and invited him to room together. The delighted stranger carried his pack inside, and so they lived under the same roof. The stranger volunteered the fact that he came from Shuntian prefecture, his surname was Yu and he went by the name Qu-E. He addressed Tao, who was slightly older, as an older brother.

Yu was not fond of sightseeing. He often sat alone in a room, his desk empty of books. When Tao was not talking with him, he did little but lie in silence. Wondering about him, Tao looked through his pack and chest: there were inkbrushes and an inkstone but no other articles. He asked for an explanation of the mystery.

Yu answered with a laugh: "Do you think that for

1. Present-day Beijing (Peking).

someone like me reading is a matter of 'waiting until thirsty to dig a well'?"

One day he borrowed one of Tao's books, shut himself in his room and copied from it furiously. By the end of the day he had over fifty pages, but there was no indication of his waiting to fold and bind them into a booklet. Furtive observation showed that he set fire to each page when he finished and swallowed the ashes. Tao's earlier puzzlement was nothing to what he felt now. He demanded to know the reason.

"I do this instead of reading," was the answer. In a few minutes Yu recited serveral chapters from the book he had been copying. Not a single word was amiss. Tao was excited by this demonstration and wanted Yu to let him in on the method. Yu thought it would not be a good idea. Tao suspected him of holding back and said so with a note of accusation in his words.

"Believe me, brother, you have not grasped my true intention. If I don't tell you the truth, there is no way to open my heart for you to see. If I come out and tell you, you'll likely be frightened of me for being a freak. What can I do?"

But Tao assured him: "It won't do any harm."

"Well, I'm not a man, I'm a ghost," said Yu. "They are awarding positions by examination now in the nether world. An examination to select examiners has been decreed on the fourteenth day of the seventh month. Candidates will enter their cells on the fifteenth and notice boards will be posted before the month is out."

"Why are there examinations to select examiners?" asked Tao.

"It is the Lord on High's considered wish. Even the most minor officials will be subject to examination. Those who

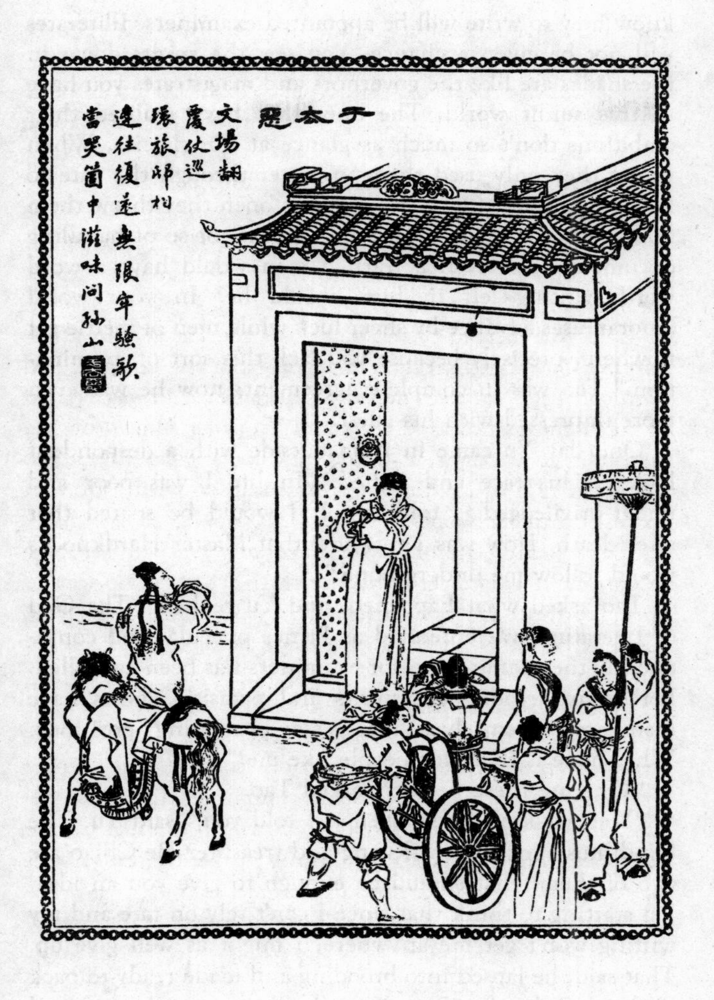
于去惡
文場翻覆仗巡環旅邸相逢往復遙無限牢騷歌當哭箇中滋味問孫山

know how to write will be appointed examiners. Illiterates will not be given a chance. You see, the spirits down in the shades are like the governors and magistrates you have in this sunlit world. The ones that have realized their ambitions don't so much as glance at the classics. When young they only used them to batter through the gate to honor and fame. Once the gate was open they threw them aside. What is more, after a dozen years or so of handling documents, not even a learned man would have a word worth writing left in him, would he? In your world ignoramuses advance by sheer luck while men of mettle get nowhere, precisely because you lack this sort of examination." Tao was in complete agreement: now he was even more impressed with his guest.

Ond day Yu came in from outside with a despondent look on his face and sighed: "In life I was poor and under-priviledged. I told myself I would be spared that after death. How was I to know that Master Hardknocks would follow me underground?"

Tao asked what happened, and Yu replied, "The God of Literature was enfeoffed as Prince of Tula, and consequently the examination for examiners has been cancelled. For many decades idle spirits and parasitic ghosts have insinuated themselves into essay-evaluating positions. What hope is there for people like me?"

"Who are these people?" asked Tao.

"You wouldn't know even if I told you," said Yu. The blind music master Shi Kuang and treasurer He Chiao are two of them: that should be enough to give you an idea. I'm starting to think that since I can't rely on fate and my writing won't get me anywhere, I might as well give up. That said, he lapsed into brooding and made ready to pack his bags. Only when Tao dragged at his arm and comforted him did he stop.

On the eve of All Souls Day (the fifteenth day of the seventh lunar month) he said to Tao: "I'm about to go into the examination cell. Please take some incense to the fields east of the city and burn it there at dawn; call my name three times and I'll be there." Then he went out the door and left. Tao bought wine and prepared fresh meat to receive him. When the eastern sky whitened, he dutifully carried out Yu's instructions. Before long Yu came, together with a young man. Tao asked his name.

"This is Fang Zijin, my good friend. We just met by chance at the examination. He has heard a great deal about you and wants very much to make your acquaintance." The three went to Tao's lodgings, where Tao and Fang exchanged bows by the light of a hand-held candle. Tao, much taken with the young man's fine, jadelike features and mild, humble manner, ventured, "I suppose Zijin was pleased with the quality of his writing."

"Just talking about it makes me laugh," said Yu. "He was over halfway through the seven assigned topics, but the minute he learned the presiding examiner's name, he wrapped up his stationery and walked straight out. A remarkable man, he is!"

Tao fanned the brazier to warm some wine and asked, "What were the assigned topics? Did you come out on top, Qu-E?"

"There was one section each on the Four Books and the Five Classics that a woman could have handled. The Policy question went like this: 'Multifarious evils have existed from ancient times, but in this day and age the treacherous and degenerate ways of men are beyond telling. The eighteen hells are not enough to punish all types of evil, nor are they large enough to hold all those found guilty.

What then can be done? The proper course might be to add one or two to the number of hells, but this is at great variance with the Lord on High's love of living creatures. Should the hells be increased or not, or is there a different course open by which evil might be purged at the source? All candidates are urged to speak out exhaustively and without reservation.' My policy statement may not have been perfect, but I couldn't have been happier with it. The topic for the Memorial was: 'A Proposal for the Eradication of Demons in the Upper Abode and for Bestowal of Dragon Steeds and Heavenly Vestment on the Various Ministers by Rank.' After that there were a 'Poem on the Imperially Decreed Theme of Porphyry Pavilion,' and a 'Rhapsody on Peach Blossoms at West Pond,' both of which dealt with the Queen Mother of the West. I'm convinced that nobody in the hall could equal my performance on these three sections." When finished speaking he clapped his hands.

"You're pleased with yourself now," said Fang laughingly. "We'll let you walk around with your head in the clouds for a while, in a few days you'll have to show what a man you are by not bawling out loud."

At daybreak Fang wanted to leave. Tao asked him to stay on as a roommate. He refused but promised to return in the evening. Three days passed without his coming back. Tao wanted Yu to go looking for him, but Yu said, "There is no need. Zijin has a good heart. Don't think he has no wish to make friends."

As the sun was westering Fang showed up after all. He pulled out a small volume and handed it to Tao, saying: "I broke my promise by three days, so I took the liberty of copying out a hundred or so of my old compositions that I'd like you to comment on."

Tao opened the book and read it with great delight, finding something to praise in every sentence. After reading briefly through one or two selections he put the book in a case. They talked deep into the night. Fang stayed and shared a bed with Yu.

From then on it was a regular thing. Fang visited every night without fail, and Tao would not have been happy without Fang. One evening Fang rushed in and said to Tao: "The notice boards have already been posted in the underworld. Fifth-Brother Yu was not selected!" Hearing these words, Yu started up from the bed and loosed a torrent of tears. The two of them had to do everything in their power to console him before he would leave off sniveling. Even then he looked at them in sullen silence, which they found unendurable.

"I just heard that Grand Circuit Inspector Zhang Fei,[1] Marquis of Huan, will come soon," said Fang. "It could be no more than a rumor started by disappointed candidates. If it is true, the literary arena may well get a good shaking up."

Yu's face lit up when he heard this. Tao asked the reason and Yu replied, "The Marquis of Huan inspects underworld functionaries once every thirty years and tours the sunlit world once every thirty-five years. The injustices of these two realms are done away with when that old gentleman appears." Then he stood up and led Fang away.

They did not return until two nights later, when Fang joyfully reported to Tao: "Aren't you going to congratulate Fifth-Brother? The Marquis of Huan arrived the night before last and tore the underworld ranking notice board to pieces. Only one third of the names on the list were

[1] A general of Shu during the Three Kingdoms period (220-280).

allowed to remain. He read all the papers by unselected candidates and was tremendously pleased to find Fifth-Brother's. He recommended him as the Maritime Inspector of South China Sea. A coach and team should be sent for him any day."

Tao served wine and congratulated him with great joy. The wine had gone several rounds when Yu asked Tao: "Is there a room free in your house?"

"What would it be for?" asked Tao.

"Zijin is on his own and has no home to return to, but he can't bear to impose upon you. I was hoping that you might give him accommodations here."

"That would be wonderful," Tao exclaimed happily. "Since we don't have many rooms, he is free to share my bed. But I'll have to inform my father first."

Yu said, "I am sure that we can depend on your father's kindness and generosity. You'll be going into the examination hall in a few days. If Zijin cannot wait for you, how about letting him go to your place first?"

Tao kept company with them in the inn, expecting that he and Fang would make the return trip together. The next day at sunset a coach and team pulled up at the gate, ready to take Yu to his post. Yu rose and shook Tao's hand, saying: "Well, this is goodbye. There is something I would like to tell you, but then again I don't want to dampen your fighting spirit."

"What is it?"

"It is your fate to see your aims frustrated. You were born in the wrong age. Your chances in this examination are one in ten. In the one after, the Marquis of Huan will appear in the world and justice will begin to prevail, so your chances will be three in ten. On the third try you can expect success." This made Tao wonder if it might not be better to give up the present attempt.

"You're wrong," said Yu. "All this is predestined. Even though you know they will be to no avail, you must weather through every one of your appointed sufferings." Then Yu turned to Fang and said, "Don't waste your time here. The year, month, day and hour are ideal this morning, so you'll be taken to your new home in my carriage. I'll make my own way on horseback." Fang bowed an appreciative farewell.

Tao's mind was in such confusion that he was unable to think of any parting instructions. He simply waved a tearful farewell. He watched the horse and the carriage until they disappeared down different roads. Regret at not sending a single word homeward to the north with Zijin came over him, but it was too late. After he had sat through all three sessions, with results that were hardly encouraging, he made the tedious trek home. He asked about Zijin the minute he entered the door, but nobody in the house knew a thing. Then he told his father of the arrangements he and Fang had made.

His father was delighted: "If that is so, your guest was here some time ago." It turned out that the old man Tao had dreamed while napping of a carriage standing at the gate. A fine young man got out, walked into the hall and bowed in greeting. The old man asked in amazement why he had come, and he answered, "Older brother promised to give me the use of an apartment, but since he had to take an examination he couldn't come with me, so I came ahead without him." Then he begged leave to go inside and meet his friend's mother. The old man was trying to keep him out with all due politeness when an old woman servant entered to say: "Madame had given birth to a young master. The old man found himself awake, greatly puzzled by his dream.

Now the younger Tao was telling of events that tallied perfectly with the old man's dream. He realized at last that his baby son was a reincarnation of Zijin. In the gladness of the moment father and son decided that he should be called Little Jin.

At first the baby was in the habit of crying at night, to its mother's dismay. Tao said, "If he is really Zijin reincarnated, his crying should stop when I go to see him." But unfamiliar faces were held by custom to be an unhealthy influence, so Tao was not allowed near the baby. But finally, when the mother's nerves could bear its howling no longer, she called for Tao.

Tao cooed to him: "Don't behave this way, Zijin. I'm here now." The baby abruptly stopped his mad squalling at the sound of Tao's voice and turned unblinking eyes on him as if to scrutinize him. Tao patted him on the head and left. From then on there was no more howling. After a few months Tao hesitated to visit the boy, for as soon as he did the boy fawned on him and begged to be held. If Tao walked away the boy would bawl uncontrollably. Tao, for his part, grew fond of the child. At the age of four the boy left his mother's side to sleep with his older brother. When his brother went out, the boy pretended to sleep and waited for his return. His brother taught him Mao's version of the *Book of Odes* in bed. The boy got through over fourty lines a night, twittering out the words like a swallow. When given essays that Zijin had left behind, he read with gay relish and learned them by heart after one reading. He was confounded when this was tried with other people's writings. By the age of seven or eight his bright, penetrating eyes showed him to be the very image of Zijin.

Tao went for examinations twice and failed both times.

In the year of 1657 abuses in the examination hall were exposed, many examiners were executed or banished, and the road to preferment by examination was thoroughly swept clean, all due to the efforts of Inspector Zhang. In the next examination Tao took an associate master of letters degree, and was soon chosen to be a senior licentiate. Despairing of further advancement, he went into retirement to teach his younger brother. He often told people: "I would not trade happiness like this for a place in Hanlin Academy."

The Chronicler of the Tales comments: "I often stop by the shrine to Master Zhang and rest my eyes on his bewhiskered, beetle-browed visage, that is somehow charged with his awesome living force. I remember also that he was known in life for the ragged thunder of his wrathful voice. Wherever his lance and horse appeared, things were sure to be set aright with a briskness that no one expected. Because the general was fond of military exploits, people put him in a class with the Marquises of Zhou Bo and GuanYing.[1] How could they know the God of Literature has such a profusion of duties that the Marquis' help has always been sorely needed! Once every thirty-five years—what a long while to wait!"

1. Two generals of Liu Bang, founder of the Han dynasty (206-6 B.C.).

37. PHOENIX SPRITE

LIU Chishui of Pingle district[1] showed remarkable brilliance at an early age and was admitted to the regional academy at fifteen. His father and mother died early, after which he wasted himself in idle pursuits. Though his family was of lower than average means, he had a fondness for ornamentation, and his bed and covers were of the finest quality. One evening he was invited to a party and, leaving his house, he forgot to blow out his candles. After several rounds of wine he remembered and hurried home, where he heard low voices in his room. Crouching, he peered into the room and saw a young man lying on his bed with a beautiful woman in his arms. Strange occurrences were nothing new in his house, which abutted on the abandoned mansion of a noble family. He realized that these were werefoxes, but was not afraid. He walked into the room, shouting "Do you think I want you sleeping and snoring on my bed?"

The two of them were so flustered that they ran off naked, clothes in arms. To his great joy, they left behind a pair of purple silk bloomers with a sewing pouch hanging from the belt. He held them in his arms under the cover, fearful that they might be taken away. Soon a mop-haired maid came in through a crack in the door and demanded

[1] In the province of Guangxi.

鳳儀
儌倖身家有富貴
先敎宜着算用循郎
君及第歸來日第一
先酬鏡裏人

the bloomers. With a laugh, Liu insisted on a reward. The maid asked if wine would do, but he did not answer. She tried to give him gold: again he would not respond. The maid laughed and left, then returned in a little while to say: "Eldest Mistress says that if you will be kind enough to return them, she will repay you with a lovely mate."

"Who will it be?" asked Liu.

"We are the Pi family. Eldest Mistress is called Eighth-Sprite, and the one lying with her was Master Hu; Second Mistress is Water Sprite—she married Master Ding of Fuchuan;[1] and Third Mistress is Phoenix Sprite. She's even prettier than the others: surely you won't find anything to object to in her."

Afraid that she would go back on her word, Liu announced his intention to sit waiting for favorable news. The maid went out, then returned to say: "Eldest Mistress sends this message: Blessed events cannot be hurried. Just now we spoke to her about it, but got cursed for our pains. All you have to do is give her some time. Our family does not give its word lightly." Liu gave her the bloomers.

Several days passed without word. One day near sunset he came home, closed the door behind him and had just sat down when his double-leafed door opened without warning. Two persons came in holding the four corners of a blanket on which they carried a young woman and said, "Now we have delivered the bride!" They laughed as they placed her on the bed, then left. He took a closer look: the movement had not roused her from her slumbers, and her breath was pungent with wine. Her flushed face and inebriated sprawl would have overwhelmed any man alive. His happiness was complete. He grabbed her feet, pulled

1. Name of a district in Guangxi province.

off her stockings, held her close and loosened her clothes. Now she was stirring. She opened her eyes and there was Liu: her four limbs were not hers to command. All she could do was complain: "Eight Sprite sold me down the river, that cheap chambermaid!"

Liu embraced her passionately: she started back at the iciness of his skin, then giggled, " 'On this night of all nights, such a n-n-*ice* man is here with me!' "

Liu followed with: " 'You angel, you! What will you do now that your n-n-*ice* man is here?' "[1] And then they took their pleasure in one another.

When it was over she said, "That shameless little hussy, defiling people's beds and then trading me off for a pair of bloomers! I'll show her!"

From then on she came, never missing a night. Their tender love flourished. One day she pulled a gold bracelet from her sleeve and said, "This belongs to Eighth Sprite."

A few days later she came with a pair of embroidered slippers set with pearls and embroidered in gold thread of exquisite workmanship. These she gave to Liu with instructions to show them to everyone he met. When Liu went out he made much of showing them to his relatives and their guests. People who asked to look paid for the privilege with wine, and so he held on to them as if they were rare commodities.

But then the girl came out one night and hinted they would have to part. Mystified, he asked the reason.

"My eldest sister is angry with me because of the slippers. She wants our family to move far away to separate me from my love."

[1] This and the preceding quote are based on a poem from the *Book of Odes*.

Liu was so frightened that he wanted to give the things back, but the girl said, "That isn't necessary. She is doing this to coerce me. If you return them, you'll be playing along with her scheme."

"Why not stay here by yourself?" asked Liu.

"My parents would be far away," she said. "The whole family, with over ten mouths to feed, relies on Master Hu to manage expenses. If I don't go along, that loose-tongued sister of mine will probably paint us in a bad light."

She did not come again after that. Two years went by, but that was not enough to ease his pangs of lovesickness. Then one day he met a young woman on the road riding an ambling horse led by an old servant. Their shoulders brushed in passing. She turned and raised her gauze veil to look at him. Her looks and bearing were exceedingly fair. In a moment a young man some distance behind her came by.

"Who is that woman? She seems to be quite a beauty." Liu praised her enthusiastically.

The young man joined his hands in deferential acknowledgement and laughed: "You flatter her too much. That is my wife."

Liu awkwardly begged his pardon.

"No harm done. After all, of the three Zhuges of Nanyang, you got the dragon.[1] There is not much worth saying about mine." Liu could make nothing of this.

"Don't you recognize the person who slept on your bed without permission?" asked the young man. Liu finally

[1] The famous prime minister of Shu during the Three Kingdoms period (220-280), Zhuge Liang, was from Nanyang district in Henan. Compared to his two brothers—who served the other two contending kingdoms—Liang was considered to be the dragon and they a tiger and a dog.

realized that he was Master Hu. The two brothers-in-law got to know one another and had great fun exchanging jibes.

"Our father-in-law has just returned," said the young man. "We were on our way to visit him. Can you come along?"

Liu was glad to go. He followed them in their zigzagging path through the mountains. Atop one mountain was a dwelling that a man of Liu's district used to go to in times of trouble. The girl dismounted and went in. In a little while several people came out to see them, saying: "Master Liu is here too!"

They went in to visit their parents-in-law and found another young man already there, resplendent in a handsome robe and pair of boots. "This is my son-in-law Master Ding of Fuchuan," said the old man. He motioned them to take their seats. Soon the board was groaning under wine and roasted meats. The talk and laughter sparkled with conviviality.

"Today my three sons-in-law are all here at once. This is truly a wonderful occasion. Also, no stranger is here: we can call my daughters out and have a family get-together."

Shortly the sisters came out. Their father had chairs set for each next to her husband. Eighth Sprite did nothing but cover her mouth and laugh at the sight of Liu. Phoenix Sprite poked fun at him. Water Sprite did not quite come up to others in appearance, but she had a calmly graceful and reserved manner. While the conversation poured forth from all around the table, she did nothing but hold her cup, a smile lingering on her lips. By this time shoes and slippers were crossing beneath the table, and the air was heavy with orchid musk. They were euphoric from wine. Liu noticed a complete set of musical instruments at the head of the couch, so he got a jade-inlaid flute and offered to play to the old man's long life. The old man was delighted and ordered the musical ones each to take part. Everyone at the table raced to get an instrument, except for Ding and Phoenix Sprite.

Eighth Sprite said, "We'll allow that Master Ding knows nothing of music, but why should you keep your fingers curled up and not show what you can do?" She threw a clapper into Phoenix Sprite's lap. Then they struck up a melody in several parts.

The old man loved it. "There is nothing better than music made by a man's own family! My young ones are all good at singing and dancing—why not let each of them show us their best?"

Eighth Sprite got up and pulled Water Sprite with her, saying: "Phoenix Sprite always acts as if her voice is too good for people: I don't dare trouble her. The two of us can sing a piece called 'Nymph on the River Luo.' "

When they had finished singing and dancing, a maid brought a golden tray holding a kind of fruit whose name nobody knew. "These were brought from Cambodia," said the old man. "They call them Temphala." He reached for a few of them and put them in front of Ding.

Phoenix Sprite was not pleased: "It isn't right to discriminate among your sons-in-law because of differences in wealth." The old man chuckled but did not speak.

Eighth Sprite said, "Daddy did that because Master Ding is from a different district. That makes him the guest. If you're going to talk about precedence, Sister Phoenix is not the only one with a tight-fisted husband."

Phoenix Sprite remained unhappy. She took off her flowery adornments, gave the clapper to the maid and sang an air called "The Dilapidated Cave." Her voice quavered and the tears ran down. When the aria was over she walked straight out with an angry sweep of her sleeves, dampening the mood of all at the table.

"The little hussy is just as wayward as always," said Eighth Sprite. They chased after her, but did not know where she had gone. Unable to face them, Liu too took his leave and headed home. He was halfway there when he saw Phoenix Sprite sitting beside the road, calling him to sit beside her.

"You're a man," she said. "Can't you do something to bring credit on your own bedpartner? 'Inside of books a golden mansion is to be found.' Please try harder!" Then she lifted her leg and said, "I was in a hurry when I left: thorns tore clear through the lining of my shoes. Do you have the ones I gave you?"

Liu pulled them out. She took them and put them on instead of her own. Liu asked for the ruined pair. A grin brightened her face as she said, "You really are nothing but a bum. Whoever saw a man hiding things from his own wife's wardrobe under his clothes? If you do care about me, there's one thing I can give you." With that, she pulled out a mirror and handed it to him, saying, "If you want to see me, search for me in your books. Otherwise, there can never be a time for us to meet again." The moment she finished speaking, she was gone.

Liu went home mired in dejection. He looked in the mirror: Phoenix Sprite was standing turned away from him, as if looking toward someone a hundred paces away. That made him think of her parting injunctions, so he refused to meet visitors and holed up in his room. One day he saw the woman in the mirror, her face toward him now, full of gaiety ready to spill over into laughter. His love for her redoubled. When no one was near, they would look at each other through the mirror. But after a month or so of this, his keen determination gradually weakened. When he went out to relax, the thought of going back often slipped his mind. Once he came back and looked at the image in the mirror. It seemed to be sniffling miserably. In a few days he looked again: now she had her back to him as before. It dawned on him that this was owing to the slackness of his efforts, whereupon he closed his door and pored over his books, not stopping night or day. In a little over a month the image was facing outward again. This was the proof of it: every time some distraction made him slacken, Phoenix Sprite's expression became forlorn, but a few days of hard study brought a smile to her face. And so he hung the mirror where he could see it night and day, as if he were in the presence of a mentor. After two years of this, victory came on his first attempt of the examination. "Now I can face my Phoenix Sprite," he said happily.

He held the mirror up and looked: there were her eyebrows so finely shaped in black, and her melon-seed teeth slightly showing. The sweetness in her face was palpable, and it was right before his eyes. His love exceeded all bounds. He riveted his gaze upon her. Suddenly the figure in the mirror laughed and said, "So this is what they mean by 'a lover in the looking glass and a sweet heart on a scroll.' "[1]

He looked about in joyful surprise, and there was Phoenix Sprite sitting beside him. He clasped her hands and asked if her parents were well. "I haven't returned home since we parted," she replied. "I secluded myself in a cave on the face of a cliff, as a way of sharing in your

[1] From the "Western Chamber Romance," a drama by Wang Shifu of the Yuan dynasty (1260-1363).

struggle."

Liu had been invited to a dinner in the prefectural seat, and Phoenix Sprite asked to go along. They went there, riding together, but people looked straight at her without seeing her. Afterward, as they set out for home, she and Liu made confidential plans to pass her off as his new bride from the prefectural seat. On their return she finally came out to meet guests and manage the household. Everyone was amazed at her beauty and had no idea she was a werefox.

Liu went to visit the magistrate at Fuchuan, under whom he had studied. There he met Ding, who graciously invited him home and treated him with lavish hospitality. "Our parents-in-law moved again recently. My wife went to pay her respects on them, and is just about to come back. I'll send a letter to her: then we can visit you together to extend our congratulations."

At first Liu suspected that Ding was also a fox, but once he made detailed inquiries into his clan affiliations, he learned that he was the son of a prominent Fuchuan merchant.

Earlier, Ding had come upon Water Sprite walking by herself as he returned from his retreat in the evening. Seeing her beauty, he gave her a sidelong glance. The girl asked if she might ride next to him on his horse. Ding was glad to oblige. He gave her a ride to his studio, where they slept together. She could enter through a crack in the window-frame, so he knew she was a werefox. She said to him, "Don't mistrust me. I wanted to put myself in your hands because of your honesty and earnestness." Ding made her his favorite and never got around to marrying anyone else.

Liu went home and borrowed a spacious house belonging to a genteel family. He prepared pleasant accommodations for his guests. He scrubbed and swept the place until it shone. The one thing that bothered him was the lack of ornaments and draperies. A night passed and a set of gleaming furnishings was there before his eyes. Within a few days, sure enough, over thirty people came bearing particolored banners and gifts of wine, in a flurry of coaches and horses that filled street and lane. Liu invited his father-in-law, Ding, and Hu to the guest house with a bow, while Phoenix Sprite greeted her mother and sisters and took them to the inner bedrooms.

Eighth Sprite said, "Now that you're a person of consequence, you don't have to hold that old grudge against your match-maker any more, you little hussy. Do you still have my bracelet and slippers?"

The girl hunted them up and gave them to her, saying: "These are still your slippers, but they are worn out from being stared at by hundreds of people."

Eighth Sprite hit her on the back with a slipper, saying: "Take that for letting Young Liu keep them." With that she threw them in the fire and pronounced an invocation:

> *When new they were just like flowers*
> *But passing time has made them wither.*
> *Such precious things must not be worn:*
> *Let Moon-Mistress fetch them thither.*

Water Sprite also said an invocation for her:

> *Once these enveloped bamboo shoots of jade,*
> *And multitudes raved when they were worn.*
> *Should Moon-Mistress ever set eyes thereon,*
> *She'd pity these slippers, so old and torn.*

Phoenix Sprite stirred the ashes, chanting:

Night after night she soared into the sky,
But then one day she left her love behind.
Now all that's left are these two slender shapes
That have been shown to all of humankind.

Then she scraped the ashes into a dustpan and formed them into ten piles. At Liu's approach, she held the dustpan out to him as a gift. It was full of embroidered slippers, all of exactly the same cut as the old pair. Eighth Sprite dashed over and knocked the dustpan to the ground. A couple of them remained until she leaned over to blow on them, causing them to vanish without a trace.

The next day Ding set out first on the long journey home with his wife. Eighth Sprite could not get enough of joking with her sister. Hu and the old man urged her repeatedly, but not until high noon did Hu and his wife go out and leave with their group.

Earlier, when they had just arrived, a marketlike crowd of onlookers had turned out for the impressive entourage. Two bandits who caught a glimpse of the beautiful lady were captivated by her, so they laid plans to abduct her on the road. Seeing her leave the village, they trailed along behind. They had closed in to less than an arrow's flight away, when her horses broke into a headlong gallop. They were left behind until the road went into a defile between two cliffs and the carriage slowed down. One of them overtook it, brandishing his sword and roaring. All her followers ran away. He dismounted and lifted the curtain: there sat an old woman. He wondered if he had accidently caputured the lady's mother, and just as he started to turn away from her, a sword bit into his right arm. Within moments he was bound hand and foot. A closer look showed that the cliffs were not cliffs: they were the gatetower on Pingle's city walls. In the carriage was the mother of Doctor of Letters Li, who had been returning from the country. The other bandit rode up from behind. One of his horse's legs was lopped off, and he too was bound fast. The gatekeeper turned them over to the prefect, to whom they admitted their guilt at the first interrogation. Questioning revealed that one of them was a notorious bandit who had been at large.

In spring of the next year, Liu passed the third-degree examination. Phoenix Sprite turned down invitations to all her relatives' receptions so as not to court trouble. Liu did not marry anyone else. Once he got the position of a ministry secretary, he obtained a concubine and fathered two sons.

The Chronicler of the Tales comments: "Alas! Immortals can be just as cold, or just as warm, as mortals! 'If you don't make an honest effort when you're young, you're asking for misery in old age.' It is a pity to be without an ambitious, beautiful woman to cast images of gloom or laughter in your mirror. My wish is that immortals to the number of the grains of sand along the Ganges River would all send lovely girls down to be married into the human world. Then living beings would suffer less than they do in this sea of poverty and bitterness."

38. HERDBOYS

TWO shepherd boys who went into the mountains came upon a wolf den. Finding two cubs in the den, they thought of a plan, and each of them grabbed one of the cubs. They climbed two trees several dozen paces apart. Soon an adult wolf came and found to its great consternation that its cubs were missing from the den. One of the boys twisted his cub's paws and ears until it yelped. The wolf looked up toward the sound, charged angrily to the foot of the tree and howled as it scrabbled at the trunk with its claws. The boy in the other tree then made his cub scream frantically. The wolf stood still and looked in all directions until it found where the sound came from, then left the one and ran to the other. As before, it howled and ran about. Then another scream came from the first tree, so it turned and dashed back. It went back and forth dozens of times, without pausing in its cries or resting its feet. Its pace gradually slowed and its howls weakened. Finally it gasped and lay stiff. For a long time it did not move. The boys climbed down to look at it: its breath had stopped.

Suppose we have a ruffian, gripping his sword and glaring as if about to pounce on someone and eat him alive. The object of his anger will slam the door and turn away. The roughneck may run himself ragged and shout himself hoarse, but there is no one to stand against him. Does this mean that he will lord it over everyone as he pleases? He does not realize that his is no more than the might of a beast: people amuse themselves by making light of it.

牧豎
狼子呼嗥踞
樹巔老狼樹
底走盤旋
休言蠢類
無知識舐
犢私情
亦可憐

39. SCHOLAR WANG ZI-AN

SUCCESS in the examination hall eluded Wang Zi-an, a renowned scholar of Dongchang.[1] Once, after a stint in the examination cell, his expectations ran high. As the time for posting the results drew near, he drank himself into a stupor, went home and lay down in his inner chamber. Suddenly a man came in and reported to him: "Mounted messengers have come."

Wang staggered to his feet and said, "Tip them ten thousand!"

His family played along with his drunkness and spoofingly calmed him: "Go ahead and sleep. We've already tipped them."

Wang went to sleep. Soon someone else came in to say, "You have been awarded the doctorate!"

"I haven't gone to the capital yet," said Wang to himself. "How could I have gotten on that list?"

"Do you forget?" asked the man. "You've been through all three examinations."

Greatly elated, Wang got up and called: "Tip him ten thousand!" His family spoofed him as before.

After a while a man rushed in, saying: "Your performance in the palace got you into the Hanlin Academy. The butler is here." Sure enough, he saw two men in clean,

[1] In Shandong province.

王子安
醉裏頻呼賞十
千東昌名士竟
拜稽首

well-cut clothes and hats kneeling at the foot of his bed. Wang called for food and wine to serve them. His family played along with him again, laughing to themselves at his inebriety. After a time it occurred to Wang that he simply must go out to flaunt his honor before the neighborhood. He shouted for one of the butlers—fifty shouts in all—but there was no answer.

"Please lie down awhile and wait. We're going to fetch him," the giggling servants told him.

More time passed, and, sure enough, the butler came back. Wang pounded on the bed, stamped his feet and cursed mightily: "Where on earth did you go, you half-witted lackey?"

"You miserable wretch!" roared the butler. "I was having a little joke with you before, but now you're cursing in earnest, aren't you?"

Wang jumped up irately, lunged at him and knocked off his hat, tumbling to the floor himself. His wife came in to help him up, saying: "How did you get so plastered?"

"The butler is an ass, so I taught him a lesson. Does that mean I'm plastered?"

"In this house there is only one serving woman," his wife said laughingly. "She cooks for you by day and warms your feet at night. What butler would wait on an penniless bag of bones like you?" His children all burst out laughing. This sobered Wang enough to make him feel he had just wakened from a dream. At last he realized the whole thing was an illusion. Still, he remembered that the butler's hat had fallen. Searching behind the door, he found a tasseled hat the size of a bowl. Everyone was puzzled.

He laughed at himself and said, "There was once a man who was jeered at by ghosts: now I've been ridiculed by werefoxes."

The Chronicler of the Tales comments: "Bachelors of letters who go into the examination cells have seven semblances. When they first go in, barefoot and carrying their baskets, they resemble beggars. At roll call, when monitors shout and lictors curse, they resemble prisoners. Going to their own numbered cells, they resemble sluggish wasps at the end of autumn in the way their heads poke out of the openings and their feet stick out from the rooms. When they come out of the arena, wearing every imaginable sort of dispirited expression, they resemble ailing birds just released from a cage. Then, as they are waiting for news of their results, they start at shapes they see in grass and trees, and their daydreams become full-blown fantasies. Now they see their hopes realized, and in a matter of moments a mansion and pavilions take shape: now they see themselves stymied, and in a blink and a breath their bones have decayed. At this juncture the restlessness of their movements makes them resemble an orangutan on a leash. Suddenly messengers come on flying steeds, but the expected names are not on the list. Their color pales dramatically, and they lapse into deathlike despondence. At this time they resemble poisoned flies that are insensible even when handled. When first defeated, their hearts are like dead ashes and their spirits are broken. They rant and rail at the blindness of the examiners and the uselessness of their writing brushes and ink, and inevitably come to such a pass that they gather up all the things on their desk and commit them to the flames. Burning them isn't enough, so they stomp them to pieces. Stomping isn't enough, so they throw them into the gutter. After this they let their long hair down and go live like hermit in the mountains, where they turn their faces toward a stone wall. Anyone who brings them essays with words like 'moreover that which' and 'previously opined' will assuredly be chased away at spearpoint. But before long, as the day of their humiliation recedes into the past and their anger fades, there gradually comes again an itch to exercise unused skills. In this they resemble a pigeon whose eggs have been smashed. The only thing it can do is fly about with twigs in its beak fashioning a nest, and then sit hatching a new clutch of eggs. People in such a situation are in mortal agony, but to those who look on from the side, they are utterly ridiculous. In an instant, Wang Zi-an's ting heart was filled with a multitude of emotions. I imagine the ghosts and werefoxes had been laughing at him in secret for a long time, so they took advantage of his drunkenness to make fun of him. No wonder his bed partner, who had her wits about her, could not help laughing. We may observe that the sweet taste of success in the examinations is but momentary, and a position in the Imperial Academy is but a transitory thing. The werefoxes who let Wang Zi-an experience all of this in one morning were as generous to him as the teacher who recommended him for the examinations."

40. FOX-GIRL CHANGTING

SHI Taipu of Mount Tai took an interest in the art of exorcism. A Taoist priest met him and appreciated his intellect enough to accept him as a disciple. He took out a boxed set of books with an ivory label: the first volume dealt with exorcism of werefoxes, and the second with exorcism of ghosts. He handed the second volume to Shi, saying: "Study this carefully: food, clothing, and a beautiful woman will all be yours."

Shi asked the Taoist's name, and he replied, "I am Wang Chicheng of Dark Emperor's Shrine in the village north of Bian city."[1]

For several days he kept Shi with him to pass on all his skills. Shi became so well versed in charms and books of incantations that people lined up at his gate to offer him acquaintance gifts. One day an old man came, introduced himself as Weng, and laid out a glittering array of cash and silken goods, saying that his danghter was gravely ill due to possession by a ghost. He begged earnestly that Shi make a personal call. When Shi heard the illness was critical, he turned down the gifts and went along to see what he could do.

After going a dozen *li* they entered a mountain village and came to the old man's house, which was a cluster of

[1] Present-day Kaifeng of Henan province.

splendid buildings and galleries. As he entered the room, a maid hitched aside the crepe curtain of the bed with a hook, revealing a girl lying inside. She appeared to be fourteen or fifteen years old. Her limbs rested limply on the bed, and her face was drawn with anguish. At his approach she suddenly opened her eyes and said, "Here is a doctor who knows what he is doing."

The whole family rejoiced at this and told him that she had not spoken for days. Shi then left the room to inquire into the symptoms. The old man Weng said, "A young man came in broad daylight and slipped into bed with her. When we went in to catch him, he was gone. In a little while he was back again, which leads us to think he is a ghost."

"If he's a ghost, driving him away won't be any trouble," said Shi. "But it might be a werefox, in which case I can't say what the outcome will be."

"No, it couldn't be that," said Weng. Shi gave them a written charm and stayed in their house that evening. During the night a well-dressed young man came into the room. Guessing he was a member of his host's family, Shi got up and asked him his name.

"I am a ghost. Everyone in the Weng family is a werefox. I took a fancy to his daughter Hong-Ting and attached myself to her for a lark. Ghosts do no damage to their inner virtues when they haunt werefoxes. Why should you interfere with someone else's attachments just to protect these werefoxes? Hong-ting's elder sister Changting is a dazzling beauty of the rarest kind. I have left that piece of jade intact for someone more deserving than myself. Wait to perform your cure until Changting agrees to marry you: when that time comes, I'll leave on my own." Shi assented.

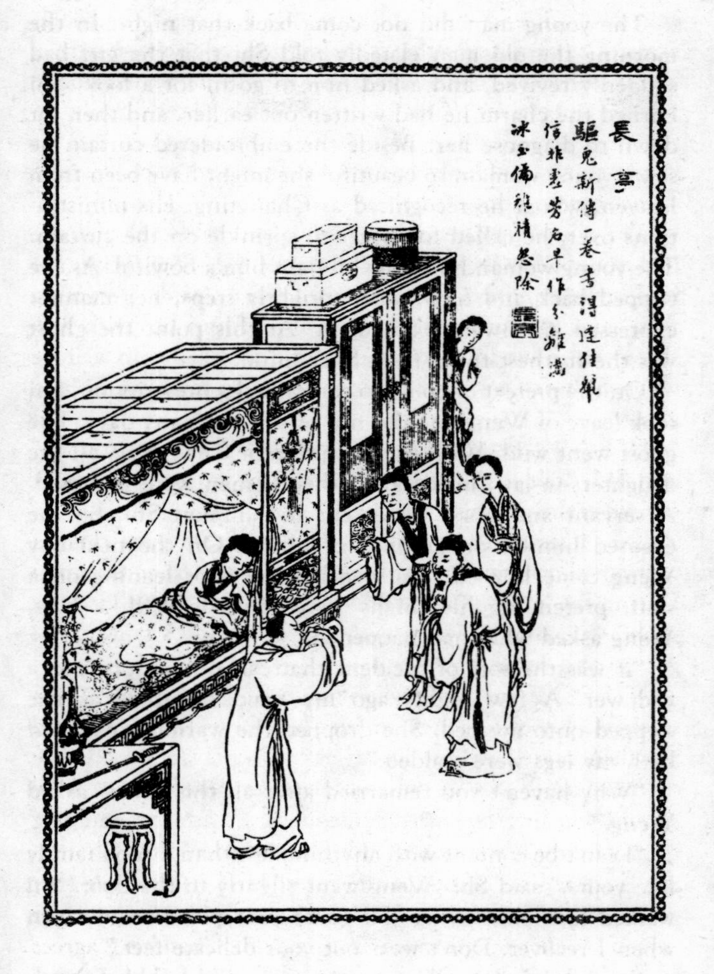
長亭
驅鬼新傳一卷書得逢佳耦
信非虛芳名早作參商讖
冰玉偏難積怨除

The young man did not come back that night. In the morning the old man elatedly told Shi that the girl had suddenly revived, and asked him to go in for a look. Shi burned the charm he had written out earlier, and then sat down to diagnose her. Beside the embroidered curtain he saw a young woman, so beautiful she might have been from heaven, whom he recognized as Changting. His ministrations over, he called for water to sprinkle on the curtain. The young woman hurriedly brought him a bowlful. As she tripped back and forth with sprightly steps, her manner expressed an inward excitement. At this point the ghost was the furthest thing from Shi's mind.

On the pretext of going to compound a prescription, Shi took leave of Weng and did not return for many days. The ghost went wild. With the exception of Changting, all the daughters-in-law, maids and other women were molested. A servant and horse were sent to summon Shi, but he excused himself on grounds of illness. On the next day Weng came himself. Shi went to the door leaning on a staff, pretending his thighs were injured. With a bow, Weng asked what had happened.

"It was the sort of accident that can only happen to a widower. A few nights ago my maid stumbled as she stepped onto my bed. She dropped the warming pan and both my legs were scalded."

"Why haven't you remarried after all this time?" asked Weng.

"I can't be content with anything less than a good family like yours," said Shi. Weng went silently to the door. Shi walked him out, saying "I'll go to your place on my own when I recover. Don't wear out your delicate feet."

Several days later Weng came again. Shi hobbled out to meet him. After asking a few polite questions about Shi's condition, Weng said, "My wife and I had a talk. If you drive the ghost away and let my family sleep in peace, we are willing to send our little seventeen-year-old daughter Changting to do your bidding."

Shi happily bumped his forehead against the ground and told the old man: "Since you treat me so magnanimously, I would be ashamed to go on coddling my ailing body." They went out the gate immediately, riding shoulder to shoulder. After examining the victims of the disturbances Shi asked to discuss arrangements with Weng's wife, for fear that Weng would go back on his word.

The old woman rushed into the room, saying: "How could you doubt us, sir? She gave him a golden hairpin used by Changting as a token of faith. Shi bowed before her. Then he gathered all the members of the family for purification and casting-out. Changting alone was hidden from sight, so he wrote a charm for her to wear on her sash and had it sent to her. That night all was still: all signs of ghosts were gone. Only Hongting moaned without cease, but the moment Shi treated her with magic water, she seemed as if she had never been afflicted. Shi asked leave to go, but Weng courteously held him back. When evening came his host urged him even more insistently to enjoy the spread of meat dishes and fruit.

The water clock had gone down two notches when the host bid his guest good night and retired. As Shi's head touched the pillow an urgent knocking sounded at the door. He got up to look; Changting slipped in, closing the door behind her, and blurted out in confused agitation: "My family is going to take revenge on you with sharp knives. Run away quickly!" Having said this, she turned straight around and walked out the door.

Shi shuddered and turned pale. He scrambled frantically

over the wall. In the distance he saw the glow of a fire. Hurrying up to it, he found men from his neighborhood who were out on a night hunting trip. He waited till they finished hunting, then went home with them.

Shi's heart seethed with outrage, but there was nowhere he could go to demand justice. He thought of going to Bian and hunting up the Taoist Wang Chicheng, but his old, debilitated father was with him at home. Day and night he considered the alternatives, but he could not decide whether to go or stay.

Suddenly one day two carriages drew up at his gate. Inside were the old man Weng and his wife, bringing Changting along. They said, "Why didn't you discuss things further with us after you went home that night?"

At the sight of Changting, Shi's resentment subsided and he kept his feelings about the past hidden. At the old lady's prompting, the two bowed in confirmation of their marriage. Shi wanted to arrange a banquet, but the old lady refused: "I have things to do. I can't sit around regaling myself with fine flavors and vintages. The old man of our house is in the final stages of senility. If there have been some oversights, I would feel fortunate if you would consider me for Changting's sake."

She climbed in her cart and they rode away. Actually, the old lady had not heard of the plan to kill their prospective son-in-law. She was not aware of it until the men returned from their unsuccessful chase. She was offended at the injustice done to Shi, and she railed at Weng day after day. Changting refused to swallow anything but her own tears. The mother insisted on taking the girl to Shi against her father's wishes. But Shi only learned of this after Changting came to live with him and he had time to question her.

Two or three months later, the girl's family wanted to take her home for a visit. Shi would not allow her to go, for fear that she would not return. From that time on, she often broke into crying fits. In a little over a year she gave birth to a son named Brilliant-Child. She hired a wet nurse to feed him; but the boy was choleric and insisted on sleeping with his mother at night.

One day her family sent a carriage with the message that the old woman dearly missed her daughter. Changting was more heartbroken than ever: Shi could not bear to hold her back any longer. She tried to take the child in her arms as she left, but Shi would not let her, so she returned alone. At her departure she agreed to see him again in a month, but half a year passed with no word from her. He sent someone to bring news of her, but the house her family once rented had long been vacant. The passing of two more years brought an end to Shi's wishing and hoping, but the child's nightlong wailing pierced his helpless heart. Then his father weakened and died, which multiplied his misery. He was incapacitated by nervous exhaustion during the mourning period, and unable to receive the condolences of guests and friends.

Shi was wallowing in a demoralized muddle when he suddenly heard a woman come into his room crying. He looked up and saw Changting in hempen mourning clothes. A great surge of grief came over him and threw him into a faint. The maid's cries of alarm brought Changting out of her sobbing fit. She cradled him in her arms and stroked him a good while before he gradually revived. Thinking that he was dead, he told her that they were now united in the underworld.

"You are wrong," she said. "I am too disobedient to win my father's favor. He hindered me from coming back for three years. That is the reason I betrayed my trust. Recently a member of my family passed by here on his way from the East Coast, and so I learned the news of your father's death. I broke off my love for you in obedience to a parental command, but now I dare not neglect the observances for my father-in-law to submit to an irrational command. My mother knows I am here, but my father doesn't."

As she spoke, her child threw himself into her arms. When she had finished speaking, she stroked him and sobbed, "I have a father, but my son has had no mother. The child also wailed and howled. Everyone in the room brushed back their tears. Changting rose and set to work putting the house in order. Shi was greatly relieved to see ample offerings put neatly in place before the coffin. However, he had been ill for some time and could not get up at once, so Changting asked his cousin to receive and entertain callers. When the funeral was over Shi could at last get up with a cane to help arrange the burial.

After the burial, Changting excused herself to return home and receive the reprimand she had coming for deceiving her father. Shi tugged at her arm and her son wailed, which moved her to stay. Not long afterwards a servant came to say that her mother was ill, whereupon she said to Shi: "I came on account of your father. Won't you let me go for my mother's sake?"

Shi gave his approval. Changting had the nurse carry the boy away to another part of the house, then went sniveling out the gate. Once gone, she did not return for years. Shi and his son slowly forgot about her. Then one day he threw open the door at the break of dawn, and Changting glided in. As Shi questioned her in amazement, she sat dejectedly on the bed and sighed, "Back in the days when I was growing up in secluded chambers, one *li* seemed far to me: Now I run a thousand *li* in one night. You can imagine how tired I am.

He questioned her closely. She opened her mouth to speak and then thought better of it. Under the weight of his ceaseless entreaties she said between sobs: "By telling you now, I'll probably make myself miserable and you delighted. A few years back we moved to Shanxi and rented living quarters in the mansion of Squire Zhao. Landlord and guests got along wonderfully, so we gave Hongting to be the young master's wife. But the young master strayed from home frequently, and their married life was by no means peaceful. When my sister went home and told our father how she was treated, he kept her at home for half a year and wouldn't hear of her going back. The young master was furious. He hired a wicked man from goodness knows where, who sent magic fetters to bind my father and take him away. Everyone in the house was horrified: within minutes they scattered to the four quarters."

Shi could not help but laugh when he heard this. The girl raged: "He may be cruel, but he's my father. You and I have been like lute and zither for years. There has been only love between us, never blame. Now my father is gone and my family is ruined. A hundred mouths are wandering with nowhere to turn. Even if you aren't sorry for my father, I thought you would at least sympathize with me. But when you heard, you hopped about with a grin on your face and didn't say a word to comfort me. It just isn't right!" She went out with a sweep of her sleeve. Shi ran after her to apologize, but she had vanished. In his dejection he blamed himself for letting her abandon him this way.

A few days later his wife turned up, together with her mother. Shi, in his joy to see them, questioned them solicitously. He was shocked when mother and daughter both went down on their knees before him, and demanded to know the reason. Both of them burst into sobs. It was the girl who answered: "I left you in anger. But I cannot harden myself now—I must ask for your help once again. I have no honor left to stand on."

"Even though my father-in-law is inhuman, I will never forget your mother's generosity and your love. You know it is human nature to delight in the misfortune of an unkind person. Couldn't you have overlooked that for a while?"

"Not long ago I ran into my mother on the road," said the girl. "It was then that I learned that your master is the man who bound my father."

"If he is, it's a simple matter," said Shi. "But as long as my father-in-law is detained, he and his children have to remain apart. I'm afraid that once he returns, your husband will weep and your son will mourn." His mother-in-law vowed to make her wishes plain, and Changting promised to repay his kindness, so Shi packed his bag right away and went to Bian. He asked the way to the Dark-Emperor's Shrine and found that Wang Chicheng had returned just a little while ago. Shi went in and opened the visit with a bow.

"What brings you here?" asked his master.

Shi, noticing an old fox tied in the kitchen by a cord passed through a puncture in its front leg, laughed and said, "This old ghoul is the reason for my visit." Chicheng asked what he meant.

"This is my father-in-law." He told his master the whole story. The Taoist would not lightly let the fox go, claiming that it was cunning and devious, but he finally gave in to Shi's insistent pleas. Shi gave a complete account of the fox's deceitfulness, which made the fox slink under the stove as if in humiliation.

The Taoist said with a laugh: "At least he hasn't lost all sense of shame."

Shi rose and led the fox outside, where he cut the cord with a knife and began to pull it out. The fox, in the extremity of its pain, snapped its teeth at him. Instead of pulling the cord out all at once, Shi did it by fits and starts and laughingly asked, "Since this is so painful, old man, would you rather I didn't pull it out?" The fox's glowering eyes flashed fire, and a livid look came over its face. When he let it go, it shook its tail, ran away from the shrine, and was gone. Shi took leave of the Taoist and started back. Three days before his arrival, word of Weng's release had reached the old woman, who went ahead to meet him, leaving her daughter to wait for Shi. When he arrived, Changting came out to greet him and went down on her knees. Shi helped her to her feet, saying, "As long as you don't forget our love, I don't care about gratitude."

"We have moved back to our old place not far from your village," said Changting. There will be nothing to hinder the exchange of messages and news. When I want to go home for a visit, I can make it there and back in three days. Do you believe me?"

"My son came into this world with no mother to care for him: yet his life was not cut short. Now I've grown used to the life of a widower. Instead of behaving like Young Master Zhao, I repaid spite with kindness. I've done everything I could for you. You will do me wrong if you don't come back. The road may be short, but if you ignore me again, it will be better for me if I mistrust you.

Changting left the next day, then returned two days later.

"Why so soon?" he asked.

"My father still won't forgive you for toying with his pride in Bian. He raved on and on about it. I didn't want to hear any more, so I left early."

From then on the women of the two houses visited back and forth constantly though father- and son-in-law made sure to stay out of touch, or so the story goes.

The Chronicler of the Tales comments: "The werefox's emotions were treacherous and unpredictable: that in itself indicated great deceitfulness. He fell into the rut of disavowing his two daughters' marriages, and from this his dishonesty can be seen. However, by maneuvering him into allowing the marriage, Shi invited his disavowal at the very beginning. Also, since the son-in-law saved the father for love of the daughter, he should have disregarded past injury and transformed the man with benevolence. Instead, he toyed with him at a crucial moment. Small wonder the werefox would not forget his anger till the end of his life. In this world there are many feuds like this between fathers-in-law and sons-in-law."

41. ROUGE

OLD Bian of Dongchang,[1] a veterinarian by profession, had an intelligent, beautiful daughter whose childhood name was Rouge. Her father intended to find a mate from an esteemed family for his beloved, precious girl, but noblemen were too proud to connect themselves with him, for they despised his low rank and lack of means. Thus the girl reached hairpin age without being spoken for.

The wife of the Gong family across the street, née Wang, was a capricious, madcap sort who often spent time conversing in the girl's chamber. One day, while seeing her friend to the door, the girl caught sight of a passing young man, commandingly handsome in his white gown and hat. She must have found him distracting, judging from the way the rippling glances of her eyes lingered after him. The young man lowered his head and hastened away. The girl's gaze remained fixed on him as he dwindled in the distance. Wang saw what was on her mind and poked fun at her: "With ability and looks like yours, young lady, I am sure there would be no regrets if you could be matched with such a man." A tinge of red spread over the girl's cheeks. She said nothing, but her pulse quickened.

"Do you know that gentleman?" asked Wang.

"No, I don't" she answered.

[1] A district in Shandong province.

"That's Bachelor of Letters E Autumn-Falcon from South Lane, son of the late Exemplar. I used to live in his neighborhood, so I know him. No man in this world is as kind and gentle as he is. He's in plain dress now because the mourning period for his wife is not yet over. If you are willing I will carry a message telling him to send a matchmaker."

The girl did not speak. Wang went away laughing. Several days passed with no news. She surmised that Wang had not yet found time to pay a visit, and she also doubted if the son of an official would care to stoop and pick up what was left in his way. She whiled away her time despondently, suffering from thoughts that would not go away, till melancholy deprived her of appetite and rest. It was then that Wang came to see her and demanded to know the reason for her illness.

"I don't know myself," was her answer. "But since the last day you saw me, I've been restless and depressed. I'm living from breath to breath. It will be all over any day now."

Wang lowered her voice: "My husband hasn't gotten back from his selling trip yet: there is nobody to get the word to young E. Is that what is making you ill?"

The girl's face was crimson for a good while. Wang joked: "So that's what it's about. Now that you are in this condition, why bother about scruples? Have him come spend a night with you first. You don't think he'll turn you down, do you?"

"Things have gotten to the point that I can't play coy," said the girl. "If only he could see far enough past my poverty and low rank to send a matchmaker over, my illness would be cured. But if it takes having a rendezvous with him, I simply won't do it!

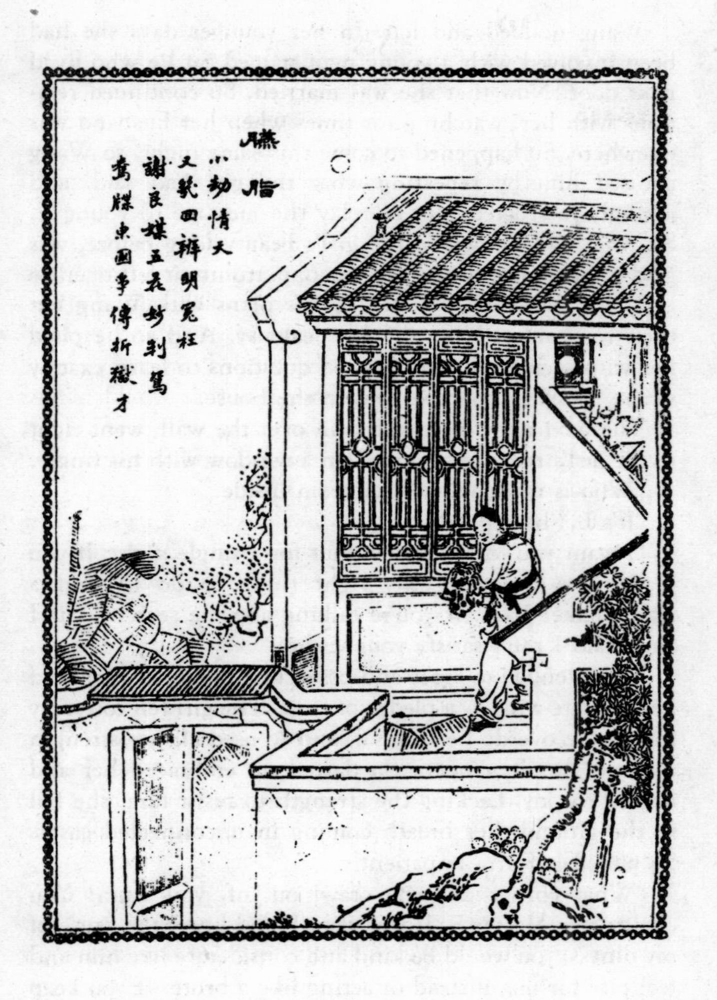
臙脂
小劫情天
又教回辨明冤枉
謝良媒五表妙判鴛
鴦牒東國爭傳折獄才

Wang nodded and left. In her younger days she had been involved with a young man named Su Jie who lived next door. Now that she was married, Su continued relations with her, watching for times when her husband was elsewhere. Su happened to come this same night, so Wang amused him by repeating what the girl had said, and jokingly instructed him to relay the message to young E. Su, who had known of the girl's beauty long before, was glad to hear this, because of the opportunity it left open to him. He thought of discussing his plans with Wang but then reconsidered, fearing her jealousy. And so he plied her with seemingly disinterested questions to learn exactly where the girl's chamber was in the house.

The next night he climbed in over the wall, went right to the girl's room and tapped on a window with his finger.

"Who is it?" came a voice from inside.

"It's E," he replied.

"I want you for a lifetime, not for a single night. If you really love me, the only right thing to do is send a matchmaker soon. If you're talking about a secret affair I am afraid I can't satisfy your wishes."

Su pretended to agree and beseeched her to let him hold her delicate wrist as a pledge of trust. The girl felt too sorry for him to overdo her refusal, and so used all her strength to push the door open. Su darted in, embraced her and begged for joy. Lacking the strength to resist him, she fell to the ground, her breath coming in unconnected gasps. Su pulled her arm impatiently.

"What corner did you crawl out of, you scum? You couldn't be Master E. If you were E and knew the cause of my illness, you would be kind and considerate like him and feel pity for me, instead of acting like a brute. If you keep behaving this way I'll be forced to scream. It won't do either of us any good to have our good names ruined!"

Fearing that his deception would be uncovered, Su dared not force himself on her any further, so he only asked to meet her again. The girl set the bride-welcoming as the time for their next meeting. Su thought that was too long to wait and asked again. The girl, fed up with his clinging, asked him to wait for her recovery. Su begged her to give him a token of remembrance, but she would not, and so he grabbed her by the leg, pulled off her embroidered slipper and left.

The girl called him back saying: "I've already promised myself to you: why should I grudge you anything? My only fear is that 'the tiger might be painted to look like a dog.' We could become the objects of vile slander because of this. Now you are holding part of my intimate wardrobe in your hand. I see no hope of getting it back. If you betray me, death is my only way out."

After Su left he went to stay the night at Wang's place. He laid down in bed, but he could not stop thinking of the slipper. He furtively fumbled in his robe and was shocked to find that it was not there. He jumped up, turned the lampshade, then shook his clothes and felt around on the floor. He turned to ask Wang, who wouldn't answer his questions, so he began to wonder if she had hidden it. She laughed deliberately to heighten his suspicions. Su could not keep it to himself any longer: he told her the truth. When his story was finished he went over every inch of ground outside the gate, candle in hand, but still it did not turn up. He went back to bed greatly annoyed, cheering himself with the thought that nobody was out this late at night and that if he had dropped the slipper it would still be in the street. He got up early in the morning and searched for it, but it was still nowhere to be found.

Now there lived on the same street a shiftless vagrant named Mao the Elder, who had once made futile advances to Wang. Knowing that Su was having an affair with her, he had the notion to catch them in a compromising situation so that he could make demands. Walking by her gate this same night, he found it unlocked and slipped inside. Just outside the window he stepped on something soft and cottony. He picked it up to look: it was a woman's slipper wrapped in a handkerchief. Eavesdropping at the window, he heard Su give a complete account of his evening. Mao congratulated himself on his good luck as he crept away.

Several evenings later he climbed the wall and entered the girl's house. Being unfamiliar with the layout, he blundered into the old man's quarters. The old man looked out the window and saw a man who, judging from the sounds and movements he made, had evidently come for his daughter. Rage swelled in the old man's heart as he rushed out knife in hand. Mao turned in great fright and ran. He was about to climb the wall, but old Bian was close behind him. In desperation at having nowhere to run, he turned around and wrenched the blade away. Behind them the old woman let out a loud scream. Unable to free himself from the old man's grip, Mao put an end to him. The girl, who by this time had recovered somewhat from her illness, was roused up by the the noise. Everyone went to the scene with candles: the old man's skull was split and he had lost the power of speech. In a short while he was no longer of this world. An embroidered slipper was found beneath the wall, and the old woman could see that it belonged to Rouge. When force was applied the girl sobbed out the truth. Not being hardhearted enough to implicate Wang, she claimed that young E had come on his own.

At daybreak charges were brought before the district court. The magistrate had E taken into custody. E was a quiet, reserved person, nineteen years of age, who got flustered like a child in the presence of strangers. Being arrested frightened him out of his wits. He lacked the presence of mind to defend himself in the courtroom. All he did was tremble, which gave the magistrate all the more reason to accept the truth of the accusations. He put the finger-vise and cane to brutal use: the pain was more than a bookishly inclined person could stand, and in this way a confession was wrung out of E. Afterwards he was transported to the prefectural court, where he received as many floggings as he had in the district.

Young E was consumed with outrage. Over and over he wished for the chance to confront Rouge and demand the truth, but when they did meet she vilified him with such fury he was tongue-tied and could not state his own case, with the result that he was sentenced to death. None of the numerous officials he was sent back and forth to for further hearings opposed the sentence.

Finally the case was referred to Jinan[1] prefecture for a confirmatory decision. At that time Master Wu Nandai was the prefect of Jinan. One look at young E was enough to make him doubt that this man was a murderer. Wu secretly sent a person to question him informally and considerately, so that he could say his piece. The result convinced Wu that E had been unjustly accused. He spent a few days before the hearing devising a strategy.

First he asked Rouge: "Was anyone aware that you had agreed to a meeting?"

"No one," was the answer.

[1] Now provincial capital of Shandong.

"Was anyone else present when you first saw young E?"

"No one."

Wu then called E to the stand and reassured him in kind tones. The scholar testified without being asked: "Once, when I was walking past her gate, I noticed my former neighbor Wang coming out of the doorway with this young woman. I quickened my steps right away to get past them. Since then I have not spoken so much as a word to her."

Master Wu roared at the girl: "You just said that nobody was with you. What was the neighbor woman doing there?" He ordered his men to prepare the instruments of interrogation.

"Wang was there," said the girl in fright: "But she really had nothing to do with him."

Master Wu adjourned the hearing and gave an order to arrest Wang. She was brought in a few days later and forbidden any communication with the girl. Wu resumed the hearing immediately.

"Who is the killer?" he asked Wang.

"I don't know."

Then Master Wu laid a trap for her, saying: "Rouge has testified that you were familiar with the man who killed old Bian. Are you trying to conceal that fact?"

"It's a lie," wailed the woman. "The cheap chambermaid got all worked up over this man. I may have said something about acting as matchmaker, but I was only joking with her. How was I to know that she would lure a lover onto her property?"

Master Wu had to question her in detail before she would repeat what she had said jokingly on that and later occasions. He called Rouge to the stand and thundered: "You claimed she did not know a thing. Now she testifies that she was going to have you two introduced. Why is that?"

"My foolishness caused my father's cruel death," the girl wailed tearfully. "Who knows how many years it will take before this case is concluded? On top of that, I have involved other people. I just can't bear it."

Master Wu asked Wang: "After you had made those jokes, did you tell anyone about them?"

"I did not," Wang testified.

"There is nothing that a husband and wife don't talk about in bed," thundered Master Wu. "How can you say that you didn't?"

"My husband was away on a long trip," Wang testified.

"That may well be, but playing a joke on someone is invariably a matter of mocking another's dullness in order to show off one's own intelligence. Who do you think can fool by claiming that you didn't tell anyone?" He ordered the use of finger-vises on all ten fingers.

The woman had no choice. "I told Su about it," she admitted.

Then Master Wu released E and had Su arrested. When Su was brought into court he testified; "I don't know."

"Anyone who Sues for the favor of a whore is not a proper gentleman!"

A severe beating was all it took to make Su admit: "It's true that I tricked the girl, but after I lost the slipper I didn't dare go back. I swear that I know nothing of the murder."

"A man who would climb over a wall is capable of anything!" Again Master Wu had Su beaten. Unable to stand up to the torture, Su finally accepted the blame.

The confession was written up and reported to Wu's superiors. There was not one who did not praise Master

Wu's perspicuity. It was an irrevocable case—as settled as a mountain—so there was nothing left for Su but to crane his neck and watch as the day of execution drew near. Still, even though Su was reckless and ill-behaved, he was a widely known intellectual in the eastern region.[1] He had heard of the civil examiner Master Shi Yushan's superior ability as well as his fondness and solicitude for scholars of talent, so he complained of the wrong done to him in a touching and sorrowful petition. Master Shi reviewed his confession, poring over it again and again, and struck his desk, saying: "This young man has been wronged!"

Then Master Shi applied to the administrative and judicial authorities of the province for permission to hold another hearing.

He asked Su: "Where did you lose the shoe?"

"I don't remember," answered Su. "But it was still in my sleeve when I knocked on Wang's gate."

Shi then proceeded to question Wang: "How many lovers do you have besides Su Jie?"

"I have none."

"Why should a promiscuous woman restrict herself to one man?" asked Master Shi.

"I was involved with Su Jie since childhood," she testified. "That is why I could not break it off. It wasn't that no one made advances to me after that, but I really didn't care to accept them."

Shi told her to name such a man in order to substantiate her claim.

"Mao the Elder of my neighborhood made repeated advances; I refused him every time," she testified.

"How is it that you've become so chaste and pure all of

[1] Shandong.

a sudden?" asked Master Shi. He ordered his men to beat her. The woman bumped her forehead on the floor until the blood ran to protest her innoncence, so he let her go. Then he resumed his questioning: "When your husband was far away, weren't there men who came claiming to have business with him?"

"There were. I let So-and-so A and So-and-so B into my house a few times to borrow money or leave gifts."

Actually A and B were idlers living in the same alley who had designs on Wang without being able to realize them. Master Shi had their names entered in the record and ordered them into court. When they were rounded up, Master Shi had them taken to the temple of the city god, where they were made to kneel before the altar. Then he told them: "A short while ago a spirit came to me in a dream and told me that one of you is the murderer. There can be no lying now that you are before the all-knowing god. If you give yourself up, there is still the possibility of forgiveness. If you speak falsely, there will be no pardon once the truth is out."

All of them claimed with one voice that they had not committed murder. The judge had wooden cangues, manacles and fetters laid out on the ground and was about to have them put on the suspects. Their hair was to be knotted atop their heads and they were to be stripped naked. All howled at the injustice of this harsh treatment. The judge ordered them untied and said, "Since you won't confess, I will have ghosts and spirits point out the murderer."

He had his men screen off all the windows in the main hall with blankets of felt, making sure that there was not the slightest crack of light. Then he had the suspects' shirts pulled down to expose their backs, and drove them into the dark, where they were given a basin of water to wash their hands. That done, he had them tied near the wall and warned them: "Keep your face toward the wall and do not move. The god will write a sign on the back of whichever one of you is the murderer."

Before long he called them out for inspection, then pointed at Mao, saying: "This is the murderer!"

Actually the judge had told his men to smear ashes on the wall beforehand and put soot into the water in which they washed their hands. The murderer, afraid that the god would come to write on him, got ashes on his back by pressing it against the wall. On the way out he tried to protect his back with his hands, thus smearing it with soot. Master Shi's previous suspicions of Mao the Elder were confirmed. With the application of ruthless torture, Mao spat out the whole truth. Master Shi's verdict was as follows: Regarding Su Jie: This man flirted with death like Pen-cheng Kuo, and he nearly rivals Deng Tuzi for lechery. On the strength of a childish infatuation, he made a wild duck out of a household fowl. When the uttering of a few ill-placed words moved the conqueror of Long to hanker after Shu, he climbed unwanted over a garden wall and swooped down like a falcon. Fancying himself an irresistible magnet to fairy maidens, he proceeded to the mouth of Rouge's grotto and finally wheedled her door open. By disturbing a lady's girdle sash, he aroused a shaggy dog. Even a rat has skin on its face, but this man had no idea of shame. He clambered after flowers, snapping off branches on the way. A man of such low conduct does not deserve the name of scholar. It was a saving grace that he heeded the feeble sparrow's cries; he had the heart to spare this piece of unblemished jade. Out of pity for her willowy frailness, he did not go wild like a March-mad oriole, but released the fledgling phoenix from his grasp, as any man of learning should. Regrettably he wrested a fragrant token from beneath her petticoat, proving how truly worthless he was! That same night a different butterfly flitted over his lover's wall. A pair of ears lurked outside the bedroom window. The petal torn from the lotus was dropped on the ground and lost, and so it was that falsehood sprang up within falsehood. Who could imagine that a second injustice would lay beyond the first. Heaven sent calamity down upon our Su Jie—a vicious beating to the edge of death. His own wrongdoing caught up to him, and his head and body nearly ended up in different places. Climbing walls and tunneling through cracks is a stain on a scholar's cap, but when a peach-boring insect tries to infect a plumtree, the fumes of injustice are not easily blown clean. Thus it is proper to show some leniency: we will spare Su Jie the rod, to make up for the cruel pain he has already suffered, and open for him the road to self-renewal by demoting him to black robes.[1]

Now as for Mao the Elder, that idle, weaselly ruffian of the marketplace: Though he met with a refusal from his neighbor girl as curt as a shuttle thrown in his face, his lustful intentions would still not die. He bided his time until a flippant young man slipped into the alley, and then a bright idea occurred to his devious mind. Later, outside an open sliding door, another wind blew his way, and he imagined himself going to meet his beloved. He was looking for homebrew, and caught the scent of fine wine. His delusions were like the heady fumes of an aphrodesiac perfume. How was he to know that his strength would be sapped by heaven, and his spirit would be carried off by

[1] Black robes were worn by licentiates of the lowest rank.

ghosts? He got on his log raft and rode the silvery waters straight toward the Moon Palace. He floated along in his fisherman's boat, thinking he knew the way to Peachblossom Spring. In the end his passionate flames were doused by a tidal wave in the sea of desire. With an unlooked-for knife coming straight at him, he lashed out, as robbers often do when backed against a wall. Even a cornered rabbit will use its teeth in desperation. He landed in this fix because he thought jumping the wall into someone else's courtyard would be as easy as 'Mr. Li wearing Mr. Zhang's hat'. Because he dropped the slipper while wrenching away the weapon, the fish swam through the net while a goose was caught. It hardly seems possible that an event so demonic should arise on the path of romance. How could a banshee like this exist in the land of warmth and softness? Mao the Elder's head shall be severed from his neck for the gratification of all.

Now as for Rouge: This girl has not yet been spoken for, though she is already of hairpin age. A fairy maiden straight from the moon palace should naturally have a bridegroom like jade. A member of the Rainbow Skirt Dancers can rest assured that a golden house awaits her. Now the mating cry of the osprey arouses her longing for a perfect mate; the time has come for Mistress Spring to wrap her up in dreams. Thinking of a likely gentleman, she resents the falling plum blossoms, and her soul goes out of her body in search of love. However beautiful other women may be, they cannot be compared to Rouge. No matter how fierce the other taloned birds may be, they all take wing at the sight of Autumn-Falcon.

A single entangling thread caused a horde of demons to converge upon this lovely girl. Once the lotus slipper was plucked away, the petal's fragrance was hard to keep.

Intruders at the iron threshold nearly smashed a precious gem.

Just as the red dots inlaid in dice are etched by tears of disappointment, a love that is felt to the bone can be a gateway to disaster. An upright tree succumbed to the axe, and a sweet young thing became a 'swamp of perdition'. But she guarded her dignity, and luckity her white jade remains unflawed. She writhed in his grasp, glad for the brocade quilt that covered her. She is admirable for refusing an intruder who was already in her room. By remaining pure and clean, she has proven herself to be a person of character. Fulfilling her wish to throw her bouquet would be an elegant closing chapter to this romance. I trust the district magistrate will play the part of matchmaker.

After the case was settled, this verdict was spread and recited far and wide.

The girl did not know that she had wrongfully blamed Young E until after Master Wu's hearing. When they met outside the hall, she sniffled guiltily, as if she had words of remorse in mind but could not yet speak out. The young man, touched by her regard, began to feel strongly toward her. But the thought of her humble origins, along with her daily appearances in court where a thousand people had pointed and leered at her, made him fear he would be ridiculed for marrying her. He brooded night and day, but could not make up his mind. The words of the verdict when it was finally delivered put him at his ease. The district magistrate had the betrothal gifts sent to the girl's house on his behalf and furnished music for the wedding procession.

The Chronicler of the Tales comments: "How great the need for caution is in hearing legal cases! Even if one could know that the plumtree was damaged wrongfully, who would think that the peach as well was decimated by mistake? Still, even the most obscure matter must have openings that let light through. Without careful thought and shrewed observation these cannot be traced. What a regret it is that people admire the wise man's brilliant resolution of a court case, while they fail to recognize the painstaking efforts of a master mind. In this world people who hold positions of authority fritter away whole days playing chess and cancel their morning audiences so as to stay beneath silken covers, never bothering their heads about the sentiments or hardships of the people. When the drums sound the opening of magisterial sessions, they sit high and mighty on the bench, silencing those who cry out for justice by slapping them into irons. Small wonder that so many injustices are hidden from the light of day!"

42. COURTESAN RUI YUN

RUI Yun, a famous courtesan of Hangzhou, was unrivalled in beauty and accomplishments. When she was fourteen her madame, Matron Cai, was ready to bring her out to receive guests. Rui Yun told her: "I am just putting my foot onto the first rung of the ladder, and I mustn't do it haphazardly. You fix the price, Mother, and I will choose the guest myself."

"All right," said the matron. So Rui Yun's price was fixed at fifteen taels of gold, and she began to see guests daily. Guests who wished to meet her had to bring acquaintance gifts. The ones gave generously were invited to stay for a game of chess and rewarded with a painting. Givers of trifles were only asked to tea. Rui Yun's name had been well known for some time; now rich merchants and men of noble houses rubbed shoulders at her gate.

In Yuhang district there lived Scholar He, famed from an early age for his talent but raised in a family of only moderate wealth. He had admired Rui Yun all along, but the thought of sharing a lovebird dream with her had never entered his mind. He exhausted his funds to buy a meager gift in hopes that he too could be admitted to gaze on her beauty with her own eyes. He worried to himself that a girl on familiar terms with so many people would not be kindly disposed to one in his straitened circumstances, but when they met and talked she entertained him most graciously.

They sat and conversed a good while and there was tenderness in her eyes. She gave him a poem that read:

What brings the seeker of rare elixirs
To knock on the Indigo Bridge at dawn?
If he hopes to find the pestle of jade
He should stard with the ground he stands upon.

Getting this poem sent the scholar into a paroxysm of joy. He wanted to have further words with her, but he left hastily when a maid came in and announced, "A guest is here."

Back home he chanted and savored the words of the poem until his soul was lost in dreams. A few days later, unable to suppress his feelings, he readied a gift and went again. Rui Yun was very happy to see him. She moved her seat close to him and murmured, "Can you arrange to have us spend a night together?"

"Devotion is the only thing a destitute scholar like me can offer to the one who understands him." This wisp of a gift stretched my meager resources to the limit. Being near to your beauty is a wish come true already. I cannot delude myself with hopes of intimacy."

Rui Yun listened in gloomy disappointment, her face turned wordlessly toward him. He sat there for a long time until the matron hurried him on his way by calling repeatedly for the girl to hurry him on his way. When he was back home, he moodily contemplated selling everything in his house to pay for a night of ecstasy, but that would mean parting with her at dawn, and what would happen to his love for her then? Thinking of this dampened his passionate impulses. Henceforth communication between the two was broken off.

Rui Yun had been months choosing a 'husband', but

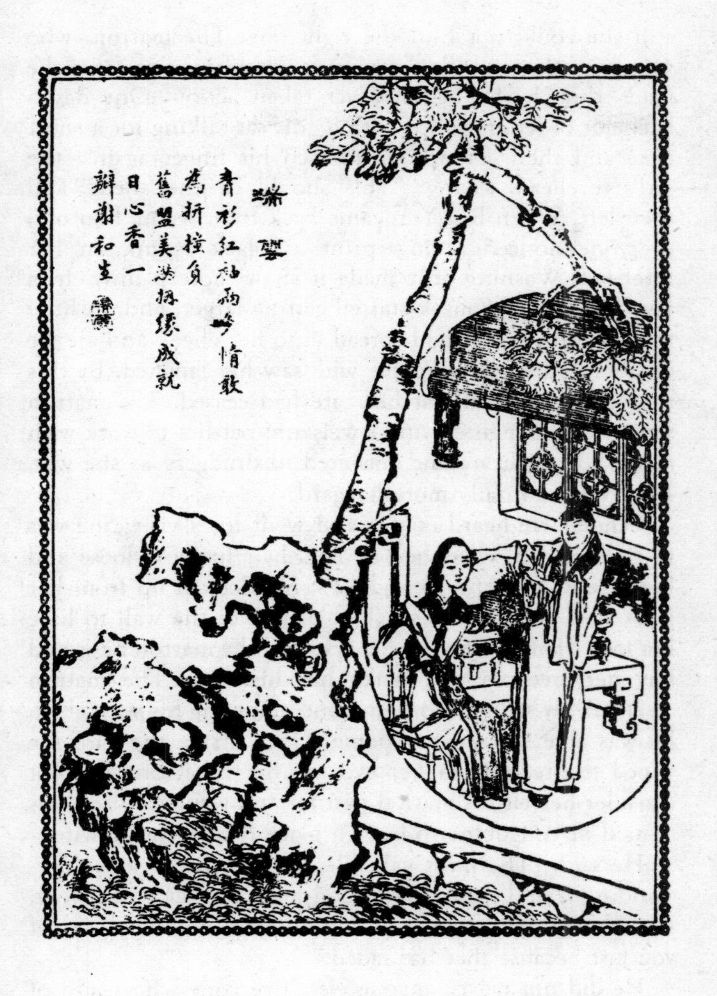

青衫紅袖兩情歡
為折撞負
舊盟美滿姻緣成就
日心香一
辦謝和生

still she could not find the right one. The matron, who was more than a little vexed, was determined to force the issue, though she had not yet taken action. One day a bachelor of letters called with a gift, sat talking for a short time and then got up. He pressed his finger against the girl's forehead, saying: "This should be cherished," and then left. When Rui Yun came back from seeing him out, everyone noticed a fingerprint as black as ink on her forehead. Washing only made it show more plainly. In a few days the inky mark started getting larger, and, in little more than a year it had spread onto her cheek and all the way across her nose. People who saw her laughed. By this time the daily bustle at her gate had ceased. The matron stripped off her finery and jewels and put her to work with the maids. Delicate and unsuited to drudgery as she was, Rui Yun grew daily more haggard.

Scholar He heard of this and went for a visit. She was in the kitchen when he saw her, hair hanging loose and her face as frightful as a ghost's. She looked up from her work and saw him there, then turned to the wall to hide her face. He felt sorry for her. He told the matron he would buy her freedom and make her his wife. The matron assented. By selling some land and emptying his strongbox, he was able to take her home. Once inside the gate she wiped the tears from her eyes on her robe. She did not consider herself his marital partner and wanted to serve as a maid or concubine to leave a place for his future wife.

He said, "The most valuable thing in life is an understanding friend. You understood me for what I was when you were in your prime of beauty. I am not going to forget you just because that has faded."

He did not marry anyone else. Everyone who heard of this ridiculed him, but his affection only grew stronger.

Nothing changed for over a year, until he happened to go to Suzhou. He stayed there in the same house with a certain Scholar Harmony, who suddenly asked him: "There was a famous singing girl in Hangzhou named Rui Yun. How are things with her these days?"

"She married somebody," answered Scholar He.

"Who was that?"

"A person very much like me."

"If he is like you, she found herself a good husband. I wonder how he paid for her."

"She was sold cheaply because of a strange affliction she had. Otherwise, how could someone like me have found a beautiful mate inside the balustrades of the gay quarters?"

"Could that person really be like you?" The strangeness of the question made Scholar He ask the meaning of it. Scholar Harmony laughed: "I won't mislead you. When I was admitted to her flowerlike presence, I felt sorry that such a sublime beauty should sink to the depths unmated, so I used a minor trick to dim her radiance and preserve her true nature, and to leave her for the discernment of a lover of beauty."

Scholar He hurriedly asked, "You were able to mark her with a touch. Are you able to wash it clean as well?"

"Why shouldn't I be able to?" laughed Harmony. "But the party concerned must ask from the heart."

He got up and sank on his knees, saying: "I'm the one who married Rui Yun."

"In this world only people of true ability can feel deeply for others, because their affections are not swayed by physical appearance," said Scholar Harmony approvingly. "I'll return with you, if I may, and deliver a beautiful woman into your hands."

So they went back together. Scholar He was going to

call for wine on their arrival, but Harmony stopped him: "Let me practice my art first. I'd like to give the server something to be glad of before we start enjoying ourselves."

Harmony asked for a basin filled with water, then traced words over its surface and said, "Washing will cure her, but the patient must come out to thank the doctor personally." Scholar He laughed as he carried the basin in with both hands. He stood waiting while Rui Yun laved her face. As hands swept over her face, it grew radiant and clean. She was just as ravishingly beautiful as before. Both husband and wife appreciated the great kindness Scholar Harmony had done them. They came out to express their thanks, but he was gone. They looked everywhere without success. Could Scholar Harmony have been an immortal?

43. LINEN SCARF, THE PEONY SPIRIT

CHANG Dayong, a man of Luoyang,[1] was inordinately fond of peonies. He longed to procure peonies from Caozhou prefecture, having heard that they outclassed all others in Shandong. It happened that other business took him to Caozhou, so he put up in an official's garden. This was still in the second month, before the peonies bloomed. All he could do was pace up and down the garden, fixing his eyes on the tender burgeons breaking through the soil and waiting for them to blossom. He wrote a hundred quatrains on "Yearning for Peonies." Before long the flowers began to form in their buds. When his funds were nearly depleted, he did not hesitate to pawn his spring clothes. He dallied there, forgetting to return. One day he hurried by light of dawn to where the flowers were. There he saw a young woman and an old matron. He scurried away, supposing them to be members of some wealthy household. That evening he went, saw them again and retreated out of sight, more calmly this time. He peered at the young woman from hiding: she was stunning in her palace robe. A thought came to him in his bedazzlement: she must be a fairy. Such a girl could not be of this world.

Hurriedly, he retraced his steps and went looking for

[1] In Henan province.

them. He scuttled round a rockery, only to run right into the matron. The young woman, who was seated on a nearby rock, looked at him in surprise. The old matron shielded the girl with her body and snapped at him, "What are you up to, you maniac?"

The scholar knelt down and said, "The mistress must be an immortal."

The old matron scoffed, "You ought to be tied up and turned over to the sheriff for talking such nonsense." The scholar was thoroughly intimidated.

The young woman gave a little laugh: "Let's get away from him." They disappeared behind the rockery, and the scholar headed back, walking unsteadily. He feared that curses and humiliation would be in store for him once the girl went home and told her father and brothers. He threw himself down in the vacant studio, cursing himself for his thoughtlessness. He felt glad that her face had showed no sign of anger: perhaps she would not give it another thought. Mingled regret and apprehension weighed miserably on him all night through, but when the sun climbed above the horizon without bringing a punitive army his peace of mind gradually returned.

But her features and voice remained in his thoughts, and fear give way to longing. After three days of this he had nearly wasted to nothing. He was sitting beside a candle in the night, his servant deep in slumber, when the old lady came in holding a jar. She held it out to him, saying: "My mistress Linen Scarf made up this hemlock potion herself. Quick, drink it."

Her words struck terror in the scholar's heart, but he recovered enough to answer, "There has never been bad blood between your mistress and me—nothing that would make her hand me my death warrant. But since your

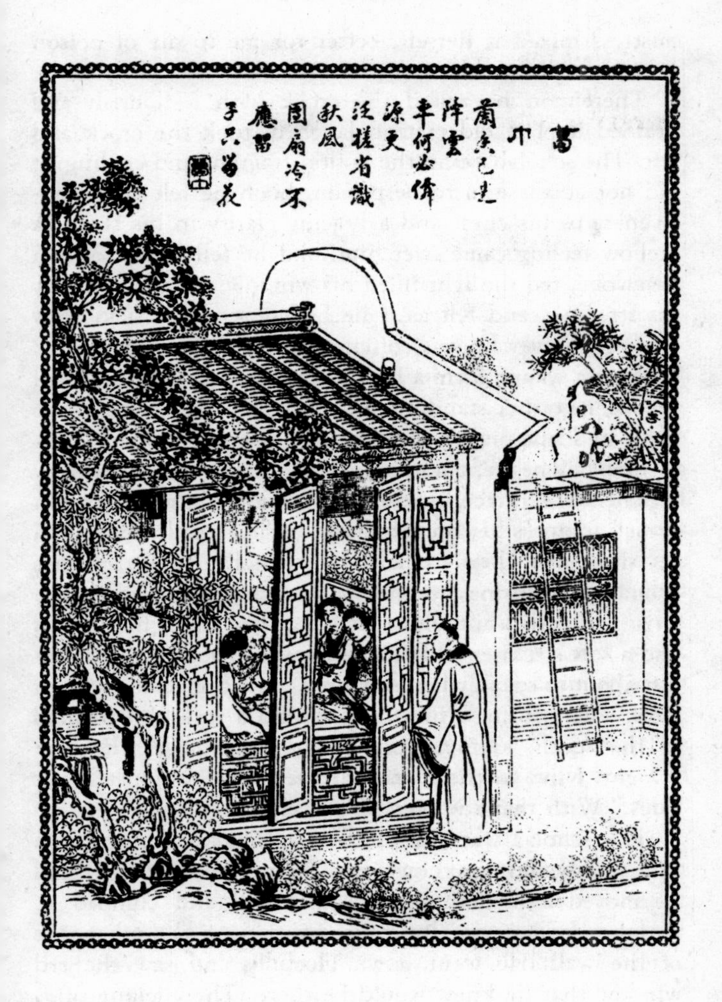
葛巾
蘭麝已走
降雲
車何必偷
源更
泛槎省識
秋風
團扇冷不
應畱
子只畱花

mistress mixed it herself, better for me to die of poison than waste away pining for her."

Thereupon he raised the crock with a flourish and drained it. The old matron laughed, took the crock and left. The scholar found the potion fragrant and cooling; it did not at all seem to be poison. Soon he felt an expansiveness in his chest and a bracing clarity in his skull. A mellow feeling came over him, and he fell asleep. When he awoke, red sunlight filled his window. He got up to try his strength, and felt as if he had never been sick. Now more than ever he was convinced that she was immortal. Lacking a way to form a bond with her, he could only call up visions of her standing or sitting and bow reverently to them in silent prayer when no one else was around.

One day he went walking. Deep in a grove he suddenly met her face to face. Fortunately no one else was there. In great happiness he threw himself to the ground before her. As she came close to help him up, he smelled a rare fragrance suffusing her body. He grasped her jade-liked wrist and pulled himself to his feet. The skin of her fingers had a soft sleekness that made his joints go limp. She was just about to speak when suddenly the old matron came in view. The girl made him hide behind a rock and pointed to the south, saying: "Climb the ladder over the wall tonight. I live in the house with red windows on all four sides." With that she bustled quickly away.

The scholar was shaken. His spirits had flown from him, and he did not know where he was going. At nightfall he moved a ladder to the south wall and climbed it. Another ladder was already in position on the other side of the wall. He went down gleefully and saw the red window that he knew would be there. The clicking of *go* pieces could be heard inside. He stood stock still, not daring to advance farther, then climbed back over the wall and went home for the time being. After a short interval he crossed over again: the *go* pieces were still clicking away. He edged up to the window and peered in. Linen Scarf sat facing a beauty dressed in white. The old matron was sitting with them, and a maid was in attendance. He turned back again. When he made his third trip, the second watch was nearly over. Crouched on the outside ladder, he heard the old lady come out and say, "There's a ladder. Who put it there?" She called the maid to help her move it away.

The scholar climbed back onto the wall but, having no way to climb down, turned back discouraged. He went again the next night and found the ladder ready for him. As luck would have it the place was still and empty. He went in. The young woman was sitting motionless, evidently absorbed in thought. Seeing him, she jumped up in surprise, leaning bashfully away. He clasped his hands and said, "I thought my blessings were too limited to ever call such a heavenly being my own. Is this night real?" He passionately took her in his arms. Her slender waist barely filled his grasp. She exhaled breath like orchid scent.

She straightened her arms and pushed him away, exclaiming: "What's your hurry?"

"You can have good things without pushing and pulling. We'll make the demons jealous if we take too long," he said.

The discussion was still underway when they heard faraway voices. The girl blurted out, "My sister Jade Clapper is coming. Hide under the bed for now."

He did as he was told. In no time a young girl came in and said with a laugh: "Is the defeated general still ready for battle? I have some fine tea steeping now. May I ask you over for a night game?"

Linen Scarf declined, pleading drowsiness. Jade Clapper renewed her offer, but would not budge from her seat, which prompted Jade Clapper to say, "Such reluctance! Don't tell me you have a man hidden in here." She pulled her sister out the door by force.

The scholar walked out from under the bed on his knees, vexed to the limit. He rifled through the pillows and mats hoping to find something she had left behind, but there was no jewelry box in the room, only a crystal as-you-will scepter by the side of the bed. It was sparkling and lovely, and had a purple handkerchief tied to one end. He put it in his robe, went over the wall and returned home. He smoothed his sleeves and lapels, on which her bodily fragrance was still clinging, and this added to his longing. But the nervous shock of hiding under the bed had planted the dread of punishment in his mind. Considering the circumstances he dared not go again. The only thing to do was to stow away the scepter in hopes that she would come looking for it.

Linen Scarf did turn up the following night. "I thought you were a gentleman," she laughed. "I didn't expect you would turn out to be a burglar."

"There was good reason for it. I only relaxed my gentlemanliness this once out of my hope for an as-I-will. Then he pulled her body against his and undid the clasp of her dress. Her jade flesh was instantly revealed, and warm scent exuded from her. As they touched and embraced, he sensed no exhalation, whether breath from her nostrils or the pungency of her perspiration, that was not sweet.

So he said, "I thought you were a fairy maiden: now I'm sure that was no mistake. I'm happy that you are kind enough to care for me. The tie between us runs through the past, present, and future lives. But I fear that your descent into marriage will end in a sorrowful separation, like in the story of Du Orchid-Scent."

"Your qualms are overdone," the girl said with a smile. "I am only a lovesick girl, and my soul has gone out to someone who happens to attract me. The main thing is for our affair to remain a carefully guarded secret, or judgemental tongues will color things to suit themselves. Since you cannot grow wings and I cannot ride the wind, a disastrous parting would be a good deal more miserable than an agreeable farewell."

Though the scholar agreed with her, he continued to suspect that she was an immortal and insisted on knowing her lineage.

"Since you take me for an immortal, why must you remember me by name?"

"Who is the old woman?"

"She is Matron Mulberry. She protected me from the elements when I was young, so I don't consider her just another servant." With that she rose to go and said, "There are many eyes and ears at my place: I musn't stay away too long. I'll slip out again when the time is right." As she was about to leave, she motioned him to give her the as-you-will, saying "It isn't mine. Jade Clapper left it with me."

"Who is Jade Clapper?"

"She is my cousin." When he pulled the scepter from his robe and handed it to her, she left. Though she was gone, his pillows and covers were suffused with a rare fragrance.

After that she came once every two or three nights. The scholar was too obsessed with her to think any more of going home. By now his pouch was empty and he was on the point of selling his horse. When Linen Scarf learned of this she said, "It hurts me to think that you emptied your purse and pawned your clothes because of me. Now on top of that you are getting rid of your mount. How will you ever travel a thousand *li* home? I have some private savings that will help you get outfitted."

"I am so thankful for your love," he replied, "Even if I put my hand on my heart and pledged every fiber of my body to you, it would not be enough to repay you. How could ever face you if I spent your fortune greedily?"

But the girl pressed it on him, saying: "Let me lend it to you for now." She dragged him by the arm to the foot of a mulberry tree, pointed to a stone and said, "Turn that over."

He did so. Then she pulled the hairpin from her head, poked it into the dirt several dozen times and said, "Dig here." Again he did as she said, and the mouth of an urn came into view. She reached in and pulled out a string of silver pieces weighing somewhere around fifty taels. He held her arm and tried to stop her, but she would not listen. Again she pulled out over ten ingots. He insistently replaced half of them, then covered the urn.

One evening she said to him: "There has been a bit of gossip the last few days. Things cannot go on as they are. We simply have to take precautions."

"But what can we do?" he blurted in surprise. "I've always been a shy, overcautious person. But now, because of you, I'm like a widow who let her guard down—I can't decide things for myself any more. I'll do whatever you say without worrying over the consequences, even if there are swords, axes and saws waiting for me."

Linen Scarf made plans to elope together, telling him to return first and arranging to join him later in Luoyang. He packed his bags and headed home, intending to get there first and then go to meet her. When he arrived, her cart had just reached his gate. They went into the hall and payed their respects to the household. His surprised neighbors congratulated them, little knowing they had eloped. It all seemed precarious to him, but she was remarkably unruffled.

"A thousand *li* is beyond the range of pursuit, and even if we are found out, I come from a good family, so my relatives won't do a thing to the man who won their daughter's heart."

She took one look at the scholar's younger brother Daqi, a seventeen-year-old boy, and said, "This one has a promising intellect; his career will overshadow yours."

The date for Daqi's wedding had been settled, but his wife died at an early age. Linen Scarf said, "You've had a peek at my sister Jade Clapper already. She is by no means bad looking, and her age is about right. If they were married they'd make a charming couple." The scholar laughed at this and jokingly asked her to be the go-between.

"If you really want her to come, it won't be hard," said Linen Scarf.

"How can you get her here?" he asked happily.

"Sister and I are very close. Send a buggy with two horses. All it will take is a serving woman to go there and back."

The scholar, fearing that past events would be brought to light, dared not agree to her plan, but she insisted there would be no harm, so he called for the buggy and sent Matron Mulberry to Caozhou. In a few days she reached there. When she came close to the borough gate the matron stepped out of the buggy, told the driver to stay put and wait in the road, then entered the borough under cover of night. A good while later she appeared with a young girl. They climbed into the buggy and started back. At nightfall the next day they stayed in the buggy, then resumed their trip at the striking of the fifth watch. Linen Scarf, who had calculated their itinerary, had Daqi go out to meet them, dressed in a formal robe. He met with them over fifty *li* from his home.

They came home with Daqi at the reins. Amid drumming and blaring, and garlands and candles, they kowtowed to each other and performed the wedding ceremony. Now both brothers had beautiful wives, and the household grew daily more prosperous.

One day several dozen mounted bandits stormed into the yard. The scholar, realizing there would be trouble, led the family into an upstairs loft. The bandits rode about the yard and surrounded the house. The scholar looked down from a window and asked, "Do you have a score to settle with us?"

"No," they answered. "But we have two demands to make. First, we hear that the two ladies are like nothing on this earth. Give us a look at them. Second, there are fifty-eight of us, and we want five hundred pieces of gold each."

They piled firewood against the base of the house and threatened to set fire to it. The scholar acquiesced to their demand for gold, but they were not satisfied and were on the point of burning the building down. Everyone in the family was terrified.

Linen Scarf wanted to go downstairs with Jade Clapper and would listen to no objections. They went down in their finest dresses. They stopped three steps from the bottom and said to the bandits: "We sisters are fairy maidens setting foot for a time in the world of dust. Bandits and brigands do not frighten us! We give you ten thousand pieces of gold, but we doubt if you'll accept it."

The crowd of bandits fell on their knees and chorused: "We wouldn't take your money."

The sisters were about to withdraw, but one bandit piped up: "This is a trick."

At the sound of his voice, Linen Scarf turned, drew herself up to her full height and said, "If you're of a mind to do something, you'd best try it soon, while there's still time." The bandits looked wordlessly at each other as the sisters went calmly up the stairs. The bandits watched with upturned faces until the two were out of sight and then dispersed in noisy disorder.

Two years later both sisters gave birth to sons. It was not until then that they gradually started telling about themselves: "Our family name is Wei, and our mother was awarded the title Lady of Cao."

The scholar thought this suspicious, since there was no noble house by the name of Wei in Caozhou. Besides, how could a great clan ignore the loss of its daughters and not make some sort of inquiry. He did not dare to pry, but kept the doubt in his heart. And so he found a pretext for going back to Caozhou. When he crossed the district line he made inquiries and found that indeed, there were no Weis among the noble clans there. Then he borrowed lodgings from his former host. Right away he noticed a poem dedicated to the "Lady of Cao" on the wall—an unsettling development to be sure. He asked his host about it. His host laughed and offered to take him to look at the lady of Cao. When they got there, it turned out to be an eave-high peony shrub. The scholar asked how it came by the name and learned that one of the host's colleagues had given it that title as a joke because it was unsurpassed in all of Caozhou.

"What variety is it?" he asked.

"It is a purple Linen Scarf."

His mind recoiled in amazement, and he began to suspect that the girl was a flower spirit.

Once home he could not bring himself to face her with the evidence; he merely told her of the poem to the Lady of Cao to see how she would react. She hurried out with a scowl on her face, called for Jade Clapper to bring their children and said to him: "Three years ago I was moved by your affection, so I offered myself to you in repayment. Now that you distrust me, I don't see how we can stay together." She and Jade Clapper lifted their children and threw them a great distance. Both of them disappeared the moment they fell to the ground. As the scholar looked on in astonishment, the two women also vanished. He cursed himself without end.

A few days later two peony shrubs sprang up where the children had fallen and grew to a foot in diameter overnight. They bloomed that year, one purple and one white, with flowers the size of saucers and petals even more numerous and finely delineated than those of ordinary Linen Scarves and Jade Clappers. In a few years they became lush, shaded thickets. When the roots were separated and transplanted, they changed into unique varieties that no one could name. From this time on the Luo River valley was unmatched for the splender of its peonies.

The Chronicler of the Tales comments: "Singleminded emotion makes itself felt by ghosts and spirits, while one who sways back and forth is not necessarily lacking in feelings. In one of his poems the Magistrate Bai Juyi was so lonely he made a flower his wife. How much nicer it would be to find one that truly understands speech! What need would there be to delve into her origins? I feel sorry for Scholar Chang, who lacked a broad view of things."

44. YELLOW-BLOOM

MA Zicai was a man of Shuntian prefecture whose family had been fond of chrysanthemums for generations. But Zicai was even more fond of them than his forerunners. When he learned of a rare variety he never failed to buy it: a thousand-*li* trip did not deter him. One day a guest from Nanjing staying at Ma's house mentioned that his cousin had a variety or two not found in the north. Ma was so excited he packed his luggage that very day and set out with his guest for Nanjing. The guest kindly got busy hunting through various channels until he came up with two cuttings, which Ma wrapped and kept like jewels.

On his way home Ma met with a fine-looking, dashing young man mounted on a nag behind a curtained coach. He moved closer to make conversation with him. The young man gave his surname as Tao. His speech was easy and elegant. He asked where Ma was coming from, so Ma told him the whole story of his trip to Nanjing.

"Both of these varieties are prime, but how they are mulched and watered depends on the gardener," said the young man. This led to a discussion on the techniques of chrysanthemum growing.

In a burst of elation Ma asked, "Where are you headed?"

"My elder sister is tired of Nanjing: we'd like to find a place to live in the north."

"I know I am poor, but you can put up in my cottage

黄英
千里萍蹤卜隱居酒
香茶氣
夢醒初良緣應為梅
花妬霎
士風流轉不如

anyway," Ma offered with pleasure. "If you don't mind roughing it, you needn't bother to go elsewhere."

Tao rode up to the coach to consult with his sister. The one who pushed aside the curtain to speak with him was a world-class beauty in her twenties. She looked at her brother and said, "I have no objection to a poor dwelling, but the yard should be spacious." Ma offered his assurances, and so they went home with him.

South of the house was a neglected garden plot with nothing but a shanty four or five beams long. Tao liked it and moved in. Every day he visited the north yard and tended Ma's chrysanthemums, which had withered. He pulled them up by the roots and replanted them: not one of them failed to survive. Tao and his sister lived in austere poverty. He took his meals daily with Ma, who noticed that they never seemed to have a fire burning in their house. Ma's wife, née Lü, was also fond of Tao's sister and gave her a quart here and a peck there by way of assistance. Tao's sister went by her childhood name Yellow-Bloom. Being an agreeable conversationalist, she began dropping in at Lü's rooms to sew and spin thread with her.

One day Tao said to Ma: "You are not well off either. I can't go on making demands on a friend every day to fill my belly. For now I think selling chrysanthemums will do for a living."

Ma, who tended to be scrupulous in such matters, listened contemptuously and said, "I took you for a spirited, high-minded man who could be content in poverty. What you are saying amounts to turning the East Hedge[1] into a marketplace. That would be an insult to these yellow

[1] An allusion to a famous line about chrysanthemums by the Jin dynasty poet Tao Qian (365-427)

flowers!"

"Earning one's own keep is not greediness," said Tao with a smile, "nor is it banal to sell flowers for a living. True, people should not amass wealth dishonestly, but, then again, they need not purposely make themselves poor."

Ma had nothing to say. Tao got up and walked out. Afterwards Tao gathered up and carried away all the broken stems and stunted plants Ma threw away. He no longer slept and ate at Ma's, except when invited. Before long, when the time came for chrysanthemums to bloom, there was a clamor that made Tao's gate sound like a marketplace. Wondering what this was about, Ma went over to observe. He saw market vendors coming to buy flowers, their carts and shoulder poles brushing past one another on the road. The flowers were all exotic varieties Ma had never seen before. He was disgusted by such aquisitiveness and wanted to break off their friendship. What was more, he was irked that Tao had kept the best varieties for himself. He knocked on Tao's gate, intending to give him a piece of his mind. Tao came to the gate, grasped his hand, and pulled him inside. The once barren courtyard had become half a *mu* of chrysanthemum beds. There was not an empty piece of ground for several rafter lengths around the house. Of all the buds swelling into bloom in the flowerbeds, none were less than exquisite. Tao had stuck cuttings in the ground to replace dug-up plants. Close inspection proved that all the cuttings were the ones Ma had pulled up and discarded earlier. Tao went into his room, brought out wine and food, and set places next to the flowerbeds.

"I am not one to abide by austere discipline when times are hard," he said. "Fortunately I have made a slight amount of money these last few days—more than enough to drink my fill."

Soon a voice called from inside: "Third-Brother!" Tao shouted in answer as he went in. Before long he brought out a number of delicacies, stewed and braised to perfection, which prompted Ma to ask, "Why isn't your sister engaged?"

"The time has not come yet."

"What time?" asked Ma.

"The forty-third month."

"What's that supposed to mean?" Ma asked again. Tao only laughed in reply.

They did not call it quits until they enjoyed themselves thoroughly. Ma went to visit the next day, and saw that the cuttings which had recently been stuck in the ground were already a full foot tall. Greatly amazed, he begged to know Tao's technique.

"Actually, this cannot be imparted with words. Besides, you would not make your living with it, so what use would it be to you?"

After a few more days, when the bustle in his gate and yard had quieted down somewhat, Tao wrapped his chrysanthemums in rush mats, loaded bundles of them onto a number of carts and left. He came back the following year, when spring was nearly halfway over, with a load of rare botanicals from the south, which he used to set up a florist's shop in town. Ten days later everything was sold out, and he went back to tending chrysanthemums. Ma learned from his customers of the previous year that they were buying from Tao again, since the bulbs they kept had all reverted to plants of low quality.

From then on Tao got richer every day. He added rooms one year and raised a new manor the next. He started new buildings when the spirit moved him, without so much as discussing it with his host. The old flower beds gave way little by little to galleries and buildings. Then Tao bought a piece of land on the other side of the wall, surrounded it with a tall wall and planted it full of chrysanthemums. With the coming of fall he carried off a load of flowers. Spring passed, but he did not return.

Then Ma's wife died. He thought of marrying Yellow-Bloom and sent someone to broach the subject. Yellow-Bloom smiled in seeming approval. All she had to do was wait for her brother's return.

More than a year went by, and still Tao did not come back. Yellow-Bloom instructed the servant to plant chrysanthemums just as he had done. The money she earned was added to her business investments. She had twenty *qing*[1] of fertile land under cultivation outside the village, and built a main residence more imposing than the last one.

Then a stranger came unexpectedly from Guangdong province with a letter from Tao, instructing his sister to marry Ma. The letter had been sent on the very day Ma's wife had died. Ma recalled with amazement that the party in Tao's garden had been exactly forty-three months before. After showing the letter to Yellow-Bloom, he asked, "Where should I send the betrothal gift?"

Yellow-Bloom would not accept his gift. Due to the rundown condition of his dwelling, she wanted him to live in the south house, as if he were marrying into her family. He refused and chose a suitable day to perform the bride-welcoming ceremony.

After Yellow-Bloom married Ma, she added a walkway

[1] One *qing* is about 15.13 acres.

leading through the dividing wall to the south house. Every day she walked over to her own house to supervise her servants. Ashamed of his wife's wealth, Ma constantly reminded Yellow-Bloom to keep separate ledgers for the north and south households so as to prevent confusion. But Yellow-Bloom brought whatever she needed for the north house from the south residence. Within half a year, Tao's possessions were everywhere in the house. On the spur of the moment Ma ordered the help to move each and every object to its original spot. He forbade her to bring them back, but before ten days passed, their possessions were mingled again. They went back and forth so many times that Ma could not keep up with them.

"Aren't you over-exerting yourself, Mr. Purity?" laughed Yellow-Bloom. This embarrassed Ma: he discontinued his inspections and left everything to her. She assembled laborers and gathered materials for a major construction project. There was nothing he could do to stop her. After several months the north and south residences were joined by continuous frame buildings and living quarters. There was nothing to mark the boundary between the two.

Yellow-Bloom did, in deference to Ma's instructions, close the gate and stop dealing in chrysanthemums. Still, they lived more luxuriously than a noble family. This made Ma uncomfortable.

"I had thirty years of purity before you imposed on me," complained Ma, "Now I'm in this world just to stare and breathe. I get my food by hanging on to a petticoat. There isn't a wisp of manliness left in me. Everybody else prays for wealth, but I pray for poverty."

"It's not that I'm greedy," said Yellow-Bloom. "But if I do not make sure that we have a fair amount of wealth, people will be saying for thousand years that my poet-ancestor Tao Qian was a born pauper whose bloodline could not thrive even after a hundred generations. Therefore I resort to this so that people will no longer ridicule our dear Magistrate of Pengze District.[1] Anyway, a poor person who wants wealth has a hard time ahead of him, but a rich person who looks for poverty can be satisfied very easily. You can squander the gold under the beds as you wish—I'm not tight."

"There is something very unseemly about throwing away another person's money," answered Ma.

"You don't want to be rich, and I refuse to be poor," said Yellow-Bloom. "Since there is no otherway, I'll live separately from you. The pure will be left to his purity; the polluted will be left to her pollution. What could be wrong with that?"

And so she had a thatched hut built in the garden and chose a nice-looking maid to wait on him there. Ma was content. But after several days he missed Yellow-Bloom painfully. He sent for her, but she would not come. The only thing he could do was to go to her. He made a habit of showing up every other night.

"Eating at your own house and sleeping with your neighbor —that's not the way a man of purity would act," Yellow-Bloom said with a smile. Ma himself had to laugh: "there was nothing he could say to that. So it was that he went back to living with her as in the beginning.

It happened that Ma travelled to Nanjing to see to a certain matter just when the chrysanthemums were in full bloom. He went by a florist's shop one morning and saw a profuse array of magnificent potted flowers. This gave him quite a start, since he noticed a resemblance to Tao's

[1] This refers to Tao Qian, also known as Tao Yuanming.

handiwork. Sure enough, the shopkeeper who came out a moment later was none other than Tao.

Ma was overjoyed. After exchanging greetings Ma stayed the night. He invited Tao to go back, but Tao said, "Nanjing is my home territory, and I'm going to marry here. I've built up some meager funds that I'd like you to take back to my sister. I'll probably make a short trip there at the end of the year." Paying no heed to this, Ma redoubled his pleas and said, "Your family is blessed with ample means. You should do nothing but sit back and enjoy it. You don't need to stay in business any more."

As they sat in the shop, Tao had servants price his goods for him. By keeping prices low, he sold everything in a few days. Then he made short work of packing his baggage, hired a boat and headed north.

Entering the gate, they found that his sister had already cleared a suite for him, with bed and bedding already in place, as if she had known her brother was coming.

Now that Tao was back, he unpacked his possessions and directed laborers in laying out extensive gardens and pavilions. He spent his days playing chess and drinking with Ma, without even befriending a house guest. He refused offers to help him find a wife. His sister assigned two maids to serve him at bedtime. After three or four years one of them bore him a daughter.

Tao was a heavy drinker, but no one ever saw him in a stupor. When a friend named Zeng, whose capacity for wine was also unrivalled, came to visit Ma, Ma instigated a drinking contest between him and Tao. The two drank mightily and uproariously, regretting that they had not met each other sooner. From midmorning until the fourth watch of night they each finished a hundred pots in all. Zheng was so plastered he sprawled in his chair and passed out. Tao stood up to go to bed, but he walked out the door and into a chrysanthemum bed instead. Like a jade mountain he tottered and fell. As he hit the ground he turned into a chrysanthemum plant with a heap of clothes lying around it. It was as tall as a man and had at least ten blossoms, each bigger than a fist.

Greatly shaken, Ma told Yellow-Bloom. She rushed to the spot, pulled up the plant and laid it on the ground, saying: "Look how drunk you are!" She covered it with the clothes and asked Ma to come away with her, warning him not to look. The next morning he went there and found Tao lying by the flowerbed. At last Ma realized that brother and sister were both chrysanthemum spirits, which was all the more reason for him to love and respect them.

Tao, now that he had revealed his true identity, drank with greater abandon. He constantly sent invitations to Zeng, and their friendship grew till nothing could come between them. Then it was Flower-Morning.[1] Zeng came to visit with two servants carrying an urn of white wine infused with herbs, which he invited Tao to share to the bottom. The two of them nearly emptied the urn without getting especially drunk. Ma stealthily added another crockful, and they finished it as well. Zeng got dead drunk and was carried off by his servants. Tao lay down and turned into a chrysanthemum again. Ma had gotten used to the sight and was not startled. He pulled up the plant in the usual way and waited beside it to watch the transformation. After a time the leaves started looking wilted. Greatly frightened, he went to tell Yellow-Bloom. She was aghast at the news.

[1] The twelfth day of the second month, traditionally held to be the birthday of flowers.

"You've killed my brother!" she said. She ran to look: the root and stalk were already shriveled. She was crushed. She nipped off the stem, put soil around it in a pot and carried it to her room. She watered it every day. Ma tormented himself with regret and felt great resentment toward Zeng. After several days news came that Zeng had drunk himself to death.

The plant in the pot slowly sent forth a sprout. In the ninth month it bloomed. It had a short stem, a powder-white bloom and gave off a winelike fragrance. They named it "Drunken Tao." It grew best when watered with wine. Afterwards Tao's daughter grew up and married into a noble family. Yellow-Bloom lived to old age without any other strange occurrences.

The Chronicler of the Tales comments: "Like Fu Yi,[1] whose epitaph was 'a man of green mountains and white clouds,' Tao ended up dying of drink. Everyone pities him, but who is to say it was not an exciting life for him? Plant this variety in your courtyard. It's as good as seeing a close friend or being with a beautiful woman. You simply have to go looking for it."

1. A Tang dynasty scholar (555-639), who wrote his own epitaph.

45. A FOOL FOR BOOKS

LANG Yuzhu of Pengcheng was the heir of a former prefect. He had been a scrupulous office-holder, and had put what income he had into collecting a houseful of books instead of investing it productively. Now it was Yuzhu's turn to be an even greater fool for books. He lived in poverty and sold every possession, but he could not bear to part with a single book from his father's collection. While alive his father had copied out the "Exhortation to Learning" by the Song emperor Zhen Zong (r.998-1022), and pasted it on his desk. Yuzhu read it aloud daily. He covered it with a gauze overlay for fear that it would become frayed.

He was not out to command a salary: he truly believed that wealth and sustenance were to be found within books. He ground away at his studies night and day, and no extreme of weather could interrupt him. He was in his twenties but did not seek a mate, expecting that some beautiful woman would come to him unbidden from inside a book. He didn't know how to make small talk around guests and relatives. He would make a few remarks, but then as the sound of his reciting started to ring out, his guest would back hesitantly out the door. Each time the civil examiner came to give a qualifying exam, he was placed at the head of the list of candidates, but he was miserably unsuccessful in higher examinations.

One day, while he was reading, a gust of wind blew his

book from his hand. As he was rushing after it, a spot of ground he stepped on gave way under his feet. He probed with his hand and found a cavity containing mouldy straw. Dug up, it proved to be an ancient cellar full of millet, which had already rotted into dirt. Though it was inedible, it strengthened his belief that the "thousand bushels" mentioned in the "Exhortation to Learning" was no lie. He studied with renewed vigor. On another day while climbing a stepladder to reach a high shelf, he found a foot-long golden model of a cart in a disorderly pile of books. He was beside himself with joy, since he took this as a confirmation of the words "golden room" in the "Exhortation." When a person he showed it to pronounced it gilt instead of gold, he was miffed at the ancients for hoodwinking him.

Not long afterward, a man who passed the examinations in the same year as his father and who was devoted to the Buddha stopped there on a tour of inspection. Someone urged Lang to present the miniature cart to him for his Buddha niche. The inspector was so pleased he gave Lang three hundred taels of gold and two horses. Happy in his belief that the promise of a golden room, carriage and horses in the "Exhortation" had come true, Lang redoubled his diligence. Still, he was already thirty years of age. When someone advised him to marry, he quoted the "Exhortation": " 'In books you will find a countenance like jade,' " and said, "I am not worried that there will be no beautiful wife for me."

Over the next few years of fruitless study, he became a butt of common ridicule. There was a rumor going round that the Weaving Maid had run away from heaven, and people poked fun at Lang, saying: "The heavenly princess must have run away for your sake."

書癡
不信書中竟有魔玉顏
金屋兩字訛
祖龍一炬雖由殺也怪
癡兒福未多

Lang let it pass, realizing it was only in fun. One evening he was reading the eighth fasicle of the *History of the Han Dynasty* and had gotten almost to the middle when he found a gauze cutout of a beautiful woman pressed between the leaves.

"Is this supposed to answer to the prediction of a countenance like jade within a book?" he asked himself, stunned. He was crestfallen and disheartened. However, a closer look at the cutout showed lifelike features. On the back the words "Weaving Maid" were written faintly in hairline characters. He thought the portrait quite marvelous and each day he placed it on a pile of books to gaze at admiringly again and again, to the point that he forgot food and sleep. One day as his eyes were fixed on it the beautiful woman bent forward at the waist, got up and sat smiling on his books. Startled to the utmost, Lang prostrated himself before the desk. On rising he was amazed to see that she was a full foot long. Again he touched his head to the ground, and this time she stepped down from the desk with statuesque poise, looking every bit as beautiful as any woman alive.

"Which goddess are you?" Lang asked with a bow.

"My surname is Countenance, and I am called Like-Jade," she said with a smile. "You've known about me for a long while, and every day you've been kind enough to look my way. If I had neglected to show myself, I'm afraid nobody for the next thousand years would trust fully in the ancients again." Lang felt wonderful.

So it was that he found himself in bed with a beautiful woman, but even though nestling among the mats and cushions was conducive to intimacy, he did not know how to play a man's part.

Whenever he read, he had her sit beside him. She told

him not to read, but he ignored her.

"Your reading is precisely what keeps you from soaring to success. Look at the spring and fall bulletins of master's and doctor's degree holders: how many of those men study as much as you do? If you don't listen to me, I'm leaving."

Lang went along with her for a while, but soon he forgot her instructions and commenced his reciting again. After a while he tried to find her, but she was gone. Without her he was bereft of spirit and senses. He invoked her with a prayer, but she showed no sign of appearing. Suddenly remembering where she had once hidden, he took down the *History of the Han Dynasty* and leafed through every page of it, until he came to the old place, and there she was. He called to her, but she did not move. Then he crouched before her in woeful supplication.

At last she stepped out of the picture, saying: "If you ignore me again, I will part with you forever." She made him set up a *weiqi* board and a dicepot. Day after day they amused themselves, but Lang's heart was simply not in it. He watched for her to go away, then sneakily grabbed a book and started skimming through it. He was afraid that she would find out, so he secretly took the eighth fascicle of the *History of the Han Dynasty* and put it among a jumbled pile of other books to mislead her. One day he was so carried away with his reading that he did not notice her return. The instant he saw her he closed his book hurriedly, but she had already disappeared. Greatly frightened, he searched haphazardly through a number of books without success. Later he found her once again in the eighth fascicle of the *History of the Han Dynasty* on the very same page. Then he prostrated himself before her and begged her to reappear, promising that he would study no more. At last she came down from the desk. She started a game of *weiqi*, saying: "If you don't master this in three days, I'll leave again."

On the third day he surprised them both by coming out two pieces ahead at the end of a game. Pleased with his progress, she began teaching him stringed instruments and allowed him five days to master a piece. Lang's hands were busy and his eyes were occupied; there was no leisure for getting sidetracked. With time the rhythm sprang to life at his fingertips: his whole body moved spontaneously to the beat. From then on she drank and played with him every day, and he had too much fun to remember his studies. What was more, she freed him to get out of the house and into society. Soon he became known as a zestful and convivial man.

"Now you're ready to go and take the examinations," she said.

One night Lang said to her: "As a rule men and women who live together give birth to children. We have lived together for quite a while. Why are we the exception?"

"I always said it did you no good to study every day," she laughed. "Even now the chapter on husbands and wives has you baffled. There is an art to 'pillowing' together."

"What art?" Lang asked in surprise. She laughed and said nothing, but in a little while she snuggled up against him under the covers.

Lang's delight knew no bounds. "I didn't suspect that the happiness of married couples had something incommunicable in it," he said.

He told everyone he met of his discovery, and there were none who were not forced to hold back their laughter. She learned of this and scolded him, but he protested, "Tunneling through walls and squirming through crannies is the sort of thing you can't tell people, but the joy of a natural relationship is shared by everyone. Why should I scruple to mention it?"

Sure enough after eight or nine months Like-Jade gave birth to a son. They hired a nurse to raise him. One day Like-Jade said to Lang: "I've been with you for two years and I've given you a son: now I can leave you. I'm afraid if I stay too long I'll bring trouble for you: when that happens our regrets will not do us any good."

Tears ran down his face when he heard these words. He threw himself down and would not rise. "Won't you miss our little baby?" he asked.

She was heartbroken also. After a long pause she said, "If you insist on my staying, you should do away with every last book on your shelves."

"Those books are your birthplace, and they are my life. How can you say such a thing?!" protested Lang.

She did not force the issue: "Anyway I know this is predestined. I had to let you know beforehand, that's all."

Prior to this, some of Lang's kin had caught glimpses of the girl, and every one of them had been thoroughly amazed. What was more, they had not heard which family he was connected with by marriage, so they went to him in a group and demanded an answer. Unable to tell an untruth, Lang simply held his tongue. People grew more suspicious. News spread as if by mail until it reached Master Shi, the district magistrate. Shi, a native of Fujian, had taken his doctorate at an early age. What he heard stirred in him an impulse to set eyes on Like-Jade's beautiful face, and so he gave an order to take Lang and the girl into custody. The girl got word of this and fled without a trace. In order to learn where she had gone, the angry magistrate arrested Lang, stripped him of his scholar's robe, and had him flogged and his hands clamped in pressure manacles, until he was within an inch of his life, but still he said nothing. Then the magistrate had the maids beaten, and they gave an account bearing some semblance to the truth. The magistrate decided that the girl was an evil spirit. He called for his coach and went to Lang's house to make a personal inspection. He found a roomful of books, too many to search through, so he had them burned. The smoke hung over the courtyard in clouds that would not disperse, gloomy as stormclouds.

On his release Lang travelled to see a former student of his father's, who gave him a letter that brought about his reinstatement as an academician in good standing. That year he won success at the fall examinations and the next year he took the doctorate. But still he harbored rage against Shi in the very marrow of his bones. He made an altar to Countenance Like-Jade and prayed to it morning and night: "If your spirit lives, help me get an assignment in Fujian."

Later he did indeed make an inspection tour in Fujian as a court-appointed censor. After a three-month stay there he uncovered evidence of shi's wrongdoings and had his property confiscated.

At that time, a cousin of his who was serving as a prosecutor had taken a concubine by force and left her in Lang's compound, claiming that she was an indentured maid. On the very same day that the confiscation case was settled, Lang declared himself unfit for office, married the concubine and returned home.

The Chronicler of the Tales comments: "All possessions in this world invite envy when accumulated and when loved give rise to deviltry. The deviltry of books was at the root of the girl's seductive magic. Lang's actions were so preposterous that it was not necessarily wrong to straighten them out, but to burn the books like the first Qin emperor was too ruthless. The magistrate's selfish motives deserved vengeful retribution. My, what an odd tale!"

46. GHOST-GIRL WANXIA

ON the fifth of the fifth month dragon boat contests are held in the Wu-Yue area.[1] Hewn logs are shaped into dragons, which are painted with scales and ornamented in gold and green. On top are sculptured tiles and vermilion railings, and the sails and banners are all embroidered satin. The stern of each boat projected upwards in the shape of a dragon tail over ten feet high. Wooden slats are suspended from these by cloth ropes, and boys support themselves on the slats as they somersault, spin and perform all sorts of stunts in constant danger of plunging into the water below. For this reason the boys are procured by cash payments made to their parents, and then they are trained to perform, so that no one can complain if they fall into the water and die. The Suzhou boats are somewhat different in that they carry pretty singing girls.

In Zhenjiang district there was a boy performer of the Jiang clan named A-Duan. At the age of seven he was unequalled for his agility and remarkable reflexes. His reputation kept growing, and at sixteen he was still at work. Then he died falling into the water at the foot of Mt Gold. His mother, who had only this one son, could only wail in misery. A-Duan himself was not aware that he had died. He only knew that two men led him away under the

[1] The area covers a part of Zhejiang, Jiangsu and Fujian provinces.

晚霞
無端幻出
空靈境
補得情天
離恨多
畢竟龍宮
何處是
居然選舞
又徵歌

water, to another heaven and earth. Looking behind him, he saw perpendicular walls of water flowing on all sides. Soon he was taken inside a palace, where a man in a battle helmet sat. The two guides said, "This is the Lord of Dragon Lair." They directed A-Duan to bow to the ground. The Lord of Dragon Lair softened the expression on his face.

"A-Duan, your mastery has qualified you for admission to the Willow-Wand Troupe," he said.

A-Duan was then led to where the view on all sides was blocked by huge palaces. As he hurried down the east gallery, a number of young men, mostly thirteen or fourteen years old, came out and bowed in greeting. Then came an old woman whom everyone addressed as Granny Xie. She sat down and told A-Duan to show off his skills. When he was finished, she taught him dances called Thunder on the Qiantang River and Dongting Lake Breeze. The din of the drums and gongs could be heard reverbrating from every courtyard. After a while the courtyards all quieted down. Granny was worried that A-Duan would not learn all the moves smoothly, so she took special care to give him long-winded instructions for each step, but he knew exactly what he was doing after one time through.

Granny exclaimed happily: "With a boy like this, our troupe will be in the same class as Wanxia's."

The next day, the Lord of Dragon Lair was to review the troupes, and every last troupe gathered. First he reviewed the Yaksa Troupe, with their ferocious faces and fishskin costumes. They struck a large gong some four feet in circumference, and their thunderous drum needed four men to hold it. They struck up a deafening chorus of yells and whoops. As they started dancing, giant waves surged across the sky above, dropping sparks of starlight that went out when they hit the ground. The Lord of Dragon Lair ordered them to stop abruptly and then called for the girls of the Nestling Oriole Troupe: all of them were sweet sixteen and beautiful. The delicate notes of mouth organs rose into the air. In an instant a cool breeze breathed across the water and the crashing waves were silent. The water slowly grew still like the everywhere-transparent limits of a crystal world. At the end of the performance all the troupers withdrew to stand beneath the west steps.

The next to be reviewed was the Swallow Troupe, made up of girls young enough to wear their hair long. Among them was a young woman somewhere around fourteen or fifteen. In the Flower-Strewing Dance she waved her sleeves and dipped her head. Then she fluttered and took soaring leaps, while flowers of all colors fell from her sash and sleeves and stockings, floating down the wind and drifting over the whole courtyard. At the end of the dance she too followed her troupe to the bottom of the west steps.

A-Duan cast a sidelong glance in her direction and lost his heart to her. He asked a fellow trouper and learned that her name was Wanxia. Before long the call went out for the Willow-Wand Troupe. The Lord of Dragon Lair gave A-Duan a special audition. A-Duan performed the dances he had just learned. His dancing was a perfect embodiment of the feelings in the music, and his every movement was made in perfect rhythm. The Lord of Dragon Lair commended his intelligence and presented him with a pair of rainbow pantaloons and a fish-whisker hair clasp of gold set with a glow-in-the-dark pearl. A-Duan bowed in gratitude, then hurried to the west steps, where each troupe drew up in its own formation. A-Duan gazed at Wanxia from afar through the crowd and she gazed back at him. Soon A-Duan edged out of rank and moved northward;

Wanxia also edged southward out of her troupe. They were only a few steps apart, but neither dared cross over the line between formations. All they could do was gaze soulfully at one another.

Then the Butterfly Troupe was reviewed. This was made up of little boys and girls who danced in pairs of matching height, age and wing color.

When all the troupes had been reviewed, the dancers walked out in single file. The Willow-Wand Troupe was to follow the Swallow Troupe. A-Duan hurried to take the first place in his troupe, while Wanxia dawdled in the rear of hers. She turned and saw A-Duan, then let her coral clasp fall. He immediately put it in his sleeve. On his return he made himself ill thinking of her to the exclusion of sleep and meals. Granny Xie served him rich and savory foods. She checked on him several times a day and tended him solicitously, but he did not improve in the slightest. She worried for him, but had no idea what to do.

"The birthday celebration for the King of Wu River is drawing near. What are we going to do?"

That night a young boy came, sat on the edge of the bed and talked with A-Duan.

"I belong to the Butterfly Troupe," he said. Then he asked with studied calmness: "Are you ill because of Wanxia?"

"How did you know?" A-Duan asked incredulously.

"She is in the same shape you are," laughed the boy. A-Duan sat up gloomily and asked what could be done.

"Can you still walk?" asked the boy.

"If I push myself I can make it," he said. The boy led him out by the arm, opened a door to the south, turned west, then went through another double door. There before them was a large expanse of lotus flowers, growing on dry land, with leaves as large as mats and flowers as large as canopies. Fallen petals were piled a full foot high around the stems.

The boy led him among them, saying, "Sit here for now," and walked away. After a short while a young beauty parted the lotuses and walked into the clearing: it was Wanxia. When they got over the happy surprise of seeing one another, they each told how much the other had been on their thoughts and gave brief accounts of their lives. Then they weighed down lily pads with stones to make them lean sideways, which did nicely for a screen, spread an even layer of petals to recline on, and gleefully lay down beside each other. Afterward, having set sundown as the time for their daily rendezvous, they parted.

Back with his troupe, A-Duan recovered from his illness soon afterward. From then on the two met every day in the locust patch. After several days they went with the Lord of Dragon Lair to the King of Wu River's birthday celebration. When they had commemorated the king's longevity, all the troupes returned, leaving only Wanxia and one other member of the Nestling Oriole Troupe at the palace as dancing teachers. For several months there was no news of them. A-Duan was miserable and spiritless. The only ray of hope was Granny Xie, who made daily trips to the Wu River palace. A-Duan asked to be taken along to see Wanxia, claiming that she was his cousin. He stayed within the Wu River gates for a few days, but the stringent palace discipline kept Wanxia from coming out of the women's section, so he went back discouraged. When little more than a month had passed, his lovesickness threatened to be the end of him.

One day Granny Xie came in mournfully to console him: "How sad! Wanxia has thrown herself into the river."

A-Duan was stunned: there was no controlling the tears that ran down his cheeks. He destroyed his hat and tore up his robe, then ran out with the gold and pearl clasp in his sleeve, intending to follow her in death. But the river water formed a wall that would not give way even when he batted his head against it. He considered going back but thought of the aggravated punishment he would receive when taken to task for the hat and robe. He was at wit's end: sweat poured off him till it trickled over his ankles. Just then he noticed a large tree beside the wall of water. He shinnied up to the topmost branches and took a mighty leap. Unexpectedly he broke through without so much as wetting his clothes, and found himself floating on the surface. Before he realized what was happening, the world of the living was before his eyes. He swam with the current until he came to the bank. Sitting momentarily beside the river he began to think of his old mother. He hailed a passing boat that was going his way, and as he reached his ward, the cottages he saw on all sides were like a memory from a previous lifetime.

Then he came to his house, where a girl's voice rang out from the window: "Your son is here."

The voice was very much like Wanxia's. In a moment the speaker came out with his mother. It was Wanxia herself. In an instant the young couple's sadness gave way to joy, while the matron's emotions ran the gamut from puzzlement and sorrow to shock and elation.

Earlier, while staying at the Wu River Palace, Wanxia had felt rapid movements in her abdomen. Owing to the severe discipline in the palace, she feared that when the time came to give birth she would be brutally beaten. On top of that she could not see A-Duan. Wishing only to end her life, she stole out and threw herself into the river. Her body floated upward until it was bobbing on the waves. A traveler's boat came along and pulled her to safety. The passengers asked her which ward she lived in. Wanxia —originally a well-known courtesan from Wu whose corpse had not been recovered when she drowned —thought to herself that a brothel was no place to go back to, and so she answered, "My husband is of the Jiang family in Zhenjiang."

The passengers rented a boat for her and took her home. Matron Jiang thought that she had come to the wrong place, but Wanxia assured her that it was no mistake. She told her whole story to the matron. The matron was quite taken with her lively, attractive manner, but worried that such a young woman could not possibly endure widowhood. Still, the girl was obedient and attentive. Seeing the difficult circumstances the matron lived in, she took off her jewelry and sold it for hundreds of strings of cash. The matron was much gladdened to learn that she had no ulterior motive. But her son was not there and the fear remained that neighbors and relatives would distrust Wanxia as her pregnancy advanced. The matron broached this subject to her.

"As long as you get your own true grandson, Mother, why should other people have to know?" This put the matron's mind at ease.

Wanxia was beside herself with delight when A-Duan arrived. The matron shared her joy and even began to question the fact that her son had died at all. She secretly opened his grave and found his remains intact, which prompted her to question him. The truth finally dawned on A-Duan, but he warned his mother not to mention it again for fear that Wanxia would reject him for not being human. His mother agreed with him, so she told the neighbors that the corpse which had been recovered that day was not her son's. Still, she continued to worry that he might not be able to father a child. But before long Wanxia gave birth to a boy that felt no different to the touch than a normal child. At last the matron was happy.

In time Wanxia realized that A-Duan was not a living human.

"Why didn't you tell me sooner? For a period of forty-nine days after the wearing of ghostly garments or dragon palace garments, a person's soul remains undissipated, just as if he were alive. If we had managed to get dragon horn glue from the palace during that time I could have joined your bones at the joints, and your flesh would have grown back. What a shame we did not buy it earlier!"

A-Duan put his pearl up for sale. A foreign trader gave a million in cash for it, which made them into a wealthy family overnight. On his mother's birthday he and his wife sang and danced between toasts. When word of this reached the mansion of the local prince, he wanted to seize Wanxia for himself. A-Duan was frightened, and he went before the prince to confess: "My wife and I are both ghosts."

A test was performed proving that the two did not cast shadows, which convinced that this was true, so he gave up his plan of abduction. He did, however, assign women from his palace to study under Wanxia in a side courtyard. Wanxia would not see him until she had disfigured herself by applying tortoise urine to her face. She left after teaching for three months, when it became clear that mastery such as hers was more than her students could ever learn.

47. FISH DEMON BAI QIULIAN

SCHOLAR Mu of Zhili,[1] known by his childhood name Changong, was a son of the merchant Mu Xiaohuan. He was intelligent and loved reading. When he was sixteen his father, considering a literary profession impractical, made his son learn business instead by taking him along on a trip to Chu.[2] Whenever there was nothing to do aboard the boat, he passed his time chanting and reading aloud. They arrived in Wuchang, where the father left him at an inn to watch over their assets. Changong took advantage of his father's every absence by picking up a scroll and chanting poems in rhythmic tones. At times like this he could see a shadow wavering at the window, as if someone were secretly listening to him, but he thought nothing of it.

One night when his father stayed out late at a party, the scholar chanted with a fervor unusual even for him. The figure of a person walking back and forth outside the window was plainly visible in the moonlight. Curious, he rushed out to get a better look and saw a fifteen- or sixteen-year-old girl—the sort of beauty that can bring a city tumbling down. At the sight of the scholar she darted into hiding.

1. The old name for Hebei province.
2. The old name for Hunan and Hubei provinces.

A few days later father and son headed north loaded with a load of merchandise. At sundown they were moored by the side of a lake and the father happened to be elsewhere, when a matron came aboard and said, "You'll be the death of my daughter, young fellow!"

Taken aback, the scholar asked what that meant. "My name is Bai," she answered. "I have a daughter named Qiulian who knows a thing or two about the written word. She says she first heard your musical chanting in the prefectural seat. Now she's so desperate thinking of you that she won't eat or sleep. I would like to marry you to her. You won't get the chance to refuse a second time."

In his heart, the scholar really felt for the girl, but he worried that his father would disapprove, and he said so frankly. The matron did not believe him and insisted that he give his pledge of honor. He would not.

The matron exploded: "Plenty of people in this world try to arrange marriages through go-betweens and don't get what they want. Now I come in person to discuss this with you, yet you turn me down. I can't think of a greater humiliation! Don't be too sure you'll make it back north across the river after this!" With that she left.

In a short time his father came back. The scholar told him of what had happened, putting it in the best possible light in the hopes that he would approve of a marriage. But his father thought there was too great a distance involved and laughed it off as the amorous impulse of a young woman.

The water at their mooring that evening was too deep for their oars to touch bottom, but during the night sand and gravel suddenly bulged up under their boat and stranded it. The father was not very alarmed at this, because every year some of the traders pulled their boats

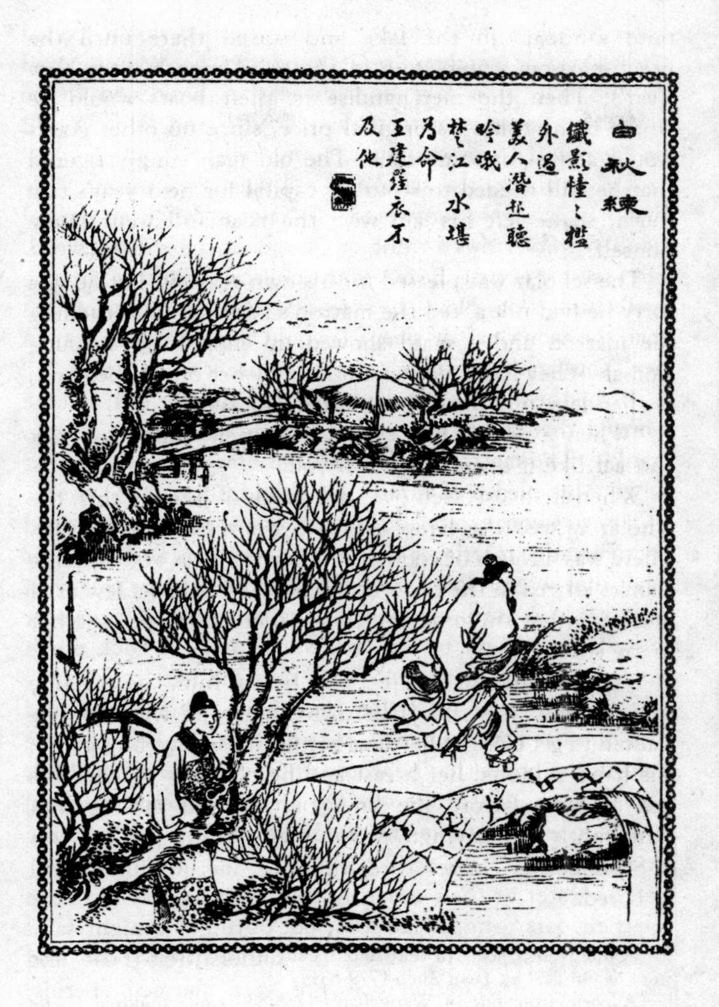
白秋練
纖影憧憧檻外過
美人潛起聽吟哦
楚江水湛
為命
王建羅衣不及他

onto sandbars in the lake and stayed there until the peach-blossom waters rose in the third month after New Year's. Then the merchandise in their boats would be worth many times its original price, since no other goods would arrive for some time. The old man simply figured that he still needed to scour up capital for next year's trip south, so he left his son with the boat and went home himself.

The scholar was pleased for his own reasons, but he was sorry he had not asked the matron's address. That evening the matron and a maid showed up supporting a young woman. They loosened her clothes, lay her on the bed and, as they left, turned to the scholar and said:

"When a person gets this sick, you shouldn't lay back and act like it doesn't concern you!"

When he had gotten over the shock of hearing this, the scholar moved the lamp closer to get a look at the girl. There was a touch of coquetry in her frailness and rippling glances stirred in the pools of her eyes. He asked a few brief questions, but she only smiled winsomely. He pressed her to say something.

" 'I pine for him but feel shy before him,'[1] is the line that fits me," she said. This drove him wild with joy. He wanted to get close to her, but her frailness gave him pause. His hand explored her breast and he playfully touched his lips to hers. Before she knew it, she was teasing him exuberantly and saying: "If you recite Wang Jian's 'Dress of Shimmering Gauze'[2] three times for me, my illness will be cured."

1. A line from a poem in the famous Tang dynasty classical tale, "The Story of Oriole," by Yuan Zhen (779-831).

2. A poem from one of Wang Jian's (768-830?) one hundred *Palace Lyrics*.

He did as she said. After only the second time through she pulled her robe over her shoulders, sat up and said, "I'm cured." As he read it the third time her coy looks were mixed with trembling. Now his soul was soaring. He blew out the candle and lay down with her.

The girl got up before daybreak, saying: "My mother will be here soon."

Before long the matron did arrive. She was naturally relieved to see her daughter sitting there in good spirits and dressed up quite presentably. The mother asked her daughter to leave, but she lowered her head and did not answer. With that the matron went out by herself, saying:

"You like having fun with this fine young man, so do as you wish."

At last the scholar got around to asking about her family background.

"Our friendship is no more than the meeting of two carts along the road," she said. "We can't be sure that marriage is in store for us. Why should I tell you about my family."

Yet the two found joy in one another and meant the vows they made with all sincerity. One night Qiulian got up at an odd hour and trimmed the lamp. She opened a book and in a moment her face turned glum and glistened with tears. The scholar jumped up and asked what was wrong.

"Your father is about to arrive," said the girl. "Just now I used a book to divine what will happen to us. It opened to 'Melody of Jiangnan'[1] by Li Yi. The mean of this lyric is not promising."

[1] The succeeding lines of Li Yi's (749?-827) poem hint that it would be better to marry a reliable boatman than a merchant who continually neglects his wife.

"The first line is 'I married a trader from Qutang'[1]: that in itself is encouraging," he said to console her. "What is so unpromising about that?"

This made her feel a bit better. She got up and took leave of him, saying: "Let's part company for the time being. When day comes all sorts of people will start pointing and staring at us."

He took her arm and choked back a sob.

"Where can I let you know if the joyous event is settled?" he asked.

"I'll have someone shadowing you all the time. I'll hear about it, whether it works out or not." He wanted to go ashore to see her off, but she refused vigorously and left.

Before long Mu the elder came back. The scholar coughed up the truth little by little. His father berated him angrily, suspecting he had entertained a prostitute. A careful inventory of the valuables in the boat showed that nothing was missing, so he gave his son another scolding and forgot about it.

One night when the old man left the boat the girl suddenly appeared. They gazed at each other longingly, but there was nothing to be done.

"Ups and downs are predestined—we should think about the present," she said. "For now I'll have you stay for two months; we'll discuss where to go from there later."

On her way out she prescribed the sound of reciting as the signal for a rendezvous. After this whenever his father went out he would start chanting, and the girl would come by herself. The fourth month ran its course, and the time of optimum prices was past. The desperate traders took up a collection for an offering at the lake god's temple. The

[1] One of the famous Three Gorges in the Yangtse River.

big rains did not come until after Dragon-Boat Festival, and then at last the boats could get through.

Once the scholar got home he fell ill pining for the girl. His concerned father had both a shaman and a doctor come to treat him. The scholar told his mother in private:

"My sickness cannot be healed by herbs or exorcism. The only way is for Qiulian to come."

At first the old man was angry, but when time only made his son's debility worse, he grew afraid. He hired a coach to carry his son, went back to Chu and moored a boat at the old spot. He questioned the people living there, but none of them knew of Matron Bai. Then an old woman came poling her boat along the lakeshore, identifying herself as the person he was seeking. Climbing aboard her boat, the old man was delighted with the glimpse he caught of Qiulian. But then he inquired into their clan affiliations and found that they were nothing but a drifting houseboat family. He frankly told them the reason for his son's illness, hoping that the girl would board his boat and relieve his son's depression for the time being. The matron would not allow it because no agreement on the marriage had been made. Part of the girl's face showed around a corner as she listened breathlessly; tears nearly dropped from the corners of her eyes at what she heard them say. At last the sight of the girl's face, along with the old man's pleading, made the matron give in.

Sure enough, when the old man went out that night, the girl appeared. She moved to the edge of the scholar's bed and sobbed, "So now it is your turn to be in the condition I was in last year! I had to let you know what it felt like, but you've wasted away so badly I can't cure you right away. Let me recite something for you."

The scholar's mood also brightened. Qiulian recited the

same poem by Wang Jian. "That was a specific remedy in your case," said the scholar. "It may not work for a second person. I have to admit that hearing your voice is exhilarating in itself. Try reciting 'All the willow wands are trailing to the west'[1] for me."

She did as he asked, and he paid her a compliment: "Wonderful! You used to chant a ditty set to 'The Lotus Gatherer' that started like this: 'Blossoms of water lily scent the spacious slope.'[2] I've never forgotten it. Please go through it once, and linger over every word." Again she did his bidding.

Just as she brought the lyric to a close, he leapt up and said, "When was I ever sick?" Then they held each other tightly, as if he had never been ill.

Afterward he asked, "What did my father and your mother say to each other? Did they reach an agreement or not?"

Qiulian, who was aware of the old man's feelings, answered straightforwardly: "No agreement."

After she left, the father came. He was very glad to see his son up and about, but he would do no more than tell him to take heart and comfort him. Then he came to the point: "She's a fine girl, but she's been at the rudder singing oarsman's songs ever since her hair has been in a topknot. I won't mention her low birth, but you can be sure she's no virgin. The young man had nothing to say.

When the old man had gone out, Qiulian came back. The scholar related his father's opinion. "I saw well enough already," she said. "In this world the more impatient we are for something, the further it recedes from us. When we

1. From a poem by the Tang poet Liu Fangping about the sorrows of a woman in springtime.

2. Line from a lyric by Huangfu Song (fl. 859).

go more than halfway with someone, they push us away. What I'll do is cause a turnabout in his opinion of me, so he will ask me instead." The scholar wanted to know her plan. The girl said: "Merchants have one aim—to make a profit. I have a method for finding out the prices of commodities. I just looked at the goods in your boat: you don't stand to gain a thing by them. Tell your father for me that if he invests in such-and-such an item he'll get three times the profit and with such-and-such goods he'll get ten times his investment. Then, when you return home and my words come true, I'll make a wonderful wife for you. By the time you come back you'll be eighteen and I'll be seventeen. There will be plenty of time to be happy together—don't worry!"

The scholar told his father the goods and prices she had metioned. The father didn't give them much credit, but he agreed to go along with her instructions using half of his remaining funds. On their return the goods he had stocked himself lost a great deal of money. It was lucky for him he had partially heeded the girl's advice, since the fat earnings on the goods she recommended were just about enough to offset his losses. This made him acknowledge the girl's foresight. The scholar laid the praise on thicker, telling how the girl had said she could make a rich man of him. At this the old man raised additional funds and headed south.

They reached the lake and stayed there for several days without seeing Matron Bai. Several more days passed before they saw her boat moored by a willow, whereupon they presented the engagement gifts. The matron would not accept any, and simply chose a favorable day to send her daughter over to the old man's boat. The old man rented another boat for his son's goblet-sharing ceremony.

After this the girl told her father-in-law to go farther south and gave him a ledger listing the goods he should invest in. The matron invited her son-in-law to make himself at home in her boat. Three months later the old man returned, bringing goods that increased two to five times in value when he brought them to Chu.

Before they set out for home, the girl asked to take along a load of lakewater. Back home she invariably added a smidgin of it to every meal, as if it were *sauce piquante.* Henceforth, every time the old man travelled south, he had to bring back several urns of it for her. A couple of years later she gave birth to a son.

One day they found her sniffing and sobbing from home-sickness, so the old man took his son and her with him to Chu. They arrived at the lake, but there was no telling where the matron was. The girl beat against the gunwale and shouted for her mother in despair. She urged the scholar to go along the shore asking for her whereabouts. It so happened that a man who fished for sturgeon had just caught a white carp. The scholar walked over for a closer look. It was a huge creature, quite similar to a human in form and complete with breasts and private parts. Impressed with such an oddity, he went back to tell Qiulian. She was greatly shaken. She told him that she had long ago vowed to set some living thing free and instructed him to pay for the fish's freedom. He went to bargain with the fisherman, who asked an exorbitant price.

"Since I've been in your family I've brought in a good ten thousand taels of gold," Qiulian said. "Why must you haggle over such a measly sum? If you insist on going against my wishes, I will throw myself into the lake and drown myself this minute!"

The scholar was frightened. Not daring to tell his

father, he stole gold to buy the fish's freedom. On his return to the boat, he did not see Qiulian. He looked for her without success until the last watch, when she finally appeared.

"Where were you?" he asked.

"I went to my mother's place."

"Where is your mother?"

In a voice halting with embarrassment she said, "I have to tell you the truth now. The fish you paid for a while ago was my mother. The Dragon-Lord of Dongting Lake had ordered her to serve on his entourage. Recently when concubines were being chosen for the palace, certain gossipy people spoke highly of me, so an order was given to confine my mother pending my return. My mother wrote a truthful memorial to the throne, but the Dragon-Lord paid no attention. He banished my mother, almost dead from starvation, near the south shore: that is why she met with yesterday's disaster. Although she is now out of that predicament, the sentence against her has not been revoked. If you love me, you can save her by praying to the True Lord.[1] If I am repugnant to you because I am not of your kind, let me hand your son over to you and leave. There could well be a hundred times more riches for me in the dragon palace than in your house.

The scholar was overwhelmed, and he worried that he would not be able to meet with the True Lord.

Qiulian said, "Tomorrow afternoon between two and four o'clock the True Lord will appear. When you see a lame Taoist, bow down to him immediately. Stay with him, even if he goes into the water. The True Lord is fond of literary men: he is sure to be sympathetic." With this she

[1] Name of Taoist deity.

took out a sheet of fine, fishbelly-white cloth and said, "If he asks what you want, show him this and reguest that he write the word 'pardon'."

The scholar waited as she had told him. Sure enough, a Taoist priest came hobbling along. The scholar prostrated himself before him. He hurried away with the scholar following behind. Then he threw his staff into the water and jumped onto it. The scholar, too, jumped after him and found it was not a staff but a boat. Again he bowed down to the Taoist.

"What are you after?" asked the Taoist.

The scholar pulled out the piece of fine silk and asked him to write the word. The Taoist unrolled it and looked at it, saying: "This is from the fin of a white carp. How did you come by it?"

The scholar dared not hold anything back; he revealed everything from start to finish.

"She is quite a delicate elegant creature," the Taoist laughed. "What makes the old dragon think he can get away with such dissipation?" He proceeded to take out his brush and write the word "pardon" in a cursive style used in charms. Then he turned the boat back and let the scholar go ashore. The scholar watched the Taoist skim away across the water, feet planted on the staff, until he swiftly dwindled away.

The scholar returned to his boat. Qiulian was happy, but cautious enough to warn him not to let a word of this slip out to his parents.

Two or three years after their return north, the old man made a trip south, from which he did not return for many months. The lake water was used up, and no more arrived after a long wait. Qiulain fell ill: day and night she gasped for breath.

"If I die," she instructed him, "don't bury me. Recite Tu Fu's 'Dream of Li Po'[1] for me once each morning, noon, and evening. Then I will not decay even in death. Wait until the water comes and pour it into a tub. Remove my clothes behind closed doors, carry me to the water and soak me in it. That should bring me back to life."

She drew a few more days of wheezing breaths and then died a lingering death. Half a month later when old Mu arrived, the scholar hastened to carry out her instructions. A little more than two hours of soaking gradually revived her. After this she was preoccupied with thoughts of returning south. Later the old man died and the scholar followed her wish by moving to Chu.

1. Tu Fu (712-770) wrote two poems with this title in which he expressed his fond recollection of Li Po (701-762). Tu Fu and Li Po were the two most celebrated poets of the Tang dynasty, when Chinese poetry reached its peak.

48. THE KING

A CERTAIN governor of Hunan dispatched a subordinate official to deliver six hundred thousand taels in revenues to the capital. On the road he and his men ran into rain, and sunset caught them between post stations with no place to stay. An ancient temple could be seen in the distance, so they went there to shelter for the night. In the morning they found that every last bit of the money they were delivering was gone. The men were bewildered and appalled. There was no one to pin the blame on. They went back and made a report to the governor, who considered it preposterous and made ready to turn them over to the law. But when questioned, the runners gave entirely consistent statements. The governor ordered them back to the scene to search for clues.

At the front of the temple they saw a blind man of peculiar aspect who announced that he could "read people's minds," so they asked him to tell their fortunes for them.

"You're here for lost gold," he said.

"That we are," said the convoy official. He told the story of the distressing event. The blind man asked for a sedan chair.

"Just follow me, and you'll find out for yourselves," he said. The official did as he was told, with all the runners following along. When the blind man said "east" they went east: when he said "north" they went north. For five days

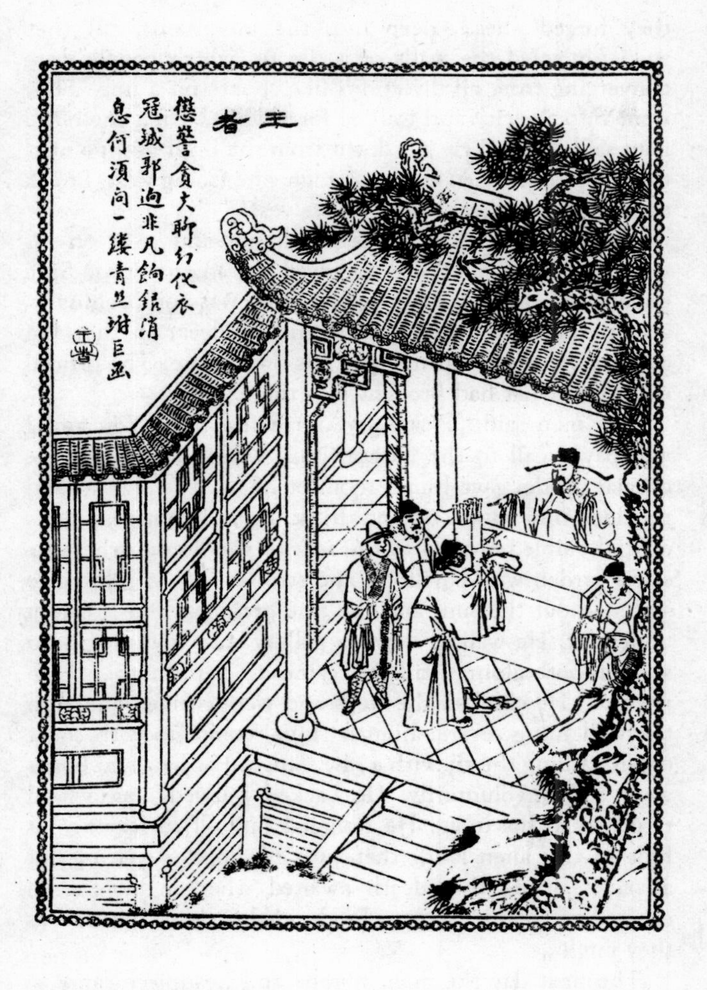

王者
懲警貪夫聊幻化衣
冠城郭迥非凡餉銀消
息何須向一縷青絲討巨函

they forged ahead, deep into the mountains, till they suddenly spied the walls of a city on which people were converging from all directions like spokes on a hub. They went into the city and walked for a while. Then the blind man said, "Stop." He got down from the litter and pointed to the south. "When you see a high gate facing west, knock on the door and ask them yourselves."

He saluted them with clasped hands and went on his way. The convoy official followed his instructions. Sure enough, he came to a high gate. As he was approaching it, a man came out wearing robe and headgear in the Han dynasty style. He did not give his own name. The official explained what had brought him there.

The man said, "Please stay for a few days. You and I will pay a call to the authorities." With that he led the official inside, gave him a room of his own to stay in and provided him with food and drink. In an idle moment the official ambled around to the rear of the house, where he saw a garden with pavilions, and strolled into it. Old pines screened out the sun, and the fine grass was like a carpet underfoot. He walked down a gallery that wound around several outbuildings till he came to yet another high pavilion. He climbed the steps and went inside. There on the wall hung several human skins, complete with sense organs, filling the air with a raw stench. His hair and bones went stiff involuntarily. He backed hurriedly away and returned to his room. He resigned himself to leaving his hide in this alien land: there was no hope of getting out alive. Realizing that death awaited whether he pressed onward or tried to retreat, he decided to let things fall as they might.

The next day the man in robe and headpiece came to summon him, saying: "Today you will be allowed to see him." The official stammered in acquiesence. The man in formal dress mounted an unruly horse that took off at a gallop, while the official trotted in pursuit. Soon they came to an outer gate that had all the marks of a governor general's *yamen*. Attendants in black were drawn up in tight, bristling formation on either side. The man in formal dress dismounted and led him inside. Passing through an inner gate, they saw a kingly man in pearl headdress and embroidered sash facing south on a throne. The official hurried forward and bowed his respects.

"Are you the convoy official from Hunan?" asked the king. The official answered yes.

"The silver is all here," said the king. "No harm would be done if your governor was generous enough to give me this trifling sum."

The official complained tearfully of his predicament: "I've already exceeded the time limit. I will be going back to face execution. What can I use to corroborate the report I will make?"

"That presents no difficulty," said the king. He handed the official a huge rolled-up letter, saying: "Discharge your mission with this: I guarantee no harm will come to you."

Following this the king assigned a brawny soldier to escort the official back. With breath catching in his throat from fear, the official was not about to argue, so he took the letter and started back. The landmarks along the way were nothing like what he had passed on his journey there. After they emerged from the mountains, his escort left him. A few days later he reached Changsha, the capital of Hunan, where he timorously reported his findings to the governor, who found this story more preposterous than the first one. He went into a rage that admitted no argument and ordered his attendants to bind the convoy official with lariats. The official untied his handkerchief and took out the letter. The governor tore it open: before he was done reading it his face paled to the color of ashes. He ordered the official untied. All he could say to him was: "The silver is a trifle. I'll let you go for now." After this the governor sent urgent dispatches to his subordinates directing them to make up for funds that had been lost in transit. Several days later he fell ill, and before long he died.

Prior to these events, the governor had awakened after a night with his favorite concubine to find that all of her hair had fallen out. Everyone in the *yamen* had been shocked and puzzled, but no one had been able to fathom the cause. What the huge letter brought by the convoy official contained was nothing other than her hair. Wrapped around it was a note which read: "Since you got your start at the district and prefectural levels, you have attained to a rank supreme among the emperor's subjects. You have taken bribes and appropriated property on innumeral occasions. The six hundred thousand taels of silver have been confiscated and are now in our treasury. You are advised to dip into your own ill-gotten gains to make good the original sum. The convoy official is innocent: no punishment shall be meted out to him. Not long ago we removed your concubine's hair as a gesture of warning. If you continue to disobey our instructions, we will remove your head anytime we choose. Your concubine's hair is enclosed as proof."

After the governor's death, people of his household began to divulge the content of the letter. Later a subordinate sent men to search for the spot, but all they could find were sheer chasms and cliffs on top of cliffs. There was not even a trail.

The Chronicler of the Tales comments: "The theft of a

golden box from beside a sleeping man's pillow, by the chivalrous maid Scarlet-Thread as told in the Tang classical tale, was a gratifying warning against greed. Still, the immortals of Peach Blossom Spring never went in for robbery. And if it really was a gathering place for men of the sword, what were the city walls and *yamen* compounds doing there? Hmmm! Could they have been spirits? If the place is ever found, I am afraid there will be an unending stream of people going there to air the grievances of the world."

49. THE BIRD NYMPH ZHUQING

YU Ke was a native of Hunan, from which district and town I do not recall. His circumstances were straitened to begin with, and after he failed to make the roll in civil examination, he ran out of money on his way home. He was ashamed to beg, though desperately hungry, so he stopped to rest at a temple to the King of Wu and prostrated himself in prayer before the image of the deity. Then he went out and lay down on the veranda. Soon a man came and led him away to see the king. The man knelt and said, "There is still an opening for a soldier in the black-robe corps. We can have this gentleman fill it."

"Good," said the King of Wu.

The man handed Yu a suit of black clothes. The instant he put them on, Yu was transformed into a crow. Out he went with flapping wings to where he saw his fellow crows gathered in a flock. They took him along to some sailboats, where they perched on the spars. The passengers in the boats vied with one another in throwing bits of meat up for the crows to catch in midair.[1] By imitating his fellows,

[1] Legend has it that people in the town of Fuchi on the Chu River worshipped General Gan Ning of the Three Kingdoms period as a folk god called the King of Wu. Several hundred crows which roosted in the trees around the King's temple were thought to be the King's sacred flock. The crows flew out to meet boats travelling the river and perched on their masts. The boatmen often threw them pieces of meat as an offering.

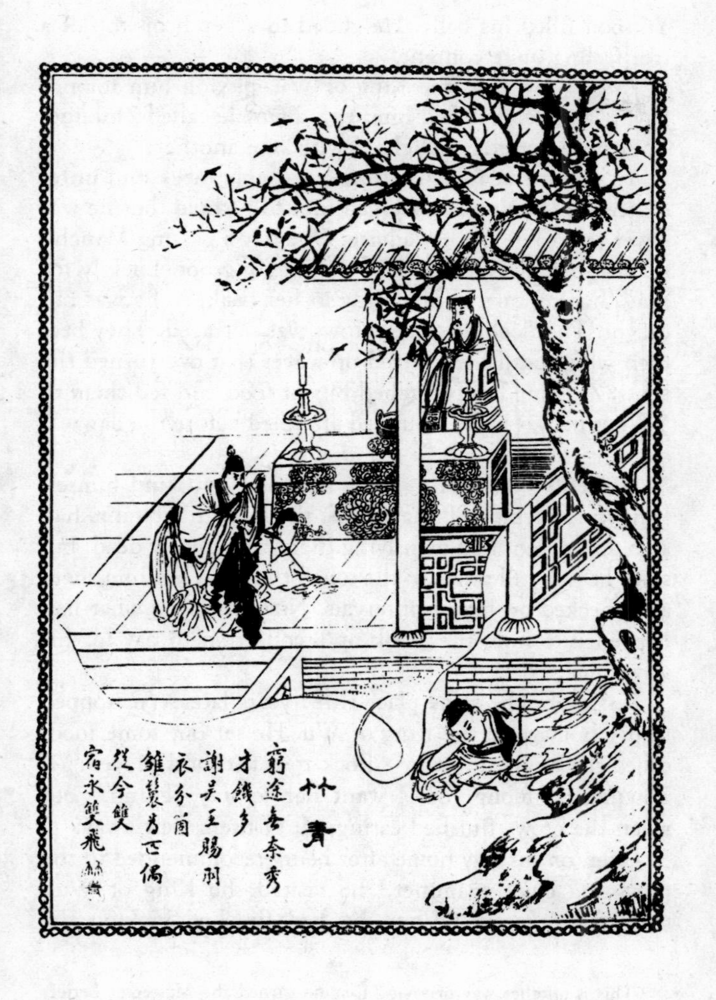
竹青
窮途無奈秀
才饑多
謝吳王賜羽
衣分爾
雛鬟為匹偶
從今雙
宿永雙飛

Yu soon filled his belly. He glided to a perch on top of a tree feeling quite content.

After a few days the King of Wu, pitying him for not having a mate, matched him with a female called Zhuqing. They were perfectly delighted with one another.

Yu's efforts at foraging were invariably meek and unresourceful. Zhuqing often urged him to be bold, but he was never able to follow her advice. One day a passing Manchu soldier shot him in the chest with a slingshot. Luckily for him Zhuqing carried him away in her beak, so he was not caught. The flock of sacred crows was outraged. They beat their wings until they stirred up waves that overturned the boats. Zhuqing busily fetched bits of food and fed them to Yu, but he was badly wounded and died before the day was out.

Suddenly, like waking from a dream, he found himself lying in the temple. Prior to this, the local inhabitants had seen an unidentified man lying there, apparently dead, but since he was still warm to the touch they had left him there and checked on him at intervals. Now, learning what had happened to him, they took up a collection to pay for his way home.

Passing by the same place three years later, Yu stopped to pay homage to the King of Wu. He set out some food, called the crows down in a flock to eat it, and prayed: "If Zhuqing is among you, I want her to stay behind." But when the crows finished eating, all of them flew away.

Later, on his way home after being recommended to the provincial chief examiner,[1] he visited the King of Wu's temple once again. When he had finished making the

[1] This is another way of saying that he earned the Master of Letters degree.

lesser offering of pork and mutton, he set the meat out as a feast for his crow friends and prayed to them again. That evening he stopped in a lakeside village. He was sitting up by candlelight when a birdlike creature came fluttering to rest before his desk. Lifting his eyes, he saw a beautiful woman of about twenty flashing him a smile as she asked, "Have you been well since we parted?"

Yu asked incredulously who she was.

"Don't you recognize your Zhuqing?"

Yu elatedly asked where she had come from.

"I'm a nymph of the Han River now: I hardly ever get a chance to come back to my own home. The crow messengers brought word twice of the state you were in, so I have come for a reunion with you."

Yu was overjoyed. Like husband and wife after a long separation, they could not contain the joy of their togetherness. He wanted to take her south with him, while she wished to invite him west, but they let the matter remain undecided when bedtime came.

On awakening Yu noticed that she had already risen. His eyes were greeted by a spacious hall lit by large, radiant candles: this was not the boat cabin he had slept in last night! He stood up in surprise and asked, "Where are we?"

"This is Hanyang,"[1] she said laughingly. "My house is your house. What need is there to go south?"

As the day brightened a flurry of maids gathered around them. Before he realized it, wine and viands had been served. Yu and his wife drank to one another across the short-legged table they set up on the roomy bed.

"Where is my servant?" asked Yu.

"On the boat," she answered. Yu was concerned that the

1. In Hubei province.

boatmen could not wait long for him. "Don't worry," she said. "I'll help you make it worth their while." And so the two of them spent their days and nights in intimate conversation. In his bliss Yu gave no thought to going home.

The boatmen were shocked when they awoke from their dreams to find themselves in Hanyang. Yu's servant went looking for him, but he was nowhere to be seen. The boatmen wanted to leave, but the knots in the mooring cable would not come loose, so they were forced to stay there together to watch over the boat.

More than two months went by before the Yu recollected his intention of returning home and said to Zhuqing: "As long as I stay here, I'm cut off from my relatives. Besides, you could say that the two of us are husband and wife, yet you have not yet been to my house. Shouldn't we do something about that?" "In the first place my going is out of the question. But even if I could go, you have your own wife back home. What would I be to you then?" It would be better to leave me here to make a home away from home for you."

The scholar complained that the distance was long and that he would not be able to come often, but Zhuqing brought out a suit of black clothes, saying "I still have the clothes you used to wear. If you miss me, put these on and you can come. When you come, I'll take them off for you."

That night a feast of delicacies was set out to send Yu off. He went to bed feeling the effects of the wine and found himself, on awakening, back in the cabin of his boat. One look outside told him that this was his old mooring place on Dongting Lake. His servant and the boatmen, who were all there, looked at him in amazement and demanded to know where he had been. He was lost in bewilderment.

Beside his pillow lay a bundle. Inspecting it, he found that it was a gift of new clothes, stockings, and shoes from Zhuqing, with the black robe folded among them. Fastened at the waist of the robe was an embroidered pouch which, when opened, proved to be filled to the mouth with gold coins. At this he set out for the south. When the boat touched shore, he paid the boatmen generously and went on his way.

A few months after his return home, his thoughts turned longingly to the Han River, so he secretly took out the black robe and put it on. Wings grew from under his arms and bore him aloft with measured strokes. In little more than four hours he reached the Han River. Looking downward as he turned a gliding circle, he noticed a cluster of buildings situated on a lone islet, so he swooped down. A maid who had seen him coming called, "The gentleman has come!"

In no time Zhuqing came out and ordered all hands to help undo his clothes. He could feel his coat of feathers split down the middle and peel off him. Zhuqing led him inside by the hand, saying: "You came just in time: I'm ready to go into confinement any day."

"Will it be an oviparous or viviparous birth?" Yu joked.

"Now that I am a goddess, my flesh and bones are more substantial. This one should be different than the ones I had before."

After several days she did indeed deliver something in a placenta so thick it resembled a huge egg. This was broken open to reveal a baby boy. The delighted scholar named the boy Han-Born. Three days later the nymphs of the Han River, all in the fresh bloom of youth, filed into the hall with congratulatory gifts of clothes, food and precious stones. Each of nymphs entered the bedroom, stood by the bed, and pressed a thumb on the baby's nose, a custom which they called "life-lengthening."

When they were gone Yu asked, "who were those ladies that just came?"

"They are my sister nymphs. The two at the very end, who were dressed in lotus-stem white, were the nymphs in the story 'A Gift of Jade Pendants on Mt Hangao.' "[1]

After a few months' stay, Zhuqing sent him off in a boat which glided forward on its own, without the use of sail or pole. On disembarking he found a man beside the road holding a horse, so he returned on horseback. From then on he was continually going back and forth. Han-Born grew with the passing years into a fine young boy—Yu's treasure. Yu's first wife, née He, who was pained by her failure to conceive a child, constantly longed to meet Han-Born. The scholar told Zhuqing of this, so she bundled up the boy's things and sent him off with his father, on the understanding that they would be back in three months.

After their arrival, his wife He developed greater affection for the boy than if he had been her own. More than ten months passed, but still she could not bear to let him go back. One day the boy fell victim to a sudden illness and died. His wife came close to dying herself of grief. Yu travelled to the Han River to break the terrible news to Zhuqing, but on entering the door he found the boy lying on the bed, ready for nap. Yu joyfully asked her how it could have happened.

1. Another legend mentions the encounter of a man with two nymphs, each of whom was wearing a sash pendant the size of a pheasant's egg. The two nymphs unfastened their pendants and gave them to him. Leaving them, he turned around and saw that they had disappeared. At the same instant, the pendants in his hand vanished.

"You stayed past the agreed time," she said. "I missed my son, so I called him back."

Then Yu told her how much his wife loved the boy, at which Zhuqing said, "Wait until I am with child again, so I can let you take Han-Born back with you."

A little over a year later she gave birth to twins, a boy and a girl. The boy they named Han-Grown and the girl, Jade-Pendant. Then Yu took Han-Born home with him. Making three or four annual trips seemed troublesome, so he moved his family to Hanyang. Later Han-Born was admitted to the district academy at the age of twelve. Zhuqing, feeling that the most beautiful feminine qualities were lacking in the human world, called the boy to her and found him a wife before she let him return. The wife's name was Goblet-Mistress, who was also the child of a goddess. After a time Yu's first wife He died. Han-Grown and his sister both went to mourn her. When the burial was over, Han-Grown stayed there, but Yu took Jade-Pendant away with him, never to return again.

50. STONE PURE-VOID

XING Yunfei, from Shuntian prefecture, had a fondness for rocks. If he found a fine-looking rock, he did not mind paying a substantial price for it. Once as he was fishing in the river something became tangled in his net. He dove down to free it and brought up a stone a foot in diameter, with finely detailed peaks and ridges on every side. He felt the boundless delight of one who has acquired a rare treasure. Upon returning home, he carved a stand of red sandalwood for it and gave it the place of honor on his desk. Whenever rain was imminent, all of the little openings on the surface emitted little clouds. From a distance they appeared to be stuffed with floss.

Then a certain local despot came to his door asking for a look at the stone. When he saw it, he seized it and handed it to his brawny servant, then spurred his horse away without a word. Xing could do nothing but stamp his feet in grief and vexation.

The despot's servant carried the stone on his back as far as the riverside, where he set it down on the bridge to rest his shoulders. Suddenly he lost his grip, and the stone fell into the river. The boss flew into a rage and whipped his servant. Later he paid skilled divers who tried everything imaginable to locate it on the bottom but were nevertheless unsuccessful. The boss drew up an open contract offering a reward to the finder of the stone and then went on his

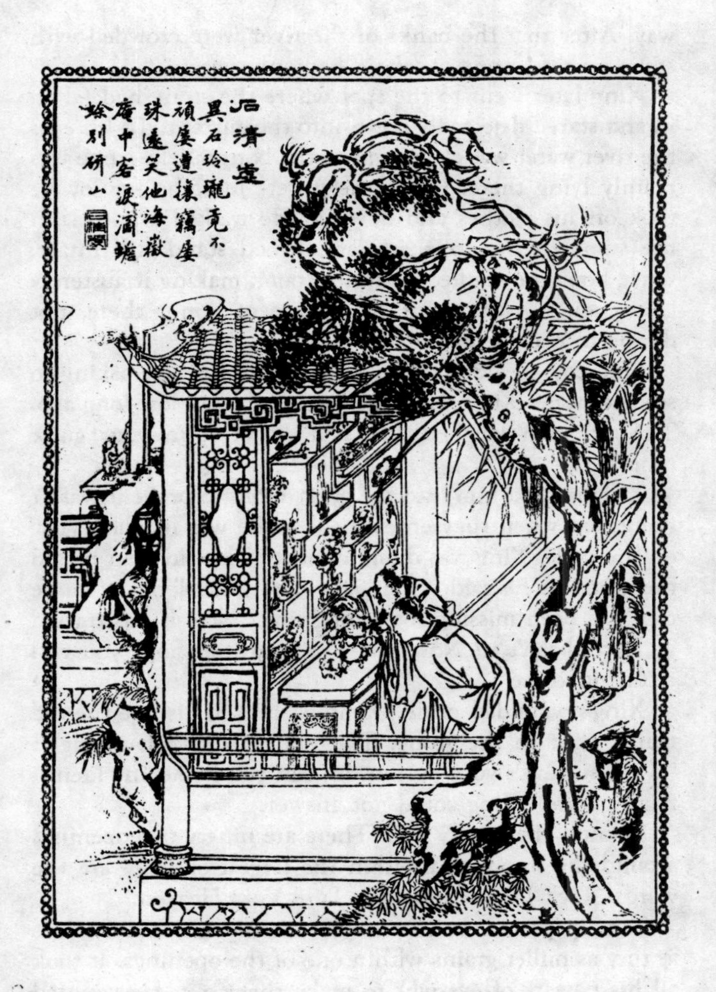
石清虛
異石玲瓏竟不
顧屢遭攘竊屢
珠還笑他海嶽
庵中客淚滴蟾
蜍別研山

way. After that the banks of the river were crowded with stone seekers, none of whom had any success.

Xing later went to the spot where the stone had fallen in and stared dejectedly down into the current. To his eyes the river water was clear right to the bottom: the stone was plainly lying there, under the water. Jumping for joy he took off his clothes and dove in. He walked ashore with the stone in his arms, its sandalwood stand still intact. Once home he readied an inner room, making it austerely clean, and set the stone in a place of honor there, not daring to place it in his living room.

One day an elderly man knocked on his gate asking to see the stone. Xing claimed that it had been lost long ago. The old man laughed and said, "Isn't it in your guest room?"

Xing invited him into the guest room to prove it wasn't there, but when they entered the stone was in plain view on the table. Xing was dumbfounded. The old man patted the stone as he said, "This is a family heirloom of mine that has been missing for a long time. Now it has turned up here, hasn't it? Now that I've seen it, I hope you will return it to me."

Xing's wounded pride prompted him to dispute the old man's right to the stone. The old man said laughingly: "Well, since it's your possession, can you name any identifying marks?" Xing could not answer.

"I know them fully well. There are ninety-two openings around the stone, and within the largest of them are the words 'Rock Decoration from Pure-Void Heaven.' "

Xing inspected the stone and, sure enough, found words as tiny as millet grains within one of the openings. It took all his powers of eyesight to make them out. He counted the same number of openings that the old man had said there were. He had no answer to give to the old man, but still he would not give up the stone.

"You had better make sure whose family this belongs to before you try to lay claim to it," the old man laughed. He raised his clasped hands politely and went out. Xing saw him out the gate. Then, when he got back inside, the stone was not there. He rushed after the old man, who was still ambling along not far away. Xing ran to him, grabbed his sleeve, and pleaded with him.

"Now that's strange!" said the old man. "How could a stone one foot in diameter fit in my hand or up my sleeve?"

Realizing that the man had supernatural powers, Xing dragged him back into the house and knelt before him to beg for the stone.

"Does the stone belong to your family or to mine after all?" asked the old man.

"It truly does belong to yours, but I beg you to part with it."

"If that is the case, the stone has been here all along," said the old man. They went to the inner room, and there it was in its old place. "The truly precious things in this world should go to those who appreciate them. This stone has the ability to choose its owner, and I too was pleased with its choice. Still, it was anxious to show itself, which made it come out prematurely before its period of calamity was lifted. I intended to take it with me and wait for three years before presenting it to you. Since you want it left here, you must give up three years of your allotted lifetime. That way you and the stone can be together until the end. Is that your wish?"

"It is."

The old man pinched the mouth of one of the openings with his fingers; the stone there turned soft as clay at his touch and the opening was moulded shut. When he had shut three of the openings, he said, "There are as many openings in this stone as there will be years in your life." With that he took his leave and turned to go. Xing beseeched him to stay, but his refusals were quite firm. He left without even answering Xing's questions as to his name.

A little more than a year later, when Xing was out on business, a burglar broke into his house at night and stole the stone, leaving all else untouched. On his return Xing was sick to death at his loss. He asked everywhere and offered to pay for information, but no sign of it turned up.

A few years later he happened to visit the Temple of Patriotic Obligation. There he saw a man selling decorative stones, and his own was among them. Xing claimed right on the spot that the stone was his own. The stone-seller did not agree, so he put the stone on his back and went to the magisterial court. The magistrate asked, "How can you prove ownership?"

The stone-seller was able to tell the number of openings on the stone, but he was at a loss when Xing demanded further proof. Xing told of the words inside the large opening and the marks left by the old man's fingers. In this way the case was judged in his favor. The magistrate was about to punish the stone-seller with a beating, but the seller protested that he had bought the stone in a market for twenty pieces of gold, and so he was released.

Returning home with his stone, Xing wrapped it in brocade and stored it in a chest. On the occasions when he took it out to contemplate it, he always lit rare incense first.

A certain board minister offered to buy the stone for one hundred pieces of gold, but Xing said, "I wouldn't give it up, even for ten thousand pieces." This made the minister angry. Working behind the scenes, he implicated Xing in an unrelated offense. Xing was put under arrest, and his property was confiscated. Then the minister sent someone to drop a hint to Xing's son. When his son told him of this, Xing vowed to die for his stone. His wife and son, however, discussed the matter and decided without Xing's knowledge to offer the stone to the minister's family. Xing did not learn of this until he was released from prison. He cursed his wife, struck his son, and would have hung himself several times if the servants had not caught him in time.

One night a man calling himself Stone Pure-Void came to him in a dream. He admonished Xing not to grieve at his loss: "I'll only be parting with you for a little more than a year. Next year on the twentieth day of the eighth month come to Haidaimen[1] at dawn. You'll be able to buy my freedom for two strings of coppers." Xing, who found this a heartening dream, took the precaution of writing down the date.

Once it was taken into the minister's house, the stone no longer emitted its remarkable clouds. As time went by no one there valued it highly. A year after, the minister died shortly after being removed from office for his crimes. Xing went to Haidaimen on the assigned day: there he found the minister's servant, who had stolen the stone and was offering it for sale. And so Xing bought it for two strings of coppers.

Years later, upon reaching the age of eighty-nine, Xing made preparations for his own burial and instructed his

[1] A gate on the southeast side of the city wall of Beijing (Peking), later known as Hatamen.

son to bury the stone with him. When he died his son carried out his last wish and entombed the stone with him. Half a year later robbers broke into the grave and took the stone away. Young Xing learned of this but was unable to trace them. Two or three days afterward he was out with a servant when he saw two men coming toward him on the road, dashing and stumbling and sweating profusely. Their eyes were fixed on the air above their heads as they threw themselves down on the ground, crying, "Mr. Xing, don't torment us this way. All we did was take the stone and sell it for four pieces of silver."

Young Xing had them bound and taken to court, where they confessed at the first interrogation that they had sold the stone to a man named Gong. The stone was brought into the courtroom. It was much to the liking of the magistrate, who ordered it deposited in the strongroom, hoping to lay hands on it later. As a clerk was lifting the stone it fell to the floor, and broke into dozens of pieces. Everyone went pale. Then the magistrate gave the two robbers a heavy beating and sentenced them to death. Young Xing picked up the stone fragments and buried them again in his father's grave.

The Chronicler of the Tales comments: "Exceptional things of any kind are a storehouse of calamity. As for the stone, his wish to die for it was fondness carried the extreme! But in the long run stone and man were together until the end: who can say that stones have no feelings? The old saying, 'A man of quality dies for the one who recognizes his ability,' is no exaggeration. If a stone can do this, how much more fitting it is that men should also!"

51. SCHOLAR JI

THE E family of Nanyang district in Henan was plagued by a fox spirit that often stole the master's money and miscellaneous articles. When anything offended the fox spirit, the disturbances grew worse. A grandson of the family named scholar Ji—an unconventional youth—burned incense and prayed for them that the disturbances would cease, all to no effect. Then Ji, to the family's amusement, implored the spirit to spare his grandfather and haunt his own house instead, but this prayer also went unanswered. "Since this spirit can assume illusory shapes, it must possess human faculties. I have made up my mind to guide it towards enlightenment," said scholar Ji. Every few days he went to call on it. Though his efforts continued to be ineffective, the fox spirit did not disturb parts of the house where he set foot, for which reason the old man often asked him to stay overnight.

At night the scholar would look into the sky and ask with great earnestness for the fox spirit to appear. One day he was back at home sitting alone in his study when suddenly the door opened gently by itself. The scholar arose and bowed respectfully, saying, "Is that you, Brother Fox?" No sound broke the stillness. Another night when the door opened itself, the scholar said, "If you are being so kind as to approach me, Brother Fox, this is the fulfillment of my prayers and invocations. What could be the harm in granting me a look at your brilliant countenance?" Again there was only stillness, and in the morning the two hundred coppers he had left on the desk were gone. That night the scholar put out several hundred more coppers. In the middle of the night there was a rustling in the draperies. The scholar said, "Have you come? With all due respect I have set out several hundred newly minted coppers for your use. I may not be well off, but I am no miser. If you are in a predicament that requires certain expenditures, there is no harm in coming out and saying so. Why must you steal?" After a moment, he looked at the money and found two hundred coppers missing. He left the remainder in the same place, but several nights passed without any more being taken. One day a cooked chicken which was to be served to guests disappeared. That night the scholar set out wine with another chicken, after which the fox spirit did not show itself again.

But the disturbances in the E house continued as before. The scholar went there and implored the spirit, saying: "You do not take the money or drink the wine I have set out. My grandfather is old and feeble: why do you keep harassing him? Please avail yourself this evening of the humble offerings I have prepared." Whereupon he arranged ten thousand coppers, a crock of wine, and the thinly sliced meat of two chickens on a desk and lay down beside it. No sounds were heard all night, and the articles were not touched. From then on, the fox hauntings ceased.

One day the scholar returned late and, upon opening the door of his study, saw on the desk a pot of wine, two roast hens on a platter and four hundred coppers all bound together with a red ribbon. Since these were the very items that had been taken before, he knew this was the fox spirit's repayment. The wine was fragrant, jewel-like in

姬生
自作穿窬自羞
慙相夫賴有室
人賢休
言狂藥
能迷性釀
酒都應如
盜泉

color and rich in flavor. When he had emptied the pot and gotten half tipsy, he felt greedy impulses stirring in his heart. He ran out the door, suddenly seized by a klepto-manic urge. He thought of a wealthy family in the village, made his way to their house and crossing over the wall. Though the wall was high, he cleared it at a single bound, as if he had wings. He went into the studio and made off with a mink coat and a gold cauldron. On his return, he placed them at the head of his bed before lying down to sleep. At daybreak, he carried the things into the inner chamber, where his shocked wife asked how he had come by them. After some hemming and hawing he told her, his face beaming happily. At first his wife thought it was a joke, but when she realized he was telling the truth, she was shocked: "You have always been an upright person. Why are you suddenly acting like a thief?" The scholar was too complacent to see angthing strange in his own behav-ior. Indeed, he spoke of the fox spirit's affection for him. It occurred to his wife that there must have been a fox potion in the wine. Recalling that cinnabar can exorcise evil spirits, she found some, ground it fine and put it in his wine. Shortly after drinking it, he let out a cry of surprise, saying: "What came over me to make me act like a thief?" When his wife explained things for him, he was shaken at losing control of his own actions. And when word of the robbery at the wealthy man's home spread through the neighborhood, he was at such a loss he did not touch his food for a whole day. His wife advised throwing the stolen goods over the wall under cover of night, which he did. Once the wealthy family got back its possessions the matter died down.

The scholar took first place in the annual examinations and was recommended to the provincial government for exemplary behavior, an honor for which he was to receive a double stipend. When the time came for posting of the results, a strip of paper bearing the following words was found pasted to a rafter in the *yamen*: "Ji so-and-so is a thief. He stole a fur garment and a cauldron from so-and-so's family. Is this exemplary behavior?" The rafter was quite high, so it could not have been affixed even by a person standing on tiptoes. The civil examiner's suspicions were aroused: with the strip of paper in hand he demanded an explanation of the scholar. The scholar was dumbfounded. No one knew of this matter but he and his wife, and, what was more, the *yamen* was tightly guarded. How could the note have gotten there? Then it dawned on him: "This must be the fox spirit's doing." Whereupon he recounted all the events leading up to this, holding back anything. The civil examiner rewarded him with a gift above and beyond the double stipend. The scholar often wondered why, though he had not offended the fox spirit in any way, it would repeatedly attempt to harm him. He concluded that this was only a petty person's shame at being alone in his pettiness.

The Chronicler of the Tales comments: "The scholar wanted to lead the wicked to righteousness, but was himself deluded by wickedness. The fox spirit's intentions were not terribly evil. Perhaps the scholar was guiding the fox spirit toward righteousness with tongue in cheek, and the fox spirit was only playing a joke in return. But if not for the scholar's good grounding in morality and help from his fine wife, he might well have ended like the woman of whom Yuan She, a knight errant of the Former Han dynasty, said: 'Once a widow has been molested by bandits, she will become a loose woman.' Whew! It was a close call!"

Wu Muxin relates this story: "In the year 1694, during

the reign of Emperor Kangxi, a certain provincial graduate serving as a district magistrate in Zhejiang was checking over the list of criminals being held in the prison there. There was a thief who, having already been branded, ought to have been released according to law. But the magistrate was unhappy that the character for 'thief' had been written in a vulgar simplified form rather than using the standard character of official fonts. He had the brand scraped away and then waited until the wound healed so that the character could be incised again according to the stroke order and form of recognized dictionaries.

"The thief thereupon improvised the following quatrain:

Peering in the speculum I hold in my hand,
I see streaks of blood trickling over my old scar.
This facial suffering would not have reoccured
Had I kept clear of your literate commissar.

"The gaolers laughed at him, saying: 'Since you're a poet why didn't you try to make a name for yourself, instead of becoming a robber?'

When young I studied truth, intent on winning fame,
But a pauper's life is never a happy story.
From money I had hoped to breed more money till
To the capital I would go to bask in glory."

Judging from this, when Bachelor of Letters Ji acted as thief, it was also because of his desire for advancement. The fox spirit bestowed upon Ji the wherewithal to make progress in his career but he returned it, and blamed himself for committing a wrong. Such impracticality! This is just for a laugh.

图书在版编目(CIP)数据

聊斋志异选:英文/(清)蒲松龄著

—北京:外文出版社,1989(1996重印)

ISBN 7-119-00977-X

Ⅰ.聊… Ⅱ.蒲… Ⅲ.①古典小说—中国—清代—选集—英文
②短篇小说—中国—清代—选集—英文 Ⅳ.I242.1

中国版本图书馆CIP数据核字(96)第06499号

聊斋志异选

王起、刘烈茂
曾扬华 编选 注释

*

外文出版社出版

(中国北京百万庄大街24号)

邮政编码100037

北京外文印刷厂印刷

中国国际图书贸易总公司发行

(中国北京车公庄西路35号)

北京邮政信箱第399号 邮政编码100044

1989年(36开)第1版

1996年第1版第2次印刷

(英)

ISBN 7-119-00977-X/I·158(外)

02400

10-E-1818P